FOR GOD AND GLORY

OTHER BOOKS BY TIM JEAL

Fiction
Until the Colors Fade
A Marriage of Convenience

Nonfiction
Livingstone
The Boy-Man: The Life of Lord Baden-Powell

FOR GOD

AND

GLORY

TIM JEAL

WILLIAM MORROW AND COMPANY, INC.
New York

Library of Congress Cataloging-in-Publication Data

Jeal, Tim.
    For God and glory / by Tim Jeal.
        p.   cm.
    ISBN 0-688-11871-2
    1. British—Africa—History—19th century—Fiction.
    2. Missionaries' spouses—Africa—Fiction.   3. Young women—Africa—
    Fiction.   I. Title.
    PR6060.E2F67   1996
    823'.914—dc20   95-52074
                                                                       CIP

Printed in the United States of America

First Edition

1   2   3   4   5   6   7   8   9   10

BOOK DESIGN BY LEAH CARLSON

To the memory of all those who died a century ago in the Ndebele and Shona Uprising of 1896, including Chief Uwini, executed by British troops; Bernard Mizeki, Christian convert, murdered by his own people; Joseph Norton, farmer, and Caroline Norton, his wife, killed by tribesmen at Porta Farm; Lieutenant Harry Bremner, 20th Hussars, Trooper C. McGeer and the other soldiers and civilians who died during the escape from Mazoe Settlement.

PART ONE

CHAPTER 1

The staff of J. & H. Ince & Co., Sarston's principal draper's, had never found Clara Musson an easy customer to satisfy. As a child, she had agonized long and hard over which bright ribbons and shiny buttons she wanted to buy. The passage of time had not made her less fastidious. But having seen her grow up, the shop assistants knew Clara well enough to suffer her whims without rancor.

Her long-dead mother had been a devout Christian, and little Clara had always been eager to please her. At the age of four, she had caused much merriment by pursuing destitute people with charitable gifts—usually dried bread and broken biscuits, which she had then thrust at them with loud demands that they eat. She had been disobeyed by bona fide beggars and by the many respectable citizens whom she had mistaken for vagrants. A deputation of angry people had dragged the young Lady Bountiful home and rebuked her parents for letting their pampered child insult them. On another occasion—and this incident had occurred in Ince's shop—Clara, aged twelve, had consoled a recently widowed assistant with the words: "Don't worry—you'll soon be dead too." The woman's shock and distress had amazed Clara. If she herself had lost a husband, Clara had known, *she* would have wanted to die as soon as possible in order to be with him in heaven. Or if she had led too evil a life to qualify for heaven, the fires of hell would at least prevent her missing him.

Ten years later, on a freezing afternoon in January 1894, Miss Greaves, J. & H. Ince's resident dressmaker, was serving Clara. She remembered the latter incident well. Even now, when she was dealing with Miss Musson, nothing could be taken for granted. Miss Greaves anticipated arguments about style and cost, and even changes of mind after "firm" decisions had been made. The dress material had been safely chosen, and now the time had come to discuss how the ball gown should be trimmed. Miss Greaves suggested a border of dark-green leaves around each of the skirt's three flounces.

"See how striking it is, Miss Musson," she enthused, holding up the trimming against the fabric. "But to look really stylish, the leaves should be edged with a little red cord. That would be so tasteful."

"So expensive too, I daresay," muttered Clara, fixing the dressmaker with glittering eyes.

"Oh, not really," soothed Miss Greaves. She turned to the milliner behind the counter. "I expect we could manage to do it for four guineas, wouldn't you say, Miss Williams?"

"I think we could just about manage that, Miss Greaves," agreed Miss Williams.

"God almighty!" cried Clara, the robustness of her expression contrasting strangely with her angelic appearance. In dark furs and with a black veil looped back from her face, her skin looked as pale as white hellebore petals touched with winter pink.

Miss Greaves swore a mental oath and steeled herself for some energetic haggling. Because Clara's father owned the town's principal earthenware works, the young lady plainly thought that every shopkeeper was out to overcharge her. Being aware of this, Miss Greaves always pitched her price too high at the outset, so she could drop it later after a convincing show of resistance.

Though Clara was unaware of it, during her childhood many tradespeople had thought her father a monster to deny his only daughter the dignity of summer silks. Instead he had made her wear cotton print dresses like a shopgirl. Only when Clara had come of age had Alfred Musson granted her a dress allowance. He was as rich as some of the county's largest landowners and yet still lived in a town house so nondescript that most members of the local gentry refused to call there. Musson's contempt for social ambitions and ostentation was well known, and while earning him the praise of fellow chapelgoers, it brought inevitable taunts of miserliness from shopkeepers.

"If madam really wishes"—the milliner sighed—"the dress could be trimmed with velvet for less money, but it would not look nearly so *distingué*."

Miss Greaves nodded gravely, impressed by her colleague's inspired choice of word. The daughter of a tradesman, however rich, would surely clutch at the reassurance of *distinguished* trimmings when dancing with the gentry at a hunt ball. But Clara laughed in a most disconcerting manner.

"The leaves are fine on their own, Miss Greaves, but I won't war something like a servant's bell rope round my waist. The idea of it!"

Clara smiled. Of course poor old Greavesy couldn't be expected to know that she could appear in a sack at a county ball and still seem a perfect vision to the one person who mattered, namely the owner of Holcroft Park. Even this casual thought of Mr. Charles Vyner made Clara feel pleasantly weak. His soft, low voice, his neat dark hair, his deep-brown eyes, and above all his gentlemanliness, had haunted her imagination almost from the day when he first called upon her. Being sure his feelings mirrored hers, Clara was cocooned in happiness.

She caught sight of herself in the big cheval glass, flanked by the two women. *They* wouldn't be going dancing or riding in carriages with gentlemen. Indeed not. Their wasted lives rose up and flapped about like crows, casting black shadows over Clara's bright mood. Thirty years in a draper's shop, twelve hours a day, and all for twenty-five shillings a week. Long ago, Miss Greaves's skin had absorbed the shop's fustiness, and it was now as dull as parchment. Miss William's back was bowed, and all her features were pinched and desiccated. It was merciful, thought Clara, that neither of them was likely to know about Charles Vyner's love for her. From the very beginning, Charles had urged her to be discreet, and Clara had been glad to oblige him. Their love, he had insisted, would grow more strongly for being their private possession until they were ready to declare it to the world. So in spite of her father's horrified objections, Clara had refused to take a chaperone when meeting Charles. In fact, practical considerations too had made discretion desirable. Charles found her father impossible to talk to and disliked calling on her at home. Since she found his mother equally uncongenial, when Clara visited Holcroft Park she usually told her coachman to approach via the stable gates instead of the carriage sweep, which was overlooked by Mrs. Vyner's windows.

Still mindful of her good fortune, Clara tried to look less brimful of hope and vitality. Yet her glowing face cried out in spite of her: I am free and you are not. I am young and loved and you are not.

Clara suddenly found that she had lost her enthusiasm for

driving a hard bargain. She smiled engagingly and said, "What about three pounds ten shillings for the leaves without the rope?"

Amazed by such a reasonable proposal at this early stage, Miss Greaves agreed with alacrity. She and Miss Williams were all smiles. They liked to gossip with their clients and lost no time in getting started now that things were settled. Clara gazed idly at the scissors and chalk on the counter's polished surface, wondering how soon she could leave without causing offense.

Then, as if lightning had struck from a clear blue sky, Miss Greaves said something that caught Clara with the force of a physical blow. "Lady Alice Heydon was in here this morning." The dressmaker's voice sank lower. "I gather that Lady Alice is staying at Holcroft Park, as a guest of the Vyner family."

Too shocked to feel the full pain of her wound, Clara stared stupidly at the brass yard measure nailed along the edge of the counter. The touch of pink in her cheeks had fled, but her white lips still held her smile in place.

Encouraged by such unexpected attentiveness from a lady whose mind often wandered, the milliner leaned across the counter confidingly. "Lady Alice's maid told me that Her Ladyship means to hunt with the Ranfurley for the rest of the season. She had such a twinkle in her eye—the maid, you understand—that I don't doubt we'll be hearing of an engagement before long."

"Well, I never," murmured Clara. "I suppose we'll have to wait as patiently as we can." Her lips ached with smiling as she buttoned her coat and put on her muff. She had meant to ask the date of the first fitting, but the dress had vanished from her mind.

She walked past two young assistants, sewing beside the stove, and then threaded her way like a tightrope walker between the coat and the hat stands. The boy who made up the parcels opened the door for her, and she went out into the street. A casual laborer was scraping frozen snow from the pavement with a shovel. She longed to seize it from him and strike sparks from the stones.

Clara tried to laugh, but an awful gasping groan escaped her. Tears spilled from her eyes. She saw herself broken and helpless, condemned forever to a spinster's life. She staggered blindly past the free library, and the old men reading newspapers by lamplight. Fearing she would faint, she grasped the railings. I won't collapse until I get home. I won't. A horse tram clattered past. On the corner, a roast-chestnut man was warming his hands over his glowing brazier. Intent on reaching him, she stumbled on, slipping on the icy snow. I've lost everything, she thought. But wasn't it worse than that? Hadn't she just found out that she had never had anything to lose? The man she would have trusted with her life had been a rat all along.

Alfred Musson's house was the last in a short Regency terrace, dwarfed by the crimson brick of the neighboring Mechanics' Institute. In his garden was a monkey puzzle tree, much loved by Clara, though if anyone had ever offered her father a good price for the wood, she guessed he would have felled it. During the last two decades, this older part of the town had been overwhelmed by new construction. But since her father gained more enjoyment from watching blungers, sifters, and pug mills in operation at his pottery works than in looking at Georgian buildings, recent developments had left him unmoved. He had made a modest contribution toward the creation of a municipal park but had never returned there after the opening, and so he had no idea that the keepers' houses and the little decorative kiosks were now grimy with soot from the town's kilns and chimneys. Pressing in around this small oasis were hundreds of huddled red-brown streets. From Clara's room, the dark spire of the parish church and the neo-Gothic finials of the Free Trade Hall were the only structures that could be seen rising above the endless roofs.

Alfred Musson was a tall man with thinning gray hair and thick grizzled eyebrows. When his mind was engaged, he seemed forbidding, but in repose his face looked kindly and worried. His clothes were often shabby, though on special occasions he dressed appropriately. The two passions in his life were his pottery works and his only child. When he returned one evening to find Clara sobbing, he guessed the cause before being told it. He felt such rage with Vyner that he was tempted to snatch up a stick and seek him out at once. But suppose he blacked the scoundrel's eye—or suffered a beating himself. Would Clara's happiness be restored? Alas, no.

That evening, father and daughter dined together, looked down upon by *Christ Walking on the Water*—the largest oil painting in the house. Clara's speech was indistinct; and most unlike herself, she spilled food on the table.

"Clara, you're drunk," he said quietly, appalled by his discovery.

"Only a drop of medicinal brandy," she muttered, pushing back her chair with such force that she all but tipped it over.

Those who knew Alfred were amazed that a man so stern with his employees should be unable to cross his daughter. But ever since his wife's death, ten years earlier, Alfred Musson had been clay in his daughter's hands. He looked at her in alarm now. Her lovely face was contorted with indignation as well as grief.

"You never wanted me to marry him—admit it, Pa. You're pleased. So don't pretend you're not."

"I'm not pleased, my dear. Really I'm not," he soothed.

But in many ways he was. Alfred had always mistrusted Charles Vyner. What sort of man could be content to live on his rents, and sit moping for months on end in his library, or go rooting around for old brown pictures in foreign churches? A connoisseur, according to Clara. Charles, she had told him, was extending the art collection at Holcroft Park and writing about it in learned journals. Few men, it was said, knew more about how to tell an early Titian from a Giorgione. Though why anybody should want to do so was beyond Alfred Musson.

Clara pushed away her plate. Her lips were trembling. "You always loathed him."

"Not at all," he lied, tightening his grip on his cutlery. Tears were running down her cheeks, though she made no sound. If she were still a little girl, he could have sat her on his lap, but now there was nothing he could do to comfort her. Torn between his longings to shout abuse at the absent Vyner and to stroke his daughter's long black hair, he did nothing, and felt all the worse for it.

About a year before Charles Vyner started to pursue Clara, Alfred Musson had heard that he hoped to marry the Earl of Desmond's daughter, Lady Alice Heydon. But the earl had evidently thought that Lady Alice could do better. At any rate, he had withheld his consent. So when handsome Mr. Vyner started to call on Clara, Alfred suspected that his recent rebuff had made him lower his sights—as he would have seen it. Manufacturers' daughters, it must have occurred to him, could sometimes bring in more money than peers' daughters. If they lacked a few social graces, no matter; these could be acquired. Imputing such thoughts to Mr. Vyner, Alfred Musson had soon feared that the young landowner viewed Clara as a poor substitute for her predecessor. Now that Lady Alice had reappeared and been welcomed back by the entire Vyner family—having apparently worn down her noble father—Alfred was not very much astonished. But he loved Clara too much to say, I told you so.

Looking at her father's lined and careworn brow and his stooping shoulders, Clara wished that he could admit he was angry with her. The fire of the brandy had stolen through her body, making her limbs tingle and her emotions veer wildly from levity to maudlin rage. Her father's mask of subdued sorrow added guilt to her other burdens, filling her with irritation one moment and sympathy the next. The poor man had never understood Charles's appeal and so pitied her. His own idea of an ideal son-in-law was, predictably, a self-made monument to thrift, combining commercial canniness with religious piety. When Clara was nineteen, her father had introduced her to several likely men, one quite attractive and already owning a share in a local works. This paragon devoted his Sunday afternoons to superintending the men's Bible class at the West Street Congregational Chapel and two evenings a week to teaching boxing at a boys' club. Though kindly, and not without humor, he had no small talk and no interests beyond business and good causes.

But with Charles everything had been quite different. He despised practical pursuits and thought the cultivation of leisure the finest way to spend a life. He had inherited a magnificent estate at the age of twenty-six and saw no reason to worry about how or why his good fortune had arisen and whether he deserved it. Few days had passed without his sending to London for books on anything from Caravaggio to cannibalism and the limits of sea power. Like many poorly educated people, Clara tended to think too highly of those who had been more fortunate in this regard. She imagined, incorrectly, that Charles's intellectual curiosity owed much to his years at Oxford. Taught from childhood that happiness not arising from service to others was self-indulgence, Clara had been captivated by Charles's zestful descriptions of visits to Florence and Rome. His passion for Renaissance painting and his tales of seeking out lost masterpieces in remote villages had made her long to accompany him. Feeling ignorant and provincial, she had been thankful to have been given this chance to improve herself.

Up in her room after dinner, Clara kicked over the artist's easel she had bought when starting life classes at the Sarston Institute of Arts and Crafts. Eager to learn, she had read numerous books on art history—all on Charles's recommendation. She had

replaced the religious prints of her childhood with vivid photogra-
vure reproductions of Botticellis, Raphaels, and Bellinis. She had
bought antique casts, odd bits of Oriental curtains, a Venetian mirror, some Chinese fans. Now these pretentious things made her
sick with self-disgust. She ripped her own charcoal sketches from
the walls and tossed them on the fire, along with the wilting flowers
and puckered fruit that had been the subject of a still life. The
oranges hissed and spat as they burned. She watched them for a
moment before going to her desk by the window. Ripping open a
drawer, she pulled out a bundle of letters. Yet the moment they
too were on fire, she gasped with horror and fished them out with
the tongs.

Her head was aching, and her thoughts tumbled about like
the cargo in a rolling ship. Why care so much for a man who no
longer cared a fig for her? But perhaps he did. Perhaps the Heydon
girl had flung herself at him again without a word of encourage-
ment; had turned up at Holcroft uninvited and been taken in out
of pity. Charles's snobbish mother might have urged the poor creature to come. Quite possible. Charles himself needn't have been a
party to it at all. All Clara's memories of Charles's tenderness
toward her declared him innocent. And how could he have written
such loving letters if he'd really intended to take back Alice Heydon? Yet even as her new hopes grew, old doubts returned. Why
had Charles persisted in keeping their friendship secret? Because
he had guessed all along that he might one day betray her, and
had therefore been keen to ensure that very few people knew
of their friendship? Then there was his failure to give any
explanation of Lady Alice's presence at Holcroft Park—a most
damning omission. But Clara knew that however painful the
truth might be, knowing it could hardly be worse than her
present uncertainty.

She took a lamp from the central table to her writing desk.
How could she compel him to see her? Since he hadn't been able
to bring himself to write a note, was it sensible to imagine that he
would willingly face the unpleasantness of a meeting? Rage and
thwarted passion made her cheeks flame. How *dare* he treat her
like this? Would he have behaved so callously if she'd been a
nobleman's daughter? Certainly not. But a grubby tradesman's girl
was another matter. She snatched up a pencil and pressed so hard
that she ripped the paper.

For God and Glory

Charles,

Meet me in the Art Gallery at three o'clock on Wednesday, or Lady Alice sees your letters.

Clara

She scrawled his name and address on an envelope; then, fearing a change of heart, she ran downstairs. Not bothering with sealing wax, and pausing only to stamp the letter, Clara ran out into the snow without a coat or boots. She reached the box in time to catch the final post.

Clara had chosen to meet Charles at the Sarston Civic Gallery because it was the only public place likely to be empty in the middle of the afternoon. The main gallery was up a flight of marble stairs, and as Clara climbed them, her heart was thumping hard. She had deliberately worn her art school clothes—a tight-waisted coat with large pockets for sketchbooks, a floppy tie, and a soft felt hat—since she thought these garments made her look adventurous and capable. She was determined not to try to appeal to his sense of pity by seeming frail or pathetic. Under her skirts her legs shook, and she knew she was breathing too fast. Absurd, she told herself, for *her* to feel nervous, since she had harmed no one. Charles should be the one to feel wretched. Yet Clara's nervousness showed no signs of easing.

In the gallery itself, he was nowhere to be seen. Clara looked around at the familiar pictures without really taking them in. The collection reflected the tastes of the aldermen and councillors who had chosen them: Alma-Tadema's *A Silent Greeting,* in which a Roman soldier placed a tender hand on his intended's arm as she gazed at his gift of flowers. In Arthur Hughes's *The Long Engagement,* two besotted lovers held hands, shielded from prying eyes by an ivy-covered tree. Similar works hung on every wall. When Clara had last been here with Charles, he had ridiculed them all. This one was sentimental, that one melodramatic, its neighbor unintentionally humorous, and so forth. Clara had never thought to question a word he said. But now his mockery struck her as cruel

11

and self-admiring. True love and piety were not to be mocked as hypocrisy by arrogant young men. Yet as she heard hurrying steps on the stairs, she feared she might faint.

Charles was wearing a tweed shooting jacket and mud-splashed gaiters, as if his visit to town had not been worth the trouble of a change of clothes. But he came toward her with a look of humble dejection on his handsome face. "You needn't have threatened me, Clara. How can you think I'd refuse to see you?"

His gentle, apologetic tones momentarily dulled her anger. "Why didn't you write me?" she asked in a shaking voice.

"Clara, my sweet Clara, try and understand my situation. I'd asked Alice to marry me before we met. When her damn-fool father suddenly changed his mind and consented, what could I do?"

"Told her you'd fallen in love with somebody else." Her words burst out in a breathless rush.

"But I'd never withdrawn my offer of marriage. Lady Alice had been working on her father all that time. She'd never stopped hoping."

"Then was it right to mislead me?" cried Clara, suddenly beside herself.

She plucked several envelopes from a pocket just as a digni-fied man in a frock coat was entering the gallery. Clara recognized Mr. Harsent, the manager of Sarston's largest bank. But had he been the Prime Minister, she could not have kept silent. She chose a letter at random and started to read in a trembling voice. " 'I can't endure not seeing you, my sweet. Please, please, my love, let me touch your hand and breathe the air where you have stood just for a few minutes each day. I must look into your lovely eyes and—' "

"Clara, please . . . we're not alone," gasped Charles, no longer suavely insouciant.

"How could you write like that while knowing you hadn't finished with her?"

"I never expected her father to relent. So of course I saw no point in hurting her a second time by ending it formally."

"What about *my* feelings, Charles? Didn't they deserve the same consideration?"

He moved closer, blocking the bank manager's view of her. Then he said in his saddest, most caressing voice, "Clara, I can't bear you to think I didn't adore you. Never in my worst nightmares did I dream of a situation like this."

Clara detected traces of normal Charles peeping through cracks in his contrite mask. He darted an oblique look at her from under half-closed lids—exactly the kind of covert glance he always employed when judging the effect he was having on anyone. But his physical presence still dazed her: the way his hair was brushed up like burnished wings on either side of his head, the confident curl of his lips, his graceful movements. And yet she felt a spasm of fierce dislike.

Clara said very quietly, "Why lie to me, Charles? You did exactly what you wanted. She was your first choice, but in case you couldn't have her, you thought you'd better have a second string. No time wasted then." Only while actually saying this did Clara know in her heart that she had been used. A wave of grief left her gasping and sniffing.

"Don't cry, Clara. I can't bear us to part like this." Again the tender catch in his voice. He tried to take her hand, but she thrust him away furiously. Her breasts were heaving as she struggled not to weep. Her sense of outrage was so great that she no longer cared what he thought. She saw her reflection in the glass of a small watercolor—a face as melodramatic as any depicted on the gallery walls. Like a madwoman, she thought, sobered by it. Would Lady Alice ever demean herself like this? She who had grown up under the gaze of gamekeepers and ditchers, coachmen and parlormaids? Of course not. Lady Alice would be an asset to her husband, however badly he behaved. Clara had imagined being proud and dignified. But now behaving well seemed a forlorn and empty consolation. Wouldn't it only make their parting easier for him if she remained stoical? And then she simply decided she had had enough.

She was turning to go, when she felt his restraining hands on her shoulders. A party of schoolchildren with their teacher was entering the gallery.

"Please let me go," she murmured coldly.

"Can I have the rest of my letters?" he asked in a low, urgent voice.

Across the gallery, immediately beneath the soft white flesh of a large Lord Leighton nude, the children were being warned by their teacher not to snigger. Clara did not take in his words as he urged them to show respect in this "temple of art." All she was aware of was a smile hovering on Charles's shapely lips. Moments before their parting forever, he was smiling—actually smiling. She couldn't believe it. He had been shameless enough to ask for his letters, having made her no apology for his behavior. It was perfectly obvious that without her threat to send the letters to Lady Alice, Charles would never have met her here. With a shout of rage, she plunged her hands into her pockets and tossed handfuls of letters up into the air. As she turned to go, she heard a burst of ragged laughter from the children. Charles Vyner was on his knees, scrabbling to retrieve his lying words.

CHAPTER 2

In the months that followed her rejection, Clara's pain and bewilderment did not fade away. Her worried father held himself partly responsible. By spoiling Clara, he believed, he had led her to expect to get whatever she wanted and had therefore left her ill prepared to endure failure or disappointment. During their largely silent meals, Alfred often recalled how happy and talkative she had been as a child before her mother died. Afterward, he had thought that her faith would enable Clara to accept her loss. And sometimes, in the years that followed, she had seemed to come to terms with it, but little incidents had kept reminding Alfred that her deepest wounds remained unhealed.

One day, three years after her mother's death, Clara—then fifteen—had been walking home with Alfred from a chapel meeting. It had been early evening, and they could see into many lamplit rooms. The area of town was a poor one, with numerous rooming houses. In a drab basement room of one such house, two children were sitting up in little cots, while their mother bent over them. ''That's the only heaven there is,'' Clara had blurted out. A few weeks later, she had stopped coming to chapel with her father, and soon she had pained him by visiting friends on the Sabbath and by playing tennis—though in deference to chapelgoers' feelings, she always wrapped her racket in brown paper on her way to the courts.

Clara's friends were mostly the daughters of affluent people—solicitors, potters' valuers, commission agents, and so forth. With them, she attended dress shows and Palm Court concerts and went on shopping expeditions. Alfred sometimes wept at the change in her. He remembered Clara in childhood begging to accompany her mother, whenever she visited sick old women or read the Bible to the girls employed in a local cardboard factory. Some of these workers had been tubercular, and this was later thought to explain the infection that had killed Mrs. Musson.

Clara knew she was making her father wretched by absenting herself from the chapel's social functions as well as from its religious services. But she could not help it. As a girl she had loved to do good deeds. But the impulse had died with her mother; and afterward, charitable acts, performed against the grain, had made her feel mean and hypocritical. She had gone on helping people only out of a sense of duty, and so had lost the afterglow that had once rewarded her spontaneous acts of generosity.

Years earlier, Clara had prayed that her bullying dancing teacher would die. And although God had not answered this prayer, Clara had never quite broken the habit of appealing for special favors. "Please let my mother live" had merely been the last and most urgent appeal of all. Yet even then Clara had known in her heart that no God could be worth believing in if He listened to individual pleas. He was omniscient, so if something was right and just, He would do it anyway, without needing to be nudged. After her mother's death, the process of praying had become synonymous with giving up hope. How could it have been right or just of Him not to have spared such a good and blameless person? Clara felt that she had been talking to herself. It was now nine years since she had prayed.

In the months after losing Charles, Clara tried, with limited success, to be rational about what had happened. She had loved him, she told herself, without knowing what sort of man he was. It was shameful to admit it, but she had probably been influenced by the romantic novels of Miss Braddon and Charlotte M. Yonge. Their humble heroines obeyed their hearts and fell for well-born heroes who, if sometimes feckless, at least always lived in elegant surroundings. And in Clara's case, surroundings had been important. The plain and ugly furniture in her father's house, the wax flowers and beadwork, the devotional texts in their heavy frames, had made Clara hungry for beauty. The drabness of the town had added to her sense of artistic deprivation. So when Charles Vyner preached his gospel of high art and hedonism, he had found a receptive pupil in Clara. How delightful, after she had admired magnificent rooms, to sit under a parasol in an open phaeton en route to a bluebell wood, there to enjoy a picnic of tender lamb cutlets on a bed of asparagus tips, followed by cold partridge and a crisp salad, all washed down with chilled champagne. Looking back on such halcyon days and on Charles's many amusing sayings, Clara told herself that without loyalty and respect between people, nothing they did together could signify a thing—and yet she still could not end her grief.

On a freezing evening almost a year later, Alfred asked Clara to come with him to a fund-raising lecture in the town's Temperance Hall. He had noticed a marked improvement in his daughter's spirits, and so felt hopeful that she would come. The lecture was to be delivered by a missionary who had just returned from Africa and had already given some very popular talks in London. Such men were received by the faithful of Sarston with almost as much adulation as was lavished upon world-famous explorers. But while Alfred knew that he could hardly expect Clara to react in that way, he was confident that she would be impressed. He had met Robert Haslam at a prayer meeting in an alderman's house and considered him superior to most missionaries.

Knowing how disappointed her father would be if she refused to come, Clara accepted his invitation. Being familiar with the jargon of evangelism, she expected to be bored. When she arrived, the atmosphere in the Temperance Hall was expectant and emotional. People wanted to be moved by tales of noble endeavor. Clara, seeing the missionary step onto the dais, was at first amused. His skin had been so darkly tanned that he looked like a Negro himself. His jutting brows and slightly emaciated face reminded her of Elijah (or had it been Elisha?) as depicted in a well-remembered child's edition of the Old Testament. As he began to speak, she stifled a laugh. His voice was strange, as if his tongue had trouble framing ordinary words; he spoke English with perfect grammar but with a most peculiar accent.

Yet the rustling of dresses and scattered coughs soon died away. Although Clara was irritated by the rapt expressions on so many admiring female faces, even she could not deny that Robert Haslam was a peculiarly persuasive man. Instead of treating them to missionary clichés about dark and degraded minds being illuminated by the Gospel, he asked his audience to consider what *they* would think if a stranger arrived in Sarston and asked them to abandon their customs.

"Would *you* give up monogamous marriage because a foreigner said it was wrongheaded? I'm sure you wouldn't—not even when he told you that in his country a man can be respected only if he has many wives and children. Or would you agree to give your house and land to the king because an African told you that only kings are entitled to own land?'' Robert Haslam gazed benignly at the well-dressed people sitting in the front row. ''Of course you wouldn't. It's hard to abandon one's own customs, even when somebody who may know better tells you why you should. That's why missionaries have to understand the people they wish to convert.'' He looked around. ''Are there any bankers here tonight? If so, prepare to be shocked. I'm afraid Africans think that thrift is evil. In my small village, if my harvest is better than my neighbor's, I'd be wise to share my grain with him. Next year my harvest may be poor and his may be abundant. Africans survive famines by sharing their grain and not by selfishly saving it for themselves.'' Again he looked around. ''There must be many shopkeepers and manufacturers here. Well, my friends, *you* won't like to hear *this*: Africans care nothing for punctuality. They've no clocks and have never heard a factory bell. They think it's better to take life easy than to rush from place to place.''

Clara felt bemused. If no way of life was better or worse than any other, how could a missionary expect people to believe that his beliefs were superior? She was pondering this when Haslam declared loudly:

''Africans ought to live as they like: owning little, sharing much, without envy of each other or lust for wealth.'' He smiled reassuringly at the puzzled faces in front of him. ''But, my friends, while I love my African brothers and find much among them to admire, I see terrible cruelty too. When I first came to live with Chief Mponda's people, Mponda had just strangled one of his wives for infidelity. Polygamy is unimaginably vile, and I am fighting it with all my strength. Mponda gives orders for twins to be murdered at birth. Tradition tells him that disaster will strike if he doesn't. He's not an unusually brutal chief, but in his eyes trial by ordeal is a perfect form of justice. So innocent people are forced to drink poison every year. And many harmless men and women are drowned or burned as witches. You cannot imagine the suffering caused by witchcraft unless you witness the horror of it yourself. Ladies and gentlemen, the conversion of a single chief to Christianity can spare the lives of hundreds and save the souls of thousands more. Unless you support missions with money, then you will be as bad as the man who sees someone dying in the gutter but does nothing to lift him up.''

Robert Haslam was soon describing his winning of the tribe's trust by treating diseases and building a watercourse. It suddenly came to Clara why his accent was so strange. The man had spoken no English for years. She gazed at him in astonishment. Without anyone of his own race to help him, this gaunt-faced man had compiled a native dictionary and translated the Bible. His description of doing this was so straightforward that she saw at once how incredibly difficult it must have been to find native idioms to match English ones, especially since numerous English words had no African counterparts.

Haslam now described an attempt to kill him. He had been invited to watch a lion hunt, and during it, a spear had been thrown, wounding him in the thigh. Since he had been standing nowhere near the cornered beast, this could only have been a deliberate attack. Clara felt a tight emotional ache in her throat. She could not help comparing the dangerous events of his life with the petty social happenings of her own. He had risked everything repeatedly for the sake of others, yet how many times, since her mother's death, had *she* run even the small risk of visiting one of her father's sick workers? Unless giving employment to the dressmakers and drapers could be said to justify an existence, what did she ever do that was of the smallest benefit to a living soul?

As the missionary uttered passages of Scripture, Clara remembered her mother's lips framing the selfsame verses, and her eyes filled. ''For what does it profit a man to gain the whole world and forfeit his soul ... I am come that they might have life more abundantly ... Commit thy way unto the Lord and He shall direct thy steps.'' For the first time in years, the meaning of these passages shone out clearly for her. She sensed that he would soon stop speaking and realized that she did not want this to happen. His voice sounded clumsy to her no longer, but rich and full and at the same time decisive. When he said a final prayer for all the suffering people in the world, the men and women around her were sinking to their knees.

Afterward, Robert's outspread hands and compassionate eyes remained with Clara as she walked wet-cheeked into the gaslit street. Charles had once told her that all acts of self-sacrifice gratified some hidden desire or eased some personal fear. Self-indulgence was a lot less devious, he had said. How trivial he seemed now.

The following day, Clara could not get Robert Haslam out

of her mind. His dedication and courage haunted her. Until now she had regarded a man of almost forty as practically in his grave. Yet when she thought of Robert, age became irrelevant. Almost for the first time in her life, she believed she had encountered a truly good man. Thinking about him, Clara remembered something she had not thought about for years. When she was four, her favorite doll had been a small Negress made of wood. She had been called Martha, and Clara's love for her had continued long after her hair fell out and her skull became dotted with holes like a worn-out brush. Without understanding why, Clara found this memory comforting.

Alfred Musson was treasurer of the West Street Chapel, and so most visiting preachers and missionary fund-raisers came to dine with him before they left Sarston. Robert Haslam was no exception. In the hall, his weather-beaten face and powerful voice had made Clara think him rugged. Seeing him again, and so close to her, she was surprised by his long, delicate features and high forehead. As he shook her hand, he said something unremarkable about being pleased to be dining with her father, and she was aware of his hand pressing hers. Though physically slighter than she remembered, he still radiated strength.

Despite his graying hair and lined face, Clara noticed a boyish untidiness about the missionary: buttons missing on his old frock coat and a tendency for his necktie to slip to one side. He also had a habit of sitting exactly as it pleased him: hunched forward or leaning far back in his chair. On his first evening at her house, Robert Haslam managed to make her father laugh while discussing that most delicate of all subjects, ''political agitation.'' Robert achieved this by luring her father into suggesting ever more barbaric punishments for union men, until at last even Alfred had exploded at the absurdity of it all.

After they had finished eating, Clara tried to get Robert to tell her more about the lion hunt and the attack on him that might have ended his life; instead he talked about lion hunting in general and the extraordinary bravery of the hunters.

''Imagine being so close that you can smell the lion's breath and hear the black tuft on his tail thumping the ground. Even then you won't be close enough to kill him with a spear.''

Robert said other things that made Clara think he was deliberately trying to understate the dangers and discomforts he had
faced. He talked about the kind of toys African children liked—
tin trumpets and skittles were very popular; and how Africans re-
acted on first seeing such civilized wonders as Eno's Fruit Salts
fizzing in a glass—they believed it would be boiling hot. Haslam
did not mention his wife's death in Africa five years before—Clara
learned this from her father after Robert had gone. Later during
this first evening, her father tried to get his guest to define how he
stood on a particular doctrine that was currently controversial
among nonconformists. But Robert sidestepped the question, saying instead something that would stick in Clara's mind.

"Christianity is really a way of life and nothing to do with
dogma. There's only one question to ask: 'Do I follow the example
of Christ's life in the way I live mine?' No other question
matters."

Alfred Musson had heard that Robert Haslam meant to spend
no more than ten days in Sarston. In fact he would stay nearly
three weeks, returning there, after lecturing in other towns, on five
separate occasions before his furlough expired.

One afternoon, a few days after dining at the Mussons', Haslam called on them again. Alfred was not at home, but Clara received the missionary in her father's library. After some
inconsequential chatter, Haslam lifted a copy of David Livingstone's *Missionary Travels* from the shelves and started to read
aloud. In Robert's chosen passage, the great man described how
he had made his own building bricks and how his wife had baked
their bread in an oven hollowed out of an anthill.

" 'There is little hardship in self-dependence, and married
life is all the sweeter when so many comforts emanate from a
husband's and wife's own hands. To some it may even seem a
romantic life.' " Robert had read these words with an apologetic
smile. But from the expression on Clara's face, it was clear that
she did not think he had any need to reproach himself. He was
still reading when Alfred returned, almost an hour later.

On the following Sunday morning, Alfred left early for
chapel with some of the other elders. Clara had not thought of
going too, until Mr. Haslam unexpectedly called for her. As she

walked beside him through the town, feeling slightly dazed, she became intensely aware of the shape of his hands and of a lock of hair that fell across his brow. She found herself telling him about a revival meeting in the chapel years earlier and her failure to declare her faith. This memory upset her more than she had expected.

"But I see God shining in you so clearly," he insisted. And then, to her amazement, the warm concern in his ungainly voice squeezed from her the admission that she had lost her faith. It was the last thing she had imagined herself telling him. Yet now that she had done so, she longed for guidance.

Robert said gently, "Seeds of belief can remain dormant for years before coming to life. Don't regret the past, Miss Musson. Our lapses and our returns to Christ are all part of our spiritual growth, like circles in the trunk of a tree."

It was a bitterly cold morning, and their breath came in clouds. As they crossed the railway bridge, a red signal light glowed in the deep canyon of the track.

"But surely," she murmured anxiously, "dormant seeds don't come to life unless the soil around them changes."

He gazed at her with understanding. "Changes can come imperceptibly, like a sea tide. Even now the change may be on its way." His eyes held hers, and for a fraction of a moment she felt that they saw each other without any barriers or pretenses. "You mustn't worry," he added softly. "Not everyone has a Damascus Road experience. Love life. Follow Christ's example. Seek and ye shall find."

At first she pretended to herself that she did not know why these words were such a relief to her. But she did know, really. If he had been disappointed by her confession, or condescendingly censorious, it would have been impossible for her to continue seeing him. But since he seemed happy with a gradual process of aspiring toward faith, she could feel relaxed with him.

In the immediate aftermath of Charles's treachery, Clara had made the acquaintance of some cavalry officers, whose regiment had been stationed just outside Sarston. Subsequently she had been invited to witness full-dress parades and point-to-points and to attend a regimental ball. The conversation of her hosts had been largely about sport and horses; and since many of them were said to have mistresses, Clara had found it hard to feel at ease with them. By their code of behavior, a born lady, or even a rich merchant's daughter like herself, was absolutely out of bounds before marriage, since she would be "ruined" if "deflowered"—more accurately, her marriage chances would be ruined. Consequently many of these young officers preferred affairs with married women.

After Charles's treachery, Clara felt that she could never risk marrying any man who she suspected might be the type to fall in and out of love. She could not endure the thought of becoming one of those wives who were obliged to turn for their happiness to children, house, and garden after their husbands had betrayed them. If she was ever to give her heart again, she would have to be sure that she was prized by an entirely honorable man. In spite of having longed to be mistress of a great house, she now thought only of being married to a man with special qualities. Her faith in love had survived but in a new form: she saw it as something sacred—more a matter of personal dedication than an arrangement bringing happiness or self-fulfillment.

When Robert had left the Mussons' house after dining there for the fourth time, Clara experienced an emptiness so desolating that she could not hide her distress. In six weeks Robert would return to Africa, and she might never see him again. Although Clara herself did not know it, her father was well aware of her feelings and was terrified by them. Since his wife's death, Alfred had become so dependent on Clara that he dreaded the day when she would eventually marry. The possibility that she might then live abroad had been his worst nightmare. Yet so absorbed had Clara been with her own emotions that she had scarcely noticed her father's distress.

After breakfast each day, Alfred usually retired to his study to go through his post and read the papers before leaving for the pottery works. Clara would listen for his tread on the stairs, so she could be in the hall in time to kiss him goodbye. On the morning following another of Haslam's evening visits, Clara moved toward her father in the usual way, but he stepped back from her. His kind, tired eyes were acutely anxious.

"You'll be seeing Mr. Haslam later, I daresay?"

"He's presenting Scripture prizes at Mill Lane School," she answered, as if the event were only of passing interest to her.

"Will you be going, Clara?"

"I've been asked, so perhaps I will." But of course she would go, and she knew that her father knew. His silence was very painful to her.

"Do you love him?" he blurted out at last. The fear in his voice both reproached and stung her. How could something so precious to her seem like death to him?

"What a question!" she replied briskly, forcing a smile. Her father's tragic expression did not alter.

"*He* certainly loves *you*."

"He's never given me any sign of it."

Her father took a deep breath, as if struggling to suppress anger. "Then why does he keep visiting us?"

"Don't be angry," she begged. How could her even-tempered and affectionate father feel such hostility? His face was flushed, and he could not keep still.

"It's unforgivable," he burst out. "A man of his age playing on a young girl's feelings. But he's so good and selfless, isn't he?"

"He *is* good, Father," she insisted.

"Is he really?" Her father nodded with heavy irony. "What's *good* about making you love him just before he leaves for Africa? Do *good* men behave like that?"

"My feelings are my fault, not his."

"Don't be an idiot, Clara. He'll ask for your hand as soon as he thinks you can't bear him to leave England. Missionaries aren't fools. They know that when they ask too soon, the woman is still too worried about foreign discomforts to say yes. She'll only lose her head when the man's about to go."

"You don't know Robert at all," she gasped out, stunned by her father's mistrust. At the same time she was wildly excited. Was he right? Could Robert really love her?

That afternoon, she went to the prize-giving. The school hall was crowded with pupils, parents, and visitors. Robert talked to the children in a relaxed and natural way about how African girls and boys spent their days, and what was expected of them by their parents and their chief. As always, Clara was moved by seeing this ungainly but mesmeric man holding the attention of a roomful of people. She could not stop gazing at him. His hair was graying, but his brisk movements were those of a far younger man.

After the prizes had been presented, the governors and their wives departed, and Clara pushed her way through the throng of children toward the platform. She found Robert talking animatedly to the new mistress of the junior school. To see him standing beside this young and attractive woman made Clara catch her breath—not because she suspected that their conversation was anything but innocent, but because in that instant it came to her that Robert owed her no special duty of any kind. It was quite possible that he respected the teacher more than her, since she earned her living and was of use to others. Clara walked away to calm herself for a moment, but cannoned into the headmaster in the doorway. He was dragging in a pretty curly-haired girl by the ear. The child looked familiar to Clara.

"Let her go," she cried. Her anger at this public humiliation of a child was sharpened by her own distress. "What on earth has she done?"

"She didn't curtsy to the governors' wives," snapped the headmaster. "Didn't even stand still, though they walked by as close as you are, Miss Musson."

As the headmaster released his grip, the girl raised her head, and Clara at once recognized her.

"Will you cane her hands, Mr. Rivett?"

Mr. Rivett drew himself up. "I think you can depend on me to know what punishment is required when children show no respect to their betters."

A year earlier, Clara had sometimes come to the school to read to the younger children when their teacher was ill. She remembered this particular child, in her spotless pinafore and carefully darned stockings. Her name was Jane Hobley, and her younger sister had recently died and been denied a church funeral—only receiving committal prayers at the graveside—and all because the vicar had mistakenly feared that the corpse might infect the congregation. Diphtheria had been given as the cause of death on the certificate, although the doctor had never visited her. The family had sworn that she died of pneumonia, but the vicar had refused to lift his ban.

Clara said sharply, "Were the vicar and his wife anywhere nearby when Jane refused to curtsy?"

"They were, Miss Musson, but I fail to see what that can signify."

While Clara was explaining, with Jane's help, she turned and saw Robert Haslam listening to her. As soon as the child had been pardoned, Robert eyed Clara with such a tender gaze that her cheeks burned.

"I might have known you'd hate injustice," he said softly. And his admiration set her pulse knocking loud and swift. He *does* care for me, she told herself. She was overjoyed and yet frightened. From the moment she had started to care for him, she had feared that a man who gave his whole life to the service of others would expect too much of those close to him. Then she reminded herself that Charles too had been daunting, in his own way. Perhaps she needed to be a little fearful of a man in order to fall in love with him.

Robert offered to walk Clara home. As they emerged in the darkening street, the lamplighter was at work with his pole and ladder, and shops were closing. Robert was intrigued by the jeweler's immense roll-down iron shutter, which was being levered into position as they passed.

"People in my village would think the English very wicked to need such a thing." He smiled at her, but Clara was unsure whether he was being serious.

"Are Africans really better people than we are?"

"I only wish they were." He sighed. "In most tribes, the basketmaker and the blacksmith are the only skilled craftsmen, so there aren't any precious objects to steal. Oxen are valuable; but every beast is immediately recognized, so only a madman would steal one. I'm afraid there's very little virtue in their honesty."

"Do they ever steal from you?"

"Never."

"But you must own things they consider precious."

"Oh, yes. But if they took my watch or even a cup or spoon, it would be obvious where it came from if they ever used it." After a pause, he murmured, "I really can't express how much I enjoy talking to you about Africa."

The coal smoke in the air made Robert cough a good deal as they walked. After the clear, warm air of Africa, Clara imagined he must find these winter days in Sarston an ordeal. She could not help noticing how much more solemn he grew as they neared their destination. Then, unexpectedly, Robert took her arm. It was the first time he had touched her except to shake hands, and the pressure of his fingers through her coat filled her with unreasoning happiness.

As they were walking along beside the railings of the little park close to her father's house, she turned to Robert. He was staring ahead, unconscious that he was being observed. They were passing a lamp, and in that startling instant, before he could compose his face, she saw a look of such anguished uncertainty that her view of him as someone far above ordinary human frailty vanished like summer dew. And her knowledge of his weakness undid her. At that moment, she knew that never, not even in dreams, had she felt anything to compare with her love for this man.

Without looking at her, he said in a voice that was both harsh and breathless, "I know I haven't the right to ask as much of anyone—only Christ had the right to ask it of his disciples—but I must ask you, Clara, though you can have no idea of the sacrifices involved. You will have to give up everything if you accept me."

"Love is not afraid of sacrifices," she whispered.

"Then will you have me?" Hope transformed him after his nervousness. She was amazed at the force of the emotion her few words had unleashed. Yet while she remained silent, he still suffered. It was intolerable that he should be afraid and looking to her for a sign. She reached out her hands in a gesture of profound sympathy.

"Yes," she told him. "Yes, my love."

Light-headed with relief, they embraced, leaning weakly against the sooty railings of the municipal park. The gas lamps glowed like blurred haloes in the evening fog.

When Alfred Musson heard the news of Clara's decision, he wept. Clara had expected grief, but not the terrible racking sobs that shook her father's body. Alfred had guessed that a proposal would be made, but he never dreamed that his daughter would accept without first discussing her answer. He was inclined to forbid the match but knew that Clara would disobey him if he did. He would also look ridiculous. Chapel elders could not with impunity pay lip service to the heroism of missionaries one moment, and the next treat them like lepers unworthy to offer marriage to decent tradesmen's daughters.

Alfred lay awake for hours each night and soon looked thin and haggard. While Clara could scarcely remember a time when he had not gone to the works unless really ill, in the days immediately after her announcement he delegated everything to his general manager and hardly left the house. Every day, he kept up his onslaught against the marriage, until Clara refused to dine with him unless he promised not to speak of it. Whatever his intentions, he usually succumbed to an outpouring of reproaches before Mrs. Gabb, the housekeeper, brought in their pudding.

His complaints, though numerous, were invariably the same: the discrepancy in their ages made such a union unnatural; Haslam had taken advantage of her youth and innocence; scores of white people died of disease in Africa every year; there were no doctors for hundreds of miles; and absolutely no society. For a woman raised in the colonies, the life would be harsh, but for a gently nurtured girl from England it would be torture. According to Clara's father, Robert was considering not her interests but only his own pleasure and comfort. And what about me? asked Alfred. "Has Robert Haslam given a single thought to the constant dread a father feels when he knows that any day he may hear news of his child's death?" Alfred was also very angry that Robert had not talked seriously to Clara about recent disturbances in South Central Africa. In 1893, a mere two years before, the white pioneers had defeated the Matabele without subduing them. And why should a proud tribe of savages, who had not yet committed themselves in an all-out struggle, be content to accept the rule of white foreigners in a country over which they themselves had long claimed sovereignty?

Her father's conviction that Robert had somehow used his greater age and experience to trick her into accepting him made Clara very angry. In her opinion, to marry a man both wiser and morally better than herself could only be to her advantage. Never again, she told her father, after becoming Robert's wife, would she feel guilty about leading a pointless existence.

"Do you want me to live in a cage?" she asked during supper one evening. "I might as well be dead if I spend the rest of my life in Sarston."

Alfred put down his knife and fork and said sadly, "You wouldn't be the only girl to marry a local man and choose to live close to a widowed parent."

"Oh, yes," she cried. "And people would applaud me. They'd praise me even more if I remained a spinster and lived with you. Noble and self-sacrificing, they'd call it. *I* call it cowardly to run away from risks. How could I turn my back on the fullest life I could ever hope to live?"

"It may be a short life," he muttered. His moist eyes under their familiar bushy eyebrows made Clara feel brutal. His hair had become much thinner recently, making him seem older and more vulnerable.

"Nobody knows more about Africa than Robert," she reassured, distressed by his unhappiness. "Of course he'll look after me."

He reached out to her across the plates to grasp her hands. "Clara, I beg you to examine your motives. Aren't you confusing love with a passion for adventure? Are you really sure you're in love?"

All Clara's tender feelings were frozen by his refusal to accept the reality of her emotions. And, as so often those days, their conversation ended in recrimination.

Alfred's last throw came two days later, when he threatened to disinherit her. Knowing he did not expect to influence her, Clara guessed that he hoped Robert might decide to delay matters, in case his haste might do lasting damage to his future wife. But Clara simply told her father, as gently as she knew how, that she would marry, with or without his consent, before the end of Robert's furlough. From that moment, Alfred's will to oppose her collapsed. If she was bent on self-destruction, what could he do?

So Robert Haslam and Clara Musson were married. Alfred wanted a quiet ceremony, and since Robert's parents were dead, there was nobody to argue with him. Certainly Clara did not want to see Sarston's richest citizens studying her through lorgnettes and opera glasses. Her father's incredulity at her choice of partner was a useful indication of what she might have expected from other affluent members of the community, and she had therefore been determined to give their curiosity no scope.

Afterward, Clara would have preferred to take rooms in Sarston, or elsewhere, until their departure for Africa; but her father would have seen that as a further act of betrayal. So a second bed had been moved into the room that had been hers since childhood, and it was here that her marriage was consummated. And in spite of the strain of being in the same house as her father, Clara was ecstatically happy. Robert treated her with devoted reverence, often murmuring endearments that sounded very like prayers to her, not that she minded in the least. He once spoke of her bed as "the altar of my passion," a phrase she thought beautiful and in the spirit of "with my body I thee worship." Their lovemaking became for her not just the greatest pleasure in her life but a perfect expression of their real union.

To please her father, she took Robert to the works one day and showed him the various processes through which raw clay passed before its final transformation into painted and glazed vessels. They examined the huge cupboards in which the pots were steam-dried, row after row of them on shelves. " 'Hath not the potter power over the clay, of the same lump to make one vessel unto honor, and another unto dishonor,' " declaimed Robert. Alfred was dismayed when the missionary expressed pity for the girl who painted the lines on cups. Her job was dull now, agreed Alfred, but one day she would graduate to flowers and be the envy of the other factory girls.

The following day, Clara and Robert drove out in Alfred's brougham onto the moors to the west of the town. The landscape was scarred by spoil from coal mines, and the pit-villages they passed were drab and grim. But Robert had been hungry for open skies. Up on the top of Hartoft Ridge, Clara told the coachman to stop, and they got out. There had been heavy rain, and the moorland was dark and forbidding. They walked along the track, stepping between puddles that reflected a stormy sky.

After walking in silence for some time, he stroked the fur trimming on the cuffs of her coat. "I'm afraid you'll need rather different clothes in Africa."

Pleased that he should want to discuss her wardrobe, Clara said eagerly, "I've been going through the catalogues of several tropical outfitters."

Robert frowned. "Don't they mainly cater for the kind of ladies who go to Africa with their husbands to shoot game? I'd prefer you to wear homelier things. A local dressmaker could run up some simple designs. Fine and fancy things don't last, not with frequent washing."

"But will I have time to get everything made before we sail? The outfitters do at least have plenty of styles and sizes in stock."

He looked her full in her face, and she knew at once that he was bracing himself to say something she would find unwelcome. "I've thought a lot about this," he said at last. "I'm afraid we can't go out together at the same time. Before I left, the tribe was about to move to better grazing. I'll have to build another house for us in the new village."

Too shocked to speak at first, she finally gasped, "Can't we live in a native hut while you're building it?"

"It wouldn't suit you at all."

"I'm not a Dresden shepherdess," she cried.

"Clara, my sweet, their huts have no chimneys. Smoke from the cooking fire seeps out through the thatch and goes everywhere. In the rainy season, the mud's terrible, even inside. They know nothing about drainage."

She grasped his arm. "I'd rather drown than stay in Sarston without you. Think what my father's going to say."

Robert slipped an arm around her waist. "I wish I could alter the facts, my dearest. I'd love you to come out with me, but it wouldn't be right. Water's a worse problem. A few weeks after the rains end, there won't be a drop for a bath. Everything has to be saved for drinking and cooking. Until I've built a storage dam, life will be unbearable."

She was so choked that her voice was scarcely audible. "Why didn't you tell me weeks ago?"

"It would only have depressed you."

"I had a right to know."

"It would have cast a cloud over our wedding. I can't believe it would have made you refuse me if you'd known."

"Of course not. But there would have been less reason to marry quickly. That's the point."

"You're wrong there, Clara. I won't be in England again for five or six years."

Clara felt an ache of disappointment in her throat. Robert was wonderfully clearheaded, but he had no idea why he had caused her such offense. By protecting her from unpleasant living conditions, he had shown a serious lack of faith in her. How many missionaries felt that their wives lacked the fortitude to share all their discomforts? Hardly any, she imagined. When Robert tried to hold her gloved hand, she pulled it away. Even as she longed for him to let her suffer in silence, he kept telling her things he ought to have said before. Apparently a schoolhouse and a chapel had also to be built in the new place. But worse than anything was his determination to delay her arrival until after the chief had been converted.

"I would like to see his baptism more than anything on earth, Robert. I know how much it will mean to you."

He refused to meet her outraged eyes, but stared at his muddy shoes. "I wish the chief had no enemies, but he does; and these misguided people bitterly oppose his conversion. They hate me, Clara." He sighed heavily. "I can't give them a chance to upset you, my dear. As soon as the ceremony has taken place, there'll be no more hostility. For both our sakes, please be patient. It may not be as long as a year. Please try to understand.''

"A year?" she repeated dumbly.

She stood motionless for a moment, then turned abruptly and walked toward the brougham. Dear God, a year. Robert walked beside her for a while, until she turned her back on him so pointedly that he stopped. When she reached the carriage, she told the coachman to drive her home.

"And the gentleman, madam?"

"He wants to walk."

The coachman did not know Robert's identity and so was only mildly surprised. In the interests of economy, Clara's father—though owning a carriage—did not employ his own coachman but instead hired a man from the local livery stables whenever he or Clara wished to be driven.

As the brougham began to move, Clara realized she was being childish and spiteful in a girlish way; but in her eyes, this did not make her situation any less tragic. How could he speak of not seeing her for a year without tears and without contrition? A separation, which would plunge her into a black midnight of loneliness—was *that* something to tag onto the end of a long list of difficulties, as though it were just another item? Perhaps she should have listened to her father. But Clara's pride prevented her from admitting such a possibility. If she'd been wrong, she would simply face the consequences.

Only moments after she had entertained such stoical thoughts, the rapid motion of the brougham and the passing moorland made her panic. Suppose Robert was never to forgive the insult to his dignity? Of course, he would *say* he did, but would it be true? Would he ever understand how much he had hurt her? Although she longed to shout out to the man to stop, or, better still, to turn around, when she thought of Robert's offense she wanted to fling herself on the padded leather and weep. While her throat was tight and her eyes smarted, she did not shed a tear.

As the brougham passed some farm buildings about half a mile from the spot where Clara and Robert had walked together, the coachman bent down from the box and tapped on the front window. She let it down a little.

"The gentleman, ma'am. He's runnin' and wavin' behind."

Clara turned and peered through the small oval rear window.

Robert was indeed running and waving; a sad, ungainly figure in the distance.

"You'd better stop," she muttered, not knowing whether to weep or laugh.

When Haslam reached the carriage, he was panting, and his shoes and trousers were plastered with mud. The coachman let down the step and opened the door, and Robert clambered in. He sat huddled in the corner, as if afraid his wife might recoil from him if he presumed to sit too close. After the brougham had moved off, Clara glanced at him, and his posture was so humble that her feelings began to soften. But she did not turn to him or give him any sign of her more forgiving mood.

"I ... I ... really ...," he gasped, still very breathless after running, "really should have warned you. I've been alone too long ... too long isolated from the company of gentlewomen. I ask your pardon, Clara, I lost my first dear wife. ... Only my concern for your safety gave me the strength ... to be unselfish enough to consider returning without you."

She was moved by his words but said quite coldly, "That's no excuse for keeping your fears to yourself."

"I was afraid I might put you off. ... I loved you so much. I couldn't endure the thought that I might lose you." He looked at her with such sad, contrite eyes that she could not help moving toward him. The next moment, he was kneeling, clumsily embracing her waist. To see her dignified Robert at her feet was so astonishing that she almost forgave him there and then. "There is another point," he murmured, resuming his seat. "I'd have little time to be with you if you come now. I'll rarely escape the saw pit and the carpenter's bench while there's building work to be done."

Robert's appearance was so slim and scholarly that to think of him bent double, wielding an ax or a pick, upset her. During the journey home, she allowed him to hold her hand for a few minutes toward the end of their journey.

Once Robert realized that he was forgiven, he was so overjoyed that he burst into tears—something she would never have thought him capable of. Only hours later did she realize that he had held his ground and got her to accept that he would return to Africa alone.

*   *   *

Clara could not remember ever being so miserable. Her days were spent in endless meditation on the theme of Robert. Sometimes her longing for his tangible presence was almost too painful to be borne. Yet in spite of her unhappiness, she found that she still had faith in her future. She told herself that people survived even after a spouse had disappeared or died; and hers was not even missing. Surely she could wait courageously for their reunion.

Just over four months from the day of Robert's departure, Clara received a letter from him. In it, Robert listed various objectives achieved and others still eluding him. There were anecdotes about the chief and his wives, and about the principal headmen. Yet whether the chief, or anyone else, had been converted, Clara was not told. Nor was this her only disappointment. Robert's concluding lines were loving, but though she read them many times to tease out every nuance, she still found them insufficiently ardent. In writing to him, she was more passionate and made it clear how much he was missed, even though she knew her letters could not reach him unless a trader rode out to his remote kraal from the nearest mining settlement.

Sitting in her room, she often recalled individual conversations and acts of love. Sometimes she walked to places they had visited and retraced their steps, as if some vestige of him still lingered there. She was haunted by him—by his ascetic, noble face, by his hands and limbs and body, by his high aims. And always she longed for his next letter. The geographical impediments to their correspondence did not spare her from feeling bitter when, yet again, the postman's visit failed to yield the thing on earth she most desired.

Another two months passed without a word, and Clara fought a losing battle against self-pity. Robert might have been dead for weeks, for all she knew. Her father never mentioned this possibility, but Clara suspected that he harbored hopes that the long silence might indeed end with sorrowful news. Certainly, when the next letter eventually came, Alfred was not pleased. Robert informed Clara that the chief's conversion was imminent and that she should plan to sail for Cape Town at the end of July, months earlier than she had anticipated in her most optimistic daydreams. She felt so rich in happiness that her father's sighs and long faces made no impression upon her.

In his letter, Robert advised her to make her travel plans in concert with the foreign secretary of the London Missionary Society, to whom he himself had already written. If no other missionaries and their wives were traveling up from the Cape to Mashonaland, the secretary, Mr. Tidman, would inquire whether any Colonial Office staff or any settlers could accompany her during the final stages of her journey. It was exciting to be advised to sew gold sovereigns into the lining of her clothes; and while she tried not to romanticize her journey, she had read too many books by Ballantyne and Rider Haggard not to be thrilled by the "Dark Continent." She had been born the year before Dr. Livingstone died, on his knees; and pictures of episodes from his life had stayed with her since Sunday school. Clara would travel by train from the Cape to Mafeking, and thence by coach via Crocodile Pools to Bulawayo and finally by mail cart to Belingwe and Mponda's kraal.

If her father could only have managed to be less fatalistic and grief-stricken, this time of waiting could have been among the happiest periods of Clara's life. But the poor man's mood was one of bereavement. Yet she still managed to distance herself enough to dream happily of her future. What Robert had struggled so hard to achieve was about to come to pass. The chief had chosen Christ, and this glorious act of faith had made it possible for Clara's great adventure to begin.

CHAPTER 3

For a week the mail cart had been rumbling through a dusty landscape of scrubby trees and unruly hillsides, carved by dry ravines. The half-caste driver gazed ahead with weary, bloodshot eyes as he whipped up his team of mules for another climb, before rewarding himself with a heavy swig of brandy.

"Hirrrie, yoh doppers! Slaagte . . . Verdommeder skepsels!" he yelled, between lashes with his long giraffe-hide whip.

Clara held on tightly as she was bounced and buffeted under the straining canvas. She had experienced discomfort before, but never for such long periods of time. All her joints had been jarred, and her rib cage ached as if she had fallen from a horse. She felt humiliatingly weaker than her traveling companions: the middle-aged wife of the Colonial Office commissioner for Mazoe District and a German mining engineer. Since both were fatter than Clara, they seemed able to absorb constant jolts and bumps while retaining contact with their seats—whereas she, to do the same, had to cling to one of the metal hoops that held up the canvas roof. Clara's lips and chin were swollen with insect bites, and her face glowed like a farm girl's; but she cared nothing for the loss of her fashionable pallor. Indeed, there were times when she knew feelings of euphoria sweeter than any experienced in her comfortable past. To her these discomforts were rites of passage into Robert's harsh but purpose-filled life; and it was a matter of pride that she could endure them bravely.

Red dust billowed in thick clouds behind the mail cart and, with a following wind, blew in and choked the travelers. It clung to the faint down on Clara's cheeks and powdered the black mustache and crinkly hair of the German on the bench opposite, giving this prosaic man a strangely theatrical appearance. Next to him, unsoiled behind her chiffon veil, sat the pale-complexioned commissioner's wife. Mrs. Hartley was in her early forties—twenty years Clara's senior. In England, she had promised Mr. Tidman, the mission secretary, to "keep an eye on young Mrs. Haslam," but so far—whether in steamship staterooms or railway carriages, or in the archaic leather-sprung Wild West–Buffalo Bill–Deadwood coach on the road to Bulawayo—there had been plenty of other people to draw Mrs. Hartley's attention. Now, in the mail cart, with only the monosyllabic German to divert her, the full force of the woman's solicitude fell upon Clara.

Copious advice was suddenly proffered on matters such as the type of clothing most likely to keep out ticks, mosquitoes, and other biting insects—all of which, according to Mrs. Hartley, could penetrate linen sleeves and woolen stockings and, it seemed to Clara, every garment she had brought. Clara was not offended to be treated like a greenhorn, but she *was* angry to find that this wife of a minor official should actually look down upon her for no better reason than her marriage to a missionary. She had been warned that the wives of civil servants, soldiers, and the richer settlers possessed more social cachet in colonial circles than a nonconformist missionary's wife. The prejudice was hurtful at first hand, less for the affront to herself than for the insult to good men like Robert.

As the evening sky burned with the improbable colors of a parrot's plumage, Mrs. Hartley questioned Herr Frübeck about the goldfields he had assessed. If she could make a successful speculation, she confessed, she would swiftly force her husband home.

"Even if he values his work here?" asked Clara.

Mrs. Hartley smiled serenely. "Just you wait, my dear. In a month or two you'll dream every night about seeing another white face—even if its owner is the stupidest man on earth."

Drained by the mail-cart's queasily mesmeric motion, Clara lacked the energy to argue. With Robert always by her side, why would *she* be tormented by longings to see other white people?

After supping on bully beef and rice, the three passengers curled up on the floor of the cart, among the mailbags. Outside, the driver and the brakeman built a fire to keep off wild beasts. While Clara watched warm shadows flickering through the canvas, she imagined Robert making love to her. A week, she told herself joyfully. Only a week, my dearest. Across the veld, a creature howled, a small sound in the vast solitude.

*   *   *

The sun had been up for an hour when the driver of the mail cart galvanized his mules into a shambling canter with a wheezing blast on his horn. Clara lifted the canvas. In the distance she saw some low buildings and a raised water tank. Belingwe Camp was a typical tin-hut African township, but Clara was ecstatic to be there. While Mrs. Hartley and Herr Frübeck would travel on with the mail cart, Clara was to complete her journey in another vehicle. Here she expected to meet her new driver, John Dukes, an artisan sent out six weeks ahead of her by the London Missionary Society to assist her husband with carpentry and building.

Along a street of tin shacks and wattle-and-daub houses, there were a store, an eating house, a hotel, a billiard hall, a feed stable, and a toolhouse. Dogs were barking madly and men shouting as the mules slowed to a trot. Mrs. Hartley powdered her cheeks before tying her veil under her chin.

The driver twisted around to address Clara between yells at the mules. "Maxim Hotel, miss? Or Mr. Greene's lodgings? Keeps a very nice bar, does Baas Greene." The man's breath reeked of brandy.

"The Maxim will do very well."

But first the mail cart halted outside the main store, which also served as the post office. The mails were being tossed out as a red-faced man pushed his way through the crowd of onlookers.

"Moses," he shouted at the driver. "D'you have a Mrs. Haslam on board?"

"That's me," called Clara, stepping down from the tailboard.

"They've news for you inside, ma'am."

Clara watched the man stride back into the store. His solemn expression had scared her.

"Nothing untoward, I hope," gasped Mrs. Hartley, following hard on Clara's heels. Around them, men were buying cartridges, candles, and canned provisions to take to distant diggings. The air was thick with the smell of paraffin and new leather. The man led the two women through the heaps of saddlery and wagon gear to a counter protected by a grille. Clara found herself facing a balding man in a tartan waistcoat.

"Sad news, I fear, Mrs. Haslam."

"My husband?" she whispered.

"John Dukes . . . He died at Tuli a month back. Bad place for fever."

"Poor man," murmured Clara, feeling too much relief about Robert to start pretending to be grieved over an unknown man's fate.

"What will you do now?" demanded Mrs. Hartley. "A lone female can't be left alone with these barroom loafers."

Clara appealed to the man behind the grille. "Will nobody take me to the mission?"

The postmaster slapped at a fly that had settled on his freckled scalp. "You'll have to ask around, ma'am."

"Precious little chivalry in a place like this," sighed Mrs. Hartley. She fixed Clara with pitying eyes. "To be perfectly frank, Mrs. Haslam, it was wrong of your husband not to come for you himself."

Clara felt blood rush to her cheeks. "Your husband didn't come for *you,*" she blurted out.

"My dear, I've made this trip dozens of times before. And unlike you, I'm not trying to find a godforsaken kraal that's not even on the map."

Clara was trembling. How dare the woman criticize Robert? Did she have the first idea about the importance of his work? And why was she ignoring the fact that Robert had relied upon Mr. Dukes to meet her? Determined to confound the woman with icy calmness, Clara was dismayed to find her voice breathless and unstable. "He couldn't ... couldn't possibly leave his people ... not for weeks on end just after the chief's conversion."

"They managed quite well before he came."

The postmaster chose this moment to thrust a printed page under the grille: it gave notice of a reward being offered for information about the fate of three prospectors who had disappeared a month earlier. "They were hunting oribi ... Small antelope. They race 'em here, like dogs, see."

The smudged photograph showed three bearded young men gazing at the camera with a hint of swagger in their pose. Africa can do its worst, they seemed to say, but we can take it. One wore a straw hat with a striped ribbon around the brim, another sported a thick leather belt with a curious clasp.

"What happened to them?" snapped Mrs. Hartley.

The man pulled a face. "Lost their way, I'd say. Died of thirst, most likely."

Mrs. Hartley shook her head scornfully, then said very firmly to Clara, "You'll have to come with us now."

"I can't do that. Someone's sure to take me . . . and if not, well, my husband is bound to fetch me in a week or two."

Mrs. Hartley studied the poster again, then turned to the postmaster. "If these men weren't murdered, I'm a Chinaman."

"It's certainly mysterious, ma'am."

Mrs. Hartley raised her veil. "Don't fool with me. I'm married to a district commissioner." She placed a proprietary hand on Clara's arm. "Frankly, my dear, the niggers have a bad time hereabouts. They grow their own food and only need a yard of cloth to cover themselves. So money means nothing. Of course they refuse to work down the mines, unless forced to."

"Forced?" echoed Clara, her stomach tightening. "Please be truthful"—she appealed to the postmaster—"was Mr. Dukes murdered too?"

The man kept his head in his ledger. "Blackwater fever, I've heard."

Clara felt Mrs. Hartley touch her elbow and begin to steer her away, past a counter heaped high with brandy bottles, toward the street. She felt shaky and confused. Her only immediate hope of seeing Robert would be to stay on and find someone willing to take her to the mission. But if she failed, and had to wait for Robert himself, how long might she be stranded in this frontier town on her own? In England, she had never spent a night away from home in a place where she was not known. She found Mrs. Hartley domineering, but the prospect of her departure had suddenly become frightening.

A week after watching the mail cart clatter out of town under its cloud of dust and flies, Clara was facing the fact that none of the miners and prospectors were willing to help her. Her hotel had turned out to be the kind of place no decent woman in Sarston would have dared put her nose into. On most evenings there was a drunken brawl in the bar or in the supper room. Since prices were astonishingly high, she had moved out into a quieter lodging house, where meals were rarely more elaborate than bread and cold meat. Without economies, the fifty guineas sewn into the lining of her skirt could not last until a remittance reached her from England.

In the lodging house, Clara dragged the iron bedstead over to the window and sat on the lumpy mattress for hours, watching for carts or coaches. Life might be quieter here, but she grew to loathe her room, with its cracked mirror and its dressing table made from a packing case. The walls and floor, even the gimcrack sticks of furniture, were crisscrossed with ant trails of sugary-looking red earth.

As the sun edged across from wall to wall with infinite slowness, Clara was tormented by Robert's proximity. If I were a bird, she thought, I would fly to him. Her heart beat faster when she imagined him already approaching. As soon as there was any doubt in his mind about her meeting up with the artisan, he would set out at once.

One hot afternoon, she walked a mile out of town to the prospectors' camp, with its tattered tents and shanties. Picking her way through the meat tins and broken bottles that littered the stubble, she gazed toward the river. Below her in the shallow water, scores of men were engaged in the tedious process of washing gravel in pans and sluice boxes. The heat was surging up through the soles of her shoes as she made for the shade of some mahogany trees.

Where the road crossed the riverbed, several girls were washing clothes in a pool; they were bare to the waist and glistened with sweat. They waved to Clara, who waved back. The rutted clay of the wagon track swam in the heat haze, as desolate and empty as it always was.

Might Robert have set out, only to meet with the same fate as John Dukes? She was pondering this cruel possibility, when her attention was gripped. Two mounted men were splashing across the ford and riding on in the direction of the town. They had clearly come from afar, and so might be passing through. As if gazing upon the horsemen of the Apocalypse, Clara uttered a faint cry and ran after them. Behind her, an ox wagon lumbered out of the mopane woods toward the ford.

When Clara reached the Maxim Hotel, she learned that the men had taken rooms and were resting. Outside, their oxen were being unyoked. Before returning to her lodgings, she left a note with the sleepy doorman. In it, she explained that she was a woman on her own, needing unspecified but urgent assistance. Would they kindly spare her a few minutes later that evening? She could be contacted opposite at Mackenzie's lodging house.

As evening drew in, diggers in broad-brimmed hats and muddy moleskins stumbled up from the river, eager for refreshment. The smell of spirits and tobacco wafted in at Clara's window. A group of Mashona girls clustered around the hotel door, calling out, "Jig-jig two sheeleeng"; they looked very young with their jutting breasts and blue bead aprons.

As a blood-red sun transformed the town's tin shacks into magical structures, Clara leapt to her feet. At last, praise be, a native boy was sauntering across from the hotel, with something in his hand.

Clara took the proffered paper nervously—a few words scrawled on the back of an old bill: "Mr. H. Fynn and Captain Vaughan will be glad of Mrs. Haslam's company this evening for dinner at the Hotel Maxim at eight." She folded the paper and slowly raised it to her lips.

CHAPTER 4

Clara's eyes were smarting within moments of her entering the smoke-filled supper room of the hotel. The smell of warm bodies and alcohol was overpowering. Seated at rickety tables, the diners were chatting and gesticulating, most of them the worse for drink. Just as had happened when she was staying here, her entrance caused a startled lowering of voices. Women were a great deal rarer than gold dust in Belingwe. One man was so eager to get a look at her that he knocked his table over.

From the adjacent bar came shouting, as if someone was being ejected. Brought up to believe that men did not swear in front of women in public, Clara had still not reconciled herself to the diggers' foul language. A group of cardplayers, who were unaware of anything but their game, seemed scarcely sober enough to know what cards they held.

The room was L-shaped, and when Clara turned the corner, she knew at once that she was looking at the men she had come to meet. They were sitting at a table near the far wall; the older of the two had his back to her, and the younger, a strikingly handsome man in his late twenties, was too interested in what his companion was saying to look in Clara's direction. She paused between two tables, suddenly scared. If they turned her down, how long would it be till others came? She could offer money, but would they accept it if they were going in another direction? The one who was a captain would be a gentleman, so an offer of money might insult him.

The man with his back to her spoke with an American accent. He was telling a rambling story about a doctor who had stripped off all his clothes to cross a swollen river. He had tied these garments to the horse's back and then clung to the creature's tail while it swam across.

''When that darn horse reached dry land, he sprang up the bank so fast my pal lost his grip on his tail. And could he catch him after?

43

No, sir. That stallion trotted right on into Mazoe township as lively as you like, with Doc Brand puffing along behind him in a state of nature.''

As she was smiling at the absurdity of this vision, the handsome man looked up and caught her eye. She blushed and tried to straighten her smile.

"Good God," he muttered, jumping to his feet. "Who'd have thought it? Incredible. You must be Mrs. Haslam. We thought you'd be some batty old widow. Come and join us. I'm Francis Vaughan." He held out a hand. "How do you do?"

His face was deeply tanned, and under his trim straw-colored mustache his lips curved into a pleasing smile. Clara took Francis Vaughan's hand and found herself smiling too. His eyes were incredibly blue. Shimmering under thick flaxen hair, they made her think of cornflowers in a summer field. Suddenly the American's chair shot back, and he too was on his feet, pressing the fingers of Clara's other hand between huge palms. His head was crowned with a mane of gray and tawny hair, swept back and secured with a leather thong in a kind of pigtail.

"Heywood Fynn at your service, ma'am." His teeth glinted between wisps of beard. He was not tall, but Clara was aware of a massive hairy chest framed by his open flannel shirt. "Now, what's this 'assistance' you're a-wantin', Mrs. Haslam?"

Three days later, seated on the swaying box of Fynn's wagon, Clara gazed across endless bleached grass to grape-blue hills. Her happiness seemed to shimmer in the bright air above flat-topped acacias and gouty baobabs. Heading north in any case, Heywood Fynn had laughed at her for imagining he might have balked at a detour. If they found elephant spoor on the way, why, then she would have to wait a few days while they tracked and shot a few beasts. Was that fair? Clara had thought it very fair indeed—so fair she burst into tears and hugged them both.

Captain Vaughan, who was sharing the costs and profits of the hunting expedition, had said that he would be happy to shoot nothing until Clara had been safely deposited on her husband's doorstep. But when Fynn swore that no ivory was going to be lost for Mrs. Haslam or for anyone else, Vaughan had simply shrugged and smiled. He reminded Clara a little of her faithless Charles; but since she was not involved with Francis, she found his insouciance amusing. Having thought all cavalry officers rich, she was astonished to learn that whenever Francis had any leave, he came up to Mashonaland from the Cape, where his regiment was stationed, to earn money as a professional hunter. He also dabbled in journalism and conducted a trade in native curios, all to reduce his accumulated mess debts.

Fynn's life also surprised her—"the best dime novel that's never been written," was his own assessment. Riding messages for a telegraph company by the age of twelve, and scouting for the cavalry by eighteen, he sailed for Africa, aged forty-four, when the West had finally grown too civilized for his taste. He could be coarse at times—not least when he ate—but Clara felt priggish for noticing it, given his kindness. He rigged up a canvas sunshade for her on the box; and when they camped near a river, he obliged his men to fetch enough water for her to take a bath. He also answered all her questions, even telling her why old Ezekiel Malatsi, his normally patient driver, sometimes spat in the face of Conate, the boy who directed the leading oxen.

Francis often rode ahead of the ox wagon. For all his cheerfulness in company, there was a brooding side to his nature. Fynn, by contrast, rarely rode his horse but slept in the moving wagon in the early afternoon and chatted with Clara when he woke.

One overcast afternoon, all three were sitting on the box. The surrounding scrub had been charred by bush fires, making the landscape look smudged and dreary. The sultry air and the rolling motion of the wagon soon had Francis drifting into fitful sleep, but he woke at once on hearing raised voices.

Fynn was saying, "Yeah, but must they give up their wives when he's made 'em Christians? That's what you haven't said, Mrs. Haslam. Does your husband make 'em do that?"

"He can't make anybody do anything they don't want to," replied Clara.

"He can say they'll burn in hell if they don't do it."

"Mr. Haslam doesn't say things like that."

Francis felt suddenly anxious for the young woman. Fynn was a very difficult man to argue with, and he made no concessions to age or sex.

"All preachers tell 'em they'll burn," Fynn insisted.

Francis said firmly to Fynn, "She said her husband doesn't say that." Francis knew that Fynn kept two black mistresses at Tuli and had recently been reproved by a missionary for going native. But how could his resentment be explained to pretty Mrs. Haslam? And by God, she was pretty! A wonderful face that was both fervent and appealing, demure and playful. Francis felt a stab of indignation. Those humorously curving eyebrows, the gently tilting nose and soft lips, were all the property of some miserable minister. The bloody waste! She was wearing a long, tight-waisted dress, checked with brown, not the kind of thing a missionary's wife could run up for herself. But could she be a lady? Out here?

Fynn appealed to Francis. "She won't say if her goddamn husband asks 'em to give up their wives."

"Of course he does," cried Clara, suddenly exasperated. "Who's ever heard of a Christian with lots of wives?"

Fynn glared at her. His gray, rather flat eyes had the same extraordinary alertness and vigor seen in the gaze of Bushmen. "Didn't they join together in good faith, them natives and their wives? What's wrong with that, Mrs. Haslam? Why should they split, and make their children bastards?"

"A man with many wives thinks he owns them like things. That's wrong, Mr. Fynn. Isn't that obvious?"

Fynn's broad face expressed vehement opposition. "Take away their wives and they'll get themselves concubines. They sure ain't goin' to keep themselves to one woman after years of doin' somethin' else."

"So it's never the right time to stop a bad habit?" asked Clara with an unshaken sense of rectitude.

"Tell me what'll happen to the children of them concubines? The fathers won't feed 'em."

Clara looked stern. "Married or not, Mr. Fynn, *no* man with twenty children can look after them properly."

"With help from his wives . . . sure he can."

"He'd hardly recognize them all, let alone have time to play with them."

"Play?" Fynn groaned. "A father doesn't play. He teaches his sons to hunt and herd. Your husband's told you plenty, ma'am, but you'd best see for yourself how these people live before you decide what's right and wrong for them."

Francis feared that Clara was about to embark on a long list of moral improvements that her husband was taking in hand. To his relief, she said pleasantly, "It's good of you to offer me advice, Mr. Fynn."

Later, when Clara was resting on her bed in the wagon, Fynn

said to Francis, "We ought to tell her what to expect, Vaughan. She's a good woman, and she deserves some honesty."

"We can't help her."

"I meant . . . make things less of a shock for her."

Francis said gently, "We can't know what she's expecting, and it's not our business. She may think it's going to be hell on earth, for all we know." He clapped the American on the back, determined to joke him out of any attempt to undermine the woman's faith in her husband. "Truth is, Fynn, some people like to suffer. Hair shirts, living in barrels . . . they've done it all, religious people, and never been happier."

"How many diggers have vanished into thin air inside a month? Six, seven? That's a heap too many to ignore, Vaughan."

"Native risings don't start like that. Not in my experience. The balloon bursts suddenly. One moment everything's sweet and peaceful; the next, hundreds are slaughtered out of the blue."

Fynn sighed deeply. "I don't want to see nothin' bad happen to her." He pulled down the brim of his Stetson against the late-afternoon sun. "Should have kept quiet, maybe. But I never could abide missionaries. All that shit 'bout sin and sinners, and saving themselves for the great hereafter. Never a word 'bout happiness here and now. That's not right for a young girl, Vaughan."

Francis did not answer. He too was mystified by missionaries. He thought of Clara, sleeping in the hot and musty space under the canvas, breathing in the reek of spirits and drying animal skins. He could imagine the rise and fall of her breasts under her cotton dress; the slight moisture on her forehead; her loose black hair, no longer pinned back severely. Clara made him conscious of everything that was wrong with his life: the lack of tenderness in it; the impossibility of returning to England until he could afford the extra expense of a home posting; the futility of hoping he might marry, lacking money as he did. And yet this missionary, with nothing but a shack in the wilds, invites a lovely, high-spirited girl to share the harshest life imaginable, and she comes running. Because she thought God had ordained it all. A pity God couldn't do some "ordaining" for a few army officers for a change. A great pity.

The more she saw of Fynn and Francis together, the more she liked them. She was impressed by Francis's ability to remain indifferent to Fynn's most sardonic remarks. At times it seemed they were playing a game, with the American going out of his way to speak disparagingly of the kid-gloved and monocled type of English officer he sometimes took hunting for a fee, implying that Francis too, if not quite kid-gloved, was refined enough to be first cousin to those stiff-necked specimens. But the hunter's keenest scorn was reserved for another group of Englishmen: colonial officials who made much of their "mission to educate and civilize." To lure Africans away from their kraals with the promise of cheap cloth and beads, and then to call this process "civilizing" them, was contemptible hypocrisy.

"Worse than butchering the Sioux and Apache?" inquired Francis meekly.

"That was *honest* butchery," Fynn had rumbled back, insisting that the only honest whites in Mashonaland were adventurers, traders, and hunters like himself, who had no pretensions to altruism. "But you, Vaughan," he had mocked on another occasion, "you're just the sanctimonious type to risk your neck for guys like me when the blacks want our blood."

Yet Clara could not think of Fynn as the gruff, tough, unsentimental man he would have had her believe him. She sensed his concern for her far too often to think him less sensitive than Francis. Certainly Fynn knew more than Francis about the bush and was not reluctant to air his superior knowledge. Often he would point into a meaningless tangle of branches, to reveal the twisted horns of a male kudu or wildebeest. Still, earlier in the day, Francis had spotted a motionless giraffe, which Fynn had missed. Francis's eye had been drawn by some tiny birds darting in and out of the creature's ears in search of parasites; and Clara had been surprised by his loud whoop of triumph, so out of character had it seemed in a man whom she had previously thought unemotional.

They did not come upon the prints of an elephant until Clara's fifth day with them. After examining the deep round indentations of a massive solitary animal, Fynn pronounced them the tracks of a rogue bull. Size apart, why was he so sure? Clara wanted to know. Because normal elephants did not go foraging alone on moonless nights. Being shortsighted, they banded together in protective herds. And how did he know this lone beast's tracks had been made at night? Because they had been crossed and recrossed by the fresh spoor of mice and other nocturnal creatures.

By midmorning, they were still hard on his tracks. The animal's droppings were moist, so he could not be far away. It being August and midwinter, the scaly mopane trees were decorated with only a sprinkling of tawny leaves. In this dead, dry world no birds sang, and not even an impala was to be seen. But within less than an hour, they were dropping down from the dusty escarpment into the fertile valley of the Kasangwa. Below them, the plumes of green papyrus reeds faded into the haze like an endless colony of egrets. Between its blue-green banks, the sandy riverbed shone a mottled silver, its surface pitted with rocks and isolated pools.

Fynn's driver, Ezekiel, brought the oxen to a halt in the bed of the river, where the huge footprints of the elephant were plainly to be seen heading upstream. Francis scrambled up onto the far bank and scanned the low hills through his field glasses. He signaled urgently to Fynn, who was soon peering at the enlarged image of a huge gray tusker standing beneath an overhanging outcrop. The elephant rubbed a back leg against the rock as if trying to dislodge something. Suddenly the creature trumpeted—a sound more savage than the roaring of a lion.

"Him plenty evil, Bwana." Fynn chuckled, looking again at the elephant. "This one's for you, huh?"

"I'll try and shoot him, certainly," said Francis solemnly. He was fed up with Fynn's automatic assumption that he would always yield pride of place to him when any difficult situation arose. Clara had now come up beside the two men. It worried her that Francis seemed unaware that Fynn's invitation to shoot the elephant had been meant ironically.

Fynn chuckled softly. "*Try* to shoot him? Brother, you'll be in trouble if you don't damn well succeed."

Clara's heart beat faster as the men loaded two guns each. Francis fumbled as he took bullets from his ammunition pouch. Surely, she thought, he'll give way now. It's just another of their elaborate games. Rogue elephants ought to be dealt with by the more experienced man. She tried to catch Francis's eye to smile at him, hoping to end his brooding mood. As if he had guessed her intention, he looked away.

Francis knew very well that Fynn expected him to back down. It was childish not to; and yet he couldn't bring himself to do so. If Clara hadn't come up at the crucial moment, he might have told Fynn to do the shooting. But with this lovely woman watching his every move, his situation had become impossible. Preserving a facade of calm, Francis checked his rifles and released the safety catch of one. Later, the slightest sound might alert the animal, with fatal consequences. At least they were downwind of the elephant, or had been before the wind dropped, so they ought to be able to approach their quarry along the riverbed in perfect safety.

Clara knew that Flynn kept a telescope in the locker under the box. With its help, she watched the two men as they reached rising ground where the long grass began to thin. They dropped onto their stomachs and began to zigzag from one patch of scrub to another. Several hundred yards beyond them, the beast lumbered toward a baobab tree, flapping his great ragged ears. Then he backed his leathery haunches up to the tree trunk and rubbed his left hind leg against the bark.

From their position, Fynn and Francis watched the same movements and were not reassured to hear the elephant's angry squeals.

"He's mad, all right," murmured Fynn, studying the animal through his field glasses from the cover of an anthill. As the elephant turned, he whispered: "Is that guy in a mess? Take a look."

Francis lifted the glasses. A dark gash extended from the creature's tail all down his left leg. The precise nature of the injury was impossible to tell.

"How will you shoot him, Vaughan?" Francis recognized the same half-playful tone, but he was not fooled. Fynn was afraid that he might after all go through with it.

Francis frowned. "Think I'll work my way round to his side to get a brain shot."

"Where will you take cover?" Francis thought about this and then pointed to several possible positions. Fynn said gently, "Let's say I come along too, huh?"

"I'll manage."

"You sure about that?" No hint of joking now. "If you miss, you're dead, Vaughan. You know that?"

Francis said nothing. Slinging one rifle across his back, he grasped the other; and holding it slightly behind him so that the barrel did not glint in the sun, he moved swiftly into a patch of tall grass, crouching as low as he could. His objective was a distant clump of thornbushes. From there, if the beast did not move away from the baobab, Francis hoped to reach a jumble of rocks to the right of a wild fig tree. Even in winter, the sun by midday was fierce; and without any breeze, Francis could feel the sweat beading above his temples and on his forehead, threatening to drip down and blur his vision.

Through her shaking telescope, Clara followed the movements of the elephant. Prehistoric, seemingly invincible, he ambled away from the baobab on a line that would enable him to see Francis from the corner of his eye, should he happen to turn a little; but the tusker's attention was fixed upon another tree, laden with edible pods. Instead of troubling to pick them individually, he leaned his forehead against the bark, with his tusks on either side, and shook the tree back and forth until pods rained down on him. Clara hated to watch and yet could not look away. She told herself that this young man was a vainglorious idiot; that she knew nothing about him, except that he was handsome, which was no reason for being concerned with anyone's fate. But her quaking stomach and shaking hands told her something else.

As the elephant examined the fallen fruits with his trunk tip, Francis sprinted for the thornbushes. His dash ended with a frantic scramble on his hands and knees that brought him safely to the concealing thorn barrier just thirty paces from the rocks he had selected for his final approach.

A sharp throbbing in his knee made him look down. Blood. He had ripped his riding breeches and gashed himself. Sweat ran down into his eyes and into the cracked corners of his dry and panting mouth. The elephant suddenly ceased his meanderings around the base of the tree and raised his trunk in the air, working it from side to side as if scenting an enemy. When the breeze had died, Francis had never considered the possibility of its return from a different quarter. As this appalling prospect occurred to him, he felt a dab of air on his neck, lighter than the touch of a feather duster. Aghast, he crumbled some dry earth and let it fall from his hand. The dust drifted sideways. Then he heard the first bellow of rage.

At any moment the beast would charge. Clara put down the telescope and prayed. Yet after more trumpeting, the elephant remained motionless, except for his ears, which flickered at intervals like the wings of a dying moth.

If charged in his present position, Francis knew he was doomed. He scrambled to his feet and ran for the rocks, which offered the only possible vantage point from which to kill the creature. His heart was pounding so violently that he wondered how he was still able to breathe. In this condition, would he ever manage to hold his gun steady? Yet he must shoot this bull in the brain if he wished to live.

Even as he ran, he imagined himself tossed skyward, gored on those cruel curving tusks, then caught by the creature's trunk and flailed against trees and rocks until his limbs were torn from his body. But somehow his legs moved under him, negotiating stones, roots, even a pile of dung, while he himself was scarcely aware of his soles making contact with the ground. *How* had he strolled into this insane predicament? Had his years spent showing troopers the way an officer faced danger left him unable to admit to any weakness?

Clara lifted the telescope again. As she gazed at the tusker, the creature suddenly and inexplicably lowered his trunk and tugged idly at a sapling, as if forgetting what had disturbed him. In a daze, Clara saw Francis sprint toward some rocks. Yards from his goal, his knee buckled and he fell.

The elephant spun around, a blur of gray menace, gashed by the arc of his mighty tusks. As Francis hit the ground, he saw his gun fly away to his left. Empty-handed now, he was wrenching the strap of his other rifle from his shoulder even while staggering to his feet. Gasping, he jammed the stock into his shoulder and stared down the wavering sight at the heaving pink triangle that was the beast's mouth. The creature loomed above him as he charged. No chance of hitting the brain from so low; and one in the lungs would never stop him. The ground was reverberating, the beast's ears flapping like canvas at sea, trunk flung upward as he roared. No hope of piercing the skull, but fire, fire anyway, between the eyes. As his finger tightened on the trigger, the brute veered aside.

Incredulous, trembling, Francis tracked the great head, passing him yards away. As one vast ear swung forward, he sighted the lethal spot and fired, hearing one moment the report and the next the earthshaking crash as the elephant's legs folded and his tusks gouged into the earth. For a moment the beast started to regain his feet, but then he staggered back and rolled onto his side.

Almost too weak to stand, Francis caught sight of Fynn, astonishingly close to him and directly in the line of the tusker's last charge.

"Good thing you shot straight, Vaughan," said the American. "I'd be dead meat now if you'd missed." He smiled. "Ought to thank you, I guess."

But Francis knew that *he* ought to thank Fynn for attracting the elephant's attention. If Fynn had fired at the creature instead of running forward, he could not have killed him from that angle, and a wound might have maddened the beast without changing the line of his charge. Francis knew that Fynn had placed himself in grave danger to save his life. He looked straight at the American. "I thought you never risked your skin for anyone."

"I don't." He grinned at Francis. "Not even you could have missed that close."

And that was that. Though Francis wanted to acknowledge Fynn's bravery, he sensed that the hunter felt guilty about letting him go after a wounded elephant—just how badly injured became apparent when they examined the carcass.

Francis felt like vomiting. Near the animal's anus was the snapped shaft of an assegai, and from there almost to the foot, the flesh was seething with maggots. For how many months had he endured this? The tusks he had paid so dearly for possessing were a poor color, too cracked and pitted for Fynn to consider removing.

When they returned to the wagon, Francis was gratified by how relieved and pleased Clara seemed. She offered to bandage his leg, but having thanked her, he said he dealt with cuts and gashes himself.

"Why did you take such a risk?" she asked at last, as he gingerly washed his knee.

Her puzzlement made him laugh. "I wanted to impress you."

"Nonsense." Her frown told him he had miscalculated.

"You might as well ask people why they gamble."

"You did it for excitement?" She was truly horrified.

"Men test themselves, you know. I'm not a freak."

"No?" Fynn's burly shoulders shook with amusement. "A man who runs at a rogue bull not a freak? Who could be crazier? Damned if I know."

They were all up on the box again when Fynn started telling Francis and Clara how, after a kill, Bushmen always carved a path, like miners, deep inside the body of a dead elephant.

"They race each other for the best organs, hacking with knives. Met a little guy near Kuruman last year. He'd lost his testicles inside an elephant—cut off by a friend who thought they were part of the creature's spleen."

"Nice story for a lady," remarked Francis.

"She don't mind. Do you, ma'am?" Fynn uncorked a flask

of Cape brandy and handed it to Mrs. Haslam. To Francis's amazement, she took a generous gulp.

"The only drink I'm used to," she confided, wiping her lips on her sleeve.

"Well, I'll be damned," muttered Fynn.

"You shouldn't keep saying that," reproved Clara, without a trace of a smile.

Was she serious? wondered Francis. This brandy-swigging, brave, priggish, fragile-looking girl? Did she believe it all: Judgment Day, the loaves and fishes? Or was she just infatuated with doing good? He groaned within himself. Either way, she was irresistible, but if he ever gave her the least sign he thought so, he would loathe himself. Like nuns and lepers, missionaries' wives were untouchable.

Since dawn, Clara had suspected that this might be the last day of her journey, but Fynn had underestimated the distance, and they were still traveling at dusk. Clara was tense with anticipation, expecting, moment by moment, to see the village looming in the half-light. The American had ridden on ahead in the late afternoon to see if he could find a shorter way; and night had fallen before he returned. Soon afterward, Fynn pointed into the gloom.

"Chief Mponda's kraal."

Ahead, Clara could just make out a low hill and a line of huts straggling across its brow. Against the paler sky, the peaked roofs of the village looked like the black serrations on a dinosaur's back. Wisps of smoke could be seen twisting upward. Women would be preparing evening meals on wood fires. A yellow moon glowed beside a great crag of jumbled granite, which dominated the village.

Looking at Clara, Francis was choked. Her face mirrored the inner struggle between fear and hope. How little she could know what awaited her. Missionaries often spoke of years of contentment among primitive tribesmen, but it was beyond Francis how any English woman, be she servant girl or manufacturer's daughter, could experience anything but misery in an African kraal.

Moonlight flowed down on the bush, silvering the wagon and matching each pair of oxen with twin shadows. The trees fell back in velvet blackness, while granite quartz glittered in star fragments where rocks shelved. Suddenly Francis lost the sense of his earlier thoughts. Rarely had the world seemed more beautiful. Clara's face bore the same wonder; it came to him that if *he* were journeying through this alien land to join a beloved spouse, he would at last know happiness.

Soon there was drumming: soft to start with, then rising to a climax, before fading once more. A solo voice broke the silence and was joined by a deep chorus. Clara remembered Robert describing the "degrading attitudes" that the women often adopted during their songs and dances. But the chanting was strange and haunting.

When Fynn shouted instructions to Ezekiel, his driver, and to the boy on the leading ox, Clara was shocked. Within sight of her destination, he seemed to be ordering his men to stop.

"We can't stop," she cried. "Not now."

"Could start a panic if we ride in at night." Fynn was obdurate. "Best camp here and ask the chief's permission to take in the wagon tomorrow."

"Why not send in the driver on foot now?" suggested Francis. "Ezekiel can give a message to Mr. Haslam, surely?" Clara smiled her gratitude.

An hour later, Ezekiel returned. He was accompanied not by Robert Haslam but by a tall, white-haired African and a boy dressed in a bleached calico cassock. As the old man caught sight of Clara, he went down on his knees and thanked God for her arrival. He prayed aloud in his own language, then added in English:

"May the good Lord bless you, Nkosikaas."

"May He bless you too," she murmured, distraught at not seeing her husband.

"You know what he called you just then?" asked Fynn. "Princess. That's what *nkosikaas* means."

The old man had stopped some distance away from her, perhaps out of respect. Clara was frantic that Robert had not come to greet her. What had happened? The boy was gazing at her without making any effort to conceal his fascination. The old man was staring too, in a most disconcerting fashion, since one of his eyes squinted and a cataract covered the pupil of the other. This must be Philemon, Robert's only native preacher. Clara had gained the impression from Robert that Philemon was exactly like an English minister. Yet here he was wearing torn trousers, a dirty old black coat, and no shoes or shirt.

"Mr. Haslam is well?" she faltered.

"Yes, mistress. He is at the cattle post for a few days."

Clara was weak with relief. She knew that the cattle grazed many miles from the village in the dry season and that Robert liked to visit the herdsmen. He was safe, and she would see him soon. Nevertheless she wanted to rage and weep. How could he have gone away, just when she was likely to arrive? What could possibly justify it?

Fynn lit a cigar and exhaled twin tusks of smoke. He said to Clara, "You'd best stay with us till Mr. Haslam meets you."

She said steadily, "I'll be safe with these people."

"With *these* people, I guess so. It's those folk yonder I'm considerin'." Fynn indicated the general direction of the singing. "That ain't a prayer meeting, ma'am."

"I don't need your advice, Mr. Fynn," she replied softly.

"D'you think she needs it, Vaughan?" demanded Fynn.

"Can't say I do," replied Francis, flicking at the ground with his riding crop.

"She'll be safe in the care of this gentleman?" Fynn glanced contemptuously at Philemon.

Francis said, "If the natives want to harm her, they'll do it whether her husband's around or not."

"Want to know why missionaries don't get killed, Vaughan? The natives think they're wizards. Don't you, boy?" The youth in calico studied the ground. "Leopard got your tongue?"

The boy half shut his eyes, as if praying. "I think Lord Jesus saves each man with his blood."

"He's saved you with his blood, has he, boy?"

"I believe he done that, yes, sah."

Fynn grinned broadly at Francis. "If that ain't hocus-pocus, I'd like to know what is."

Francis frowned. "Sounds like Holy Communion to me."

Fynn threw down his cigar butt. "Reckon I'm the odd man out." He sighed as if suddenly too weary to go on arguing. "Better be gettin' your baggage, ma'am." Then he began shouting instructions to Conate and Ezekiel.

As the Africans lifted down her things, Clara moved closer to Francis. Around them, cicadas sang.

"That was very kind of you, Captain Vaughan."

"I hope it was." Francis felt wretched. He did not want to leave her here any more than Fynn did; but to force her to remain with the wagon against her will would simply be to humiliate her.

"My husband will be here tomorrow or the day after."

Francis knew that she was trying to be brave. "I'm sure he will," he said with a smile.

A bat flitted low over Clara's head, but she scarcely noticed. Francis found her unhappiness distressing. He would have liked to shake her husband until his teeth rattled. He said gently, "I wouldn't mind starting a new life myself. Most of us would leap at it if we had the guts." She gave him a smile of heartfelt gratitude that he would treasure for a very long time.

Flanked by the gangling ancient and the calico boy, Clara walked into the night, as Conate and Ezekiel staggered after her with the luggage.

PART TWO

Robert Haslam woke when the stars were still out in a mother-of-pearl sky. A white mist hung over the land. In a few hours the heat would be fierce; but now, just before dawn, Robert shivered. Expecting Clara at any time, he would not have left the village even for a few days, had not compelling events forced his hand. His favorite mission boy had either gone into hiding or been abducted, after being accused of sorcery. His life was probably in danger.

When the missionary crawled from his tent, his Bushman servant, Dau, was still curled up close to the ashes of the night's fire, but he stirred as soon as his master moved. Dau searched in the fire's ashes for its glowing core. Then, with his face almost touching the ash, he blew a tiny flame into life and fed it with twigs and kindling. As the fire burned he sat back and grinned, eyes screwed up against the smoke.

It being winter, the cows were lean and there was no milk to be had. Because the days were short, the cattle were watered before dawn to give them more time to search for pasture. Already in the riverbed the herdboys were digging holes and scooping up water into long wooden troughs. The cows lowed as they smelled the water, and the boys sang to calm them when they plunged forward. A younger boy walked by with three goats. These pastoral scenes made Robert feel that he shared a dusty road with Jesus in a land like Galilee.

The sun was up by the time Robert and Dau slid down the crumbling bank into the riverbed. The dust raised by the departing cattle still hung thickly in the air. A group of young men had remained behind. With much shouting and laughter, they were breaking a young ox for riding.

The man Robert was in search of, and yet dreaded to find at the cattle post, was not among them. Robert had arrived too late the previous evening to look for Nashu; but this morning he found him with ease. The witch doctor was basking in the sun, in a spot where the floods had cut away the bank, leaving tree roots curling in the air like snakes. He had been smoking wild hemp and was red-eyed. As the missionary approached, he coughed and spat. Still squatting, he bellowed with strange politeness:

"Welcome, Umfundisi."

"Thank you, Nashu," Robert answered in Venda. It always surprised him that Nashu should call him "teacher" when everything Christian was anathema to him. The witch doctor—or nganga—was sitting with two other men: Rozi, his informer, and Makufa, the chief's ambitious son and heir.

"Why is that dog here?" asked Makufa, eyeing Dau.

"Don't call him that. You know very well why I brought him."

"He'll find no tracks here," said Nashu.

Robert could never understand how Venda people could think Bushmen scarcely human—mere dogs, in fact—and yet fear their formidable tracking skills. Dau had been owned by a Venda headman, who had beaten him almost to death before dragging him into the bush for lions to dispose of. Found barely alive, he had been brought to the mission, where he had remained.

"Why will Dau find no tracks?" asked Robert.

"Ganda was never here," said Rozi, refusing to pollute himself by uttering the mission boy's Christian name.

Robert looked from man to man, each one as still as a Buddha, with his knees folded under him. Were they really recent murderers? Nashu, with his kilt of monkey skins and his smallpox-pitted face? Rozi, whose pointed skull looked like a coconut? Makufa, so handsome in his leopardskin kaross? In the past, they had forced dozens to undergo the ordeal and drink poison, so why make an exception of poor Simon? The innocent vomited. The guilty—and they were far more numerous—did not. Robert thought of Simon's naive and trusting nature, his delight in pleasing. He longed to roar out his grief at the boy's disappearance.

Two weeks before, Chief Mponda's baby son by his youngest wife, Herida, had died of diphtheria. Herida was the witch doctor's daughter. Since witchcraft was blamed for roughly a third of all deaths in the tribe, it had surprised nobody when Nashu, whose duty it was to seek out witches, had detected a witch in this case. Robert had suspected that Nashu would accuse a relative of Chizuva, Mponda's principal wife. This was because Chizuva's family stood to gain most if her husband converted to Christianity. As a Christian, the chief would put away all his other wives, including Herida, leaving Chizuva as sole wife. Nashu and his family expected to be the tribe's principal losers if the chief converted— and not just because Herida would be divorced. Her father's services would no longer be required as mediator with the ancestral spirits, as rainmaker, or even as seeker of witches. The missionary would have become the tribe's spiritual leader.

Having thought that Nashu would accuse an adult member of Chizuva's family, Robert had been taken aback when her thirteen-year-old nephew had been named. Since Robert's fondness for the boy was well known, Nashu had obviously meant his accusation to hurt the missionary. When news of Simon's peril had reached the mission, it was rumored that he had fled to the cattle post, so Robert set out at once.

Now he noted with distaste the magical amulets of lions' and lizards' claws around Nashu's neck. "Where is he?" His anger made him so breathless that his intended roar came out as a whisper.

Nashu pulled at his thin beard. "His brother is with the young men." He waved his zebra-tail fly whisk in the direction of the warriors. "Perhaps he knows."

"Why do you say that Simon bewitched Herida's child?"

Nashu's wizened face creased into a shocked grimace. "You know very well, sir, that we ngangas never reveal our medicines."

"I'm not interested in that. Did you *see* Simon betwitch Herida's baby?"

"I did not."

"Did anyone see him do it?"

"What if they didn't? I see things in here." He raised a hand to his forehead.

"You threw your bones and they told you?"

"Bones tell nothing unless the spirits move them."

"So God moved the bones to tell you that Simon killed the child?" Robert's anger made him tremble.

"The spirits spoke through the bones, Umfundisi."

"Spirits? Evil spirits, don't you mean?"

"I protect the people from evil spirits, sir," said Nashu, as if deeply hurt by such disrespect.

Rozi, who had been struggling to contain himself, burst out:

"The boy you call Simon, he looks at a paper and speaks the words of a man who died years ago. This man was born in a goatshed and came alive after dying. Ganda talks to his ghost."

"He prays to Jesus Christ." Robert corrected him fiercely.

Rozi shouted, "He entered Herida's hut at night and said words. I saw him."

So Simon had prayed for the sick child. How cruel that the boy's good intentions might have cost him his life. Robert remembered Simon shortly after he first came to live at the mission—a boy of five, laughing when he saw people on their knees, praying. "Is your God under the earth, master?" He had tried so hard to understand everything.

Robert hurried away to question Simon's brother, but the young man was too frightened to say anything. Robert and Dau spent the rest of the morning searching vainly for Simon's tracks, which the Bushman knew from memory. In the rainy season, witches were sometimes drowned in the river close to the cattle post. Perhaps executions by other means took place there in the dry season. But the riverbed was too densely crisscrossed by cattle tracks for Dau to draw any conclusions. Certainly, if Simon was still alive, Nashu would be eager to kill him as a warning to other wellborn persons who might be thinking of baptism.

Robert was acutely anxious about Clara's arrival. In his letters to her, he had claimed in good faith that Mponda would soon accept Christ. Yet would Nashu have dared strike directly at the Christians if Mponda was really about to convert? It seemed unlikely.

Robert knew he should have left a note for his wife in case she arrived during his absence. But what could he have told her? Not the real reason why he had gone away. To confess the danger of their position within days of her arrival would be unforgivably cruel.

As his Cape cart rattled homeward across the bushveld, a herd of hartebeest was on the move. Usually their tarnished copper coats and graceful movements spoke to him of the Creator's purpose. But not today. They moved as a herd, obeying brute instinct. And the people were no less caged and confined. Inexperienced missionaries might see these blinkered men and women as free children of nature. Yet in any village they cared to visit, they would find evidence of total conformity. Every pointed roof and every granary for a thousand miles would be the same, every pot and mat identically designed. Custom dictated the great events and the smallest minutiae of their lives. No deviation was possible without the chief's consent. Unless Mponda accepted Christ, the tribe would remain pagan forever. This was what Robert most dreaded having to tell Clara.

O Lord Jesus, he prayed, if Mponda has turned against Thee, incline his heart once more toward salvation, so that those he rules over may be redeemed and know the joy of serving Thee. May Thy Holy Spirit enter and transform us all, including Thy humble servant Robert Haslam.

CHAPTER 6

After Philemon had lit the lamps and left Clara in her husband's house, she gazed around her in bemusement. In the yellow lamplight, the room looked mean and cramped. Clara lifted the oil lamp and saw above wattle-and-daub walls a roof thatched with tambookie grass, like any native hut. Crawling along the rafters were large brown spiders with long, hairy legs.

The floor felt gritty underfoot. She lowered her light—no boards, only smoothed and beaten mud. Around the glass chimney of her lamp, a dense cloud of moths and insects bumped and fluttered. The unglazed windows were covered with stretched calico. For sitting, there were just a rush-bottomed ladder-back and a Windsor chair. Some crude shelves accommodated Robert's books. Moffat's *Apprenticeship at Kuruman,* Charles New's *Life, Wanderings and Labours in Eastern Africa,* Livingstone's *Missionary Travels,* Shakespeare's sonnets, a life of Charles Wesley, a Tennyson collection. Could this be all Robert needed to pass his evenings? The strangeness of the room and her husband's absence made her feel locked in a dream. Why had he gone to the cattle post at a time when he must have been expecting her? What could justify such a visit?

On the table below Robert's books were a tin box and a large Bible with brass hasps. It was open at the 139th Psalm. "If I ascend up into heaven, thou *art* there: if I make my bed in hell, behold, thou *art there. If* I take the wings of the morning, *and* dwell in the uttermost parts of the sea; even there shall thy hand lead me, and Thy right hand shall hold me." As she read these words, Clara could hear Robert speaking them in his rich, vibrant voice. She lifted the lid of the box and found pens, paper, and several marble-backed notebooks. There were also statements of account from various traders and letters from the directors of the mission society. Under these were several photographs. In one, Robert was standing with some Africans in front of a square thatched house. In another, he was in shirtsleeves, working on a building with another white man. Two photographs were of a young woman. In the smaller one, she was wearing a long striped dress and was standing in a group of naked African women. Her fair hair was cut short, and she was gazing unsmilingly at the photographer. "Ruth 1886" was penciled on the back. Ten years ago. In a larger, studio portrait, Ruth was leaning against a balustrade, wearing more elaborate clothes. Her hair was long. The picture was undated. Perhaps it had been taken in England shortly before she came to Africa. She looked happy rather than apprehensive.

As Clara studied the unsmiling picture, she realized she could not even answer the most basic questions about the woman. For example, had Ruth ever become used to the life? Had she often been ill before fever finally carried her off? Or had she died from another disease entirely? It seemed incredible to Clara that she had never questioned Robert directly about his wife's last days. Considerations of delicacy had influenced her, but only up to a point. The truth, she now admitted, was simpler: she had never dared ask anything that might have obliged her to estimate the risks involved in becoming the second Mrs. Haslam.

The bedroom was divided from the sitting room by a curtain of sacking. A massive mahogany bed dominated the room, and Clara had to wonder whether Ruth had died in it. She pushed aside the mosquito curtains and lay down. Eyes closed, she summoned up Robert's lean and muscular body and imagined him murmuring endearments.

At length she left the bedroom for the lean-to shed that housed the kitchen. A cloud of gilded insects moved with her lamp. Metal bins contained flour, oatmeal, and sugar; there was a meat safe hanging from a rope, a well-scrubbed table, an earthenware water filter, and a wood-burning oven. Ants swarmed everywhere, except on the table, which was protected by cans of water under each leg. Rattraps were scattered on the floor.

A door led out into a small fenced area. Beyond a sprawling woodpile was the privy. Gripping the lamp more tightly, Clara crossed the yard and went into the tiny hut. From beneath the seat came the furious buzzing of flies. The smell made her gag, but she swallowed at once, before doing what she needed and tipping down earth from the bucket.

Having eaten with Fynn and Francis earlier in the evening, she did not regret having rejected Philemon's parting offer to cook something for her. Instead she drank some water in the kitchen and splashed her face before going to bed. Since marrying Robert, she had resumed her childhood ritual of praying before sleeping, but, tonight, tears of loneliness leaked from behind her clasped hands. She had not lain long in the dark when an eerie squeaking in the thatch began to grate on her nerves so badly that she was obliged to relight the lamp.

Determined to root out the nuisance, she fetched a broom from the kitchen and placed a chair on the dressing table. As she clambered up, a rodentlike creature scuttled into the thatch. Clara struck out at it fiercely, and something fluttered to the ground. She jumped down and turned it with her foot. Not a rat at all, but a bat, and a hideously ugly one. Its single twisted tooth made it look more like a small devil than one of God's creatures.

Wishing profoundly that she had stayed with Fynn and Francis for the night, Clara returned to bed. After an hour or so, she fell into a fitful sleep, in which breathings and snufflings outside the flimsy calico windows entered her dreams and merged with images of her weeping father. Sometime before dawn, she was awakened by the sound of light footfalls in the next room. Her heart sounded too loudly in her ears for her to judge exactly where the intruder was. She had been led through the village in darkness and had only the vaguest idea about her immediate surroundings. Not knowing whether screams would bring aid or encourage the stranger to bludgeon her to death, she lay as still as she could.

"Master, help me," she heard someone call. "It is me, master. It is Simon."

Only a boy, rejoiced Clara, amazed that this child should be speaking English. Relieved and thankful, she leapt up to comfort him. But as she approached in her white nightdress, the boy let out a shriek and fled. She gave chase at once, horrified to have driven away anyone in trouble. Before she could catch him, the boy darted through the kitchen and out into the yard, where he scrambled over the reed fence. By the time she emerged in the lane, it was deserted.

A light breeze rattled the fronds of the banana plants. Clara looked in desperation between the moonlit huts. Perhaps Philemon lived in one. Clara called his name, softly at first, then louder. A woman crept out from the nearest enclosure and looked at Clara and froze with horror. Her hair was greased and twisted into strings like a mop. A man followed her, wearing nothing at all. Other men and women came out of huts and stared at Clara. She backed away and tripped over a horn stuck in the ground. A man pointed angrily at her and began waving his arms. Others joined in. Several of the men had spears in their hands. Whether they were angry to be woken or were cursing her in a more sinister way, she had no idea. A strong smell of sweat and cowhide wafted from them. One of the shouting men had glazed and damaged eyes and a dusty, hairless body. Helpless to communicate with these people, Clara simply walked back into the kitchen yard and into the house. Inside, she listened in case the shouting people came closer—though what she would do if this happened, she did not know. In fact silence returned very quickly.

In bed again, Clara could not sleep. Somehow she had imagined that Robert's villagers would be different from the natives she had seen in other remote places. But they had looked just as scruffy and underfed as any of the tribes along the way. Could she really have expected Robert to have transformed them? What a fool I am, she thought. What a silly little fool. She was still tossing and turning when the first cock crowed. Not long afterward, the bleating of goats made further rest impossible.

It was still early morning when Philemon arrived with bread and coffee. Philemon might look like an old tortoise, with his wrinkled scalp and nodding head, but she had rarely been more pleased to see anyone. She had soon blurted out an account of the night's happenings.

"Who is the boy," she asked, "and why was he so scared?"

Philemon shrugged his shoulders. "He's master's houseboy. He ran away, Nkosikaas. I cannot say why."

Clara was sure that Philemon knew a great deal he had no intention of telling her. "How can we find him?"

"I will ask many people where he is."

"Chief Mponda will surely help us."

Philemon said, quite sharply, "Nkosikaas, you must wait to see chief till master returns."

"The boy may be dead by then."

"We will ask at the school and at the mission. Then master will be here, and he will tell all you wish."

As Philemon led her through the village, Clara screwed up her eyes against the dazzling sunlight. Philemon's reluctance to talk to the chief seemed inexplicable. A new doubt assailed her.

"Has Mponda been baptized?"

"Not yet, Nkosikaas."

"But he has accepted Christ in his heart?"

Philemon lowered his eyes. "You will please ask master."

Clara followed him in stunned silence. In his letters, Robert had been so confident of Mponda's conversion.

A film of blue wood smoke rose through the thatch of the round, windowless huts. Women were carrying bundles of firewood or big black pots on their heads. Others were using besoms to sweep goats' dung away from the bare earth in front of their huts. Small groups of men were smoking or chatting in the shade of the few trees that had not been chopped down for fuel.

As Philemon approached a large shedlike building with a taller box structure added at one end, he pointed proudly.

"Our church. Master builded with his own hands."

A sudden rush of emotion swept over Clara. That a remarkable man should have labored to produce this ramshackle building was both sad and moving. Sad because he would know only too well the limitations of his workmanship; moving because he had nevertheless persevered. The spirit, not the outward form, was what mattered. Stenciled letters were plainly visible on the walls of Robert's church. The place had been made out of old boxes and packing cases. At last she understood what a blow the death of the carpenter John Dukes was going to be to Robert.

Next door to the chapel was the schoolhouse, its sagging walls plastered with crumbling clay. About a dozen boys and girls sat on earth mounds; their desks were upended logs. Most of the pupils were eleven or twelve years old. They wore calico loincloths or gray blankets draped from their shoulders like plaids. The children's teacher was the youth who had come with Philemon to the wagon to greet her the night before.

As Clara entered the school, this boy said some words of greeting, which everyone repeated. The teacher's name was Paul, Philemon told her. He was seventeen and lived at the mission. He had been a Bulawayo shop boy before his conversion. Philemon looked increasingly agitated as he talked to Paul in Venda. The only word Clara recognized was "Simon." Philemon then questioned the children, but Clara could see from his expression that no satisfactory answers were given.

While Philemon and Paul talked together, the children looked slyly at Clara and giggled. She turned to Philemon.

"What are they saying?"

"That your skin is as white as a flower, Nkosikaas. That you are like a queen."

Clara smiled. "I can't believe that's all they're saying, Philemon."

"They say that you are thinner than we like our beautiful women." She turned in surprise, not having realized that Paul also spoke English. If Philemon had spoken to Paul in Venda, it was only so she would not understand what they were saying.

There was something immediately attractive about Paul's smiling face. He was wearing a gray flannel shirt without a collar and a pair of much-patched striped trousers. He lowered his eyes. "They also say your skin looks soft and they would like to touch it."

"They should not say so," said Philemon, who lost no time in leading Clara across the lane to a fenced compound on the other side.

After pushing open a gate, they crossed an abandoned vegetable garden and headed for a long, low clapboard house.

"This is the mission, Nkosikaas."

A sick man was lying on the dilapidated veranda at the back. They walked past him into a room that ran the length of the building. Some people were lolling on mats or blankets on the floor, while others sewed or read books at a table. All wore frayed and dirty items of European clothing, but they themselves looked cleaner than the people in the village. The room echoed with noise and laughter. At Clara's appearance, silence fell.

A boy of eight or nine came forward and bowed low. "We welcome you here, our mother." These well-rehearsed words turned out to be all the English he knew. His name was Matiyo. As he walked away, he hid one of his hands. Later, Clara saw that most of his fingers were missing. His stepfather had caught him stealing and burned away half his hand. After being nursed at the mission, Matiyo had begged to stay on and had finally been accepted as one of "God's children." Everyone who lived at the mission, regardless of age, liked to be called a "child of God." According to Philemon, this elevated a person far above the casual mission servants, who worked for payment in food or cloth.

While most of the women wore crude dresses of white or blue trader's calico, a large and imposing female, whose face glistened as if freshly oiled, stood out in a dress of printed fabric with a matching headdress. As Clara approached, the woman closed her book and rose from the table. Clara was taken aback when Philemon introduced her as Queen Chizuva, Chief Mponda's principal wife. She could speak no English but smiled and squeezed Clara's hand. The queen was attended by a female relative and a male slave, who fanned flies from her face.

"Does she know about Simon?" Clara whispered to Philemon.

"Of course. Simon is not just master's boy. He is the queen's nephew."

"Would anyone dare harm the queen's nephew?"

"Very few, Nkosikaas. You need not worry."

The groans of the man on the veranda could be heard. One of his feet was grotesquely swollen. Sweat stood out on his forehead as repeated spasms racked him. Darker in color than most of the people around him, he was a Damarara, according to Philemon, so nobody could understand much of what he said. He had been wagon driver to a Dutch trader, who had abandoned him after his foot was crushed in an accident. He had refused an amputation and was not expected to live. A mass of flies covered his bandages and his exposed skin.

Fighting back feelings of nausea, Clara asked Philemon if anybody would fetch some water. A tall, stooping woman, who suffered from a chronic nervous affliction, bustled out, and soon reappeared with a little water in a bowl. Clara moistened her handkerchief and began to dab the man's forehead and lips. She asked his name.

"Everyone calls him 'Footman,'" replied Philemon. "He knows this name. Even says, 'Footman is sick,' in Dutch. 'Banja sick'—very sick—he says."

When she had done all she could for this gaunt, big-boned man, Clara folded the damp handkerchief and gave it to him. Unaccustomed to kindness, he seized her hand and loaded her with thanks—not one word of which was comprehensible to her. As tears seeped from his sunken eyes, a sudden suspicion overcame Clara. She turned to Philemon.

"Are any of the people at the mission ordinary Venda, or are they all unfortunates and outsiders?"

Philemon frowned. "The queen is not unfortunate. We have also the son of a headman. But Nkosikaas is right—most are slaves here, children of widows, or helpless people. Mabo—she brought the water—Mabo fled from the Matabele and came here just bones. But Jesus loves poor outcasts. We must show people that we are generous. Who will understand the love of Jesus if we are not kind to everyone?"

Walking back alone to Robert's house under a pulsing midday sun, Clara was so shocked by the state of the mission that she no longer knew what to think. How could she ever have imagined that Robert's tribe had been magically transformed in a few years? But she did not blame her husband for misleading her; she blamed only herself for underestimating his problems.

A great stillness had fallen in the village. Men and women were sleeping face downward under the eaves. Only the hens and pigeons were active, pecking at morsels in the dust. Yet through the trembling waves of heat, a solitary woman was approaching Clara. A length of cloth, secured above her waist, fell in classical folds to her ankles. She moved with a dancer's grace, like a reed swaying. Her naked breasts swelled beneath an intricate necklet of woven fire.

Everyone else in the village—men, women, and children—had followed Clara's movements with their eyes, but not this beauty, who looked only straight ahead. Then, just as she drew level, she turned and stared at Clara with a hatred that the Englishwoman had never before seen on any face.

CHAPTER 7

That evening, a girl arrived from the mission with a boiled fowl and rice for Clara's supper. Soon afterward, the boy Matiyo ran in, shouting, "Master, master," and gesturing to Clara to follow him.

Matiyo strutted ahead of Clara, proud to be guiding the white woman. Thinking only of Robert, Clara was scarcely aware of the evening village scenes: the families eating outside their huts, the men sitting apart under the trees.

Clara felt faint and unsteady. She wished that she could stop and lean against something for a moment. What was happening was wrong. Robert should have come to her, not gone to the mission first. She wanted so badly to let love overwhelm her on seeing him, but how could she be anything but self-conscious in front of so many inquisitive people?

A crowd had gathered by the veranda of the mission, where some sort of altercation was taking place. An albino girl of three or four was surrounded by angry people. A woman wearing nothing but a leather apron was pointing at the child and demanding something from someone whom Clara could not see. Then she heard Robert's voice, deep and insistent, rejecting whatever the woman was asking—this much she deduced, though understanding not a word of the language. As the dialogue grew more intense, Clara could barely keep from rushing up to her husband. I've waited for months, she longed to say. Isn't it my turn? But she realized that the child was probably in danger.

A spear-wielding man with cicatrices on his chest began to harangue both Robert and the woman. Meanwhile the blotchy pink-and-white child clung to the leg of the woman, as Robert stood listening to the man with extraordinary calmness.

Paul, the teacher, was standing near Clara. "Tell me what's happening," she whispered.

"The mother—that's the woman," he explained, "—she says the mission must take her child. Her husband says by tribal custom the child should have been killed as a monster long ago. He says he would have killed her himself if her mother had not begged him to let her grow a little. He only spared his daughter because his wife promised to give her to the white man. Today she comes to give her child to the missionary to rear."

The mother remained perfectly still while her husband ranted on. She was very solemn, as if she had spent all her emotions and was now resigned to endure the worst. As Robert started to speak again, Clara's eyes were riveted on him. He was talking and gesticulating exactly like the people around him. She turned to Paul. "What is he saying?"

"Master pretends he is very shocked. He asks the woman, 'You don't like her? Don't like your own child?' 'That's right,' she says. 'I hate her.' Master tells her, 'You can't be the mother, then.' She begs him to take the child from her. 'No,' says Master. 'You must be patient another year. And you, father, you must let this child go home with her mother. And mother, of course you love her! We can see that! You will nurse the child for *me* for another twelve moons and then bring her back and I will train her.' "

The mother rose, and the little creature stretched out her arms and was carried away, knowing nothing of the momentous debate.

"Master is so clever." Paul chuckled. "The child stays with her mother, and the husband will not kill her."

As the crowd parted, Clara saw Robert smiling down at a boy who was clasping his hand.

Paul said happily, "Simon has come home. Master found him."

A tightness in her throat made Clara swallow. While she had been thinking negative thoughts about the mission, Robert had been selflessly helping others and putting their concerns before his own. Just then he caught sight of her and waved.

"Clara, my Clara," he called out joyfully as he hurried toward her.

Clara wished that they could be far away from all the curious eyes that were fastened upon them. She moved to kiss her husband on the lips, but he did not bend his head; so their first kiss, which she had imagined as intense and lingering, turned out to be little more than a perfunctory brush against her forehead. To her amazement, she found herself babbling about her journey when all she wanted was to ask why he had not come to her as soon as he reached the village, and why he had gone away in the first place.

On their way to the house, the crowd followed them closely; it included the mission "children" and villagers whose greased bodies glowed warmly in the evening light. A girl whom Clara had not seen before walked just behind Robert, as did the boy called Simon, almost as if impersonating a page and a bridesmaid.

Once home, Simon and the girl went into the kitchen, leaving Clara alone with her husband. Flies buzzed and vibrated, a dying moth flopped around. Clara wanted Robert to hug her tightly and kiss her, but all he did was hold her hands in his. Her fingers looked very pale against his darker skin. The next moment, he sank to his knees. She thought he would beg her forgiveness for having been at the cattle post when she arrived. But instead he cried out, "Almighty and most merciful God, we thank Thee for this reunion. We beseech Thee to bless us and keep us in health and harmony, serving Thee till our lives end."

She thought of how he had just saved the albino and of his love for Simon. She saw how thin and exhausted he looked; but she still wished his first private words had been personal rather than religious. Robert rose to his feet and said humbly, "I wish I'd been here when you arrived. You see, I had to find Simon. He was in danger."

"Was I in danger too?" she whispered.

"With Paul and Philemon to care for you?" He smiled serenely. "Nobody could have been safer."

Relief and gratitude flooded through her. "Why was Simon so frightened?"

"Africans often are." His voice was warmly reassuring. "Their minds are plagued by ignorance and superstition." And then, at last, he drew her to his chest, his deep, rich voice resonating in her own body. "How strange everything must seem to you, my dearest. We all have to strive to be especially patient here." He looked into her eyes as if dazed by what he saw. "If you only knew, Clara, how I've longed for this day, how impatient I've been, how much I've missed you. When Philemon told me just now that you'd been alone in Belingwe, I couldn't believe it. My own dear wife had been friendless in such a place? It was unthinkable. If the faintest rumor of John Duke's death had ever reached me, I'd have come for you at once." She shut her eyes and let herself rest passively in the circle of his arms. His breath was warm on her cheek.

Even in the twilight, Clara could tell that Robert had changed. His cheeks were hollower, his eyes deeper-set. He wore an old city shirt without a collar and stained moleskin trousers. His big leather belt emphasized how thin he had become, but his eyes shone as steadily as before. A lock of iron-gray hair fell over his face as he bent toward her. And this time his kiss was as tender as she had hoped. He had once said, ''When we kiss, our souls are open to each other,'' and she prayed that he still believed it. She could feel the throbbing of his heart as he pressed against her. His lips set a delicious apprehension fluttering under her skin.

There was an old copper-framed mirror in the bedroom, and as Clara brushed her long black hair, she gazed into its spotted depths and saw a face that scared her: pale and haggard, with eyes dazed by desire. She wanted Robert so badly that all the questions she had meant to ask might never have existed. She undressed quickly, not wishing him to see the insect bites on her legs or to be found struggling with buttons when he came in. Then she lay waiting. A great hollowness occupied the center of her being, a void of desiring tenderness that longed to be filled.

Robert entered, stripped to the waist, the gray and white hairs on his chest still damp from washing. He brought warm water with him and shaved, peering into the same mirror. She liked the idea of his face replacing hers in those speckled depths, like one fish gliding after another in a pond. But when he got into bed she saw that he was not aroused. Her heart contracted. She thought: He no longer cares for me as he did in England. Just to look at me made him tremble then.

She wanted to press against him and yet was afraid to do so in case he would think her unladylike, indelicate. Their lovemaking, she had always half feared, would remain a sacrament to him only for as long as she appeared angelic. He lay beside her without moving, and at first Clara feared everything had changed. Yet when he finally turned to her, it was with a sharp moan of desire. When she felt his penis throb against her thigh and his arms tighten around her, she knew such wild relief that nothing afterward could quite compare with it.

Later, Robert knelt on the earth floor and thanked God for his wife's homecoming.

Robert had already got up by the time Clara woke the following morning. She dressed and went into the kitchen, where Simon was taking a freshly baked loaf from the oven. He placed it on a wire tray to cool and lifted a blackened coffeepot from the stove. The boy looked very smart in a crisp white shirt and neatly pressed shorts.

"Where is master?" she asked, a little disappointed that Robert had not waited to take breakfast with her.

"At the mission, missus. In early morning, sick people come to see him. You will have coffee? I cook an egg for you?"

"Bread and jam will be enough, thank you. And coffee."

She smiled appreciatively, although the boy's domestic competence slightly unnerved her. Before arriving at Mponda's kraal, Clara had missed Robert so much that she had barely thought about what she would do with her time. Simply being with her husband would be enough to make her happy. They would walk together under shady fruit trees; they would read aloud to each other; she would make curtains, embroider cushions, and beautify the house. But there was neither garden nor orchard to walk in, and the bush was overgrown and dusty. Nor could sewing be expected to occupy her for long. A nurse would at once feel useful, but she herself had never learned anything in the medical line.

Simon said in his sweet, soft voice, "I have made fig jam. You will eat, missus?"

"Yes, please."

Though she smiled at the boy, she feared that if she started to make jam, he would not be pleased. What I must do, thought Clara, is learn the language as quickly as possible, so I can work in the school.

She asked casually, "Did the first Mrs. Haslam teach the mission children?"

"Yes, missus. I was six years old when Mrs. Ruth taught me my letters."

"Was she liked by the children?"

"Oh, yes, missus. All us boys and girls loved her."

Simon's teeth shone brightly in his black face. His voice was low and guttural in a pleasing way, and his English was excellent. But was he telling the truth, or what he imagined she would like to hear? If Ruth had been stern and unsympathetic, Clara doubted whether he would tell her.

She said lightly, "Why did they like her, Simon?"

"Mrs. Ruth was kind and laughed with us. We all cried for long time when she died."

Clara frowned. Perhaps Robert's memories of Ruth would make him reluctant to see anyone else following in her footsteps. As in other matters, she would have to feel her way before making a move.

Simon cut a slice of bread and placed a jar of his homemade jam beside her plate. What wonderful composure, thought Clara. His unobtrusive movements would have done credit to an experienced waiter. It was puzzling that such a self-possessed boy should have been terrified in this very house only two nights earlier. Could it just have been superstition and ignorance, as Robert had suggested?

As Simon was pouring coffee into her cup, Clara murmured, "Why were you so scared the first time I saw you?"

Simon jerked away the pot, splashing coffee onto his shorts. "I did not know you would be here, missus."

"Why had you run away from the village in the first place?"

"I was afraid of a sorcerer." He dabbed at himself with a cloth.

"Are you still afraid, Simon?"

"No, missus."

"Why not?"

"Because Lord Jesus will protect me."

"Why didn't you trust Lord Jesus before you ran away?" Simon avoided her eyes. "Well?" she insisted.

His eyes remained lowered. "I do not know, missus."

Clara said softly, "Surely you know why you feel safer now."

"Master has told me he will ask Chief Mponda to protect me." The boy was still uneasy. "Master said I must not worry you, missus."

"You haven't worried me," lied Clara, dismayed that Robert had warned Simon against being open with her. Unless he could share his problems with her, how would she be able to help him?

When Robert returned an hour later, he smiled delightedly to see his wife relaxing in his small sitting room. She was surprised that he had not asked what she thought of her new home. He must surely be anxious, in case she was disappointed.

"My brave girl," he murmured at last, as if making excuses for a favorite daughter. "How could you know that women who go out at night are considered witches? I hear you kicked over one of their fertility horns."

His amusement shocked her. "Is it funny to be thought a witch?"

"They'll think you're magical whatever you do. White women are rarer than eclipses and more frightening. Primitive minds have no sense of logical causation. Any unusual event— even the death of a cow—can explain illness or misfortune. The Venda see omens everywhere. Your arrival was bound to bother them."

"You should have been here to warn me. Will they harm me, Robert? One woman looked as if she wanted to kill me."

"I expect she'd quarreled with her husband." He was smiling again, and now she was annoyed by it. "White people's spirits are considered terribly dangerous. Only a madman would risk freeing one by killing its owner."

"If everything's so safe and amusing," she burst out, "what was Simon scared of?"

"Magic, my dear." Suddenly he looked sad and weary.

"Isn't the boy supposed to be a Christian?" she asked.

"He *is* a Christian, but before his baptism, his life was dominated by magic. Don't be angry, Clara. I can't help the way Africans think. They'd deny that grass is green before doubting the reality of magic. Simon believes in Jesus, but his pagan past still tugs at him." Robert got up from the table. "Come with me for a moment."

Clara let herself be led to a hut less than twenty paces from the house. A man was lying prostrate under the eaves. He was covered by a blanket and lay very still.

Robert said under his breath, "His name is Kefasi Chimutsa, and he's been ill for a week. This morning, his wife called in the nganga—that's the local priest and healer. Afterwards, she swore to me in all seriousness that the nganga had just removed three hundred beetles from her husband's brain. She'd seen them fly away—every one. She said they'd been placed in Kefasi's head by a woman who lives six miles away and never leaves her home. I could argue with Kefasi's wife till doomsday, but I'd still fail to shake her belief in this diagnosis.''

As they returned home, Robert seemed almost cheerful, but Clara was very distressed by what he had just told her. How could anyone hope to make converts out of people who believed such nonsense? Although she already knew the answer, she braced herself to ask him whether the chief had converted. Suddenly the thought of hearing him tell her that he had suffered a crushing reversal made Clara feel ill. In addition, it occurred to her that if she pushed him too far, Robert would probably be tempted to give her answers that were soothing rather than truthful. Only by seeming undismayed by her new surroundings could she hope to be told what he was actually thinking; and openness between them would be vital for their future happiness.

As it happened, Clara did not have to wait long before Chief Mponda's name cropped up. Later the same morning, a messenger visited the mission. The chief, he said, wished to make the acquaintance of his missionary's wife. With a keen sense of anticipation and not a little nervousness, Clara put on a high-collared silk dress and helped Robert to press his ancient frock coat.

Mponda's stronghold was at the top of a fortified crag a mile from the village. Its lower slopes were strewn with boulders and thick vegetation. All gaps and crevices between prominent rocks had been filled with dry-stone wall, forcing the chief's visitors to ascend by a single winding path. The morning was very hot, and Clara was glad to be carrying a parasol. What she would do with it later, when the path became steep and she needed both hands, she had no idea.

Never having met an African chief, Clara was excited. She decided not to ask how Mponda might be dressed, since it would spoil her surprise. She imagined him in a leopardskin kaross, with a headdress of ostrich feathers, and he would also be wearing a necklace of rough-cut gems or tiger's teeth; his hut would be as big as a barn.

Far below them, a procession of women was snaking along the same path, carrying earthenware pots on their heads.

''The day's supply of water,'' explained Robert. ''There's no spring on the hill.''

"What an inconvenient place to live," she remarked, trying to imagine what it would be like to climb a steep hill with a heavy jug on her head. Not for the first time, Clara admitted to herself that the chief must be a frightened man.

As if reading her mind, Robert murmured, "Mponda's father was butchered by his uncle. So one can't blame him for being cautious."

"But that was years ago, surely. He wouldn't live up here unless expecting an attack soon."

"You mean by the Matabele?" Robert shook his head dismissively. "I very much doubt it."

In fact, Clara had meant an enemy closer at hand—possibly the very one responsible for terrifying Simon. But she decided not to press the issue.

At the top of the scarp, a ridge stretched ahead. Immediately before them was Mponda's compound, ringed about with a stockade of wooden posts and guarded by a group of warriors, who stepped aside to let Robert and Clara pass. Robert pointed out the chief's hut in the center and the surrounding dwellings of his wives. Stretching out along the ridge, behind this royal stockade, were the huts, granaries, and stock pens of members of his household.

Mponda's hut, though larger than most, was, to Clara's chagrin, like any other inside: the same circular depression where the fire burned, same beaten-clay and cow-dung floor, same soot-blackened thatch, mud chicken coops, baskets of grain, and bundles of skin bedding. The chief was sitting on a simple wooden stool, while a white-haired counselor squatted in the dirt at his feet. In spite of the heat, Mponda wore a sheepskin skullcap and a tattered cloak that left his chest exposed. He was a large and muscular man of forty or so. His face was proud, sensitive, and wonderfully expressive. He was attended by a boy and by an old woman with breasts like empty seed pods.

What ought to have been the African equivalent of an English presentation at court was just a grubby hole-in-a-corner greeting. The dramatic pictures in old missionary magazines of encounters between Livingstone and Sekeletu, and between Moffat and Moselekatse, had led Clara to imagine heralds shouting, drummers drumming, and women and warriors lining up around the chief's enclosure.

The only ceremony—if it deserved the name—took place outside, when they emerged briefly for Mponda to present a sheep to Clara. She in turn handed him a box of cigars, bought in London on Robert's instructions. Then they trooped back into the hut, where Clara was soon coughing in the smoky atmosphere. Robert was offered a gourd filled with foaming millet beer, but Clara was given a tiny cup of undrinkable coffee. She felt more indignant when a boy brought in chunks of meat for the men and nothing at all for her. Venda men and women did not eat or drink together, but an exception ought surely to have been made in the name of hospitality for a missionary's wife.

Robert sensed Clara's feelings and was upset on her behalf. But since Mponda hated anyone to converse in a foreign language in front of him, Robert could not explain to Clara that an informal meeting was a greater honor than a ceremonial affair. Her lovely face looked sad and disenchanted—a pity, since Mponda was observant and very easily hurt.

"My chief," Robert was saying in Venda, "how can I know that my people are safe?"

"Umfundisi, do you speak of the boy Simon?"

"Yes, great leopard. I fear that he will be threatened again."

"I have told Nashu I have eyes all round my head. He is placing himself in the path of a buffalo if he harms God's children. I have said this to him."

"What was his answer, my chief?"

"The old wolf obeys the leopard's roar."

The old man sitting at Mponda's feet nodded vigorously, applauding his ruler's omnipotence.

"Will Makufa obey you too?"

"We have not spoken. He has bought guns, Umfundisi ... my own son." Mponda's voice was thick with grief and anger.

"Who would sell guns to him?"

"Men who work for the white man's company."

"Black men?"

"Black policemen, Umfundisi."

"My chief, how many rifles has your son bought?"

"Many."

"As many as there are huts on the plain?"

"Yes."

"Do your spies know where Makufa will hide his rifles?"

"At Mount Rungai. In the caves."

Robert nodded, despite suspicions that these guns had been

invented by Nashu and Makufa to terrify Mponda. They clearly hoped to delay the chief's baptism by making him believe he would need to arm his warriors before he could risk inflaming his pagan opponents by converting. And what a clever hiding place they had chosen for their fictitious guns. Because the spirit of Mwari, creator of earth and air, was said to inhabit the Rungai caves, people would be far too frightened to go there, to look for guns or anything else.

"My chief, will you seize the rifles?"

Mponda shook his great head sorrowfully. "They are guarded by Mwari's priests."

"They are ordinary men."

"*You* think they are ordinary men. *I* think they are. But my people say they speak with Mwari's voice. What can I do, Umfundisi? If a priest is killed while I search the cave, how many friends will I lose?"

"Who has seen the guns with his own eyes?"

"They are in the caves, Umfundisi. You must believe me." Mponda sighed aloud. "My headmen must have guns too. I cannot be washed by Jesus till I give them guns. My son Makufa is too strong."

"Each day you delay, great leopard, more people will doubt your strength. Give yourself to Christ now. Why did Nashu dare accuse Simon of witchcraft? Because he thinks you will not punish him. So who will suffer next? Paul or Philemon? Even me? But when you wash away your sins, what will people say? 'Our chief is strong. The great leopard fears nothing. Lord Jesus is with him.' "

Mponda looked guilty and embarrassed. "I will send warriors to protect God's children. No one shall harm them."

"My chief," urged Robert, "you must not send guards. Your friendship is the only shield we need. The moment you admit that you doubt our safety, we will be in real danger."

Mponda smiled sadly. "There is a Venda saying: The ape denies his red bottom because he cannot see it. My friend, I cannot see my enemies, but I am wiser than the ape."

As Robert was about to reply, the old courtier jumped up in alarm. A little snake was wriggling around the wall of the hut. Neither a puff adder nor a mamba, it looked harmless. But a snake entering a hut was thought to prove that a witch was present. With astonishing speed for a man of his bulk, Mponda seized a stick and flung it with deadly aim. The snake's back was broken, and second blow killed it.

"Yebo, yebo, Ewe—E-hea!" cried the white-haired counselor delightedly, jumping up and down. The old woman joined in, her breasts flapping against her ribs.

Almost as fast as he had killed it, Mponda snatched up a knife and skinned the snake. He held up the dangling skin for a moment as if about to fling it from him in disgust. His attendants cheered, even the old woman. Then Mponda laughed loudly and tied it around his skullcap like a striped ribbon. With one compelling gesture, the chief had derided the very possibility that Clara might be a witch. Before Robert could offer his congratulations, a young woman burst into the hut and started to scream abuse.

Robert raised a finger to his lips, then whispered to Clara, "Don't worry. I'll explain later."

Mponda yelled back insults, but the girl was not cowed. Instead she eyed him with blazing reproach; and then, with a movement so swift and unexpected that Robert would have missed it had he turned his head for a moment, she prostrated herself at the chief's feet. After a tense silence, she rose and left without another word.

Thankful that the young woman had gone—but shaken because it was she who had glared so strangely the day before—Clara was very curious to know what she had been saying to the chief. Was she his daughter or a concubine? And why was Mponda abjectly downcast now? Clara longed to be told at once, but Robert was doing all he could to cheer up Mponda—at least that was how it looked to her. But when a sad silence became embarrassingly prolonged, Robert admitted defeat and, to Clara's delight, took his leave.

Outside, Robert held Clara's hand. "You do see, my dear, don't you, that I couldn't explain anything in there? We couldn't speak English in front of him. He may live in a hut, but he's a king, and easily offended." Before the path began to drop steeply, he drew her closer to him. "I'll tell you what happened when the snake came in."

"No, no," she cried impatiently. "Tell me about that woman."

"Her name's Herida, and she's Mponda's third wife. If anyone can stop him converting, it's her."

So *that* was why she had stared at Clara with such hatred. Of course she would loathe the wife of the man who was trying to take away her husband. "What's going to happen to her?" murmured Clara.

"When Mponda's a Christian? She'll have to go home to her father." Robert made this sound like a minor inconvenience.

"Was Herida begging just now?" Clara found this possibility very upsetting.

"Demanding, not begging, I'd say."

"Lying in the dust . . . demanding? Oh, Robert!"

"To put him in the wrong, don't you see?"

"I'd say she loves him."

Robert said dryly, "There's very little romance out here. Her father wanted an alliance with the chief. That's the long and short of it."

"Maybe they fell in love later." Robert's lack of sympathy astonished Clara. How could he not have been moved by the woman's misery?

As if reading her mind, he said gently, "Don't upset yourself by imagining that she feels as you do. Polygamy breeds envy and resentment . . . never love."

"There must be exceptions." Clara could feel her cheeks burning.

He shook his head. "Venda widows are always happy to be taken over by a dead husband's brother."

"Always? How can you be sure?"

"Because all marriages are arranged here. Herida's family will find her a new husband in no time, and if she's his only wife, she'll be happier than before. She didn't put on that act because she's lovesick. She's the witch doctor's daughter. *That's* why she's so cussed. Mponda's baptism will finish her father's power. Of course she hates Christians and will fight to stop Mponda converting."

As if the last word on the subject had been spoken, Robert resumed his descent, turning to help his wife when the path became precipitous. Going down was harder than coming up had been, but her aching muscles did not prevent Clara from brooding. How could he so lightly dismiss a young wife's outraged dignity?

Near the bottom of the slope, they sat down on a large rock to rest their legs. Robert offered Clara his water bottle, which she took without a word. He told himself that her reluctance to accept opinions based on his long experience of Africans need not be a blow to his pride. Hadn't he been drawn to her in the first place because she had known her own mind?

She was studying him closely with her bright, slightly quizzical eyes. "What were you arguing about? You and Mponda?"

"Word for word?" he asked, trying to sound lighthearted. "I can't possibly repeat it all." However hard she might press him, he was determined not to frighten her. To tell her about Makufa's rifles before knowing whether they existed would be cruel and pointless. He decided that he would relay to her an earlier conversation with Mponda. "The best of friends have their disagreements, you know. *I* think he should be baptized at once, but *he* wants to wait till after the rains . . . December or January. Of course I argued with him."

Clara's enchanting face expressed puzzlement. "He must have his reasons, surely."

"Oh, yes. He's sure if the rains are late, his baptism will be blamed. They'll say the ancestors are angry with him."

"So he's being sensible?"

Could he detect a hint of gentle mockery? Robert's eyes met hers calmly. "I'm afraid he isn't sensible. The tribe's female initiation rites take place soon. Girls are cut between their legs in a loathsome manner. A few will bleed to death. Mponda won't ban these mutilations till he's a Christian. Of course I want him to hurry up."

Against her wishes, Clara found herself doubting this explanation. What if Mponda wanted to keep all his wives and had no intention of becoming a Christian? Would Robert still be crawling up the hill to plead with him three years hence? And would there be a single child left at the school by then? As if in a shaken kaleidoscope, her memories of Robert lecturing in England to adoring audiences became jumbled with recent vignettes: Robert chewing meat in a filthy hut, cajoling a half-naked autocrat, ignoring an unhappy woman. Clara knew she had upset her husband and longed to put matters right as soon as she could, but how could she possibly hide her feelings when faced with discarded wives and terrified houseboys?

*　　*　　*

That evening, after their return from the crag, dark clouds began to mass, and there was thunder and lightning at dusk. But after a loud blustering storm of wind and dust, only a light shower fell, and the following morning all the promising signs had vanished. By eight o'clock, the day was already scorchingly hot. Guilt gnawed at Robert as Clara dabbed her forehead with a handkerchief. He should have given her a better idea of what to anticipate, but he had expected their love to compensate for every discomfort.

As a young man in Africa, he had himself been shocked by the modest scale of many mission stations, so Clara could not be blamed for feeling the same. Missionary societies were the real culprits—exaggerating their successes in order to attract donations and so exciting unrealistic expectations. Yet Robert still felt wounded by Clara's attitude. He had worked from dawn to dusk for four months to build their house. The chapel and the school had taken him as long again; and now he was laboring like a coolie to finish the village dam. Eventually, he told himself, she would start to recognize his achievements. To have made converts as dependable as Simon, Paul, and Philemon was a feat most missionaries could not boast even after a dozen years in the bush. Yet in half that time he had also compiled the first Venda dictionary and translated the Bible. With a core of regular worshipers at the mission and a dozen children regularly in school, the mission's prospects were outstanding. If Mponda would only embrace Christ, Clara would soon view everything in a different light.

In the meantime, if anything could get her involved, it would surely be the school. But as he led Clara in its direction, he froze. Ahead of him were two members of Mponda's bodyguard. If the chief really felt obliged to protect his friends like this, his power must indeed be crumbling. It was now more urgent than ever to visit Mount Rungai. The sooner Robert could establish that the rifles were an invention of the witch doctor, the sooner Mponda would realize that Nashu and Makufa were making a fool of him. Robert dreaded telling Clara he must go away for a while; but he dreaded even more the consequences of Mponda's vacillation.

Outside the school, an old man was sitting under a tree, smoking hemp or dagga. His pipe was a primitive hookah, with the stem attached to a reed going down into a cow's horn full of water. As he sucked at the horn, he laughed and spluttered to himself.

The school delighted Robert. The transformation of wild and uncontrolled children into biddable pupils in a few months was a process he never tired of witnessing. Yet so long as the tribe's initiation rites took place, the school's civilizing effects would continue to be thrown away when puberty arrived. Only the chief's baptism could change this.

"Why do their parents let them attend?" whispered Clara, plainly entranced by the children.

"So they can steal the white man's secrets," confessed Robert. He had decided to respect her eagerness to understand things; he would be honest whenever he could without alarming her.

"Is that *really* why they let them come?" Her disappointment was greater than he had expected.

"I'm afraid it is. But imagine you were illiterate and saw people reading. Wouldn't you think it a kind of magic? A scary ability, but very desirable to possess. Many villagers think white men own wagons and horses because they can read. So they weigh up the dangers and advantages, and some of them decide to risk letting their children come here to learn."

"It's sad to think of parents worrying about your bewitching their children."

"I know." He sighed. "Before the children come here, lots of parents tell them. 'Keep to the old African ways. Don't pray in school; just pretend to. Don't let the white man steal your heart and make you despise your mother and father.' It takes a long time before the children trust us."

"Poor Robert. It's not easy, I can see that."

Her sympathy brought a lump to his throat. He managed to smile as he said, "I hope I didn't you give the impression that they don't enjoy it here. The boys love using carpentry tools, and the girls are very keen to sew and bake."

Later that morning, as they were walking to the mission, Robert and Clara passed a boy of three or four with a bloated stomach and a weeping sore on his leg. He was sitting listlessly in the dust, watched over by an older boy.

Clara's dark eyes sought Robert's imploringly. "How awful. What can we do for him?"

"Nothing at all, unless his mother brings him to the mission. Imagine the row if we kidnapped him. And suppose I succeed in persuading her, and the boy dies anyway—it's a deep ulcer, so he probably will. What do you think will happen?"

"You'll feel all the better for knowing you did what you could to save him."

He shook his head sadly. "You're wrong, Clara. I'll feel worse. People will say he died because I took him; and children with better chances of recovery won't be brought to me by their parents."

Robert braced himself for a fierce argument over the child, but she surprised him by walking on in silence. When they reached the mission, she merely announced that she felt tired and was going home to rest.

On Robert's return in the early evening, he found Clara reading in the dark little sitting room. She had put on a red satin dress, and he was touched that she had taken this trouble for him. She looked so sadly out of place that he was momentarily speechless. His back ached from too much digging, and his feet were leaden. Dust was sticking to his sweat-soaked skin, and he felt too messy to kiss her. So accustomed was he to seeing no faces but black ones that Clara's skin, with its subtle gradations of pink and white, and its frame of raven hair, made him think of an exotic bird or flower. Her presence in this dingy little room became miraculous.

"My darling," he groaned, holding out his hands to her. "If you only knew how much you mean to me . . ." As he thought of Ruth's death and the long years of loneliness afterward, hot tears blinded him, and he felt such a fierce longing for future happiness that he was terrified by the possibility of losing Clara's love.

"What is it?" The look on his face startled her.

"Forgive me," he choked. "You're unhappy. I should have prepared you for life here. Everyone's depressed at first in Africa." He smiled lovingly. "Our labors sometimes seem fruitless, but they never truly are. Even when we fear failure most, a hidden power is at work. Conversions often appear to arrive out of the blue, but really it's thanks to this heavenly power."

Clara looked at him and shook her head. "No," she said. "I think a hidden power may give us the strength to persevere, but it is thanks to *our* efforts that success finally comes."

Upset to have offended her so soon after a moment of tenderness, Robert replied in a voice that was furry with emotion. "You're right. None of our efforts are vain in God's sight. Will you help Paul with the school? Please, say yes. They're our seed corn, the children . . . our best hope." He broke off awkwardly but saw at once that he had affected her.

"Oh, Robert, I'll certainly try. Of course I will. But don't expect too much, and I'll have to learn the language first."

She stepped a little to one side to make room for him to come up beside her in the cramped little room. As she held out her arms, he marveled at her grace. Every turn of her head, every movement of her shoulders, was lovely to him. He embraced her in her red satin dress, dirty as he was, and thanked God for their love.

CHAPTER 8

In the hot and dusty months before the rains, many people came to the mission suffering from sore eyes. Robert treated them all with a weak solution of nitrate of silver, which cleared up cases of ophthalmia but was useless against serious conditions such as glaucoma. Lacking any formal training, he had consulted widely among medical men, but his own observations had taught him most. He warned every one he could against the dangers of hookworm. Make yourselves sandals out of bark or leaves, he told them. But hardly any one did, although he explained over and over again that hookworm larvae entered their bodies through the soles of their feet. Like many parasites, they bred in human excrement, but all his urgings to villagers to dig latrines had fallen on deaf ears. Among his many anxieties was the fear that Clara would think he had never tried to change the insanitary conditions.

As Robert approached the veranda, where Philemon had lined up the patients, his thoughts were focused upon his wife rather than upon the diseased bodies awaiting him. Of course age-old African attitudes could not be altered in under a generation, yet because Clara had thought him a mover of mountains, he knew she was secretly disappointed. But today, as ever, the trusting hopefulness of the waiting sufferers touched him deeply. God's power to breathe faith into deformed humanity never failed to give him joy. Grateful patients accounted for half his Sunday congregation.

Robert applied a watery solution of opium to the vast distended breast of a woman afflicted with elephantiasis. This would do nothing to cure her but might give relief for a while. Nashu, the tribe's nganga, knew as much as Robert about local anesthetics and a great deal more about poisons and their antidotes. But the nganga infected wounds by plastering them with dung and made deep incisions with a dirty knife to let out spirits. The breast that

Robert was examining had been lacerated in this very way, and the skin was still tight and red around the scars. In time, it would become coarse and wartlike, and the swelling would harden. Robert knew of no cure. His next patient was a boy with yaws. His skin had erupted into a mass of pimples, exuding a yellowy viscid fluid. As Robert sprayed carbolic acid over the boy's infected groin and armpits, he praised him for not crying out.

To his right in the line stood a woman who had recently threatened the mothers of several of his schoolchildren. Robert squared his shoulders. Most patients showed respect by covering themselves with a kaross when coming to the mission, but this dyed-in-the-wool pagan was completely nude except for a tiny apron and a felt hat. She was holding a rusty machete, as if expecting an attack. Robert pointed angrily at the weapon.

"Never bring such things to the home of God's children."

A frightened little boy was hiding behind her. Shock gripped Robert's stomach. This was the very child Clara had begged him to help. When the boy died, as he soon would, Robert feared that Clara would see it as grounds for a more general pessimism about the mission. Robert bent down to examine the child's diseased limb. The smell was so nauseating that he gagged. What he had at first considered to be a single sore was part of a chain of ulcers of the kind that often turned cancerous. Attempts to dry them out were usually futile. A better diet and frequently changed dressings could help; but the ulcers were just as likely to grow larger. The boy's eyes were dim, and his skin had that peculiar dull and crepey appearance usually present in hopeless cases.

Before starting to wash and bandage the leg, Robert said a prayer. Why *this* boy, when so many others, with better chances of recovery, might have been brought to him? God's will be done, of course, but it was difficult to see how anything good for Christianity could arise from this little chap's arrival.

Last in the line was old Footman, still alive but, as long as he refused an amputation, doomed to get steadily worse. The poor man was clutching a square of dirty cloth as if his life depended on it.

Philemon said reverently, "Mrs. Robert gave it to him . . . her handkerchief, master."

"I see," murmured Robert, moved by Clara's gesture and not at all surprised that she had never mentioned it.

*　　*　　*

Since shortly after breakfast, sweat had been running down in the small of Clara's back and between her breasts like tickling insects. By midafternoon the heat was even greater, and although there was nowhere to escape it, something hard and obstinate in her nature saved her from self-pity. But nothing had staved off her misery after Robert walked away from the sick boy. Could she even continue to see him as the man she thought she had married? Despite feeling so wretched, she had not spilled out her anger and unhappiness in case he would think her too frail to be told the truth about her new surroundings. To live in ignorance would be the worst fate of all.

When Clara calculated that school would be ending for the day, she set out to meet Paul, for her first language lesson. She had paid a secret visit to him the day before, shortly after the encounter with the sick child, since the young teacher had seemed the obvious person to approach for help. So while Robert had thought her resting at home, Clara had been urging Paul to persuade the boy's mother to bring him to the mission. Today, of course, Clara was eager to find out what had happened.

When she reached the school, Paul was playing a game with his pupils. They stood in a line, holding on to one another's waists. A child with a cloth in her hand was pretending to be a parent or a teacher. A boy standing slightly apart from the line was a wild beast—for what else could his aggressive lunges mean? He too had a cloth. Each child in turn left the line and tried to fetch a pebble from near the beast without allowing him to flick them with his cloth. Meanwhile the mother did her best to protect her children, and the beast himself was soon leaping around trying to avoid being flicked by *her* cloth. The game proceeded, with terrific shrieks and yells.

Paul came up, smiling broadly. Clara found herself smiling too.

"Do you want to play with them, Mrs. Robert?"

"Is it a lion they're running away from?" she asked.

"No, no." he laughed. "A crocodile. You didn't see his teeth go snap-snap-snap? The children must fetch water from the river without being eaten. If the mother hits the crocodile with her cloth, he must let that child go, even if he has caught him."

So Clara took the mother's cloth and darted back and forth, flicking and lunging in defense of her charges. She was soon breathless and red-faced, but she kept going even after several children had been snatched and dragged off to the crocodile's lair.

When the game was over, the children remained in line, singing and shuffling along like a snake.

Clara dabbed at her moist brow and gasped, "Did you manage to see the sick boy's mother?"

"Yes, I did, Mrs. Robert, and she agreed to take him to the mission. I think he will be there now." Paul looked sadly at Clara. "He is very sick, Mrs. Robert. Maybe too sick."

Though disappointed by Paul's prognosis, Clara still found his calm, unhurried manner soothing. After he had given her twenty basic words to learn and explained their meaning and pronunciation, Clara asked him to tell her the words for "get better soon." She repeated these several times. He's not going to die, she told herself, not if I can help it.

As she was leaving, it suddenly occurred to her to ask him if, like Simon, he too had enjoyed being taught by Ruth.

"Mrs. Ruth was a very good teacher."

Clara smiled wryly. "That's not what I asked you." She leaned closer. "I won't tell anyone what you say."

"I enjoyed her lessons till she became sad."

"What changed her?"

His eyes followed a line of ants crossing the floor. "Her baby died, Mrs. Robert."

"Did she die giving birth?"

"No." His reluctance to say more disturbed her.

"How *did* she die? Was she ill?"

"You must ask master, please. I am sorry, Mrs. Robert."

At these words, a peculiar unease took possession of her. She found it hard not to run in search of Robert the moment she was outside. She *had to* know what had happened. But if she took to her heels, these superstitious people would probably suspect her of hurrying away from the scene of some evil deed. So she forced herself to walk at an even pace.

Waiting for Robert to return home, Clara felt unpleasantly sticky after playing with the children. She summoned Simon from the kitchen and told him she wanted a bath, but to her amazement the boy was grumpy and put out. After a long wait, she went to look for him, without success. She was lying on her bed when he returned at last. He was breathing hard and staggered under the weight of a large jug. After bringing in two more, he poured them into the tin hip bath at the end of the bed. When Clara thanked him, he did not even nod an acknowledgment. Still worried about Paul's refusal to tell her how Ruth had died, she shrugged off his behavior and got into the bath.

Simon heard his master first and ran out to greet him. When Clara came upon them, Robert was showing the boy an insect in a glass vial and they were talking animatedly. Robert was explaining how this tiny creature distilled water in the bone-dry atmosphere. Clara, who had no interest in insects, suspected that Simon's fascination might be put on to please his master.

She was in the sitting room when they both came in. Simon set down a bowl of water and began to wash Robert's feet, his manner quite different from his earlier gracelessness.

Desperate to question Robert about Ruth's death, Clara turned to Simon. "Leave us," she cried, more sharply than she had intended. The boy did not obey at once but waited for Robert's confirming nod. Even when he got it, he paused at the door. Suddenly Simon began gabbling in Venda. His anger was remarkable. Robert replied gently, also in Venda, and at last Simon went out. Believing that she had been the butt of his complaints, Clara felt her cheeks glowing fiercely.

"My dearest," Robert said hesitantly, "it's my fault for not saying anything . . . but you really shouldn't have asked Simon to fetch water in the afternoon. He and Hannah, the girl who helps him, must be told how much is needed before they go down to the well in the morning. A young man is humiliated if he has to draw water alone." Realizing she was angry, he attempted a placating smile. "When my dam is finished, we'll have piped water for all our needs."

Clara shook her head impatiently. What was all this rigmarole about something as trivial as fetching water? She said briskly, "I'd have been perfectly happy to wait till tomorrow for a bath, if Simon had explained things. Instead he was rude and complained to you."

Robert's mouth hung open for a moment. "Simon rude? I hope when you get to know him better you will . . ." His voice trailed off as he saw how strangely she was looking at him.

Clara's eyes were very bright as she whispered, "You never told me what happened to Ruth."

Robert sat shocked and dumb, his feet still in the bowl of

water. At last he murmured, "We lost our newly born son. Ruth had fever at the time. She was unhappy afterward . . . no, worse . . . I mean despairing. Malaria makes everything seem so dark and grim." Tears stood in his eyes.

Clara blurted out, "You mean she killed herself?"

He said rapidly, "She took the Cape cart and drove off toward Belingwe. The cart was found a few days later on the road . . . one of the mules too."

"And Ruth?"

"Not a trace." He gazed down at his feet and spoke awkwardly and yet as if he had often rehearsed his answer to this very question. "Sadly, it's not uncommon to get lost. I've heard of a dozen people straying from the track in search of water or guinea fowl." His eyes met hers briefly. His voice shook as he continued: "Two months later, some Bushmen came to Mponda . . . not at this kraal, but the old one. They'd found a white woman's skeleton in the bush. They showed me some hair and a few rags of clothing. They were Ruth's. She'd died of thirst, they thought."

Clara felt sick. "You're sure they didn't murder her—the tribesmen?"

Robert shook his head. "If they had, they'd have stolen the cart and never come near the village."

"Did you find her body and bury her?"

"Yes." He stood up, blinking away tears, and began to dry his feet, balancing awkwardly all the while.

Clara imagined the distraught woman blundering into the bush, deliberately walking on until lost. "Did she leave any kind of message?"

"Nothing at all. God knows what went on in her mind. She never kept a journal."

Clara was too overwhelmed by the horror of Ruth's death to give him the sympathy he deserved. She said, "Why didn't you tell me any of this before we married?" Her voice was breathless and accusing.

He raised his hands in entreaty. "She didn't kill herself, Clara. I swear to God she didn't."

"She must have been at her wits' end to go off like that— on her own, Robert, without a word to anyone. What am I meant to think?'

"That grief makes people do mad things." He stared at her with suffering and contrite eyes. "I couldn't bear to tell you."

Her brow darkened. "If lovers can't trust one another, who can?"

"Be fair to me, Clara. What would your father have said if he'd known?"

"Damn my father! Ruth killed herself or died trying to run away from you. That's more than a social blot to hide from Papa." She was shouting and could not stop. "It was monstrous not to tell me."

"But you knew she died out here. I told you that." His attempts to mitigate his obvious fault only fed her anger.

"Yes! But not that she'd gone dashing into the bush on her own. And that isn't all you failed to tell me." Her words were racing now. "You said the chief was virtually a Christian." A stab of anger goaded her. "Christian, my foot. That old pagan! And as for the mission ... it's just a soup kitchen for derelicts." She rushed into the bedroom and slammed the door, shaking the whole house.

Her heart was still pounding as she flung herself down on the bed. She thought: Now he knows what he's done. But soon the hateful satisfaction of punishing him began to fade. She had tried for days to remain calm and accepting of her new life, but at the first real test she had lost control of herself.

As Clara lay in her hot and airless little room, she imagined another unbearable evening, just like this one. Ruth and Robert had been arguing. Later, in the darkness, the distracted woman crept out to the stable to harness the mules and drive off into the moonless bush. And who could blame her? Clara could hear Robert pacing back and forth on the other side of the wall. On and on. Where could Ruth have found peace in a tiny house like this one? And still he paced.

At dusk, as the calico in the window was beginning to glow pink, Clara found herself thinking of Francis. His smile had been so frank and cheerful. How strange that her earlier prejudice against army officers had blinded her to his decency until they were almost due to part. Now he and Fynn already seemed to belong to some remote period of her life. Her eyes filled as she recalled Francis comforting her by saying that scores of people wanted to start new and more adventurous lives but lacked her courage.

Suddenly the bedroom door burst open, and Robert was standing in the opening with staring eyes. She feared he was about to weep, but when he spoke, his voice was low and dignified.

"Remember this, Clara: A single soul saved for Christ is a richer prize than the greatest earthly fortune. Paul and Philemon can testify to that. As for my poor mission house . . . the Son of God was born in a stable."

"He didn't choose to live in one later," she muttered.

Robert regarded her with such sadness that she regretted her bitter remark. He said, "It's not easy to build a house or chapel in a place like this. You expect a great deal."

"Did Ruth expect as much?"

Ignoring the sting in her words, he said calmly, "She came from a large family. Her father was not a wealthy man."

"You knew my background when you pursued me."

He said pleadingly, "I loved you, Clara . . . I still do. Please try to accept the past."

"Accept it?" she stammered. "What help is that? What help is anything now?"

She pushed past him and walked out into the evening air. As in a dream, she saw the whimsical arrangement of huts and pathways, so incredibly different from the ordered solidity of Sarston's streets. The darkening shadows and wisps of smoke spoke of peace and continuity. Did people out there in their huts ever dread to go home? Did *they* feel as lonely as a stick or stone? Behind her, somebody had lit a lamp in the house. A fan of yellow light glowed on the dusty earth by the door. She turned and saw Robert looking out and Simon holding the lamp behind him—the man of God and his devoted acolyte. Did they now wish she had never arrived?

I must calm myself, thought Clara, as they sat down to their meal in the kitchen. Unless I can, I'll end up running away like Ruth. The strips of mutton Simon was slicing from the chief's gift sheep smelled excellent. The boy had skillfully flavored the dish with roasted monkeynuts and herbs, and Robert's pride in his cooking was understandable. As she ate, Clara felt petty to have wanted Robert to rebuke Simon for his rudeness. It was a small thing, really. As the boy stood watching her, Clara smiled at him.

"What did you hope for when you first worked for Mr. Robert?"

"When I came to master, my one wish was for a gun," admitted Simon shamefacedly. "At last I had saved up money to buy one from a trader. I brought it home. My own gun! It was like a dream. I got up each night to make sure I really owned it. I was always admiring and polishing.'' Wide-eyed wonder gave way to religious awe. ''But now that I love Jesus, I never think of it.''

Robert was smiling like a doting parent. It did not seem to cross his mind that Simon might simply be saying this to please him. Earlier in the day, Robert had shown Clara the marks on the kitchen wall that Simon used in order to tell the time by the position of the sun's shadows. ''Such ingenuity!'' He had chuckled, adding that one day he might surprise the boy with a watch—a gift that Clara feared might cause envy and resentment in the village. Could the boy consider himself safe from threats simply because he was Robert's servant? Increasingly she had to wonder about Robert's judgment. When he wished to describe the terrible difficulties he had faced, he could be coldly analytical about Africans' motives. By contrast, his view of individuals was often rose-tinted and uncritical.

In the bedroom, Clara was careful to conceal her body when she slipped off her clothes. But when Robert took off his own, his erect penis was jutting eagerly. So soon after the revelations about Ruth, Clara prayed that he was not going to speak to her of a wife's duty to her husband. To her relief, he put on his nightshirt and then knelt in silent prayer for several minutes. His face was so solemn that Clara braced herself for more unwelcome news.

At last he murmured, ''Tomorrow I have to go away for a few days. Food gets very short in the dry season, but happily I can provide meat for the mission with my gun.'' He got into bed beside her, being careful not to touch her legs with his. ''Perhaps you'll feel more kindly toward me when I return. Paul and Philemon will be on hand whenever you need them. Hannah will be living in the house.''

''What about Simon?'' she asked.

''I'll need him with me,'' he acknowledged.

To her surprise, Clara felt no bitterness that he had chosen to leave her behind. They might well benefit from a time apart.

Clara woke during the night and saw that he was still awake and listening to the night sounds of the village. His face, composed and resolute in the moonlight, bore the expression he wore after he had been praying.

The sun was shining when she next opened her eyes, and

Robert and Simon had already gone out. Clara found herself alone with Hannah, who spoke no English and had not yet been fully trained by Simon. The girl was laying the table as Clara went in to the kitchen. After putting the salt and pepper under the tablecloth, Hannah poured milk into a jug, straining it through a filthy cloth. When Robert returned for breakfast, Clara told him what she had seen.

Robert smiled tolerantly. "Hannah meant no harm. She wouldn't understand the purpose of filtering. I expect she saw Simon straining the milk and thought it was a magical procedure to ward off witchcraft. Why should a charmed cloth need to be clean? As for the cruets, she probably thinks they have to be on the table to protect the food. Under the cloth or over it makes no difference." He touched Clara's hand reassuringly. "Just get Paul to come over here after school, and he can interpret for you. He'll want to come anyway."

"You're sure?"

"Of course. He's in love with Hannah. I only took her on here so he could see more of her. Her parents are very suspicious of Christians."

Before Robert went out to load the Cape cart, he held Clara's hands, and this time she did not pull away. She found it touching that he should want to help Paul and Hannah, and was pleased that he should look upon their love with sympathy. Just as she was beginning to wonder whether she had been too hard on him the night before, he spoiled things by saying earnestly, "Please keep a diary, my love. Ruth didn't, so I had nothing to send to her parents."

"I wouldn't want you to be embarrassed a second time," she said sarcastically.

He wagged a finger at her. "You know what I mean." But she didn't know at all. Was he implying that she would be in danger while he was away? Or were they always in danger? He frowned as if another irksome thought was troubling him. "I'm embarrassed to ask you this, Clara, but . . . please don't give your sanitary towels to Hannah to wash. She might be tempted to sell them to an nganga as a fetish. Also, bury your nail clippings or any trimmed hair. People think they gain magical power over a woman if they get hold of something that was once part of her body."

"I'll be careful," she promised, astonished by these grotesque warnings but knowing that they were probably necessary.

"I've left a letter on my table," he told her quite casually. "But please, open it only if I'm not back in two weeks."

Her heart thudded. "You're not going to shoot lions?"

"No, no. Just buck and guinea fowl." His smile stiffened. "You really mustn't worry. I never do myself. While we're useful to God, no harm can come to us. It's as simple as that."

Is it really? Clara wanted to ask. What makes you so sure? But with no desire for an argument before his departure, she kept silent and followed him into the lane, where he kissed her on the cheek and blessed her before clambering onto the box of the cart, where Simon was waiting.

Seeing her husband sitting up there, his profile outlined against the blue sky, Clara was reminded of a statue, so still was he. Robert lifted the reins in his beautiful long-fingered hands, and for a moment he was the man she had loved in England: brave, self-denying, and invincible in his faith.

As the mules began to pull away, she wished that she had never thought him infallibly wise and good. Nobody ought to be placed on a pedestal beyond teasing and contradiction. His parting words had cried out to be challenged. But she had kept quiet to protect the sense of dignity that he found so vital. But what he had just said was untrue. If harm *did* finally come to him, of course he would not believe that he was no longer serving God's purpose. Martyrdom was both the ultimate curse *and* the ultimate mark of God's favor.

A gray lizard with a bright-blue head and an orange throat blinked at Clara from the rafters. It was a few hours after Robert's departure, and already she felt too hot to move. Outside the kitchen door, a chameleon's mouth opened in an ugly pink gash, and its tongue shot out to trap a fly. In the lane, a goat was shifting its feet in the hot dust.

I can do nothing. I have nothing I can do, Clara thought. I *could* write to father in case I die. But saying what? A few comforting lies? Or the truth? Better a chatty day-by-day account filled with details of pet parrots and monkeys—didn't resourceful settlers always write home about such jolly creatures? "I call them Jack and Jill and they live in a comfortable nest. Such cheery antics all day long and then cuddling up for the night so sweetly." And finally a sad denouement: "Jack and Jill have been eaten by a leopard."

The stifled wail of a baby carried clearly on the still air. The next moment, it might be a beaten dog or a bleating goat. Clara forced herself to get up from the Windsor chair and go into the kitchen. She picked up a knife and cut some slices from the dark-red stands of dried antelope meat hanging from the rafters.

On her way to the mission with the meat in a cloth, she was made slightly uneasy by the presence of two men with spears, standing across the lane in the shadow of a hut, but the feeling faded as she sensed the cheerfulness of people all around her. A mother was shelling a mealie cob onto hot ashes and giving her delighted children the charred popcorns as they burst. Girls sang together while grinding dazzling-white meal between stones. A stream of talk, work, and movement flowed on every side of her.

Out of the sunlight, she stood blinking in the gloom of the mission's long room. The boy with ulcers was sitting on the floor in a corner, looking frightened and unhappy. Mission children, like Matiyo, were nowhere to be seen. Clara sought out Philemon.

"Why is that poor child being neglected?"

Philemon regarded her like a grave old stalk. "I have today bandaged his leg with my hands, Nkosikaas. Master bandaged yesterday."

"Why is he alone?"

"His mother is a bad woman."

Clara folded her arms. "Did he choose his mother, Philemon? Please tell the others to be kind to him. What is his name?"

"Homani, Nkosikaas."

Clara asked for milk to be brought and then approached the child. Holding out the cup, with a smile on her face, she spoke his name. Homani cringed from her at first but, when she least expected it, scuttled rapidly toward her like a crab.

Philemon noticed Clara's dismay. "His legs are too weak to carry him, Nkosikaas."

Unable to remember the words for "get better," Clara offered the cup in silence. The child snatched at it, spilling some and drinking the rest in a few noisy gulps. It was the same story when she held out the strips of meat.

"All hungry children grab at food when they first come," soothed Philemon.

Like starving animals, thought Clara, watching Homani cram

the meat into his mouth. His face was wizened and looked incredibly old, with its hollow eyes and prominent cheekbones.

"He must put on weight," she said. "I mean to come back every day to see him."

Leaving the building, she was alarmed to spot the two armed warriors watching for her. "Who are they?" she whispered to Philemon.

"They are Chief Mponda's bodyguards."

"Then why aren't they guarding him?"

Philemon smiled. "The chief has told them to protect you while master is away."

"Does he suppose I'm in danger?"

The old African's brow became deeply furrowed. "He wishes to honor you, Nkosikaas."

She moved closer and implored, "Is my husband really shooting game for us?"

"Master did not tell you?" Philemon's gentle surprise seemed almost a reproach.

"Tell me what?"

Philemon's cataract-covered eye was turned in her direction, as if he had no desire to continue their conversation. At last he said, "Whatever he told you, *that* is what he is doing now."

As usual, Philemon had avoided telling her what he knew, but there was still one way she could learn what was going on.

Back in the house, Clara passed the kitchen door. Inside, Hannah was cleaning out a saucepan, using Robert's hairbrush. With no hope of making herself understood, Clara could only smile and walk on. Soon she stood next to Robert's writing table and gazed at the letter propped against the inkwell. She felt its thickness as if estimating the number of sheets within. *"Clara. Only to be opened in the event of my failure to return."* With a sudden movement, Clara ripped open the envelope. Only fools chose to remain ignorant when they could choose to pick the fruit of knowledge.

> *My dearest Clara,*
>
> *Since you are reading this, it follows that I have not returned as expected, but this need not mean I am dead. Trust in Him who*

never fails us. It is quite possible that I am being held against my will.

Her eye raced on over the paper as her hand groped for the support of the chair behind her.

> *Mponda believes his son has bought rifles to use against him. He will not risk being baptized until he is sure that he can defeat Makufa. In my view, the rumor about these guns is being put about to scare the chief. I must either prove that the weapons do not exist or abandon any hope of converting Mponda this year.*
>
> *The chief has ordered men to watch over you, but you must not stay at Mponda's kraal without me. Philemon will take you in the ox wagon to Belingwe. Leave all arrangements to him. Christ be with you till we meet again, be it on this earth or in a better place.*
>
> *Ever your loving husband,*
> *Robert*

After reading the letter, Clara felt both betrayed and humbled. It was horrible to find that she had treated Robert with little sympathy at a time of crisis, and it was monstrous of *him* to set out on a perilous journey without giving her the opportunity to say a proper farewell. Too dazed to think of her own danger, she gazed ahead of her in blank dismay.

CHAPTER 9

Shortly after leaving Clara, Robert collected his Bush-man guide, Dau, and soon the Cape cart was clattering past the public meeting place, or khotla, and heading north. About fifty people stood gathered in the shade of the great kachere tree in the center of the open space. Every month, Mponda came down from his hilltop to arbitrate in disputes and impose fines for a wide variety of crimes, including murder. Robert reined in his mules and cast his eyes heavenward. This was definitely not what he had wanted. His one longing was to get on as quickly as possible in order to prove that there was no arms cache at Mount Rungai; but since Mponda would already have seen him, it would be impolitic to rush by without a word of greeting.

The dignity of this small court was always touching: the wit-nesses standing when addressing their chief, and Mponda himself speaking only when his clerk asked for a verdict. As Robert jumped down from the cart, proceedings were drawing to a close. While he pondered when to approach, Mponda waved away those around him, except for his son Makufa, and beckoned to his missionary. Though alarmed by Makufa's presence, Robert sat on a stool just vacated by a headman.

"Umfundisi," murmured Mponda, "my son has asked me how I will justify myself to my father's spirit if I change the customs of my people."

Robert turned toward Makufa, who had risen to his feet and was looking down on him menacingly. The missionary realized that he and Makufa were being invited to compete for Mponda's belief and trust. Robert said amiably to the chief's son, "If Mponda becomes a Christian, you think that the spirit of Chief Khari, his own father, would curse him. Is that right, Makufa?"

"It is, mfungu."

To call him "white man" instead of "teacher," or "umfundisi," was a deliberate insult. Robert could feel the blood mounting to his cheeks. "It's a foolish idea, young man."

Makufa thrust out his smooth, well-muscled chest. "Why is it foolish, mfungu? Khari would want us to live like our ancestors."

Robert smiled stiffly. "Are *you* living like your ancestors, Makufa? You hunt with a rifle, you ride horses and own a gasogene lamp. You covet my ox wagon and Cape cart."

Makufa tossed his head contemptuously. "Guns and lamps are not customs."

"That's true," conceded Robert. "But it's foolish to speak of Khari. He never heard the word of God, and so he never refused it, as you have done. He might have accepted it, for all you know."

Makufa's eyes blazed. "Khari loved his tribe's traditions."

"Our Queen in England loves her people's traditions, but she doesn't imitate the cruel behavior of her barbarous ancestors."

The apparent normality of relations between Mponda and Makufa was unnerving. A stranger seeing them together would have found it hard to credit that the father believed his son had plotted against him, and that the son thought his father a traitor to his own people. Robert was not deceived by the playful little glances that Mponda sometimes exchanged with his handsome son. These looks were really taunts: Didn't I tell you the teacher would have an answer for anything you might fling at him?

Makufa finally lost his temper. Spitting out the stem of sorghum he had been chewing, he jabbed an angry finger at Robert. "How can you say you love my father?"

Makufa would murder every Christian in the place if he became chief, but Robert was too angry to feel frightened. Because this arrogant youth had delayed his father's baptism, Clara's illusions had been shattered. Robert got up from his stool to be level with Makufa. He found it hard to breathe.

"Do you doubt that I love your father?"

Every movement of Makufa's shining body expressed distaste and superiority. "Tell me this," the youth demanded. "If Matabele warriors attack my father, will you lend him your guns and bullets?"

"You know I can never become a party to fighting."

Makufa threw up his hands scornfully. "So you would let

his enemies kill him? You are his friend and teacher, but you would let them do that?''

''I would pray for him.''

''Oh, yes!'' jeered Makufa. ''And while you did that, the Matabele would stab him. A fine way of helping.'' He turned to Mponda. ''Is that how a man who loves you should behave?''

Mponda toyed uneasily with the ivory bracelets on his wrists. Robert was horrified. Could the chief's faith in him be so easily shaken? Mponda caught his eye and asked quietly, ''If I came to you for help, Umfundisi, what would you do?''

''Welcome you, my chief,'' said Robert, ''and give you food and clothing.''

''Yes, yes . . . and if the Matabele followed me to your house and said, 'Give Mponda to us so we may kill him,' what would you do then?''

''I would stand in the doorway and say, 'If you wish to take Mponda, you must kill me first.' ''

''That's very good!'' Mponda chuckled, touchingly relieved. ''What do you think of that, Makufa?''

''Think?'' his son sneered. ''*You* should try to *think,* father. Didn't we have gods of our own before this white man came? Has he ever met this Jesus he babbles about? Not once. Jesus is just a name in that big book of his. Tell me, father, if his God is so mighty, why can't he change me into a Christian at once? If he did that, I wouldn't have to suffer a fool like your Umfundisi for months.'' The young man picked up his assegai and stalked away, flinging his leopardskin over his shoulder.

Robert anticipated a furious outburst from Mponda, but the chief said sorrowfully, ''When I become a Christian, I shall have to kill him, or he will kill me.''

''Of course you can't kill him.''

''He has killed many men.''

''So have you, my chief.''

''Warriors must. But I have sworn to kill no more.''

''Then you must keep your promise.''

''You whites strangle men with a rope if they kill. If Makufa kills again, I will strangle him.''

''You will not, Mponda.''

''Maybe he will kill you, Umfundisi.''

''I am not afraid to die. Are you?''

Mponda whispered fervently, "I believe in Jesus."

"Then will you name the date for your baptism?" Robert waited in an agony of tension.

"You know I cannot tell you until my enemies are in my hand. You know what I wish, Umfundisi." Mponda's face conveyed blank misery.

Robert knelt down beside him and said tenderly, "Mponda, these are Jesus' words: 'Come unto me all ye that are heavy laden and I will give you rest.' You will be at peace when your sins are washed away." He remained kneeling for several minutes before returning to the cart.

As they were driving away from the khotla, Simon pointed to some children playing with a top made from a whittled stick and the broken shell of a calabash. Children usually delighted Robert, but today their laughter could not lift his spirits. Even if there were no rifles at the Rungai caves, this would not mean that Makufa's opposition was at an end. Mponda would certainly be thankful if the caves were empty and unguarded, but he still might not feel strong enough to pledge himself to Christ. And while the chief delayed, the last rags of Clara's respect were being blown away. Would she try to leave the kraal? First Ruth, then Clara. As if a long-chained beast had slipped his leash, fear of a second desertion overcame Robert.

"Are you ill, master?" Simon touched his hand.

Robert shook his head and ruffled the boy's hair. "Only a toothache," he replied, and it was not quite untrue. For several weeks an eyetooth had been troubling him. He said sweetly, "When we get back, I want you to try your hardest to please my wife."

Simon did not comment. He had been happier before Clara's arrival. Robert had brought Simon with him in case Nashu or Makufa was tempted by the missionary's absence to make a second attempt to abduct the boy. Clara, by contrast, would be perfectly safe, with Mponda's guards watching her every move.

On the fifth day of their journey, Robert guessed that they were within three days of Mount Rungai. But Dau doubled that. It was beyond Robert how the Bushman could tell. Stretching to the horizon on every side was an unvarying sea of coarse blond grasses. At random intervals, berry-yielding moretloa bushes and white-thorned mimosa rose above the waving tufts.

One afternoon, Dau pointed to a hole at the root of a certain bush. Across the opening a spider had made a web. Robert and Simon were puzzled. Dau beckoned to them and then thrust his hand through the web, into the earth. He withdrew it at once, holding up, like a conjuror, a large frog.

Robert applauded. "Who but a Bushman would think of searching for a frog under a spider's web?"

Dau grinned. "After he makes his hole, he will not come out for months, so spiders are safe to use his hole for webs."

Simon cooked the frog over the resinous branches of the same bush, and the flesh tasted like delicately flavored chicken. A few hours later, Robert began to feel ill. Since the others did not suffer, the frog could not have been to blame. He felt nauseated, and his head throbbed painfully. His tooth chose this moment to nag at him.

As they approached the next water hole, Simon was driving while Robert slept. Dau nudged the boy and pointed into the trembling haze. Simon went rigid. What he had taken to be drinking antelope were really warriors, sitting on the ground behind their cowhide shields. The "horns" he had seen were spears. Before waking Robert, Simon said a prayer: Please God, I know it is sinful for these men to sit behind their shields and threaten travelers at a drinking pool, but do not let my master speak too harshly to them. Jesus spoke harshly to evildoers, and it ended badly for him. Please make my master pleasant and not angry. Keep master safe, or his enemies will kill me and all the Christians. Do not let bad men harm us for the sake of Jesus Christ. Amen.

Walking unsteadily under his old green umbrella, the missionary approached the waiting tribesmen. Simon tagged after him. God must be watching him, the boy thought. Otherwise he would not dare hold up his head so disdainfully. But Robert did not feel disdainful. He wanted to fall down and beat his fists on the earth. Mount Rungai was being guarded against intruders. The rifles were there, and rebels were assembling. What else could explain this attempt to deny travelers access to water? At last God seemed to have deserted him. The chief's conversion would not happen this year or even next. Clara would abandon him. The Christians would be driven out.

A man wearing a long bead necklace stepped forward. "Little toto, we will give your mfungu water if he will turn back."

"Why must he?" asked Simon.

"No one may visit our holy mountain."

"He has visited it before. Why can't he see it again?"

Another man rose and said very gravely, "Our god Mwari forbids him. White men have dug there with picks and have angered the spirits. Mwari did not put pretty things in the ground to be stolen by foreigners."

"My master has no use for gold. He will not dig."

"He is white and will defile the sacred shrine."

Robert closed his eyes. There was no help for it—they would have to turn back. This water hole would be not the last to be barred. He knew what he and his companions would suffer if they journeyed on—the cracked lips and blackened tongues, the agony as their blood thickened.

That evening, after Dau had lit their campfire, Simon wept with relief.

"I thought we would go on until we died."

The sun had just gone down, and the pale sand and grasses were still stained a reminiscent pink. What courage the boy had shown! Robert squeezed his hand and murmured, "Dear child, I would never risk any life but my own." Simon said nothing, but his eyes were troubled. Robert knew that where he led, the boy would follow. It was not possible for him to risk his life alone. His tooth was still hurting, making it hard to think.

"Those men who stopped us," he asked Simon, "weren't their faces flatter than yours?"

Simon nodded. "Maybe they were Ajawa, master. They weren't Venda or Makalaka."

"They were Manganja," declared Dau, who rarely volunteered anything unless sure of it.

Robert sighed. Whether Ajawa or Manganja, those men had come from the north. And if people from far afield were guarding Mount Rungai, Makufa and Nashu were involved in something larger than a plot against a single chief.

Scores of whites had been murdered by the Matabele three years earlier, but until now, Robert had believed the northern tribes were incapable of emulation. He thought of the smoothness of his wife's throat and the softness of her breasts. What could he say to Clara now? Had he even the right to keep her here? The smallest sounds grated on his nerves: Dau chewing tobacco, the cry of a night bird, the cracking of burning logs. He began to pray, and ended with a repeated refrain: From battle and murder, and from sudden death, Good Lord deliver us.

After Robert had been gone for a week, Clara's life had settled into a routine. In the morning she would go to Philemon for an hour's language lesson, and when school was over she would spend another hour with Paul. She also helped the women at the mission with their dressmaking, despite her misgivings about this popular activity. One morning, while Clara was demonstrating how to cut a pattern, Herida stalked past the veranda, a picture of dignity and grace. Coiled around her straight and slender body was a thick string of beads, from which hung a kilt of pressed bark. Elephant-hair bracelets on her wrists and copper bangles on her legs completed an outfit that showed off her body to perfection. Yet if she ever enrolled at the mission, her first task would be to sew a strip of shoddy material into a shapeless garment for herself.

Since the day when Clara first gave dried meat and milk to little Homani, he had not improved. His skin was still dull and his pixie-like face was no less pinched. His arms and legs were like sticks, and with every breath he took, the skin between his ribs seemed to be sucked in. His eyes welcomed her greedily when she came near him, and after she went home she could not get him out of her mind. It made her feel utterly helpless. But how much worse it would have been if it were her own child lying wasting away. When Robert had proposed marriage, he must have known the dangers that any baby of theirs would have to face. But again he had kept silent.

Clara went up to Philemon, who was helping Chizuva with her copybook. "Why isn't Homani gaining weight?" she demanded.

As usual when pressed about anything, Philemon looked reflective for several seconds. He then drew a wiggling shape in the air. "Perhaps he has a worm inside him."

"Big, big." Chizuva laughed, delighted to have understood enough to be able to contribute in English.

Ignoring her, Clara asked Philemon, "Can't you give him medicine to get rid of it?"

"Only master can do that. He has special scales, and weighs out just enough poison to kill the worm. If I give a tiny bit more, I will harm the child."

Chizuva's laughter had convinced Clara that there could be another explanation for Homani's condition. So for the next two days she sat with him while he ate. Only on the third day did he no longer snatch at his dried meat, and by then he was definitely a little fatter. As her suspicions hardened into certainty, Clara looked around her in disgust. Could Christians have stooped low enough to steal a sick child's food?

Philemon seemed concerned when she complained to him, but he was not outraged. In the dry season, he explained, when the only milk in the village came from the mission's cows, people valued dairy produce very highly. Homani was an outsider, whose mother was a well-known enemy of the mission, so naturally a boy like Matiyo was bound to resent a stranger's getting more milk than himself.

"Each day people come begging, Nkosikaas. If all get their desire, we Christians will soon be hungry."

"That would never do," she murmured.

By the end of the week, there was no denying how much better Homani looked. When Clara changed his bandages, the sores were definitely smaller. The pride and satisfaction in his strange little face as he watched her delighted reaction reduced her to tears.

In spite of her pleasure over Homani, Clara was too bound up with her worries about Robert to experience a more general contentment. Even if she managed to forgive his lack of compassion for little Homani and his deliberate attempt to mislead her about his present expedition, would she ever be able to trust Robert again? His failure to be frank about Ruth had been shameful, and yet, because of his present peril, she felt guilty. And if he was dead, it was herself she would not forgive, for spending the days of his absence in listing his shortcomings.

When she entered the mission the following morning, an argument was raging between Chizuva and someone partly hidden by Philemon's back. The old man stepped aside, and Clara saw it was Herida. As soon as the young queen spotted her, she advanced angrily, hurling abuse all the time. Clara asked Philemon for a translation, but he drew in his wrinkled old neck, more than ever reminding her of a tortoise, and muttered, "I cannot tell you, Nkosikaas."

"You must," she demanded, more enraged by his obstinacy than by the woman's insults.

Philemon sucked in quivering cheeks. "She says she has cursed you."

"What sort of curse?" Clara was too surprised to be angry.

"She says you will be sterile."

Clara could not help laughing. "Tell her I'm grateful. Go on, Philemon. I'd hate the anxiety of giving birth here."

When this was relayed to her, Herida looked as if she might faint. Sterility was a disaster for an African woman. Her husband would reject her, and her family would probably refuse to take her back. Herida whispered something.

"What does she say, Philemon?"

"That you are cruel to mock her, Nkosikaas. You have a husband who never will turn his back."

Clara was dismayed to see this harpy of moments before melting into tears. "Tell her I was offended but didn't intend to hurt her. Please apologize."

Herida's expression softened as Philemon spoke to her. She looked wonderfully regal in a blood-red cloth that covered one breast and fell in pleated folds to her ankles. She began to speak again, in her rich and husky voice.

At length Philemon said, "Herida won't believe you're sorry unless you ask master to tell Mponda not to send her away. She says she will come and learn to be a Christian woman if Mponda lets her continue to be his wife."

Upon hearing Herida's promise, Mponda's senior wife, Chizuva, began to shout. When Philemon could make himself heard, he told Clara that Chizuva was warning her not to be fooled by Herida's vows to become a Christian. Personal advantage was what Herida had in mind. Although this was plausible, the prosperous plumpness of the chief's senior wife and her sanctimonious manner appealed less to Clara than the younger woman's emotional volatility. Hadn't Chizuva come to the mission out of self-interest too? Christianity seemed set to make her the chief's only wife.

A shouting match began between Philemon and Herida. Clara guessed it must be about whether Herida could stay and learn. The arguing ended only when Herida stormed from the room. Clara touched Philemon on the arm. "Did you refuse to let her stay here?"

Philemon shuffled uneasily from foot to foot. "I cannot allow her. Only master can decide."

Clara's eyebrows shot up. "You're refusing to teach her the Gospel? Oh, Philemon."

"She is our enemy's daughter, Nkosikaas."

"We must forgive our enemies."

Philemon burst out, "If Herida comes, Chizuva will not be a Christian anymore. Mponda will never be baptized without her."

The old man looked so unhappy that Clara did not argue, but she doubted whether Herida would continue to accept defeat as meekly as she had today.

Early the following morning, Clara and Philemon walked through the village to the well. The old preacher's language lessons helped her most when he described village scenes in Venda. Like distant shadows, Mponda's guards brought up the rear, using huts and bushes to keep out of sight whenever possible. Out in front, a group of women from the mission were walking with empty water pots on their heads.

It was not long after sunrise, and the slight dampness in the air intensified the smell of fowl droppings and rotting garbage. From a distance the funny little woven-grass fences and thatched granaries struck Clara as picturesque, as did the people: half-grown children, all legs and smiles; men standing around, leaning on spears; graceful women carrying loads on their heads. Yet closer to them, less edifying details intruded. The thatch was rotting; in a darkened doorway, a woman was shaving her pubic hair with a shard of glass; a baby with snot smears on its upper lip was sticking handfuls of chicken droppings and earth into its mouth. Outside a hut, a woman was squeezing the milk from her breasts onto the ground.

"Her baby died last night, Nkosikaas," murmured Philemon.

How many tragedies had happened since her arrival? Clara found her ignorance distressing. Inside the blacksmith's hut, the man himself and his assistant were forging an ax. One fanned the coals with goatskin bellows while the other hit the red-hot metal with a hammer, grunting with every blow. The men gazed at Clara with undisguised suspicion.

"Why do they stare so, Philemon?"

Philemon seemed embarrassed. "Our own women never come near when they are menstruating. The men think a white woman does not know that her blood can spoil new metal."

Her own menses had started the day before, and she wondered how the men had known or even suspected. She was still puzzling over this, when Herida came into view, approaching between the huts. She was preceded by a boy driving a black goat. Her left leg was bandaged with a bloodstained rag.

"What's wrong with her?" asked Clara.

Philemon asked a few questions and then explained that Herida's leg had been cut by her father. The witch doctor had caught the blood in a horn and rubbed medicine into the wound. Herida's blood would now be mixed with another medicine. But try as he might, the preacher could not get Herida to disclose the use to which the mixture would be put. Although understanding only a word or two, Clara could not help watching Herida's beautiful face. Her nose tilted upward becomingly, and her long and narrow eyes gave her a slightly Oriental appearance—though she was not inscrutable. Her moods were wonderfully clear, whether sadness, roguish good humor, or indignation.

Philemon asked, gently, "Where are you taking your goat?"

"To sacrifice him."

"Why?"

"To appease the spirit that has bewitched my husband."

"That's untrue, child. Your husband is not bewitched."

"Umfundisi, *you* sacrifice to the spirits, don't you?"

"No."

"Then how can you be safe from bad spirits?"

Philemon said quietly, "No spirits can harm us, Herida; only the bad desires in our own hearts."

"Which spirits do you speak to, Umfundisi, when you talk to the air?"

"Only one. The spirit of God, the father of Jesus Christ. He watches over all of us."

"Is he watching now?" Herida looked about her uneasily.

"Not one hair falls from my head that he does not see."

Herida shuddered "How can that be? Where is he now?"

"He is everywhere."

"I cannot see him."

"You can talk to Him if you pray."

"I do not know how to."

Just as Clara was asking Philemon to promise to teach Herida how to pray, a commotion broke out on the path ahead. Some men jumped forth from the long grass, and staves flashed as they began to beat the mission women. A pot fell to the ground and smashed. Screams rang out as women were thrown to the ground. Like a spindly Quixote, Philemon ran forward bravely. Clara dashed after the old man and overtook him, shedding combs and pins from her streaming hair. As in a happy dream, the attackers recoiled as she bore down on them. But though scared at first by her white face, the men soon stood firm. One naked warrior even stepped toward her. Clara's heart was banging so hard against her ribs that she fancied they must hear it. Philemon's feet flapped behind her, sounding as sadly ineffectual as an old bird's wings. But firmer steps were following. Herida's angry voice rang out. Clara turned and saw her waving the men away.

The aggressors stood crestfallen beside the path, while the Christian women scampered off in the direction of the well. Just when the danger seemed over, more shouting erupted. Mponda's guard belatedly sprang out from the long yellow grass. Seeing Herida apparently commanding the attackers, they pointed their assegais at her breast. Clara screamed and dashed to place herself between Herida and the chief's men. Very slowly, Mponda's guards lowered their spears. As they did so, the malefactors jumped back into the bush like startled bucks.

Still breathing in gasps, Philemon smiled at Herida. "You see how Jesus Christ saves us?"

She smiled back at him with gentle mockery. "Jizzus won't protect my marriage if Mponda drinks his blood." She laughed softly. "The white woman saved me, old man, not your Jizzus."

Clara resolved to do whatever she could to aid this brave and touching person. Herida had taken a huge risk in helping the Christian women. Her father would be especially angry.

After Herida had left them, Clara turned to Philemon. "If Mponda must have one wife, why can't it be Herida?"

"Nkosikaas," he objected, amazed at her obtuseness, "Herida was not his first wife."

"Does that matter? All Mponda's wives were married in the proper tribal fashion, I'm sure."

"You must talk with master, Nkosikaas."

"But surely you must have your own opinion, Philemon? If

the chief had been a Christian when he took his second and third wives, then of course his first wife would be his only true one. But Mponda was a pagan when he married all three, so each has an equal claim.''

Even as she spoke, Clara knew that the old preacher's opinions about Herida did not matter. Robert was the one who had decided the issue in Chizuva's favor, without even considering which wife loved the chief most.

The rains were late, and when the wind blew from the east across the dried-up riverbed, clouds of tawny dust would rise and fling themselves upon the huts. On such a morning, Clara struggled back from the mission to find that the housemaid, Hannah, was plastering the floor with a mixture of liquid cow dung and clay. She ran out again and, coughing and choking, dragged Paul back from the school.

"Witchcraft?" He laughed. "No, no, Mrs. Robert. Nothing lays the dust better than dung. Kills fleas too."

Already Hannah was giving the vile-smelling mess a surface of glassy smoothness with the help of a length of wood.

"How long till it dries?"

"Very soon it will be hard," promised Paul.

"And smelly?"

"No smell, Mrs. Robert." He laughed again, and Clara could not help joining in. She enjoyed her lessons with Paul much more than those with Philemon.

Paul was easily embarrassed. And because a number of words had two or more meanings, depending upon which syllable was stressed, the opportunities for misunderstanding were numerous. *Mala,* for example, could mean both bowels and cold; *libe* could be sin or cow dung; and *tsetla,* yellow or bladder. When Clara unwittingly pronounced words in their lewder sense, Paul would look away and mutter about the importance of correctly emphasizing this or that vowel.

"But what's wrong with *pholo* with the stress on the last letter?"

"It doesn't mean health, Mrs. Robert."

"What does it mean, Paul?"

"A man's . . ."

"If it's important I know, you shouldn't make me guess, should you, Paul?"

"His penis."

Why he should be so embarrassed, when large numbers of men in the village walked about with their penises exposed, was a mystery to Clara.

Sometimes she tried to impress Paul by increasing her vocabulary from other sources. Recently she had asked Matiyo for the name of a particular lizard. "Kaya," he had replied. So when Paul came to teach her, she pointed to an identical lizard. "Kaya," she announced confidently. Paul laughed uproariously. Matiyo had been ignorant of the name of this variety of lizard and, when pressed, had replied, "I don't know." That was what *kaya* meant.

Clara found Paul's love for Hannah very affecting. He knew so much more than she, yet Hannah had a serenity that he entirely lacked. Nothing rushed or flustered her. She was not upset by Paul's laughter when he found her using a sock as a coffee strainer or misapplying one of the other mysterious household contraptions. While working, she moved about so softly on her bare feet that her presence was strangely calming. Her lighting of the kitchen fire each morning struck Clara as miraculous. Hannah could blow longer and more powerfully than seemed possible for a girl of her slenderness. If she found a pin or button on the floor, she always placed it on the table. Even spent matches were preserved in this way. Clara thought her a model of trustworthiness.

Whenever Paul came over, he would watch his loved one with a devoted smile. He delighted in repeating for Clara some of Hannah's ingenuous remarks about white people. Why did they wash themselves so often and use so many implements to eat a simple meal? And why did they nibble at their food instead of taking big, satisfying mouthfuls? Paul's laughter was never condescending. "I too once asked such things, Mrs. Robert." His good-natured cheerfulness was a tonic to Clara. A gap between his front teeth made him look much younger than his seventeen years. Five years earlier, Paul had been a shop boy in Bulawayo, selling alarm clocks, concertinas, patent medicines, canvas trousers, and cricket bats.

"Until master came to buy lamp oil, nobody told me where all these wonderful things were made. Master drew pictures of factories and steamships. He said if I lived at his mission, he would teach me." Paul's voice grew thick with emotion. "Master opened my eyes. I might have grown up proud to kill a man."

Clara thought of boastful soldiers at home with their campaign medals. Paul's admiration for Robert made him forget what ordinary white men were like. It also left Clara with a guilty feeling that Robert might be a far better man than she had given him credit for.

During the second week of his absence, the noise of drumming started to persist into the early hours of the morning, making sleep impossible and setting Clara's heart racing. Was an assault on the mission imminent? Or even on her? The attack on the women near the well, coupled with Robert's letter, had filled her with foreboding. Paul reassured her about the drums. He said they were summoning the adolescents to prepare for their initiation rites, but Clara still felt nervous enough to ask him to sleep in Simon's shed until Robert returned.

So Paul moved in. Though he understood the drumming, he too had no love for it, having his own reasons for dreading the initiation rites, especially the girls' ceremonies: the boyale. Paul had tried hard to convert Hannah to Christianity, but he had failed. Her parents wanted her to be circumcised, and she herself believed that she would be a real woman only when she was. In Paul's eyes, she would be siding with the pagans and rejecting him. But he knew she would cause her family great pain if she refused to attend the boyale. In that regard, Hannah knew exactly what his faith had cost him. When his father had been on his deathbed, Paul had not been able to ask the ancestral spirits to accept the dying man's soul, as a good son should. Instead his Christian duty had obliged him to inform his father that he had worshiped the wrong god all his life and ought to repent at once, before it was too late.

"You tried to convert him as he lay dying?" Clara was aghast.

"Of course I did." Paul looked hurt and puzzled. "It was my last chance to save his soul."

"Were you successful?"

He shook his head sadly. They had just finished their meal of sadza, the local stiff porridge, and Hannah now brought in bowls of water for their hands.

"You can go and join her," Clara murmured to Paul; but he declined. Men did not prepare food with women or clear it away.

"When did you start to believe in Jesus?" she asked as Hannah left.

"In the church in Bulawayo. Master took me. People were

kneeling in front of a cross. I didn't know what it was. It was dark, and there were shining nails in the wood. I thought they were God's eyes. I believed this till master explained.''

Clara sighed. So much more thrilling to see God's eyes gleaming like a lion's than to share a white minister's decorous vision of the deity. After a long silence, she walked to the door and looked out. A shooting star traced a chalky line across the heavens. The drumming and dancing were echoing across the village. This was the only time of day when the heat was not intolerable. She longed to watch whatever was going on but knew that Paul would not let her. After all, she was his master's precious possession.

''Mponda's men would surely protect us,'' she pointed out.

''They'd be poisoned if they didn't. But what would people say if they saw them with us? They'd say Christians can't feel safe if they need to go everywhere with the chief's men. Who would want to be a Christian then?''

After telling Paul to go to bed, Clara went back to the door, eager to feel a breath of cool air on her face. To be free again. Free! A longing to escape from this terrible error of hers and start again tantalized her. It would be as if she had never gone to the Temperance Hall that evening, never heard Robert speak. On the returning steamship's deck, people would gaze at her intently. Behind her widow's veil she would be mysterious—a woman who had lived and suffered without paying the price of age or ugliness. The idea was both frightening and pleasurable. Had Charles already married? Would Francis be in England? She covered her face in shame at feeling so little for her husband.

In the kitchen, Hannah was humming to herself as she filled the kettle, using a jug to pour water down the spout. Amazed that nobody had shown the girl what to do, Clara lifted the lid and was rewarded by a shrill peal of laughter. Hannah took the lid and held it in front of her face as if to hide her embarrassment; then she peeped around it with a delighted grin, for all the world as if she had just played a joke on the white woman. Clara had thought her demure to the point of primness, but the girl's dimpled cheeks and mischievous eyes made her think again.

A cock crowing under her window woke Clara to another burning-hot morning. In three days' time either Robert would be back or she would be arranging her departure with Philemon. When Clara was dressed, she went to the door and peered through the shimmering haze between the huts. The chief's men were nowhere to be seen. Refusing to allow herself to be a prisoner, she stepped into the lane and headed in a direction she had often seen people take but had never tried for herself.

She scrambled across a barrier of rocks and tangled undergrowth into a network of frowzy grass paths. A displeasing smell reached her nostrils. Before actually seeing human excrement, she noticed the dung beetles scurrying hither and thither. In her ignorance, she had stumbled on the place where villagers went to relieve themselves. She hurriedly retraced her steps.

At the mission, Clara went in search of little Homani. He was not in the corner where he usually lay, nor could she find him in the kitchen or by the cowshed. As she went out onto the veranda, Philemon came up beside her, muttering about how happy everyone would be when the rains came.

He scratched his fuzzy white hair. "Do not judge us as we are today, Nkosikaas. Soon the oxen will return from the cattle posts and the women will scatter seed after the plow."

"Where is Homani?" She was too shaken by the child's disappearance to respond to Philemon's remarks.

"His mother has taken him." The old man's voice was low and inexpressive.

"Couldn't you have stopped her?"

"She came with angry people, Nkosikaas."

"He was so much better. Even his legs were—" She broke off, her voice wavering. The child's recovery would have given her more satisfaction than anything since her arrival. She had let herself believe that if she could only save this little boy, other good things might follow.

Later that day, she found Homani outside the hut where she had first seen him. He was sitting on the ground, playing with two other children. His bandages had come undone and were trailing in the dirt. Some sticky-looking red substance had been smeared all over his sores. He turned his head aside when he saw her, knowing she was angry and upset. His mother emerged from her hut and started shouting. Clara walked away with smarting eyes.

As she entered her own house, she paused in the musty sitting room to let her eyes adjust to the dimness. An odd noise was coming from somewhere beyond the kitchen: a sound like a wounded animal, rhythmic, anguished, and searing. The kitchen itself was empty, and the door into the yard was flapping on its hinge. A rush of courage took her outside, where she found the door to Hannah's lean-to ajar. Light was gleaming on a sweat-drenched back, which rose and fell as the sound became more breathless and urgent. Under the man's body were open female knees. Hannah's. Whose else could they be? Heartbroken, Clara told herself she should not be surprised because Paul wasn't what she'd thought him. Not pure, not innocent, but a flattering hypocrite like Simon. She imagined greeting a returning Robert: ''Oh, by the way, that sweet Bible boy of yours . . .'' But already she knew she never would. It was his tragedy too, poor Robert—a tiny part of it.

On a shelf above the bins of maize flour were some dark bottles. She clambered up onto the table and snatched one down. The usual rough Cape brandy sold in Belingwe. As she reached for it, out of the corner of her eye she spotted a naked man spinning on his heels in the doorway. Before she could turn, he was gone. But he had not been Paul. She was sure of that. This man had been taller, more muscular, with a line of raised scars on his chest. Shame at doubting Paul overwhelmed her. No longer wanting to drink, she replaced the brandy on the shelf.

She slept that afternoon and woke to hear Paul asking when she had last seen Hannah.

''About midday.'' Clara rubbed her eyes, surprised that it was already getting dark. ''Isn't she here?''

Paul shook his head. He looked as if he had been crying. ''I think she has gone to the girls' camp. For the boyale.''

''I'm so sorry,'' murmured Clara.

Paul shook his head again and presented her, from behind his back, with a scrappy bouquet of leaves. ''Herida asked me to give it to you.''

''What for?''

''You boil the leaves and drink the water.'' Paul lowered his eyes. ''It is for the girls who cannot have a baby.''

Clara smiled in spite of herself. ''Can you thank her, please?'' Paul was confused and embarrassed. ''It's because Herida laid a curse on me,'' she explained. ''Now she's trying to lift it.''

Just then the drums struck up again, the long, low introductory thumps followed by staccato beats that drowned out every other sound.

*   *   *

Hannah did not return the following day, and in the evening, abandoning his misgivings, a distraught Paul said he meant to go and see the dancing. "Hannah will be there."

"What are you going to do?" Clara asked anxiously.

"I will bring her back."

"Against her will, Paul? You can't do that."

"She was taken against her will, Mrs. Robert." The fact that Paul was probably mistaken alarmed Clara. He was certainly angry enough to try to drag Hannah out from the midst of a swaying mass of excitable people. And yet Clara was so eager to see the dances that she had no intention of saying anything that might discourage him.

As she and Paul set out for the clearing where the boyale dances were taking place, darkness was falling. The subdued radiance of the stars lit the twisting track dimly and helped them elude Mponda's guards. Occasionally, a nightjar fluttered up from near their feet. The drumming and singing were growing louder. Soon they could hear the scuffling of the dancers' feet. Sparks from the ceremonial fires were rising high into the blackness. Urgently wanting to know how dangerous these people could be, Clara pulled fiercely on Paul's arm to make him stop. In a moment they would be leaving the shelter of the thorn trees and mongongo bushes.

"Paul," she whispered, "did you ever hear why Simon ran away?"

"Nashu tried to make him take the poison ordeal." Grasping Clara's hand tightly, Paul hurried her on.

At the end of the scrubby bushes, they came to a halt. Ahead of them in the firelight, about a hundred young men and women stood in opposite rows, with nothing but a simple cloth wrapped around their waists. Soft drumbeats set them moving, slowly at first. Both sexes danced into the middle, in a figure that reminded Clara absurdly of a Sir Roger de Coverley. Yet soon the pace increased, and they began a series of complicated hops and agile sideways skips that threw their little skirts high. The rhythm was beaten out on a row of large and small drums. As it became faster, the dancers shrieked and shouted as they jumped in the air. The girls' naked breasts shook and quivered, and the boys thrust their hips at their partners in a mime of lovemaking. The earth answered their feet like a great drum. Clara caught her breath. This is how they ought to be, not bent over copybooks. Such power and grace of body, muscles twisting like snakes under their shining skin. Her nerves tingled at the insistent drumming; the upraised voices made her spirits soar.

And then she looked at Paul. His normally placid face was scored with anger. He tried to sound calm but had to shout to make himself heard. "Now they forget hunger, even death, but later nothing is changed. They will be sad then."

Clara felt indignant. "Is that what Robert says?"

Paul did not answer. His eyes were fixed on a female dancer near the drums. Clara suddenly recognized Hannah. The fever of the dance was sparking lightning from her body, shaking it from within. Before Clara could stop him, Paul was pushing his way through the crowds of swaying and gyrating people. She saw his arm raised as he struck Hannah, and then he was struggling with other women, who were trying to protect her. In the scuffle, Paul and several women fell against the drums, knocking them over. A threatening silence fell.

A man screamed abuse at Paul, and others ran at him. Clara started in his direction, fearing he might be lynched. As she reached his side, two furious men were being held back by a dozen others, and Paul was shouting at a sobbing Hannah.

The sight of so many somber faces in the firelight chilled Clara to the bone. She took Paul's arm, and, unresisting, he let her guide him through the crowd. She did not know how she overcame the urge to run.

Paul was coming away without Hannah, but he was lucky to be coming away at all.

CHAPTER 10

Garbed in his full panoply of monkeys' tails, eagles' feathers, and leopards' claws, Nashu solemnly approached the place of circumcision, followed by men bearing the sacred vessels. These contained the ashes of countless foreskins, linking today's candidates with past generations. Never had the nganga felt a greater sense of responsibility to his tribe and a greater sense of dread.

So the young schoolteacher had damaged the drums at the boyale dances after insulting the initiates. And why had he dared commit this sacrilege? Because he believed that the chief would soon be washed with the white man's most powerful medicine. No less painful to Nashu was his own daughter's treachery. Herida had been seen outside the white woman's door, dressed in one of the white sacks worn by the mfungu's converts. What a fool to imagine she would remain the chief's wife if she pretended to believe the mfungu's wicked nonsense. The white man would never let an nganga's daughter be the chief's only queen. Her folly and disloyalty made Nashu want to bite the earth and howl.

Not far from Nashu, the chief's son was exhorting the boys to be brave. Many days ago, Makufa had promised that before the male circumcision rites took place, he would tell Nashu when he would strike against his father. Around the tall young prince, the naked boys clustered in a fearful little semicircle. As Nashu sharpened his knife on the stone at the foot of the ancient mugumo tree, Makufa left his charges and came over to him.

He squatted down beside the nganga and whispered with a heavy sigh, "I cannot kill my father."

Nashu eyed him scornfully. "But you know very well that every chief who is washed with this medicine one day sells his land to the white men. Isn't it the same story wherever a preacher settles? He is one man alone, so people suspect nothing. But soon come the traders and the farmers with their fences. If people argue, soldiers come and shoot them. I never lie to you, Makufa. The white men will make us pay to live in our huts. This has happened in Bulawayo and Gwelo.''

''Lord of the Spirits, I know you do not lie.''

Nashu shuffled closer like an old eagle. Blood-red disks had been painted on each side of his eyes. ''The white woman is dangerous too,'' he rasped. ''She took a child and cursed him when he ran away. She told the young teacher to smash the boyale drums. Now she is stealing my daughter's heart. She will bewitch us all when Mponda takes the water medicine.''

''My father will never take it.'' He smiled grimly. ''There will be no one alive to give it to him.''

Nashu spat scornfully. ''How can we kill the mfungu when he is far from here?''

''We will kill the others in their wooden house when they sing. The mfungu will die too if he returns, but he will vanish when he hears what we have done.''

''The woman also dies?'' Nashu gestured obscenely with his knife.

''All of them.''

''What will your father do?''

Makufa shrugged, as if his father's actions were scarcely worth considering. ''We'll tell him that Mwari's messengers ordered their death. We needn't be there. I'll say the rebellion started by itself. He knows Mwari has decreed that all the whites must die.''

''Very well,'' said Nashu. ''Let it be done on the next day they sing.''

After Makufa had returned to the clay-painted boys, Nashu gazed up at the gnarled and mysterious mugumo tree. His father had brought him here as a boy when the village had been two days' walk away. He had not yet been circumcised and had longed for his penis to be freed from its hood of flesh so he could be a man. His father had said, ''Where Mwari placed his hand this tree sprouted. From its branches you can see Mount Rungai, Mwari's home.'' They had climbed up together into the leaves. Far away to the east across the bush had been a blue hill. Young Nashu had wept with joy at the sight of Mwari's home. And now all this might be sold to the white man, and the ancestors' sacred tree be felled.

Four moons ago, when Nashu had heard that three young

white men had come north from Belingwe and were digging near Mount Rungai, he and Makufa had hurried there and killed them as they slept. Another day or two, and they would have desecrated Mwari's natal cave. But the white men were like soldier ants. More and more would come; and then what could he do? Nashu felt a dull pain in his heart, as if he were fighting a force that pressed in on him from the air itself.

"God is everywhere and knows everything. There is none righteous among you, not one. Little can you know what grossness shrouds your minds. Your ignorance is a fog through which you wade in filth and sin."

Nashu had sometimes listened to Philemon, the traitor, spouting his master's words, and had been dazed by the man's blasphemous conviction. *How* could he believe that a white man without a father, born in a goatshed, was really God? The man's lies made Nashu long to kill him. How could it be right to have one wife only, when a chief needed many wives in order to have many children and thus be a power in this tribe? And without many wives to grow food, a chief could neither give feasts nor feed slaves and strangers. And what was this talk of a man requiring salvation for himself alone? Had he no duty to others? Unless men and women shared grain in a famine and sowed and reaped together, the tribe could not survive. Nashu's whole body ached with grief. Only one course was open to him. The land must be cleansed and these foreigners wiped from the face of the earth.

He beckoned to the first of the candidates to come forward. A desolating thought possessed him. Was it possible that the children of these boys would one day worship the white man's God and never come near this holy place? His throat ached at the thought.

The first boy lay down, and Makufa parted his legs. There would be three cuts. Nashu pulled the foreskin clear of the glans and sliced cleanly from right to left. A white ridged line suddenly turned brilliant red. The boy looked up at him with icy stoicism. No longer need he bow to an older person or be touched on the head in greeting. Nashu cut again, and his spirit leapt with the joy of a trust fulfilled. As the boy floated on waves of pride and pain, Nashu marked his forehead with white clay to protect him from the evil ones.

*   *   *

Early in the morning, Clara had sometimes gone with Hannah to fetch milk from the mission. But now when Clara went, it was alone. To the amusement of the kitchen boys, she would sit on one of the stools and pull at the stiff teats, her cheek resting against the cow's warm belly. She loved the milky smell of the filling pails and the animals' docile eyes. On one such morning, arriving at the mission gate, Clara stumbled on what she took to be a pile of rags. She looked down and gasped to see, staring up at her, old Footman's lifeless eyes. His face was thick with blood and flies. A ragged hole gaped where his throat had been.

She stood swaying dizzily for a moment before running to summon Philemon. Shaking uncontrollably, she watched the old man hurry off in search of the chief's men. But when he came back, he was alone. For some reason, the bodyguards had not followed Clara's movements as usual. Strange too was the silence that blanketed the village. When Philemon had gathered together enough people to bring in the body, Clara watched the sad procession as it approached the veranda. With a prickle of terror, she recalled the sullen faces of the boyale dancers.

By the time Paul came to help dig a grave, there was more ordinary activity in the village, and Philemon was no longer obviously on edge. But then some warriors in war paint were seen near the khotla, and everyone became scared again. The boy Matiyo was sent racing off toward the chief's crag, and a long and nerve-racking wait began, with everyone fearful that Mponda might already be powerless to send help.

Clara went out to the little cemetery beyond the cattle kraal, where Paul was digging. "If only master could be here," he sighed as he rested on his spade.

"What would he do?" asked Clara. She tried to dig but stopped abruptly as the spade jarred against the brick-hard earth. She had been troubled for a day or two by pain under her right toenail, and the sudden pressure made it throb sharply.

"Master always knows what to do," insisted Paul.

"He's just a man like you," said Clara.

Paul shook his head. "Master makes everyone brave. You should see him when there is danger."

Clara stared into the shallow grave and found herself longing for the reassurance of Robert's physical presence. He had lived through so many menacing situations that he would know at once if they ought to leave. She pressed her foot down on the spade, but the pain under her nail was a pinprick to the stab of truth that seared her mind. If Robert was dead, the men who had killed him would already be closing in. Unless he returned, there would be no hope for anyone else.

Matiyo came back from the crag shortly before noon, accompanied by two men sent by the chief. They were not the ones who had watched over her before, and they carried short stabbing spears but no guns. Clara shared the general sense of disappointment. Mponda had not deserted them, but he was clearly unwilling to make Footman's murder grounds for an immediate trial of strength. Clara's dread deepened when Chizuva slipped away without a word.

Yet not everyone was upset. Mabo was absorbed by her knitting, and several women were sewing calmly. The kitchen boys, Serame and Jonas, sang as they chopped logs into fuel for the oven. They reminded her of pantomime pirates—Serame in his rakish, greasy gray tam-o'-shanter and Jonas in his dress coat held together by part of an old quilt. They had come here through trust in Robert rather than faith in Jesus, and Clara hated to think of their confusion if the white man's magic failed. But was she, perhaps, getting everything out of proportion? A helpless old man had been murdered, but should that mean the world was coming to an end? His death need be linked neither to Paul's behavior at the boyale dance nor to the events that Robert feared.

By the time she sat down to eat sadza with Paul and Philemon, Clara was a little calmer. Then Jonas came in with water and said that Footman's precious handkerchief could not be found.

Understanding the general sense of this without translation, Clara asked Paul, "What does it matter if the thing's disappeared?"

"It was yours, so people may use it to harm you."

"You know that's all nonsense."

But Paul did not look as though he knew any such thing, and Clara recalled Robert's warning to bury her nail clippings. Robert's two-week absence had one more day to run. Tomorrow would be Sunday, but Clara doubted whether any people would come to chapel from the village. Everyone would know about Footman's murder and the attack on the women. Probably only the mission Christians would be there.

Herida chose to present herself at the mission in the early afternoon of this inauspicious day. She was enveloped in the white sacking she had been wearing for days. Ignoring the distress around her, she demanded to be taught. Mission "children" screamed in her face. How dared she come, when her father had murdered poor Footman? Did she think she could come and be a spy in their midst? But Clara told Philemon to remind the women that Herida had protected them only days before. "Explain that Nashu will not attack us if his daughter is here."

After a long discussion, Paul and Philemon agreed that Herida could remain. Yet seeing how loftily the young beauty looked at the men and women around her, Clara was not sure that she ought to have argued her cause quite so strongly. Herida even refused to speak to her when Paul was nearby. He was a lowly Makalaka, a "mere thing," while she was a queen. At her urging, Philemon relayed to Clara Herida's justification of the harsh but entirely proper requirements of rank. These would of course make it impossible for her to learn to sew. Servants alone required such skills. Nor would she be able to read and write unless Philemon could give her his undivided attention. Though shocked by such arrogance, Clara was ready to make allowances for an unhappy woman.

Later that afternoon, Herida noticed that Clara was limping and caused astonishment by indicating that she wished to examine the white woman's foot. She looked at it closely and then shouted something to Philemon, who borrowed a needle from one of the sewing women.

"You have a jigger under your nail," murmured the old preacher, handing over the needle to Herida. "The young lady wishes to remove it for you. She wants me to tell you that until today she has done such a thing only for her husband."

Clara thanked her in Venda and gritted her teeth as the delicate probing began. Herida said something to Clara, and Philemon murmured, "She says that burrowing fleas can breed enough to eat away a whole toe."

"Don't tell me that!" Clara laughed.

With remarkable dexterity, Herida swiftly picked out a tiny sac of grubs and crushed it between her fingers. Clara was grateful, though she knew Philemon was still suspicious of Herida's motives.

Footman was buried in a calico shroud, which had to be sewn up by Clara since the other women were against wasting good cloth on a man without relations. After conducting the burial, Philemon overtook Clara as she paused by the cattle kraal fence.

"He is in heaven now," said the old man, and added, almost in the same breath, "Herida is clever. She thinks her father will depose Mponda, but she guesses the chief still has a chance to win. She makes friends with us in case he does." Philemon's face crinkled with disapproval. "She wants to cause mischief for Chizuva too."

"That doesn't mean she hasn't thrown in her lot with the Christians," replied Clara.

"Against her father?" asked Philemon with unconcealed skepticism. "Why is that, Nkosikaas?"

"She may think it's the best way to keep her husband."

Philemon made a show of considering this, but from the tortoiselike retraction of his leathery neck, she knew he was unconvinced. "She will be Judas, Nkosikaas. You will see."

It was just after sunset, and a bloody stain hung in the sky. Clara was walking home with Paul, while little boys shooed goats into their kraals and scrawny hens into their huts for the night. From far away they heard a stuttering beat, as if of muted drums. As usual at this time of day, a light breeze came dipping down from the chief's crag, whispering so quietly it seemed as if the earth itself were breathing. Already soft stars were smiling.

Paul was the first to realize that the distant thudding was not being made by drums.

"Master's mules," he screamed, flinging up his arms and starting to run.

"Dear God!" cried Clara, in joy and gratitude.

Women looked up in amazement from their cooking, and old men gaped. The white woman was chasing the little schoolteacher through the village.

As Clara undressed, she was in a daze. Only days ago, she had imagined what it might be like to return to England without Robert, and now she could not believe she had ever thought it. Incredibly, it was possible to wish one had never met a man and yet almost at the same moment to be glad one had. Robert had been extraordinarily quiet and gentle with her since his return. Minutes before, he had put his arms around her and kissed her neck lightly at the nape. Then, gazing at her with sorrowful intensity, he had kissed her lips softly again and again. She felt herself responding as he stroked her naked body with the tips of his fingers. She was safe now and need not feel tense or frightened. By the time he began to take off his own clothes, Clara felt radiantly expectant. But just as they lay down on the bed, the evening drums started up. In that instant, Clara felt a change in him, not just the tension in his face but a sense that he was withdrawing from her.

The drumming went on, and though they were both naked, he did not stroke or kiss her anymore. Instead he sat on the edge of their bed with his head bowed. A lamp in the adjacent room cast a yellow square on the bedroom floor. When he raised his head, his eyes were intent and sharply focused, but not on her. Something beyond her seemed to absorb him completely—or so she thought until she realized that he could not bear to face her.

"You must tell me," she murmured with a sinking heart. "Please, Robert. I must know."

And so he told her, not sparing himself, or her, anything. The rifles; the defended hill; the men from the north; the probability of an uprising. It was all laid out before her, without any attempt at mitigation. By the time he finished his recitation, she was shivering, and her mouth was very dry. Yet she was excited too.

Her voice shook. "Does it mean we'll be able to leave this place?"

He raised his heavy-lidded eyes, plainly knowing how much his answer mattered to her. "I'm sorry, my love. We'll be much safer here than on the veld. Mponda will defend us."

"You think he will?"

"I do."

She looked at him expectantly, her voice scratchy with hope. "Suppose we face up to the dangers of a journey and go away . . . Surely they'll patch things up, father and son. If *we* are the problem, we owe it to them to go."

He stared at her in astonishment. "But, Clara, we owe it to them to stay. How else can we set an example and influence them for good?" His voice throbbed with certainty. "When God is testing us, we cannot run away."

So there was to be no escape after all. As Robert reached out and touched her breasts, she felt her cheeks burning. How could he fondle her like this after being the cause of such disappointment? But her anger was short-lived. What a hypocrite I've been, she thought: praying for his return, but only so long as he could save my life. And now that he's made it clear he can't, am I going to wish he'd never come back?

For Robert, the truthtelling appeared to have been entirely beneficial. As if they had magically returned to the time immediately before his revelations, his face resumed its rapt solemnity. Her own desire to make love had not survived his revelations, but if he took pleasure in her body, should she deny it to him after his long abstinence? And who knew how many more times there might be? Very few, perhaps.

After they had made love, he fell asleep at once; but she lay awake, listening to the bats in the thatch, as her husband's sweat and semen dried on her body. She tried to build a bridge between this night and others that might lie ahead, but she could not do it. Her future was unimaginable.

On no other Sunday since her arrival had Clara seen even thirty people in the little wooden chapel; yet today more than that had already assembled outside. Before Paul rang the bell, a broad phalanx of warriors was snaking toward the building. Most were daubed with clay colors and carrying weapons. None had been near the place before. As they shuffled past the doorway, Clara turned to Robert with a wildly beating heart.

"Don't they wear paint when they fight?"

"Red ocher? That's right; and blue shining stuff on their heads—it's mica dust mixed with grease."

Clara caught her breath as she saw the glint of blue on their shaven heads. "Why are they wearing it now?"

"To protect them from the power of the white man's God." Robert smiled encouragingly and took her arm.

Clara was still standing in the doorway, eyes screwed up against the sunlight. Remembering their lovemaking of the night before, Robert's heart was filled with tenderness. She looked lost and heartbreakingly young. He took her hand and said gently, "When I first came to live with Mponda's people and washed my hair, they thought I was washing my brain. The soapsuds, you see. They're very easily frightened. You should remember that."

But frightened people often lash out, she thought, as she and Robert caught up with Simon and Paul. They were leaning against a broken fence that bordered a dusty enclosure. Inside, a woman was braiding a child's hair. Clara's hand tightened on her husband's arm. How could Robert suppose that his words would ever matter to these people? *If we are murdered, people will carry on just as before.* To her right, a man was urinating against a tree and a boy was chopping wood, just as on any other day.

Simon and Paul were in their best clothes, and both were scared. The stiff and ceremonious way in which Robert was walking seemed ominous to Clara.

He spoke, in his hoarse, slightly awkward voice. "Dear friends, these are Our Lord's words to his disciples in Saint Luke's Gospel: 'When ye shall hear of wars and commotions be not terrified. Though they shall lay their hands on you, do not meditate before what ye shall answer: for *I* will give you a mouth and wisdom, which all your adversaries will not be able to resist.' "

As they approached the chapel, Clara wanted nothing so much as to run back to the house. But what good would it do? She would be found wherever she hid. As Robert embraced them all and said a prayer, Clara wondered how she would survive the tension of this moment, let alone endure the minutes to come. Robert intoned:

The Lord is thy shade upon thy right hand.
The sun shall not smite thee by day,
Nor the moon by night.
The Lord shall keep thee from all evil:
The Lord shall keep thy going out and coming in,
From this time forth and for evermore.

They entered the building, and Clara was conscious of smelling rancid fat and old leather. The warriors had placed themselves in the seats immediately behind those that the converts always occupied. Not being used to furniture, they sat as if on the ground, with their feet on the benches and their knees drawn up to their chins. A dog was wandering among them, yelping as it received blows in the ribs. As usual, there were mothers with squalling babies on their backs, and strangers who had come out of curiosity. But these people had been careful to sit in the back rows. They seemed unusually quiet.

Robert recited the Lord's Prayer in Venda and then, eyes on the armed men, declared in a friendly, encouraging voice:

"I know you feel suspicious. I understand that. But it really isn't as hard as you think it is to believe in something you can't quite understand. I'll show you what I mean." He pulled an egg from his pocket like a conjuror. Everyone was very still. "Just look at this egg. If I break it, only a yellow slime comes out." He cracked the shell and let the contents splatter on the floor. He reached down and touched the broken yolk. "Just slime. But place an identical egg under the wings of a fowl, and in no time at all a living thing is born. Who can understand how a little warmth can make a chicken out of slime? I certainly can't explain it, but I don't deny the fact. Some of you can't understand why Lord Jesus died for your sakes. But please, my friends, be like the hen. Place that fact in your minds and hearts, as the hen places the egg under her wings, then dwell upon it and take the same pains, and something new and wonderful is sure to hatch out."

They then sang a hymn, which Robert had translated from the English:

Thy Kingdom come, O God,
Thy rule, O Christ, begin;
Break with Thine Iron Rod
The tyrannies of Sin.

Robert was always moved by the vigor of African singing, and today the shrill, defiant voices of the female converts made him feel brave and joyful. Looking at the poor, half-naked pagans, with their ocher-painted bodies, he no longer feared death at their hands. The way they were stealing covert glances at one another and seemed loath to lower their eyes told Robert that they were afraid to be in the white man's spirit house. A moment's inattention, and they might be bewitched or forced into some action against their will. He had been so certain that they had come as enemies that no alternative had occurred to him until now. And yet if Mponda had really decided to espouse the Christian faith, it would be perfectly natural for people to come here in order to show their chief that they were not ill disposed.

Robert caught Clara's eye and smiled. He knew how disillusioning she had found earlier visits to the chapel. Once, a man had called out to a friend to give him sweet reed during the blessing, and several women had snored throughout the service; on the same occasion, a group of men had smoked hemp noisily, and a chameleon had fallen from the rafters, provoking an uproar. But today he sensed that their shared danger had restored Clara's faith in his vocation. And this, he told himself—along with their very survival—he owed entirely to the power of the Holy Spirit.

Sometimes when Philemon preached, Robert thought him too tolerant of his listeners' foibles; but now when the old man rose to speak, he railed most bitterly against the evils of circumcision and blamed the Venda for bringing all their present ills upon themselves.

"Look upon the panting oxen," Philemon cried in his strangely high-pitched voice. "Have *they* sinned against Thee, God? Have the dying plants sinned, or the trees and grass blasphemed? Nay, brothers, they have not. So why does God deny us rain? I will tell you. It is because of the evil of the boyale that God punishes us all. Who can deny it?"

A club clattered to the floor, and Robert braced himself for the warriors' reaction to Philemon's call to repentance. A man jumped up and lifted his assegai. Its point was aimed at Philemon's heart. Robert jumped up, his finger jabbing the air:

"You will burn if you cast that spear . . . forever and ever. And your children will know eternal fire."

In the eerie silence that followed, the young man gasped out a deep sob, and his spear fell from his hand. Someone behind him began to moan. Then, one by one, others started to weep, so that soon the chapel was filled with the rustle of people murmuring aloud. The very sound, thought Robert, that had filled the upper room at Pentecost, a rushing mighty wind. Within him, like a resurrection, faith and courage blazed. Mesmerized by the missionary's eye, men and women gazed in awe, then hid their faces. Clara's spirit soared. They were saved. Joy filled her heart. At the moment of crisis, Robert had not failed her.

Compassion and pity lit his features. These ignorant children had sinned and blasphemed, but they should not be punished. No, he would intercede for them. Christ had died for all mankind, so why should they be denied His bounty? As if stilling stormy waters, Robert raised a protecting hand.

CHAPTER 11

For almost a month after Robert's triumph in the chapel, there was hardly a breath of wind, a circumstance the villagers attributed to the white man's magic. The metal of sky and hill and the rough stubble of the thorn trees had fused into a gray so uniform that it was impossible to tell where sky and land met. For hours on end, the people lay in their dark huts or rested under the shade of their grain bins. The stars hung large and low. Only days before, there had still been mice to dig up, but all had been eaten now, and Clara was shocked to see women reduced to stewing rotten figs. At night, she heard hungry children crying. They reminded her of Homani, with their stick-like legs, running noses, and overlarge eyes.

In these dusty days, as the rains failed to come, Robert strode purposefully through the village on his way to Mponda's crag as if he alone could see beyond the hard times. He spent most of his days with the chief and was optimistic about his progress toward conversion. Clara tried to put out of her mind the violence that seemed more likely to materialize if Robert succeeded than if he failed. But from a personal perspective, she found his renewed confidence much more attractive than his anxiety before he had gone away. He really seemed a man inspired. God had worked through him in the chapel and would do so again. How else could she explain what she had seen with her own eyes? The warriors had come, determined to commit murder, but they had been thwarted by a power greater than their own.

When Robert touched her, she imagined she could feel this new force emanating from him. When she saw him working on the village dam, she was overwhelmed by how hard he himself labored in order to inspire his African diggers. At the mission, he was constantly harried by sick or hungry people. His resilence amazed her. And when he came home in the evening too tired to talk, she understood and did not press him. Remembering how his silences had once exasperated her, she was surprised by her new tolerance. Can I be falling in love with him again? she wondered. Yet quite often she feared for him. He believed so completely in Mponda's coming conversion that Clara worried about how a serious setback to his hopes might affect him. Mponda was vitally important to Robert, but Clara could not understand her husband's absolute faith in him. If she could only share Robert's optimism, they could be as close to each other as they had ever been. Yet one particular doubt prevented that. Why should Mponda choose to oblige Robert by deciding to be baptized before the rains? What the chief stood to lose was crystal clear. If he accepted Christ too soon, he would risk being blamed for extending the drought. Knowing how sensitive Robert would be on this subject, she felt acutely anxious before finally putting this point to him.

"But can't you see, Clara?" he demanded, in a deep and resonant voice. "When God decides that the moment has come, nobody on earth can resist Him." However, earlier in the day, he had admitted that Mponda had been complaining about God's unfairness in denying to black people the goods that white people had enjoyed for generations. How long, he had demanded, would God allow this injustice to continue after he had been baptized?

"What did you say?" asked Clara, disturbed by the gulf of understanding that this anecdote suggested.

Robert smiled. "I explained to him the quite different values of spiritual and material wealth."

"Did he appreciate the distinction?" asked Clara faintly.

"Why shouldn't he?" asked Robert, evidently nettled by her question. "Former believers in witchcraft have great respect for things they can't touch or see."

Though far from reassured, Clara did not say so. Often she found herself wanting to talk of less weighty matters, but when she tried to gossip about Hannah or Chizuva, Robert rarely responded. In England, a wife whose husband was bound up with his work would have her circle of friends to fall back on, but not in this wilderness. On many nights Clara lay reading by lamplight long after Robert had fallen into an exhausted sleep.

Of all the things that pained her in the village, Clara found the people's sullen expressions the worst. Robert had long since become hardened to them, and he encouraged Clara to learn from him. Yet she felt that he was wrong not to contradict the widespread rumor that he had stopped the rain. And what would have been lost by pointing out that the chief's conversion would not threaten all their old customs?

Unless villagers were sick, he rarely spoke to individuals. When not with Mponda, Robert would generally be working on his dam, across the dried-up riverbed. His aim was to create a reservoir large enough to provide the Venda with water for their fields throughout the dry season. The dam was half a mile from the village—an ideal spot, given the many hours he spent there, for any would-be assassin to seek him out. Robert's literal belief in God's protection terrified Clara. He was sure that no harm could come to him until his work was done, and therefore he saw no need to cajole or reassure opponents.

Early one evening, a group of Mponda's counselors came to the mission and begged Robert to allow their chief to take part in the witch doctor's rainmaking rituals. Their bodies were lubricated with grease and mica dust, and they wore cloaks of spotted cat and silver jackal. Behind them trailed a swarm of small flies. Clara moved closer to hear what these men wanted. She had started to make good progress with the language and every day understood a little more.

Robert greeted his visitors courteously. But with a heavy heart, Clara recognized his cruel-to-be-kind expression. He wished he could help them, truly he did; he could understand their distress; indeed, he shared it; but no missionary on earth could help them unless they first opened their hearts to God.

One counselor said that if Robert would allow Mponda to help them make rain just once, then they would come to church as often as he liked. Everyone knew that the chief's absence would damage the ritual.

Robert shook his head sadly and said, "I'm sorry, but Chief Mponda must act according to his conscience. He is a free man."

"He is your creature, Umfundisi," objected one of the older men. "You have bewitched him."

Clara was impressed by the restraint shown by the counselors. When at last they shuffled away, sad and disappointed, she longed to call them back. They could have understood little of Robert's reasoning and would think him vindictive. To them his decision looked like a death sentence.

That afternoon, Robert had told Simon and Paul to smear beeswax into the thatch of the mission house to make it waterproof.

And only moments after the counselors had gone, he urged them to get started. He himself clambered up onto the thatch to help.

"Master expects big rain soon," Paul explained joyfully, revealing the gap between his front teeth.

"Do you believe everything he says, Paul?"

"Master is God's prophet, Mrs. Robert."

Though Paul's Christian faith had cost him Hannah's love and many friendships, trusting Robert was still second nature to him.

While Clara often worried about Paul, and also about Simon, whose dependence on Robert had become greater since their time away together, she felt far more anxious about Herida. Her father, Nashu, was surely planning to punish her. Yet Robert rarely addressed a word to her or even smiled in her direction. He often told Clara how upset Chizuva had been after Herida was permitted to learn at the mission.

When Robert climbed down from the roof, Herida was regaling the mission "children" with a comical fable about a warthog and a hyena. While they were still quaking with laughter, she placed a thimble on the end of each of her fingers and tapped out an astonishingly complicated and catchy rhythm on the table. Dazzled by her performance, Clara offered congratulations. Robert walked away.

Speaking slowly so that Clara would understand, Herida whispered, "Those men who came to your wooden prayer house. Makufa sent them to kill you all. I know he will try again." Without waiting for a response, she returned to her group of admirers.

Robert, who had not heard what Herida had just said, came up to his wife and murmured, "You know she's only pretending to be a Christian. Already she's put off dozens of ordinary people from coming here."

Though shaken, Clara said fiercely, "Why believe her enemies instead of her? She's just told me that those men in the chapel came to kill us on Makufa's orders."

Robert's eyes narrowed. "Her father probably asked her to tell you that. It's meant to scare me so much that I'll stop trying to convert Mponda."

Clara felt sick. And the awful thing was that she couldn't think of a single argument that would change his mind. In the end it was a matter of trust. She trusted Herida, and he didn't.

Before she could stop herself, she blurted out, "Mponda's right to wait till after the rains. Perhaps you should civilize the

Venda first, before trying to convert them.'' She paused, realizing that she had mouthed the ultimate blasphemy. The idea that colonization ought to precede mission work was anathema to him. She cried, ''How can any good come of a baptism that leads to killing?''

''You think there's no killing now?'' he demanded. ''A month ago, just yards from this house, a man thrust a spear through his wife's throat. His supper wasn't as he wished. And today he's still free. Not even shunned. He paid four cows to his wife's father. She was lazy, he said. Four cows were too many.'' Robert's voice shook. ''How can I civilize *him*? Only God's Grace can do that. If Mponda falters, his people will wade in blood for generations. Think of the twins who'll be murdered, the children whose top teeth grow first, the so-called witches, the mutilated girls.''

After Robert had left for the dam, Herida came up to Clara and took her hand. Her beautiful face was full of sympathy. She asked huskily, ''Would you like to see a bride prepared by her women?''

Without hesitation, Clara said she would. Paul stared at her with a worried frown. ''Master will not like you to watch pagan ceremonies.''

Clara said firmly, ''You took me to the boyale dances, Paul.''

He looked away. ''I think you will not like the things they do. But if you go, I will come with you.''

Herida made shushing movements in his direction. ''Ey-ye! Men can't see a bride prepared.''

''I will wait outside,'' muttered Paul.

As they approached a newly built hut, separated from its neighbors by an area of burned grass, they were greeted by the sound of the full-throated singing Clara had heard with Paul at the dancing.

Herida took Clara's hand again. ''For girls life is sad, they tell us in their song. When we marry, our husbands won't let us dance with our friends. Instead we must grind mealie meal till our arms ache. Before marriage, there are hopes and dreams; after it, life is harder. They tell the bride, Be fruitful. Fill your homestead with children. May your enemies drink sand, and may all disease be burned up in the sun.'' Herida paused as the tone became plaintive.

Clara understood the next verse as they sang to the young bride, "Don't forget you leave at dawn for your husband's village." She turned to Herida. "Must she go far?"

"Very far. Three days' walking. They say, 'Don't forget you have a mother, don't forget you have a father. You must go when the sun rises.' "

"Does this girl know the man she's going to marry?"

Herida laughed. "How could she?" She paused and studied Clara's face. "No girl ever does. Her first husband is chosen when she is a child. Did you know your husband?"

"I thought I did."

As soon as the singing stopped, Clara followed Herida into the hut. Some of the women were anointing the naked bride with oil; others were braiding her hair and threading beads among the braids. Next they took red earth and pressed it onto her skin, as if making a cast of her whole body. They molded her breasts, and fashioned a muddy crown, before handing her a green bough exuding sap.

"Leaves from the milk tree," murmured Herida. "The leaves are her unborn children. She will take them to her husband. . . . I took leaves to mine."

Herida's eyes were moist, and Clara realized with a jolt why she had been brought here. I too was married, Herida was silently telling her. Why should my marriage, which was performed with all the proper rites, be set aside because your Christian customs are different?

Clara said gently, "Mponda may decide to keep all his wives."

Herida shook her head. "He will keep one only. You will tell your husband I am a Christian woman. You will tell him, please?" The urgency of the question shook Clara.

"I'll talk to him about it, yes," she promised.

Herida laid her tear-stained cheek against Clara's for a moment and then left her in the hut with the bride and her attendants.

Given Robert's prejudices, a particularly favorable moment would have to be found in which to talk to him about Herida. But since his toothache had recently been spoiling his sleep, that mo-

ment might not be for a while. As they were finishing their breakfast, Simon ran in with the news that Nashu was about to make
rain on the khotla.

"What a surprise!" muttered Robert sardonically, pointing
to a ridge of heavy cloud that had been thickening since dawn.

As they were walking between the huts, Clara asked, "Why
shouldn't they pray to their gods for rain?"

"Because their gods are false ones." Robert's amazement at
her question was unfeigned.

"How can we blame them if they think the same of our God?"

He was very angry. "They came to kill us in God's house.
You told me so. Then do *not* tell me I mustn't blame them for this
and for that."

The nganga was dancing as they arrived at the khotla. On
his head Nashu wore a cap of baboon skin. Around his neck, waist,
and ankles hung many strange objects: cowrie and tortoise shells,
teeth and claws of wild beasts, strips of skin and inflated gallblad-
ders. Nashu was sailing through his dances, twisting and jumping,
quivering and contorting. Then he beat the ground with his hands
and feet and sprang up as if grappling with an unseen foe. His leaps
became wilder, and sweat poured from him. The women began a
shrill ululation. With a great leap, Nashu whirled high in the air
and fell prone to the ground, where he twitched and shuddered.

As soon as he was on his feet and breathing evenly again,
Nashu lit a small fire and burned some herbs and strips of hide,
chanting all the while. Only when he stopped did Robert greet
him.

"What a lot of medicines you have here."

"You think I should not make rain?" The menace in the
witch doctor's voice was naked. His face was wizened, but his
eyes radiated immense power.

Robert said calmly, "Only God moves the clouds."

"Of course Mwari makes the rain," growled Nashu. "But
what use is that unless my medicines persuade him to send it down
to earth as well?"

"Send it down? All you do is wait till you see clouds. Then
you burn your charms and take the credit for what God does by
Himself."

People pressed closer to the disputants, listening attentively
to the debate, nodding eagerly as Nashu made his points but looking darkly at Robert whenever he spoke. Clara had understood

enough of Robert's remarks to wish he knew the meaning of fear. He was deliberately annoying this dangerous man.

Nashu flicked at the missionary with his giraffe-tail fly whisk. "You whites believe in medicines too. You give them to a sick man. If he gets well, you boast how you cured him. But maybe God did it all. You can't tell. It's the same with my rainmaking."

"Of course it isn't. A man takes a pill and we see it go into his body. But your medicines never go near the clouds."

"Maybe *you* can't see them well enough to observe it. You can't see your Jesus up there either. But you still say he's there."

Loud laughter greeted this sally. Robert asked, "How can you be sure you've ever made rain? Have you, for instance, made it rain on one spot and not on another?"

"Why would I want to do that? I like to see the whole country green and all the people glad."

More loud laughter goaded Robert. "You deceive both them and yourself," he shouted above the jeers.

Nashu suddenly drew himself up straight and chanted in a singsong voice: "I make sickness do my bidding on men and cattle. I end life when I choose. I can blight the crops and dry up the milk of cows. I can make my enemies run like bucks chased by dogs." The nganga's followers gazed at the missionary with horrified sympathy, as if to say: Now look what you've done. But Robert simply turned away with a dry laugh. Nashu roared, "Before the new moon shines you will die."

Robert spun around. "No rain will fall till Mponda is Christ's follower." Ignoring incredulous mutterings, he pushed through the ring of scandalized spectators, carving a path for himself and Clara.

Behind them, Clara heard Nashu declaim to the crowd: "I am the hyena. If I dance, what will you give me?" The people cried joyfully: "We will give you a dead body."

Hurrying after Robert, Clara gasped, "How can you possibly know when the rains will come?"

But Robert did not answer her.

They were passing the blacksmith's hut when she saw a dreadful spectacle. A goat had been skinned alive and was tottering about, dying in its pink and bleeding nakedness. Robert looked for a stone.

After splitting its skull, he wiped his hands on the earth. Blood was splattered on his shoes. He said without anger, "When they make a bellows from a goat's skin, they think the creature must be skinned alive. Otherwise the metal spoils. Only Christ can end such cruelty.''

At that moment, a man flung a stone. Meant for Robert, it hit Clara above the temple. She saw a flash of light and fell. The cicadas went on with their grating song. Waves of heat still shimmered. Something warm was trickling from her hair across her cheek. She looked up at the sky as if an angel might help. Instead she saw Robert. He lifted her like a child.

A week later, Clara—out and about for the first time since her injury—was walking with Robert to the dam. Whenever she spotted any movement, however small, between the huts or in the scrubby bushes, Clara felt faint. Her head still hurt if she moved abruptly. Robert had stitched her wound skillfully, and the scar did not show through her hair. She was taken aback to feel so frail and vulnerable. It seemed incredible that two weeks earlier she had tried to chase a group of warriors near the well.

The cracked mud of the riverbed stretched away for miles on either side of Robert's sturdy bastion. Would grass ever sprout again, or trees break into leaf? Closing her eyes behind her veil, Clara tried to imagine a lake shining here. The rains were two months late already; maybe they would simply miss a year. It had happened before.

"Look," commanded Robert, pointing to some ants running about with their usual mindless vivacity. He seemed as pleased as if he had created them himself. "You know they can make water out of the oxygen and hydrogen in their food?" Clara nodded dumbly, and did so again when he showed her that the leaves of the mimosa trees were furled as tightly now, in the heat of the day, as they were at night. "How well God fits his humblest creations to live in this world."

Are we humans so well fitted? she asked herself. People are hungry here. They die of numerous diseases. Can that be part of God's plan? And if Mponda fights his son, and Herida lives out the rest of her life in misery, what will that prove about anyone being fitted for anything? But Robert was invulnerable. In his ragged waistcoat and cut-off moleskin trousers, he still looked like an Old Testament prophet. If he went back to England, he would again inspire the faithful. And why not? He was as selfless now, and as dedicated, as when Clara had first seen him. *I* must be the one who's changed, she thought.

Waves of heat were rising from the mud as if from a great oven. Although the building of this dam was an incredible feat, Clara could not find the words with which to praise him. Instead she blurted out what was uppermost in her mind. "Why *can't* Herida be Mponda's one wife when he converts?"

Robert said firmly but pleasantly, "If she'd married her husband first, I would accept her gladly." He reached for her hand. "Imagine the chaos if we don't have one firm rule for everyone."

Across the dried-up river, close to the spot where a dust devil had just swept by, Robert spotted something square and white beside some fig trees. Through half-closed eyes he made out a second pale shape. Wagons. Traders. Dear God, why now, when the moment could hardly be worse? These men could be drunkards or skeptics. They might insult the chief and tell him missionaries were fools. Something worse occurred to Robert. After the attack on her, Clara might want to go away with these strangers. He could hardly breathe at the thought.

Clara was staring at the distant wagons with tears spilling from her eyes. Had his own problems blinded him to the depths of her suffering? Her tears of thankfulness made Robert's heart ache. Her skin was burned brown, and her hair had lost its luster. He prayed that the newcomers would not pity her. If they did, she would know it. But what could he say to arm her against condescending sympathy?

He said insistently, "I want you to understand that Mponda's baptism is only weeks away. Things are different now."

CHAPTER 12

As soon as Makufa had heard that two white men, a white woman, and six black men wearing red hats and sand-colored short trousers had arrived outside the village, he called a meeting of headmen in the chota, or men's house. These men were mainly his supporters, and all were opposed to Mponda's plans for baptism. Makufa loved the chota's curving thatch and the way it dipped and crested like a bird's back. The roof swept out from the sides of the building to form a wide veranda supported on wooden posts. Inside, wattle ribs showed through the clay.

Nashu had told Makufa that the traitors with the red hats were exactly like the black soldiers he had seen six months before in Bulawayo. These men carried guns and obeyed whatever orders the white people gave them. They counted how many people lived in different villages and then asked them to give grain or animals so they would be allowed to go on living in their huts. If any nganga killed a witch, the black soldiers came and choked him with a rope. If anyone called another person a witch, he was shut up in a stone house. Makufa had heard of such injustices but had looked upon them as misfortunes confined to the lands of the Matabele and the Tswana. Now he wanted to go out and kill these people, before they could contaminate his tribe. Years earlier, Nashu had predicted such humiliations if Mponda was foolish enough to let a missionary settle at his kraal.

The defeat suffered by his warriors in the white man's spirit house had made Makufa determined to avenge their disgrace. The white man's religion had been designed to part Africans from their land without a struggle. They were asked to love their enemies and to turn their other cheek. Nashu had heard a bitter joke in Gwelo. "When the white man came here, he had the Bible and the black man had the land. Now the black man has the Bible and the white man has the land.'' These Christians were clever and dangerous. Their strength was disguised as weakness.

Nashu rose and raised his hand. Between the leathery folds of his face, his dark eyes glinted. ''My friends, I thank you for coming to this council. Mponda has permitted our enemies to enter the village. Our ancestors are weeping, but I ask you to raise no weapon now. Friends, it is the inexperienced ox that kisses the ax. If we kill these people, many soldiers will come to slaughter us. We must act together with all our brothers. We must kill the white men in every part of our country. We cannot strike alone. When the day of vengeance comes, you will know it. Till then, be calm. The earthworm is slow, but he reaches the well.''

A rumble of assent greeted these words. Makufa could make out eyes and teeth gleaming in the chota's dim interior. He stepped forward and said, ''These people are very evil. They say our sacred customs are wrong and that we live in darkness. Would *we* go to a foreign place to steal goats and land? Never! The missionary tells us that his god has a son but no wife or concubine. Who has heard such nonsense before? This god's son died and moved a great rock away from the cave where he was buried. He asked his men to drink his blood. The white men tell our children such things.'' Makufa looked around, pleased by the revulsion his remarks had caused. ''Nashu says we must not kill the newcomers, and I agree. Other white men will know that they have come here. But the missionary can be killed without danger as soon as the others have left.'' He drew himself up and shouted, ''If a man fouls your hut, you do not thank him.''

Chiweru, an old man who, until recently, had advised Mponda, clambered to his feet. ''Nkosi, what will the chief your father do if you kill his umfundisi?''

''He will awake from his madness,'' said Makufa.

''Will the chief not kill you?''

''No. The mfungu's spell will be broken, and my father will thank me.''

Nashu took Makufa's arm. ''I cannot agree with you, Nkosi. Nobody must die in this kraal until I tell you that Mwari wishes it.''

Makufa stayed silent rather than risk quarreling with the nganga. Because Nashu claimed to be able to speak for Mwari, he could invent any divine command that suited him. Makufa knew that Nashu had his own reasons for saving the missionary, the foremost being his desire to oust Mponda—a goal the nganga would achieve only if the missionary converted the chief. Not until then would the tribe's headmen agree to depose Mponda. Loving his father, Makufa wanted at all costs to prevent his conversion. If the missionary could be killed in time, Mponda would not be able to drink the fatal medicine.

Each day, Makufa prayed to his grandfather's spirit for help. Afterward, he would put on his black ostrich feathers and war paint, steeling himself to cleanse the tribe. The missionary had used magic to defend himself in his spirit room, but he would be easier to kill in his own square house. That was where the blow should be struck.

The wagons had stopped at the center of the khotla and were already surrounded by several hundred Venda by the time Clara and Robert came on the scene. As Clara pushed through the crowd with a thumping heart, she caught glimpses of tall black men wearing red fezzes, blue tunics, and khaki shorts. These men were forcing back curious onlookers with the stocks of their rifles.

The two white men were sitting on camp stools in front of their wagons like fashionable people watching a play. She let out a cry of disappointment. One of them was about fifty, bald, short, with a snub nose and a trim mustache. His companion was in his late twenties, with sleek black hair and large dark eyes. Both were total strangers, as was the third person, a fluffily feminine woman who sat close to the younger man. Blond curls spilled out from under the brim of her new bush hat. If only Francis and Fynn were sitting there instead!

Strangely, Robert seemed relieved at the sight of the visitors. "The stocky fellow is the native commissioner for the district," he explained, "Arthur Bullock by name. He thinks missionaries ruin Africans if they teach them anything at all. The villagers call him Bwana Baboon, because his face is as red as a baboon's bottom."

"What about the others?"

He shrugged. "Never seen them. Settlers, I expect."

One of the uniformed men was shouting, and soon many of the younger women in the crowd were pressing forward. As a drum was heard, they began to dance.

Robert's face was angry. "The same story every time he comes here. The women get cloth and beads if they dance for him."

"What's wrong if they're willing?"

"He likes to gape at their breasts and thighs."

"Is that all?" she muttered, thinking of the whores in Belingwe, with their refrain of "jig-jig two sheeleeng."

The women were wheeling fast enough to lift their modesty aprons away from their thighs. The fat man began to toss coins and beads to the dancers as a preliminary to telling the prettier ones to dance closer to him. When he pointed out two particular dancers to his majordomo, Clara felt less sanguine about his intentions.

Robert and Clara lunched with the newcomers at a table set up between their wagons. The young couple turned out to be a bankrupt French count and his English wife, who hoped to start afresh as tobacco farmers. The commissioner had a gruff and bullying manner. At present, he was undertaking a survey of all the villages in the region. "My Domesday Book," Arthur Bullock called it, and made no secret of the fact that it would enable the colonial administrator to estimate how much hut tax could be levied from the local people.

Robert's fork froze on its way to his mouth. "Why should they have to pay anything to live in their own country?"

The commissioner bit into a chicken leg and mumbled with a full mouth: "It's so they can have schools and roads. These things aren't free."

"That isn't why you want to tax them," objected Robert. "It's so you can force them to work in the mines."

"Nothing wrong with work, Haslam. Africans are lazy devils." Bullock picked a strand of chicken from between his teeth with a prong of his fork.

"They're free men and women," snapped Robert.

"Free?" The commissioner chuckled. "Free to live in rags and die young? What if they want a pair of boots or a bar of soap?"

"They can work for a few days to earn money."

Bullock drained his wineglass. "That won't do for a mine owner or a railway contractor. They want men for a year." He smiled reassuringly at the young blond woman. "Even my friends here will need men for months at a time on their farm."

As the Frenchman nodded, Robert rounded on him. "It's

shameful to tax poor people simply to force them to work far from home.''

''A sad necessity.'' Bullock sighed, refilling his glass. ''No colony prospers without a regular workforce.''

''Prospers?'' sneered Robert. ''Who'll prosper? Not these poor people here.''

Bullock shifted his weight on his camp stool and remarked jocularly to Clara, ''He's a hard man, your husband.''

''No, Mr. Bullock, an honest one.''

Bullock sniffed. ''I can see that you're well suited. But then I could be wrong.'' He smiled disagreeably. ''I thought the same about the first Mrs. Haslam. But ... I mustn't go repeating old rumors.''

After an uneasy silence, the count began to talk about his tobacco-growing plans. His countess turned out to have been a ''slavey'' in a London boardinghouse before catching her aristocrat. Her name was Nina, and her toughness and determination were in contrast to her sweet appearance. She had brought a new sewing machine to Africa, and laughed as she promised to defend it with her life. Clara had often yearned for the relief of talking honestly to a woman of her own race, but faced with Nina's bright optimism, she knew she would have nothing to say to her.

Before lunch ended, the commissioner promised he would call on Robert and Clara at the mission in the afternoon, bringing with him all the mail that had piled up for them at Belingwe. The prospect of reading letters from her father made Clara tearful. Since Bullock would be leaving Mponda's kraal in two days, she could no longer postpone writing letters of her own. Already she knew that she would not be riding away in one of the commissioner's wagons. To save the mission from Nashu's vengeance, she would have to stay on with Robert and somehow persuade him that the nganga's daughter ought to remain Mponda's wife.

While Clara was waiting for Bullock to arrive with the mail, Paul said to her, ''The first time I saw Bwana Bullock, he was carried in a chair by six Matabele men. My mother told me he owned the country.''

''Were you angry?''

''I thought he was a ghost or a god.'' Paul smiled wistfully. ''Now he gives me pencils and paper for the school.''

Clara could guess why. There could be few boys in the colony who spoke better English. Paul would make an excellent clerk.

Perhaps she should warn Robert of her suspicion, but first she had something more urgent on her mind. As soon as she could steer Robert out onto the veranda, she asked, "Will you tell Bullock about Makufa's rifles?"

He shook his head and said, "Suppose Bullock sends for soldiers. They'll arrive in a couple of months, and the guns will have gone by then, so they'll burn all the huts here because this is a rebel village."

At that moment, Bullock came through the gate, closely followed by two of his policemen. Paul and Simon ran forward and took the mail sack.

"Here is something for you, master," shouted Simon, holding up a square parcel. "And what is this little one? Is this my watch?"

When Clara was handed her letters, she could not bear to read those from her father until she was alone. But one posted from Natal she did open and read while Simon and Paul were still pestering Robert to unwrap various packets.

Dear Mrs. Haslam:

I must regret that Mr. Fynn and I were unable to return from the Somnabula Forest by way of Mponda's kraal. Much though we wished to do so, our supplies were too low to permit it. But no doubt you are now well settled in your new life and will hardly have missed a visit from us.

I had expected my regiment's posting to be over before now, but we are detained here in Natal for a few months more in case the Boers kick up a fuss. If they keep quiet, I should be able to come up north again one last time for some shooting and drop in on you. Otherwise I shall have to wait to make Mr. Haslam's acquaintance and to renew our own in the Old Country.

> *Believe me with kindest regards,*
> *Yours sincerely,*
> *Francis Vaughan*

Clara stared at Francis's letter. What possible meaning could the civilities of ordinary life ever have for her again?

On getting back to the house, she read through her father's letters and found them more upsetting than she had anticipated. Every day he had feared that she was dead, every day he had hoped for news and every day he had been disappointed. Recently he had spotted a dark-haired young women in the street bearing such a striking resemblance to her that he had called out Clara's name, only to be faced, as she turned, by a stranger. Until taking up her pen, Clara had imagined writing to him honestly. But now she realized that even if she could be sure of coming home alive, it would still be pointless to tell him anything that would increase his anxiety while he waited for her. So she wrote a warm and optimistic letter, wondering, as she did so, whether Robert had always been wrong to keep things from her.

The following morning, Countess Nina, in a sky-blue fitted outfit with a matching bonnet, gave a demonstration of revolver shooting. Her husband had set up an array of tins and bottles and proudly summoned the Haslams and Commissioner Bullock to watch as his young wife knocked them down at an astonishing rate.

"She shot a lion last month," he told Clara, admiringly. "He was an old one, who came near our camp at night. But our boy, he misses with his rifle, and Nina, she says, 'If you will take all night, here goes!' and she shoots him in the neck at ten paces."

The commissioner applauded loudly and swore that all white women in Africa ought to learn to shoot. Then he smiled lugubriously at Nina and added, "Always keep one bullet back. Never fall into the hands of savages alive."

"I thought you killed all the rebels in '93," said Nina with a tight little frown.

"They were given a bloody nose," agreed Bullock, adding sotto voce for Robert's benefit, "though not by me, you understand."

Unlike the commissioner, the small crowd of villagers watching the proceedings from a discreet distance did not applaud or smile as Nina snapped off the necks of wine bottles. Their sullen faces scared Clara. We know why you have learned to shoot so well, they seemed to say. We know that blacks are your real targets.

Noticing this glowering audience, Bullock started to harangue Robert about the ill effects of educating Africans. "Makes them discontented. Look at the blighters.'' He stabbed a finger in their direction. ''They don't know if they belong to the whites or the blacks, so they live in bars and stores and learn to cheat and drink.''

Robert looked at the man pityingly. ''Wherever they go, my boys and girls will lead others to Jesus.''

Bullock turned to Paul. ''What about you, my boy? Will you do that?''

''Yes, sah, I will.''

''Why not come and work for me, eh? I'll pay you forty shillings a month and your board. What do you say?''

All eyes were upon Paul. Forty shillings was a fortune. Paul owned no more than two old shirts, a pair of shorts, and a theadbare blanket, worth perhaps two shillings altogether. The commissioner was promising him a world of untold luxury.

At last Paul said, in a tone of quiet apology, ''I think I will stay here, thank you very much, sir.''

Bullock said sharply to Robert, ''Very touching, I'm sure, but you're wrong to let him stay. He'd earn an honest wage with me and even get a government pension.''

''He'd be hated by his fellows.''

''Don't fool yourself, Haslam. He's hated already. Bush kaffirs can't stand mission boys.''

''You're behind the times, Bullock. His chief will soon be converted, and Paul will become a valued adviser.''

The commissioner grinned derisively. ''Pigs'll be flying too. I'll ask the lad again in a month or two.''

Robert glanced at Clara with tears in his eyes, as if to say: Now do you understand what loyalty is? She too had a lump in her throat.

Before the count's ox wagon trundled away into the brown and dusty landscape, Nina sent a boy to the mission with an invitation. She would be honored if Mr. and Mrs. Haslam would come to see them at Mungora in the autumn. By then they should have built their house.

Mungora was eighty miles away—nothing by African standards. But though Clara knew they would never visit their new neighbors, the image of wasp-waisted Nina, defying a continent with her little gun, moved her.

* * *

155

The following day, the commissioner's wagon also departed. Soon afterward, Clara heard someone tapping lightly at the kitchen door. Herida was standing outside, by the woodpile.

"You have asked your husband, my missus?" she inquired breathlessly. As usual, hoping to please Clara, Herida had put on her ugly mission dress. "He will let me be Mponda's one wife?"

"My husband hasn't decided," she replied after a brief silence.

Herida stared at Clara as if unable to bear the pain. "You lie to me," she said in a dull, flat voice.

"I swear I'll go on trying to persuade him."

Hope shone briefly in Herida's eyes. "Tell him this, my missus: A man's parents choose his first wife, but *he* chooses the others. So why must Mponda put away the wife he chose for love and keep the one his parents chose? You will ask this, please?"

"Of course I will." Herida's humility upset Clara more than her arrogance ever had. If she could only explain to her why Robert hated polygamy, perhaps Herida would stop seeing his beliefs as a personal attack.

Yards away, flies were buzzing loudly in the privy as the sun beat down. Herida said brokenly, "Your man has no heart. My child died, my only child. Will your husband stop me bearing another baby for my beloved? Ask him what I have done to offend his God. Why must I lose my man now, as well as my child? Tell him I will pray to his Jizzus every day."

"Listen to me, Herida: *I* want you to keep your husband."

Herida grasped Clara's arm. "Then why won't he listen to you? Aren't you good to him? Does he breathe hard and shiver when he lies down with you?"

"You don't understand how he thinks."

Herida was offended. "You are wrong. All men are dissatisfied unless their wives prepare their bodies." She lifted her dress and squatted. "You see? When we are little girls we pull our lips down. Look." Blushing, Clara glanced down at Herida's hanging labia—like a drooping pink butterfly. "You show *me* now?" demanded Herida.

"It isn't the custom in my country," faltered Clara, who was especially embarrassed since, because of the heat, she had stopped wearing underwear weeks before.

Herida demanded sternly, "Do you put your feet around his

back when he pushes? Do you hold him in your mouth? Do you play at love till he moans for you?''

Clara shook her head. How could Herida understand the inhibitions of Sarston? "My husband likes me to seem . . ." She broke off helplessly, not knowing the Venda words for "pure" and "angelic." Did they even exist in the English sense?

Herida clasped Clara's hand. "No man loves his wife till she conceives. Did you drink the medicine I brought?"

Clara said, "My husband loves me, and I won't stop trying to persuade him." Then she turned back into the house, leaving the young woman standing alone in the sunlight.

CHAPTER 13

Two days after the white official and the young man and woman had gone, Makufa decided to act. For months he had been eager for this moment, yet now that it had come he was afraid. But with his black war feathers on his head, he swore not to show his fear to anyone. Shortly before dawn, he had killed a goat under the dark branches of the sacred mugumo tree, offering beer and blood to the ancestors. "Nyalhuana, ancient mother, guard these warriors," he had prayed. "May the morning star preserve us."

And now, just outside the village, with his men around him, Makufa could see a spark of light above the peaked roofs—the morning star. "O light of initiation and all beginnings, help me," he murmured. "May I live to save my father and cleanse this tribe."

To feed his anger, he thought of the fat, red-faced bwana who had made the women wriggle and shake for him. Although he should have been hacked to death, Nashu had warned against the killing of whites. But Makufa knew he must kill the teacher to save his father from the disgrace of baptism. The men sent to the chapel to murder him on the last singing day had failed because they had stared straight into his eyes. But if he was sleeping, his eyes would be closed. Rather than defy the nganga directly, Makufa had ordered a dozen followers to kill the missionary, while he himself attacked the spirit house and the mission. Later, he would tell Nashu that hotheads had run amok.

As his warriors crept through the sleeping village, Makufa knew that he could not rely upon their silence any longer. It would raise their spirits if they could sing and make a noise. Great courage was needed to attack people who were protected by powerful fetishes. On entering the lane where the white man lived, Makufa ran out in front of his warriors and raised an accusing finger.

"Mfiti," he growled, pointing at the missionary's house. And again he uttered the terrible word meaning witch: "Mfiti."

A long hiss of execration arose, and the members of the surrounding circle spat several times over their left shoulders. Now they were ready.

Clara had first stirred shortly before dawn as a wedge of pale light was thrusting itself under the bedroom door. She was eager to make one last appeal to Robert on Herida's behalf; but since he had been tossing and turning for most of the night with a raging toothache, she knew she would have to wait. His renewed groans suggested that oil of cloves and brandy had finally failed him. He had been suffering for weeks, delaying in case the abscess healed. The tooth in question was a front one, and Clara had been surprised to hear that he had struggled to save it in case its loss made her think him ugly.

The worsening pain sent him stumbling out into the storeroom where he kept his box of tools. He returned with some nippers, like those employed by cobblers to pull out brads from the soles of workmen's boots. She took them from him and said a silent prayer as he lay down on the bed and braced his head against the backboard. His gum was discolored and swollen, and she feared that the doomed tooth could not be shifted without her jarring its neighbors. To get more light, Clara unpinned the calico in the window and lit a lamp.

She tightened the nippers on his tooth, but he roared so loud that she let the tool fall from her hand. He yelled, "Pull, woman! Don't stop, for the love of God."

Before trying again, Clara was aware of shouts outside. With a knee jammed hard against her husband's ribs and her left hand clamped on his brow, she squeezed and wrenched with all her strength. Eyes starting from his head, he flung out an arm and caught her in the stomach. Falling, Clara kept her grip on the tooth, and a pistol seemed to detonate in her hand. She lifted the lamp and peered into his mouth. The tooth had splintered, leaving half its root behind.

Robert groaned as blood leaked from his damaged gum. Again she was aware of unfamiliar sounds coming from the lane, a strange hissing or spitting, as if angry geese were being driven past. But her need to stop his pain as quickly as possible prevented her from looking out. She forced back his head and was thankful to find enough tooth sticking above the gum to give her a purchase. This time she yanked from side to side, making no attempt to spare him, risking all on haste. His jaws champed on the metal, but she did not stop. At last a fierce rotation of the wrist met with no resistance, and her hand flew up.

Tears stood in Robert's eyes as she exhibited the stump. She was trembling too much to trust her legs. Her nightdress was liberally splashed with blood. And as she stood towering over her husband like an avenging spirit, she did not see the awestruck black faces at the window. Nor did she register the witnesses' terror as they dropped to the ground and made their escape.

A lopsided smile parted her husband's lips. "Bless you, my angel. Bless you."

Just then they heard a loud roar, apparently coming from the village. Simon entered without knocking.

"They attack the mission, master," he gasped. "Many men. You must come."

As the boy ran out again, Robert sprang up from the bed and started to pull on his trousers. Clara stared at him in horror. "Are you crazy, Robert? You'll only be killed."

He did not answer, but prayed for a moment and then picked up his shoes and ran barefoot into the lane.

Before opening the school each morning, Paul went to the mission to help Philemon with his minor jobs. Today he had been asked to burn ticks off the mission's few surviving sheep. The poor creatures looked like diseased puffballs, with their dusty, matted coats. Paul hated the way they struggled to escape his hot iron and was sickened by the unpleasant smell of burning wool; but he never complained. As the light grew brighter, he thanked God for another day. When he had first learned about heaven, he had wondered what held it up there in the sky. Surely it must rest upon a pole like the center post of a hut.

Because the sheep were penned at the back of the mission, Paul saw nothing when Makufa burst through the boundary fence at the head of a gang armed with spears and knobkerries, but he heard the angry roar and ran inside to help block up the doors and windows.

Old Philemon had also heard the yelling. Telling himself that

Christ had never shown fear, he walked out onto the veranda, closely followed by Mabo. As she limped up beside him, he ordered her to go back in. Makufa's men were surging across the deserted vegetable garden, raising a great cloud of dust. They were shaking their weapons and chanting so fiercely that for a moment Philemon's courage failed him. To his amazement, the crippled Mabo lurched forward, gesticulating wildly at the advancing rabble.

"Jesus, Jesus, come quick!" she screamed.

"Keep quiet," begged Philemon.

"I not afraid. Jesus goin' punish these pagans." She darted forward with her usual uneven gait: one shoulder dipping down level with her waist and then, with her next step, jerking up again. "Jesus has stopped your rain. Wait and see what he'll do next. He'll burn you all."

For a moment the advancing men wavered, astonished to see this ungainly figure defying them. Philemon took advantage of the respite to shout, "Go away from here. Do not desecrate the home of God's children."

An eerie silence followed, then the chanting started again, much louder than before. A thin, wiry man ran forward, brandishing a long spear. His mouth gaped open and his eyes squinted upward as if he had been smoking dagga. He took long strides, and arched his back to cast his weapon. It rose high in the air. Philemon dragged Mabo toward him. The spear thudded into the earth and vibrated where she had been standing.

Bundling Mabo in front of him, Philemon hurried back into the mission and bolted the doors. He and Paul barricaded the window with a table and ran on through the mission building and out through the kitchen, taking Chizuva and Herida with them, hoping to hide them in the grain store. Philemon called out to the boys Serame and Matiyo to run into the bush. Herida argued with him, angrily insisting that Makufa was her father's friend and could not intend to harm her.

"He thinks you betrayed your father by coming here," cried Philemon, seizing her arm. But she pulled away and ran out. Chizuva and several other women went to the grain loft, to hide behind the sacks and baskets, but Herida was not among them.

Philemon ran back into the house and cannoned into Paul, who was dragging Simon along with him. The boy was holding a gun.

"Little fool," snapped Philemon. "They'll kill you if you fire at them."

"They'll kill us anyway," screeched Simon.

"Then face your Maker without blood on your hands." Philemon wrenched the gun away from him and sent the boy after the others, who were already streaming past the cattle kraal. Philemon shouted, "Think of master's grief if you're hurt."

A splintering crash resounded through the building as the long-room table was flung away from the window. Paul and Philemon stood frozen. A scream seared the air behind them. Paul spun around. Herida was struggling in the arms of two men. Philemon jerked the gun barrel in their direction but turned so rapidly that he fell over his own feet. The discharge of the gun in the confined space stunned him. He was choking on powder smoke and could see nothing. Someone was moaning.

Paul watched little dolphins of blood leaping up from a hole beside his navel. He knew he was making a strange sound but could not stop it. He called out, "Master, help me!" but it was only Philemon who bent over him. "Master is coming," he soothed, kneeling beside the wounded teacher. Tears were flowing from the old man's eyes. "In Christ we are made new again," he sobbed.

A warrior with black ostrich feathers on his head burst into the passageway from the kitchen. Makufa was carrying a knobkerrie and a spear. The unexpected sight of the two traitors on their knees amazed him. They would try to enchant him as the white man had done in his spirit house. Best kill them before they could.

As he leapt forward, Philemon tried to shield his dying friend with his body. "Christ forgive you," he croaked. Makufa avoided Philemon's eyes as he raised his club. The old wizard might still try some magical trick. Philemon's last sight before the club struck the base of his skull was of Makufa's strong white teeth and shining skin.

Robert knew the chapel was on fire long before he reached it. As he came up to the burning building, he did not stop to look. The plume of smoke drew his eyes skyward. Rain clouds were gathering. Running toward the mission, he prayed that no storm would break; not yet; not even to save the chapel. Rain was to have been God's reward for Mponda's conversion. The continuing lack of it was his punishment for delaying.

The gate loomed ahead, and Robert darted through it. At least the building itself looked unharmed, but the absence of any people was sinister. In the compound, a vulture hopped a few yards and scrambled into the air. A body was spread-eagled on the veranda. Robert heard footsteps and turned. Clara was not far behind him.

"Go back," he shouted, touched but dismayed at her rashness.

On the veranda, Robert gaped in horror. Paul's stomach had been ripped open and his eyes gouged out. The missionary flung himself on the ground and howled. As Clara recognized the body, she also screamed. Paul could have gone away with Bullock. Could have been safe and prosperous all his life. Through a fog of grief, she recalled her lessons with him, the night they had been to the dancing, how gullible and kind he had been.

Please God not a massacre, moaned Robert, staggering to his feet. The long room was deserted. In the storerooms, he stumbled over someone on the floor. It was Chizuva, not dead but cradling Philemon's head in her lap. He had been brutally beaten but was still breathing. Robert heard someone vomiting on the veranda. Clara, he guessed, feeling sick himself.

"Where is Herida?" he gasped, shaking Chizuva.

"Makufa took her."

"Was she alive?"

"Yes."

"Where are my poor boys?" He stared at her beseechingly. "Where is Simon?"

"Matiyo and Simon are hiding in the bush. Mabo and the others too."

Robert bowed his head and wept with relief over Simon. He wrapped Philemon in a blanket and made sure he was no longer losing blood. Then he covered Paul's body. Ants were already swarming into the dead youth's mouth and nostrils.

The sky grew darker as rain began to spit. Gusts of wind agitated banana fronds and dried grasses. Robert yelled at the sky. "No, rain. Not yet. Please God." His words vanished on the strengthening breeze. Clara clutched his hand.

"I must see Mponda," he told her.

"You'll leave me alone here?"

"Makufa won't be back."

"How do you know?" she shrieked. "Don't baptize Mponda. I beg you. Herida must remain his wife. Don't—"

But already he was running toward the gate. "Go back," he roared. "Go back."

When Robert returned from the chief's crag later that day, he was transformed. There had been a brief shower, and he was wet and dirty, but his face was radiant. Clara guessed at once that Mponda had agreed to be baptized. Nothing else could explain how the haunted man of three hours earlier had been replaced by one serenely sure of himself. She thought of Herida and wanted to weep. Nashu would never forgive Robert or Mponda for the insult about to be done to his daughter. Makufa would try to oust his father afterward. But when Clara said all this, Robert shook his head vehemently. "These murders would never have happened if Mponda had accepted Christ six months ago."

"Oh, Robert," she wailed, "they happened because people feared he *would* convert."

"Once the thing is done, they'll have no further use for intimidation."

"They'll fight one another instead."

"Nonsense. They'll respect Mponda for getting off the fence. If I don't convert him now, the time may never come. Can God want that?" His face was very close to hers; his eyes were glittering and angry. "The early fathers were imprisoned, spat on as the lowest of the low. But the highest prince of all, the Roman emperor, became their brother in Christ."

Robert dug Paul's grave alone as his final service to his young disciple. He sweated heavily, and another brief rain shower wet him more, but he was too exhausted to change his clothes. Paul's funeral took place at dusk, as bats skimmed above the huts. The theme of Robert's address was: "He did not die in vain." "At last, dear friends," he declaimed, "the chief has decided. Tomorrow he will wash away his sins."

A cheer went up, followed by loud hallelujahs. Never had Simon been more excited. Clara wondered what he expected from the ceremony itself. That God would come down and speak? And yet, as always when the converts sang, she was moved. They had suffered and endured pain and terror, but they had not lost hope.

Above them, the Southern Cross shone brightly. The clouds

had thinned to raglike streamers, and the threat of rain had receded. Robert pointed to the gleaming cruciform pattern of stars.

"Like the cross on Calvary. See how our blessed Savior watches over us." Paul's death, he told them, had convinced the chief that further delay would only incite the enemies of Christ to bloodier acts. "This is our great day."

In the early evening Simon found a club and several spears on the ground outside his master's bedroom window. When Robert was shown these weapons and the marks of many feet, he thanked Christ for saving him and Clara. "Poor pagans, they think their spears scare us."

"Jesus is our rock," agreed Simon with shining eyes.

That night, Clara was awakened by a terrifying dream. Paul came toward her, his face thick with ants. She reached out for Robert, but her hand encountered emptiness. A dim glow came from the next room. Her husband was measuring medicines by lamplight on his small set of scales. He was shivering so much that his teeth chattered. After mixing quinine with water, he added chlorodyne and drank it down.

"Pile up blankets to make me sweat. I'll need plenty of water to drink. It's only fever." She led him back to bed. His skin felt very hot. He held his head in his hands and said, "If I don't baptize him tomorrow, they'll say Nashu stopped me with his spells."

Soon he was dozing, but as she turned away, he began muttering to himself. Clara piled up blankets, aware that Nashu's best chance to stop the baptism would be to kill Robert tonight, while he lay helpless. Moment by moment, she expected spears to thrust aside the calico windows.

As time limped on, her hopes revived a little. If Robert was too weak to baptize the chief in the morning, public faith in him would collapse and Makufa would no longer see him as a threat. An unconverted Mponda would stay wedded to Herida, leaving nothing for Nashu to avenge.

At the base of the lamp by the sick man's bed, a circle of singed moths struggled to resume their quest for death. Robert tossed and turned, as if he too were struggling to keep a fatal tryst. Clara prayed that his strength would fail him.

After one of the incoherent outbursts that punctuated Robert's sleep, Simon came and sat with his master. Clara went into the neighboring room and, against all odds, fell asleep soon after sitting down. She dreamed that Paul was dancing with Makufa, who held a knife behind his back, but Clara could not cry out a warning. When she woke, the cicadas had started their endless shrilling. A knot of fear gripped her stomach. Please God let me find Robert delirious.

But he was propped up in bed, looking pale and emaciated, and would crawl to the khotla, she guessed, if he had to. His sunken eyes burned with resolution. After Simon had shaved him, Robert stood unaided for a moment, then swayed, and would have fallen without the boy's steadying arm. Clara looked away in anguish.

"I'll have to be carried in a chair." His lips formed the ghost of a smile. "They'll think it's part of the ceremony." He lay back and closed his eyes.

Before the chief came to escort Robert to the khotla, a bizarre figure limped up the lane, so heavily bandaged about the head as to be scarcely recognizable. Clara identified Philemon only by his old swallowtail coat. He was hobbling on two sticks and was followed by Mabo, Matiyo, Serame, and all the other mission "children." The women wore white dresses, and the boys and men white shirts. They sat outside on the dusty path and began to sing:

A re binelung Yesu,
Hoba ke eena Moloki.

Sing the praises of Jesus,
He alone is our Savior.

As Robert called out a greeting to his people, Clara's heart opened to him against all logic. She thought him a gambler with the tribe's future, but his faith had never faltered. No danger had diverted him from his purpose. "We are all immortal till our work is done," he liked to say, really speaking of himself.

When Mponda's bodyguards carried Robert onto the khotla, no women were pounding grain or sweeping their yards, no men were making baskets under the trees. Those who had not had the heart to come out and witness their chief's apostasy remained in their huts. According to Philemon, Nashu had put it about that the chief would drink a male child's blood. Those who knew that some magic liquid would be poured on the chief's head were puzzled that he had not shaved off his hair. How would the medicine reach his brain? Wouldn't it run down his temples?

Clara stood close to the mission party, whose members were singing more joyfully than ever. Jesus had exalted the humble and meek. The proud had been cast down. The "dogs" and outcasts had become the chosen ones. While they sang, many old men in the crowd wept with grief.

One white-haired veteran shouted, "We did not steal the teacher's ox or fuck his wife, so why does he hate us? Why does he shit on our customs?" Another cried, "We worshiped Mwari before the white man came. We never asked him to come. Did *we* force our ways on *him*?" These speeches were greeted with sympathetic groans.

Robert sat slumped in his chair, as if too weak to respond. Then very slowly he raised himself. "God, whom you never cease to injure, is merciful even to the worst of His children. He will forgive your sins, if you repent."

"Hallelujah!" shouted Philemon through his mummy-like covering of bandages.

Then Mponda strode into the khotla. Cries of greeting rang out: "Ete, Baba." The chief wore a lion's skin slung across his broad chest and shoulders. His stride was leisurely, and when he halted, he looked around as if inspecting soldiers.

"Ngikubona," he said in his low, rich voice. "I see you." Clara loved this ancient greeting. "My friends," he asked, "will you be converted today? Do you dare run as fast as me?" He smiled. "Or do you want to see what happens first? That's what baboons do. When they find a promising place for food, they push ahead a young one in case there are snares. If the child is caught, they run. If he finds honey, they grab it from him. Will you grab Jesus from me, my friends?" A long moan of dissent greeted his words.

Robert sat swaying in his chair. "You must begin, master," begged Simon, splashing him with water from the baptismal ewer.

Like a boxer who has taken a heavy punch but still wants to fight, Robert staggered to his feet. Neglecting to command the chief to renounce the devil, he gasped hoarsely:

"Peter Zacchaeus Mponda Ngombe, I baptize thee in the name of the Father and the Son and the Holy Spirit, Amen. And I mark you with the sign of the cross. . . ." He scooped a cupful of water onto Mponda's head and traced a cross. "Be not ashamed to confess the faith of Christ.'' Robert tottered, before collapsing onto his chair.

So it was done. The chief had been baptized; and as if to emphasize the dangers now facing Mponda, his bodyguards raised a wall of oxhide shields between his royal person and his grieving subjects. The mission party sang the hymn ''In Christ I'm now a man!'' With nothing else to do, Clara followed the Christians home. Half-naked men with angry faces were pressing in on her. She was kicked and jostled, but she kept walking.

At home, she shed tears of frustration. If Herida was still alive, where was she, and what would happen to her now? How long would Makufa and Nashu hold off before making a second murderous attack?

That evening, Mponda placed armed men outside his missionary's house. Robert was racked by fits of shivering so violent that at times he could scarcely breathe. Again Clara piled blankets on him, and again Simon came to help when she was exhausted. The boy administered a dose of quinine, but Robert had difficulty keeping it down. His face was grayish yellow and his breathing very shallow. Clara knew that if he died, Nashu's magic would be given the credit for a great triumph. Mponda would be ousted, as the creature of a defeated deity, and all the Christians would be driven out or killed.

Robert's next bout of sweating left him weaker than ever. Clara longed to ask Simon if he thought his master was sinking, but her fear of what he might say dissuaded her.

Shortly before midnight, she heard shots and shouting coming from beyond the khotla. She peered out and was relieved to find everything peaceful in the moonlit lane. The chief's guards were smoking together, apparently unconcerned.

Much later, Clara was sleeping in her chair, when Simon touched her on the shoulder. ''The chief is here, mistress.''

She woke up to fear. Mponda stood and watched over Robert for a few minutes and then came into the room where Clara was sitting. His authority seemed to fill the little house.

''Soon we will have rain,'' he announced, rubbing his hands, then sat in the chair that Clara offered. ''I said to Umfundisi long time ago, 'These people will never believe by just talking to them. They will stay pagan unless I use a whip to make them believe!' '' He chuckled at the memory. ''Umfundisi was angry. 'Christians don't thrash people,' he said.'' The chief chuckled again, but almost immediately became solemn. Clara could not fathom him. She was about to ask about Herida, when distant shooting began again.

"Are you safe from your enemies, sir?" she blurted out.

"A chief is always safe."

"Is Herida safe too?" she whispered.

Mponda's face suddenly became grave. "She will marry my brother."

"But she is not in danger now?"

"She is in my kraal." His displeasure was obvious.

Clara longed to question the chief about Herida's feelings toward his brother, but his expression persuaded her instead to ask why he had suddenly decided to be baptized. He looked at her sorrowfully, as if to say: Can a man speak of such things to a woman?

A long silence followed, and Clara had all but given up hope of a reply, when he said, "We Venda have a legend. God commanded the chameleon to save human beings from a bush fire. 'Lead them across the river,' ordered God. But the chameleon was too slow, and the fire burned all the people black. When they reached the river, they found only a few drops of water left. The most selfish people had used it all and become white, so the rest were left with just enough to wash their palms and the soles of their feet."

"What a bitter legend."

"Wait, Mrs. Robert. In the beginning I believed Umfundisi wanted ivory like other white men. When he was kind and did not ask for anything, I guessed he hoped to cheat us more easily later. Then, when he built houses and a dam, I thought: Perhaps he truly likes us. But is he mad? His Jesus story is so strange. Yet he owns wonderful things: a magic lantern, a telescope, a music box. Can anyone be mad who has so much? Would he come all the way from his own country just to tell us lies?" He gazed intently at Clara. "Sometimes he begged me with tears in his eyes to believe him. He said I was like the suspicious dog in our proverb that ran away when a man threw a bone, fearing it was a stone." He fixed an eye on her. "Now I will no longer run. I trust him."

So faith in Robert, rather than faith in Christ, explained his conversion. Clara felt intensely anxious on the chief's behalf. He had split his tribe and gambled everything on Christ's magical protection.

"Were your men shooting earlier this evening?" she asked.

"Some bad men were trying to scare me. Pah! My mother frightens me more." He laughed and then looked sad. "Even to my face, people have said things I used to kill for. One man said, 'I have seen chiefs like you eat grass from the anus of a goat.' He meant: Mponda will lose everything. Another man said, 'A toad does not run in the day unless something's after it.' Meaning Baba Robert had scared me into his church." Mponda lifted his large hands. "I will not harm them for words alone. But for deeds, they will bleed." His clipped enunciation gave his words a biting emphasis. Just as Clara was expecting more anger, he flapped his lionskin cloak like tawny wings. "Chizuva says you can sew with a machine. Will you make me a coat and trousers from this skin?"

She smiled uneasily. A lionskin suit would be as hot and bulky as an Eskimo's clothes. But he was looking at her with such eager anticipation that she felt obliged to say yes. He clapped his hands with delight. The finished clothes, she sensed, would matter less to him than the fact that she had made them.

He looked her up and down. "You are too thin, Mrs. Robert. I will send you some breast of zebra. You will tell me what else you need?"

"Other people need more."

He grinned. "But are they so nice to talk to?" Clara found herself smiling back. She could not help being charmed by the unexpected compliment.

Robert was still sleeping when Mponda rose to leave, but the chief stood by his bed for a while.

"Our friend will be better soon," he whispered, ruffling Simon's hair.

Passing through the sitting room on his way out, Mponda pointed to various items, mentioning with pride that he possessed a set of teacups and a Staffordshire jug shaped like the Duke of Wellington's head.

It came to Clara only after he had gone that this man, with his few pieces of china, also owned several thousand head of cattle, a large cache of ivory, and the mineral rights to a wide territory. All this he had put at risk for Robert's sake.

In the morning Philemon hobbled over from the mission to warn Clara against leaving the house. Mponda was confronting his enemies on the khotla. What Clara ought to do if matters went badly was not discussed. The old man looked at her sadly from under his wreath of bandages.

"Will you take Paul's place in the school now, Nkosikaas?"

"I don't know yet. I'm sorry, Philemon."

He sniffed sadly, as if he had expected this answer, and then tottered away toward the mission.

At midday, Herida burst in on Clara. Her eyes were streaming. Her father was being humiliated on the khotla and had been forced to confess his fraudulence.

"He never lies or cheats," cried Herida in a choking voice. She spoke so fast that Clara could understand only isolated sentences. "The spirits chose him as an nganga. He could not refuse. . . . Please, my missus, you will save his life?"

With Robert too ill to help, did she have any choice but to try? Clara was followed into the lane by Simon, who caught at her dress. "Don't go, Mrs. Robert. Nashu deserves to die."

But Clara had made up her mind. Herida had lost her baby and her husband. She must not suffer the loss of her father too. On the khotla, the crowd was so thick that Clara was soon separated from Herida. As she pushed forward, people moved aside, afraid of her. The heat was unendurable, and the crowd clustered most thickly under the few acacias that dotted the open space.

Mponda sat beneath the tall kachere tree in the middle. In a semicircle behind him stood men with guns. At first Clara was uncertain whether he was their prisoner or their commander. But as a man was dragged out from under the shade of the acacias and flung down on the burning earth in front of the chief, it was clear where authority still lay. Two men leapt on the prisoner and tore off his clothes. Stripped naked, he was forced to squat like a toad in the sun. Headmen came out from the throng and abused him, pointing with their fingers, threatening him with whips and spears, before ranging themselves behind the chief's tree. Others came forward, but more reluctantly. Loyalty was being coerced under threat of execution.

As she came closer, Clara recognized the naked man as Makufa, the chief's handsome son. Philemon blamed him for Paul's murder; but though Clara had loved Paul and hated his killer, she felt nauseated as she watched the young man's limbs being stretched out on the burning soil and tied to wooden pegs. She had heard of bound men being covered with black ants. A fire was burning nearby, its flames scarcely visible in the sunlight. Heated blades came to mind. But the chief's attention shifted to another figure pegged out on the ground.

Clara was unsure of this man's identity until she saw beside his body various gourds, bones, and bladders, his magical paraphernalia reduced to pathetic rubbish. The nganga was weighed down by heavy stones on his chest. Mponda strode up to Nashu. The chief had a basket in his hand, from which he tipped horns, teeth, feathers, a necklet of rats' skulls, and a green snake.

"Are these yours?" Mponda thundered.

"You know they are." Nashu's voice was high-pitched and very clear.

Mponda pulled a knife from under his skin kaross. Clara's heart leapt, and she thought she would faint. The chief knelt next to Nashu and raised his knife. The crowd caught its breath. As the blade flashed downward, Clara shut her eyes. Dazed with shame at having done nothing, she forced herself to look again. Expecting to see the nganga jerking in his death throes, she was overjoyed to see him push away the stones. Mponda had used the knife to sever his bonds. He pointed to the nganga's possessions.

"Burn them."

When Nashu hesitated, Mponda nodded to a burly man with a whip, who stepped forward and lashed the nganga across his shoulders. Nashu staggered, stunned by the pain, then bent down as if complying. He picked up the snake and an armful of other things. But when he reached the fire, he looked around as though in a trance. The crowd watched the snake twisting and turning above the fire. People gasped and backed away. A few screamed in panic. The man with the whip lashed Nashu again. The witch doctor tossed the snake aside and threw something else into the flames. The fire exploded. There was pandemonium as smoke billowed across the khotla.

Nashu fled toward the trees, hoping to find safety in the fleeing crowd. But Mponda ran faster. He caught him a few yards from where Clara was standing. She was sure the nganga would be murdered. The chief was followed closely by a handful of his retinue. As they closed in around Nashu, Clara flung herself in front of Mponda and shouted, "Show mercy, great chief!"

Mponda, who was holding Nashu by the throat, looked at her in anger and amazement, then flung Nashu down next to his possessions. "Burn the rest." Clara sensed that the chief was angry with her because he had never meant to do more than humiliate the nganga.

People hid their eyes and backed away as item after item was dropped onto the fire by the nganga: powders, bones, charms, strips of fur and flesh. But though Nashu grimaced and chanted, nothing else occurred to alarm the onlookers.

The nganga cried out in anguish, "Who will care for the ancestors now?"

But the crowd did not rally to him. They were subdued and shaken. Their spiritual leader's magic had failed. The chief's new medicine had triumphed. An altercation was taking place under the kachere tree. Mponda and his men were shouting angrily at each other. While they had been chasing Nashu, Makufa had been spirited away. Mponda grabbed the whip from his henchman and beat Nashu in front of the crowd. Clara lost count of the blows. Only when the nganga screamed for mercy did the chief release him.

A few hours later, it was known throughout the village that the chief had gone in pursuit of his son and that Nashu and an unknown number of headmen had fled into the bush. Clara went to the mission to tell Philemon what she had seen. On finishing her account, Clara asked him, "Will Mponda catch Makufa?"

"Not if he can join up with Nashu. The nganga is too clever for all of us."

"Would you like him to be dragged back and butchered?"

Philemon raised a hand to his bandaged head. "Of course Mponda should have killed him. When Nashu kills Mponda, you will see that too, Nkosikaas."

"Oh, Philemon," she murmured, "what about forgiveness?" Even as she spoke, she thought of Paul's forgiving nature and his trust—not just in Jesus, but in people too. Where had they got him in the end? She had come to ask Philemon what he thought would happen next, but she feared she knew.

CHAPTER 14

obert knew he would soon feel stronger, but at present he still wept over trifles and found the ordinary sounds of village life intolerably strident. Though his illness had been a great trial, in more important matters God's hand had clearly been at work. The great rains had been held in check. Now, when they came, they would be greeted as a divine reward for Mponda's baptism.

Without going to the window, Robert could imagine the pale, burned-out blue of the sky darkening to gray and purple along the horizon. Neither bird nor lizard moved. A silence charged with latent energy hung over the village. Soft rumbles of thunder muttered across the plain. Within days, the rains would be lashing down.

One afternoon, Robert walked with Clara as far as the base of Mponda's crag. He had not intended to go beyond the well, but there was a light breeze; and with Clara at his side, he felt able to strike out farther than usual. Rounding the shoulder of the spur that led to the crag, they saw an almond tree in full flower—an exquisite drift of pale pink against the dusty bush. How African trees could burst into spring flower under a scorching sun after six months without water was a mystery that filled Robert with joy. Some women walked by, bearing on their heads long trusses of grass for the new chapel's roof. They were singing.

"Just listen to them," he said. "They know the best is to come."

Far away across the scrub, a bush fire was winking, no brighter than a burning cigar. Clara could imagine the savage heat at its center and the stampeding wildebeest and impala. Somewhere out there too, Nashu and Makufa would be planning their return.

That afternoon, Robert and Clara rested together in the house. Clara lay on their bed and tried to read a novel—a society romance by Mrs. Braddon called *The Lady's Mile*. Why did these fictional men and women care so much about social distinctions? Was a gentleman in a silk top hat less bizarre than a tribesman with feathers on his head? Suddenly she saw the story of Jesus as if through Venda eyes. A white boy, born, in a stable, of a human mother but no father except God, had taken away all the evil in the world by allowing himself to be nailed to a piece of wood.

As his wife closed her book and lay staring up at the dirty thatch, Robert felt a great welling of love. How marvelously kind she had been when he was ill. For the first time since his illness, he wanted to make love to her. Tiny beads of moisture along her hairline and on her upper lip in no way discouraged him. The heat was a shared privation, just as the divine reward for their steadiness would be a shared joy. When the rains broke and the people saw that God had repaid their chief's faith with a blessing on the earth, Clara would recognize her suffering as a necessary part of God's plan.

Seeing the attentive, tender expression on her husband's face, Clara closed her eyes. The thought of sexual intercourse in this terrible heat held scant attraction—all the less when she thought of poor Herida. When Robert reached out a hand to her breast, she said, "What's the chief's brother like—the one Herida must live with?" The hand withdrew.

"He's called Moeti. I don't know him."

"Will she have to share his bed?"

"Of course."

"That's horrible if she doesn't love him. Imagine it, Robert."

"It happens all the time with arranged marriages. But that's all coming to an end now. Mponda's baptism spells the end of treating women like things."

The rebuke in her hazel-flecked eyes hurt him. She asked unexpectedly, "Remember that dreadful man Bullock? What were the rumors he taunted you with?"

Robert felt as though he had been punched. He said, "Ruth fell in love with Bullock's predecessor, a man who was nothing like him . . . younger, kinder. She may have been trying to join him when she ran off."

Clara was speechless for a moment. "You didn't say a word about this when we talked about her."

He was sweating freely. "Some things are best forgotten."

"I don't agree. It would have comforted me a lot to know she didn't mean to die."

"I felt too humiliated to be honest with you." He waited for another humbling blow, but her expression softened.

"What happened to the man?" she asked, almost kindly.

"He was recalled by the Colonial Office, and Bullock took his place. He'd been his deputy."

When she murmured, "Poor Robert," he sensed he had grown smaller in her eyes.

He went to the kitchen and returned with a glass of brandy, which to Clara's amazement he drained in a couple of swallows. "Perhaps I shouldn't have married again," he muttered, searching her face anxiously for a hint of denial. "I didn't mean to fall in love with you. But when you explained to me about your mother's death, I couldn't help myself. I thought: I can actually do something for this lovely girl. She longs to regain her faith. Perhaps I can restore it to her."

Clara's cheeks were flushed with anger. "You married me to save me?"

"No, no. I worshiped you . . . almost blasphemously. I wanted you with me all the time. It wasn't only selfishness. Your life was empty—you said that yourself. You hungered for a purpose. I believed the simple life here would bring you back to God."

"Oh, Robert, Robert," she cried, "what on earth does that mean? Perhaps I only wanted to have my mother back again—not my faith at all."

He sighed heavily. "Hasn't Mponda's conversion made *any* difference to you?"

"It's made me frightened for him. The rebels won't give up."

Clara thought of Countess Nina and her husband. She had failed to tell them about the rifles or about any of her fears. Until Paul's murder had thrust reality in her face, she had denied common sense and even ordinary notions of duty to others. If she could only reach the two of them and tell them everything, they would be able to protect themselves. But the count and countess might as well be on the moon, for all her chances of reaching them.

Later that week, on an oppressive afternoon, indigo clouds piled up on the horizon, while lightning flickered fitfully. Clara had observed similar formations many times before and had come to see them as examples of nature's playfulness rather than real auguries of rain. As she walked into the village, Herida was being dragged between the huts by a brutal-looking man, who struck her repeatedly. Clara shouted at him, and he spun around, momentarily releasing his grip. Herida fled. Pursuit did not occur to her persecutor, who was big and clumsy.

The sky was closing down like a black ceiling as Clara hurried after her friend. A shattering detonation reverberated across the heavens. A sigh of wind heralded a distant hissing sound. While Clara followed Herida toward the mission, a splatter of isolated raindrops rapidly became a thick curtain of water. Clara was soaked within moments. Joyful children splashed in and out of puddles between the huts. The air felt miraculously cool.

Clara approached the veranda as two women burst from the house. They were locked together, hands grasping for advantage, wrenching and scratching at each other. On the edge of the veranda, they tripped and fell into the mud. One of the women wore a long, opulent garment that had become split across the back, while the other, who seemed to have been dressed more scantily to start with, was naked. This other was Herida. Mission "children" ran out. People from the village pushed through the fence to watch. There were gasps of amazement as they identified the combatants. Queen Chizuva held the advantage for a moment before Herida rolled on top of her, bare bottom uppermost. She brought her thighs down on each side of Chizuva's torso, straddled her, and then plastered handfuls of mud into her eyes and mouth.

"Steal my husband," she yelled.

"Insult the queen?" choked Chizuva, arching her back and managing to grab Herida's hair. Then she dragged her down and bit deeply into her shoulder. Herida screamed, and the crowd cheered.

Philemon hobbled forward and tried to get between the women, ending up on his rear for his pains.

"Ladies, ladies—are you mad?"

"She stole my husband," cried Herida.

"He's *mine!*" shrieked Chizuva.

Both women's faces were torn and bleeding. Herida was trying to cover her nakedness with a filthy scrap of cloth.

"Do not bring shame on yourselves," pleaded Philemon, horribly embarrassed. He tried to grasp Herida's arm, but she pulled away.

"My new man uses me like a baboon," sobbed Herida. "In and out of me twenty times a day."

"Silence!" implored the old preacher.

Having said her piece, the nganga's daughter limped away

toward the gate. Clara pursued her through the rain, her feet slipping on the greasy layer of thin mud that covered the entire path. She walked beside Herida for a while before reaching out a hand.

"Are you angry with me, Mrs. Robert?"

"No."

Herida surprised her with a tearful smile. "I had to hit her."

In answer, Clara squeezed her hand. They were very close to the house now.

Robert knelt down in his pitch-dark kitchen and thanked God for the rain. Mponda would be the hero of the hour. Even Clara would see the change. The missionary lit a lamp and crossed to the stove. The sound of the rain hitting the thatch was extraordinarily loud. He used up half a candle in lighting the fire, so much water was coming down the chimney.

When Clara returned, her green dress was clinging to her body and her face glistened. She stood in the doorway emptying her shoes, and Robert's throat tightened; she looked sleek and sinuously lovely in her soaking dress. As Robert moved toward her, smiling tenderly, Herida stepped into the room. His mouth hung open. She was stark naked and covered with mud.

"What are you doing here, child?" Robert's voice was breathless with reproof.

Clara said firmly, "She can't go back to that brute."

"Moeti is the chief's brother."

"I don't care who he is. I saw him hit her."

Rain was dripping through the thatch onto the dung floor, liberating a farmyard smell. Robert fetched a towel and wrapped it around Herida to make her decent. "Why did he hit you?"

"Because I ran away. He touches me all the time—my breasts, under my apron. I feel sore from him."

"I'm sure he'll tire of you as soon as he's more familiar."

"For God's sake, Robert," cried Clara. "She doesn't love him, and he wants her body all the time."

He let out a long sigh. "I'll talk to Mponda. Of course I will."

"She stays here till then," said Clara. Meanwhile Herida stood in front of the stove as if in heaven. Later, Clara bandaged her shoulder and sat with her.

Across the room, Simon was ironing sheets. The smell of the warm linen and the spicy tang of a relish he had made from caterpillars and herbs created an atmosphere of ordered homeliness. Outside in the lane, frogs were croaking loudly—snoring, as Simon aptly described the noise.

Herida stayed in the house that night and the next. When her new husband had first beaten her, she had run into the bush and slept there among the "things of the night." Since these included spirits as well as wild beasts, Clara realized how truly wretched Herida must have felt.

"You were mad to take such risks," she whispered.

Herida's lids drooped. "My love hurts me badly. I fitted so well with Mponda; he was not too heavy for me, nor too light, and our bloods sang. Moeti crushes my life out every time he gets on me. Why am I treated like this?" Great tears formed in her eyes.

Clara could think of no reason why such a graceful, loving person should receive anything but respect. Yet Robert said that Herida's marriage to Moeti had been according to tribal rites and she ought not to have deserted him. They were on their way to bed, and Robert's tone was almost pleading.

"Please don't think I'm not sorry for her. But if pagans start to jettison traditional obligations, they'll take concubines instead of wives. We mustn't undermine their tribal rules until Christian morality is widespread. Think what will be said if we encourage her to desert Moeti."

He had spoken so gently that Clara did not stop him when he ran his hands over her breasts. What could she ever suffer at his hands in comparison with Herida's daily ordeals?

A few days later, there was a break in the rains, and the sun shone. The yard was a muddy morass, alive with frogs and millipedes. Birds twittered in every thorn tree and swooped down upon the hosts of insects emerging from the earth. Now that new grass was growing, the oxen had been driven in from the cattle posts. Robert and Clara savored the astonishingly pungent smell of the damp earth as they walked into the fields to watch the men driving their teams, with their wives behind, guiding the plows. In less than a week, blackened shambas and dusty hillsides had become as green as English fields. In dusty places, where nothing had flourished before, children were collecting mushrooms.

"We thank Thee, O Lord, for bringing new life and hope to our world," declaimed Robert, with uplifted palms.

The villagers were building shelters close to their gardens, and many would remain there until harvest time, hoeing weeds and scaring away birds and beasts. The pale smoke of cooking fires rose in slow blue columns. Close to the path, an old woman was digging holes with a tiny hoe and sowing maize seed picked from a few precious cobs.

Yet the scene did not bring Clara happiness, for she was thinking of Herida's tulip-petal skin suffering at the hands of her grotesque man—a suffering that would begin again if she went "home."

That evening, when Robert was leaving the mission, he was confronted by the lumbering bulk of Moeti, with a rhino whip in his hand. Robert sprang away, but Moeti caught him on the back of the calves, inflicting three raised welts. Even before this assault, Robert had wanted Herida to leave his house. Now he was determined that she should do so soon. Whenever he went to the mission, Chizuva subjected him to a fierce tirade for allowing her attacker to stay under his roof.

Robert consulted Mponda that Sunday after an open-air service on the khotla. Could the chief, please, speak to Moeti and tell him to treat Herida more kindly? With two other wives, surely he could satisfy his appetites with them for a while and give Herida a rest? To Robert's relief, Mponda was genuinely distressed by Herida's unhappiness. As he bowed his head, Robert could almost feel the weight his broad back was already carrying.

Mponda placed a hand on his friend's shoulder and said sorrowfully, "Umfundisi, I am sorry he hit you. But would you be glad if I told you not to sleep with your wife and took her to my house to live?"

Robert blushed. "If you explained why my attentions displeased her, I would thank you for your advice."

Mponda smiled fondly, like an older, wiser brother. "Moeti is not like you, Umfundisi. Perhaps he will hurt you again. He will go around saying that you won't let men sleep with their wives. Do you want to give him that big stick to beat us? Send Herida back to him. Do it for my sake and for your sake."

"You must give me a few days."

Robert knew he had no choice. The mission would lose many adult pupils if husbands ever gained the impression that their wives, learning there, might never return home. So Herida would have to return to her husband soon. But how could this decision be broken to Clara without his earning her lasting anger?

Despite the rains, no maize would be harvested for several months, and people still came to the mission for food. In the past, Clara had always been upset by this daily trickle of pathetic supplicants, but Herida told her not to be sentimental.

"How do some people manage to make their grain last them through a long drought?" she demanded, putting down the piece of cloth she had been cutting.

"Maybe they had more to start with."

Herida shook her head vehemently. "They eat less and think ahead. Some people even eat their seed corn." She pulled an imbecilic face to illustrate what she thought of such folly.

Clara suspected that Herida might be more sympathetic if she herself had ever encountered such a fate. One afternoon, a long-faced man came to the mission and bowed humbly as he watched Clara unwrapping dried dates.

He opened his eyes very wide. "Dear me! How clever white people are! What a lot they eat. Are these the delicious sweet things I have heard so much about?"

"They are not delicious," Herida announced. "They taste like dung, and we give them to our goats."

When he shuffled away empty-handed, Clara felt dreadful. "So cruel of you! He was only trying to please."

Herida imitated him brilliantly: " 'Dear me! What is that food which clever white people have?' " She laughed loudly. "I hate fawning. Don't you?" And when she came to think of it, Clara had to admit that Herida was right. She *did* dislike the beggars who fawned.

Herida helped Clara in many ways and never stopped telling her interesting facts of a kind that Robert would never have thought it proper to mention, such as how a polygamous husband behaved at night.

"Does he wait till the wife he starts with has gone to sleep before going on to the next?"

"Unless he wants trouble, he waits."

"There's open jealousy between the women?"

"Eeayay! You can't imagine, Mrs. Robert. When Mponda used to leave Chizuva's hut for mine, he first waited for her to sleep. But sometimes she pretended, so when he got up, she grabs him. 'Where are you going?' 'To piss.' When he comes back, later, she pretends to wake up—she never went to sleep. 'Dearest, make love to me. But why does your penis dangle like a baby's? You didn't piss. You screwed Herida.' And she starts wailing."

From Herida, Clara also learned about the male initiation ceremonies. How after the circumcisions all the foreskins were collected and burned, and their ashes mixed with semen and herbs, so the next generation of young men could be anointed. "The semen must be fresh, so two men make it together." Herida said such things in the same matter-of-fact way that she explained rubbing bats' dung into her labia to make them as long as bats' wings. Widows often had other women come and slip their fingers into their vaginas to relieve their frustration. Even wives whose husbands were away at the cattle posts would do the same. Clara tried to imagine such things being mentioned in Sarston. People would faint at the very idea.

Clara no longer found it odd to enjoy being with a young woman who smoked hemp in a small wooden pipe and believed that bats' dung improved her genitals. Herida could spit, very discreetly, an astonishing distance. She had sparkle, charm, and intelligence. And because Herida knew that Clara had begged for her father's life on the khotla, she adored and trusted her. She particularly loved to quiz her about English ladies. Did the grandest ones really do nothing? Couldn't they make a pot or plaster a wall? "Poor things," she said, chuckling. Herida's laughter made Clara lighthearted too. She made up her mind to teach her English and imagined taking her to England on Robert's next furlough. What would Herida make of dressmakers and trams? She would look marvelous in an elegant fitted outfit. But this was a private fantasy she shared with no one.

Every afternoon, currents of warm air boiled up from the land, forming storm clouds, which in due course emptied themselves on the valley with spectacular effect. After such storms, Robert always went to examine his dam, checking that no damage had been done. What he had dreamed about had come to pass: a lake had formed, almost a mile long and half a mile wide. Fishermen were scrabbling about in the shallows, digging into the earth. Watching them, Robert marveled at God's goodness. The

Almighty had caused fish to burrow into the mud of the drying riverbed, so that now, months later, villagers could dig them out alive when food was needed most. Thank you, Lord.

His eye followed the sweep of a fish eagle's descent. In some elephant grass, no more than a hundred paces away, Robert's astonished gaze fell upon a Matabele warrior. His stillness was so extraordinary that it was several seconds before Robert grasped what he was seeing. He too kept as still as he knew how. The man had apparently gone down to the water to drink and was leaving now. He wore a traditional black headring and carried a short assegai. Robert could not have been more shocked if he had seen Ruth's ghost. The Venda usually hid in their rock caves and blocked all the entrances the moment any Matabele were reported within fifty miles of their villages. Something very strange was happening. Since the warrior exhibited no particular wariness, Robert guessed he could not be alone. Should he warn Mponda at once? In his confusion, he hardly knew what he feared more: that Mponda should know that the Matabele were here, or that he should be entirely ignorant of their presence. Robert swung around in alarm. Light footfalls were coming from behind him.

"You must be very proud," said Clara, gazing at the lake.

"We must leave," he whispered.

"Is anything wrong?"

He told her that he had seen an armed warrior in the grass, which was an unusual sight by the dam. He did not mention that the man had been a Matabele. "He may be quite harmless, but we mustn't take risks."

Robert was desperate to see Mponda, although he feared that the chief's first question would be: "Have you sent Herida back to my brother?" Entering the village, Robert took a deep breath and turned to Clara. "Do you know how long Herida expects to stay with us?"

"You mean she must go?" The color fled from Clara's cheeks.

"I'm sure she knows she must return to Moeti sooner or later."

"Why must she? Dear God, Robert! Moeti hit and raped her."

"Dearest, please listen. She's shamed him by running away. He'll behave well now. He's sure to."

"Nonsense," cried Clara. "He'll be angry enough to kill her."

"Not with everyone watching him."

"Herida still loves Mponda. It's not as if she's properly married. A third wife!''

"We're not in England, Clara. Her father's gone. A woman starves here without a husband."

"We could feed her."

"Along with all the other discarded wives of men who become Christians?"

"Yes," she shouted.

"All right," he murmured, frightened by her anger. "If he misbehaves again, we'll look after her. But she must give him one more chance. Mponda insists on it."

When Robert had left for the chief's stronghold, Clara ached with anger. *Why* wouldn't he insist that the chief take Herida away from his brother? Robert had the courage to stand up to anyone. The problem was that he valued Mponda's friendship more than his own wife's wishes.

It was two in the morning, and Clara had lain awake for hours, listening to the rain in the thatch and the ceaseless cacophony of the frogs. Robert had been gone since the late afternoon and had not returned. She told herself he was sure to be safe, for who would dare kill the devil incarnate?

At the same time, Clara could not help hoping that Robert was still absent because he was close to persuading Mponda that Herida had a right to choose her destiny. Just after two o'clock, she went into the yard and watched Herida sleeping calmly in the lean-to room next to the kitchen. At that moment, she believed that if Robert brought back good news she would love him as much as she ever had.

But the minute she saw his figure framed in the black square of the doorway, she knew her hopes had been vain. Unaware of her presence, he rested his forehead against the doorframe and began to sob. Such desolation could have only one cause, she thought. Mponda had abandoned his new faith. For an instant Clara's hopes leapt again. Herida would be taken back by the chief, Nashu and Makufa would be forgiven, the Christians would no longer be seen as the tribe's enemies, and Robert could become a teacher of ordinary things. She lit a lamp and led him like a child to the bed.

"What happened?"

"We must leave." His voice was small and numb.

"Leave?" She could not believe it.

He looked at her despairingly. "The Matabele are killing whites near Bulawayo. The Venda will soon join in. There are Matabele warriors here with Mponda's blessing."

"Will Mponda kill women and children too?" She was too shocked to think of anything else. The folklore about Matabele murders in the '93 rebellion haunted every white in southern Africa.

"How can you think that of him? He'd rather die. But when troops are sent to punish the rebels, he'll fight them."

"Couldn't he stay neutral?"

"He hates the hut tax as much as anyone." Robert bowed his head very low. "It's the end of everything I've worked for. The ngangas are in charge now. Nashu invited the Matabele here. Mponda's a dead man if he doesn't join the rebels."

"No, he isn't," she cried. "If he takes back Herida as his wife, Nashu will forgive him."

"You'd ask Mponda to deny Christ?" Robert stared at her with absolute incomprehension.

After a silence, she said quietly, "In these circumstances, yes." His eyes filled with tears, but he did not speak. She said gently, "When do we leave?"

"A week or two. Mponda's taken a great risk in warning us."

"Can we take Herida with us?"

His gaze was pitying. "Remove her from her own people for life?"

"Just for the present."

"We won't come back. Haven't you understood that, Clara? Herida's place is with her own tribe, not in some white town."

Tears were running down Clara's cheeks. She tried to think how she might protect Herida, but nothing occurred to her.

Two days later, soon after dawn, there was a commotion in the yard.

Robert sprang out of bed and ran out, with Clara following. Herida was being dragged away by two men.

"Don't hurt her," yelled Robert.

Herida's confusion was painful to see. "Must I go with them?" she asked several times, looking to Clara as if begging for some contradiction. But all Clara could think to do was kiss her. Like Judas, she thought. She slipped a garnet ring off her own finger and pressed it into Herida's hand. Seconds later, Herida was led out into the lane. Clara followed for a few yards but then could bear no more and ran back into the house.

Later that week, Robert learned from one of the boys at the mission that Herida had once again run away from her husband. He said nothing to Clara but hurried up the steep path to Mponda's kraal to question Moeti and the chief. He learned nothing more than that Herida had left two nights earlier and had not been seen since. The bush had been searched around the village, but the rains had washed away Herida's tracks. Whether her father had returned for her or she had attempted to travel on her own was unknown. Robert could not even establish whether she had taken food and clothing with her. It was clear to him that Mponda had many things on his mind and was deeply unhappy.

At the chief's kraal, Robert saw many more Matabele. When he inquired how many of these strangers had arrived, the chief refused to say. His manner was so brusque that Robert did not ask again. But before he left, he did manage to take Mponda aside for a moment.

"My friend, let us pray together."

Mponda shook his head, not angrily but with great sadness. "There is a stone where my heart should be. I cannot think of Jesus."

The following morning, several hours before dawn, Robert was awakened by someone calling his name very softly. Clara stirred but did not open her eyes. Outside, Robert found Mponda, waiting alone close to the wall of the house. The missionary took the chief around to the kitchen door. In the blue darkness, Robert could see Mponda's head like a bronze sculpture, the scoop of his eye sockets and wide cheekbones just discernible.

The chief touched Robert's hand. "There is a plot to kill you, Umfundisi. You must go without delay. Makufa has returned."

Robert's hand shook as he lit a candle with a spill from the stove. As he placed the light on the kitchen table, he saw that the chief's face was wet with tears. "Mponda," he said, "do you really think Makufa would kill me?"

"Not while I am with you, but, my friend, I leave very soon." He reached in the pocket of his old black coat and produced a crumpled photograph. Robert held it up to the candle. Three black men had been hanged from the branches of a tall tree. Their heads and necks were twisted at odd angles; their feet were tied together at the ankles. A dozen or so white settlers were looking on. Most wore slouch hats and smoked cigars. They struck deliberately negligent poses. "They put a noose around their necks and order them to climb up and tie their own ropes to a high branch. Then they shoot at them with buckshot till they can bear no more and jump."

"How can men be so evil?" groaned Robert.

"We should look in our own hearts too, Umfundisi. I have terrible news." Mponda held out a ring, which Robert recognized as one of Clara's.

"Where did you find it?"

Mponda's mouth puckered. "On Herida's hand." He covered his face and said brokenly, "She killed herself with a knife."

Robert murmured, "Will you pray with me . . . for her?"

Mponda shook his head. "We killed her." He dropped the ring on the table, and as he did, Robert heard someone behind him.

Clara was gazing at him. "You sent her away." Her words were quiet but fiercely accusing.

Mponda said, "*I* told him she must return to Moeti."

Clara picked up her ring and handed it to Mponda. "It was my gift. Bury it with her."

Clara wept for a long time after Mponda had gone. She thought of Herida's vivacity, her smiles and her courage, how bewitching she had been. And *I* let her go. I recognized her misery and did not cling to her when the men came. Despair washed through Clara like a great river, in which she wished to drown.

CHAPTER   15

Now that the rains had come, people were busy in their gardens outside the village, hoeing down the weeds and heaping earth about the roots of the growing maize. They drank beer in the fields and danced in the evening to celebrate the return of the cows from the cattle posts.

Several days after learning about Herida's death, Robert and Philemon were sitting on the rocks above the well, listening to the gurgle of water as the women filled their jars.

When Robert asked Philemon whether he thought everyone at the mission should leave at once for Belingwe, the old man shook his head. "What could we eat in a strange place? We have planted our maize. How could we harvest it if we go?"

"But should the young ones come away with me?"

Again the grizzled head moved in dissent. "They would be in greater danger among the miners at Belingwe. The Matabele will only murder whites and the blacks who serve them."

Robert was distraught. If the friendship of white people was going to endanger Africans, ought he to take Simon with him? The thought of leaving the boy behind caused a physical pain in his chest.

Philemon said in his soft, rasping voice, "When you are gone, master, they will think we are helpless. Why should they hurt us then?"

"Who can read evil minds, Philemon? What good did it do them to kill Paul?"

"That is true, master. But if Mponda lives, he will protect us on his return. Far from here, who will care if we live or die?" Sunlight speckled his deeply lined face. "And tell me this, master: if we go away, how will you find us again?"

"My dear friend," said Robert, linking arms with him. "While *you* are here, Christ will be here too."

As Robert entered the mission with Philemon, he no longer felt a traitor. To take these people away with him would be as dangerous as to leave them here. When everyone had lined up to say a personal farewell, Robert saw them through a blur of tears. Matiyo gave him a Christian cross made of new leaves, woven cleverly together, Serame had cooked him some sweet maize cakes, Mabo had sewn a flannel shirt, and Dau had decorated a calabash. Clara arrived as three children from the school presented a posy of wildflowers. A small group of invalids whom Robert had treated arrived with a fish from the lake.

A more poignant leave-taking took place early the next day, just before dawn. After handing over his first copybook and his best drawings of animals, Simon clung to Robert for almost half an hour before agreeing to release him. Clara could not endure the sound of his sobbing and went outside. Robert was more than a father to the boy, having been benefactor, friend, and teacher. But at last, after much muted talk, Simon mastered his grief sufficiently to face the inevitable.

As dawn broke, Mponda and most of the men in the village were also preparing to set out. They would go north, while Robert would head east. The stars were still glowing, and light from many lanterns shone palely through the canopies of the chief's wagons. His men all carried spears and axes, and their bodies were daubed with white clay. Their voices rose and fell in harmony as Mponda prepared to brave the future. Clara was sorry she had not had time to make the lionskin suit he wanted. Instead she gave him a silk scarf. Robert's gift was a small leather-bound New Testament— proof that he would teach Mponda English when peaceful times returned. The chief's memento for Clara was a necklace of leopards' claws, and for Robert, an ivory cane. The two men embraced before Mponda climbed onto the box of his wagon. "You must go soon, Umfundisi," he warned.

When Mponda touched the leading oxen with his whip, Robert cried, "God bless you, my chief."

He stood alone, gazing into the blue-gray bush for a long time after the wagons had rumbled off. The singing had become very faint when he finally turned. Out of loyalty to his friend, Robert had made a point of not asking where he meant to go. By remaining ignorant of such things, he could never betray Mponda if soldiers came.

Soon after the chief's departure, the Haslams clattered across the khotla in their Cape cart. Clara, though sad, was relieved to be leaving a place where she had lost many illusions. Their first objective was to warn the French count and his wife at Mungora. Like Clara, Robert felt guilty to have said nothing to them about the rumors of rebellion. If anything had happened to these settlers, their blood would be on his conscience.

Along with food and water, Robert and Clara took spades, ropes, and sand in case they became bogged down. In this light vehicle, drawn by a pair of mules, they expected to travel in the morning and to rest during the afternoon storms. Yet from the first day, mud sucked at the mules' hooves and adhered so thickly to the wheels that they had to be scraped every few yards; and after showers the ground became so sloppy with unabsorbed water that the cart slithered on the slightest slope.

The world was astonishingly greener than the parched terra-cotta landscape of a month before. The mopane trees had put out tender pinkish-blue shoots, and extraordinary aloes displayed spikes of waxy red. Even the huge gouty baobab trees, with their broad distended trunks and spindly branches, had struggled into leaf.

By midday, clouds began to throw dark shapes over the land. Choosing their moment and moving fast, Robert and Clara could often pitch their tent and find the mules some cover before the first rain came whipping down. Despite the discomfort of their low and leaking tent, Robert wanted to make love on their first night. Clara pleaded exhaustion. In fact, Herida's death had bled away all her sexual feelings for him. She thought: If I could only believe that Robert's work offered something positive to the Venda, I might still be able to forgive his betrayal of Herida. Even his best qualities had become warped for her—his determination seeming to be obduracy and his courage fanaticism.

At night, their campfire was meant to keep wild animals at bay, but Clara feared it would attract humans. In this flat and almost treeless country, an enemy would find it child's play to follow them by day and strike by night. But Robert still trusted in God's protection. Because he sympathized with African anger, he could not imagine it directed against him. African custom decreed that land could never be sold, but only be loaned. Yet whole tribes to the south and west had become squatters on their own land. Since the new "owners" were settlers whose farms had been "granted" to them by the British Chartered Company, Robert thought it natural and inevitable that the Matabele and the Venda should have decided to fight.

In the evenings, when the rain stopped, Robert lit a fire with dry kindling from the cart. He boiled water to make maize porridge and shot guinea-fowl to roast. They slept in their clothes, and when a lion roared or a jackal yelped, Clara was conscious of being separated from the savage world by only a width of canvas. Shadows cast by the firelight made her half expect to see the silhouette of a man. Their female mule was in heat and had to be tethered apart from the male, whose braying disturbed their nights.

On the third day, they reached a swollen river and took several hours to find a drift where the water was shallow. The river ran along a valley between hills with crumbling sides, like cake cut with a blunt knife. A track followed the stream's course, and they passed along it between thorn scrub matted with bur grasses. The possibility of ambush made Clara beg Robert to load a gun. Although she had little confidence in her marksmanship, it comforted her to have the weapon on her knee.

The following morning, in open country, she thought she saw a family of warthogs through the shimmering haze. As the cart came closer, the hogs looked more like impala and then like no animal at all. Doves were cooing gently in the heat. Clara began to shiver. Twenty or thirty people were approaching. She lifted the gun.

"Just country people," Robert told her, placing a restraining hand on her gun.

"Why are there no women among them?"

"I expect they've been hunting."

Clara longed to believe him. The sun glinted on the tips of spears and flashed on armlets and bits of finery. When she clearly saw the warriors' lean and scarified bodies, she tugged hard at Robert's arm. She recognized Nashu and again struggled vainly to release her gun. The nganga's men started to chant and shake their spears. As some ran forward, Nashu raced in front and gestured with his wooden staff to hold them back.

By the time the tribesmen reached the cart, they were walking again; and though they still looked menacing, with their spears and axes, Clara sensed that the danger was over. An hour later, she was still shivering as if she had a fever. Nashu would have spared them only because she had begged Mponda not to kill him. Just chance, blind chance, she thought. If she had arrived on the khotla ten minutes later, her appeal would never have been made and she would be dead beside the cart. She could find the hand of God nowhere.

Their brush with Nashu persuaded Robert to travel in the rain, when no natives cared to move about. As the mules crawled through a slanting downpour and flinched at zigzag lightning, Robert said that the Venda thought lightning was a bird with a tail like a cock's.

"A woman recently told me she saw this bird. It landed in a puddle and then ran up her hoe and scratched her." He smiled at Clara. "As a domestic fowl, the greatest forces of nature can seem manageable."

Until you destroy their beliefs, she thought. If death could be held at bay by charms, and a strong enemy defeated with the help of his own nail clippings, even a weakling might brave life's perils.

As they came closer to Mungora, Clara looked forward to sleeping under a watertight roof and being warmed by a fire that did not smoke. There would be mosquito nets, chairs, lights in the evening, even edible meals. Some years earlier, Robert had visited a mine in this region, and now he recognized the massive escarpment to the east. It was crowned with great piles of granite, like a giant's toy bricks. They passed a burned-out pump house and a mine shaft with the windlass smashed. Whether the miners had fled or been murdered, there was no means of knowing.

The next morning, Robert struggled up into the branches of a fig tree and saw what he took to be the count's farmhouse, apparently unharmed, at the base of an ironstone ridge. Not long afterward, they came across an outhouse, burned to the ground. The fire had been extinguished by rain, so its age was hard to judge, but Robert reckoned from the bulk of the ashes that it had been alight a day or two earlier. It came to him at once that the fire could have been used as a threat to drive the occupants from the house for fear of being burned alive.

Some vultures flapped away on their great sooty wings. The birds had been feasting on two tribesmen who had been shot dead and still lay with their shields and spears beside them. The smell was vile. Cartridges were scattered in front of the house. By the door was a large pool of dried blood. Inside, trails of blood were everywhere: on the floor and on the walls, even splashed on the window glass. Robert shouted, "Anyone here?" but his words died in the empty rooms. He followed a thicker trail of gore into the next room, where chairs and tables had been overturned. The place was littered with empty bottles, half-eaten tins, and ransacked boxes. Some rooms were half finished, with only a few floorboards laid across the joists. Clara thought of the high hopes the couple would have had when they started to build. A smashed sewing machine lay on the floor of the kitchen and, near it, a little silver gun that Clara remembered well.

She ran outside, where Robert found her in tears. High in the trees, plantain-eaters were screeching.

"Can we go?" she implored.

"I have to find them."

Robert stumbled upon two male servants at the back of the house. They had been sliced open and their intestines strewn around. A cloud of flies led his eye to a rocky slope. He forced himself to walk toward it. The count's body lay pitched backward across a rock. His face and forehead had been blown away by his own gun. He must have fought till his last few cartridges. Three Africans lay a dozen yards away, so badly decomposed and gnawed by wild beasts that Robert abandoned any thought of burying them.

A vulture, alighting in a misasa tree, drew him to an area of flattened elephant grass. And there she lay. Nina had been killed by a spear, which was still lodged in her back. She rested on her front, her fair curls looking as they had done when she was alive. He could not see her face and was glad. Her eyes and lips would have been eaten by termites. Butterflies clustered like flowers on a blackened arm. Several fingers had been severed to facilitate the theft of her rings. A sob formed in his throat as he recalled her lighthearted boasts. He hoped that her husband had died before knowing her fate.

After reciting prayers from the burial service, he collected the couple's personal papers for their next of kin. An episode that had seemed to last hours had actually been over in less than ten minutes.

"We killed them by saying nothing," choked Clara.

Robert did not answer. What could he say? It was very likely true. He knew there was no point now in going to Belingwe. The miners would have been murdered too. As for trying to survive in the bush, or attempting to travel directly to Bulawayo, both courses would be fatal. Their only realistic option was to return to Mponda's kraal. At least they had friends there. And even if Mponda did not return for many months, the fact of his former support for the mission might still afford a measure of protection.

In the swaying cart, Clara wept herself to sleep. She dreamed she was a child, breakfasting in the nursery after her mother had dressed her. As always, her mother's presence was soothing. Later, she was in chapel, breathing in the reassuring smell of horsehair hassocks and polished wood while the preacher droned. But when she woke, she was cold and wet, and knew that she was going to die horribly. Rain was dripping from the cart's leather hood in streams, while the bush spread drably all around as far as the eye could see.

PART THREE

CHAPTER   16

When Simon saw two columns of white men riding toward the village, he ran home joyfully to put on a clean shirt and his khaki short trousers. Although they were not like the men in tall fur hats he had seen in one of his master's books, he knew they were soldiers because they had guns. Some wore dark-blue tunics with flaps of braid across their chests; the rest were clad in earth-colored jackets and wide-brimmed hats.

As he raced home, Simon was angry to see women and children running from their huts in terror. It was insulting and silly. Why would these white men want to hurt them? Had master ever tried to do that? It was true that the fat bwana and his policemen could be brutal, but they did not kill people—as Nashu and Makufa had tried to do to him.

Simon observed the soldiers from behind some mongongo bushes, and an hour slipped by while he watched them putting up their tents in straight lines and stacking their weapons in mysterious pointed piles. Everything intrigued him. Why, for instance, when their horses were taken off to graze, were three or four men always sent along to guard them? They must surely know that there were no warriors in the village. Perhaps they had heard that enemies were approaching from somewhere else?

The white men owned two big guns, which had each been drawn by six oxen. Several smaller guns had been pulled by mules, and these were being taken to the corners of the camp and placed in shallow pits. Men were cutting down thornbushes and placing them like walls around the tents. Simon felt sad that these men had not come before his master's departure. Perhaps they might still find and protect him.

Simon was wondering whether to seek out the soldiers' leader, when he heard behind him what he took to be a snake slithering in the bushes. As he turned, a large hand clamped over his mouth and another lifted him into the air. He tried to bite and kick, but the hand tightened so hard that he let himself go limp as a matter of self-preservation. The man was very black and smelled of fish. A Makalaka. Simon felt faint with humiliation. A stinking dog was carrying him off just as he was about to gain the help of the white men.

Captain Francis Vaughan ended his inspection of the sick-horse lines. Red-billed tickbirds were feeding on the animals' backs, and he gave the troopers in charge a dressing-down for poor grooming, but his heart was not in it. Over and over again his eyes returned to the path that led from the village to the dam. He was haunted by his memory of the missionary's young wife vanishing into the night beside a white-haired old native. Unless she was soon walking toward him up that path, he would have to assume the worst.

It was less than an hour since he had sent Fynn and six men to the mission to collect Mrs. Haslam and her husband—too soon to draw firm conclusions, but in his heart Francis already sensed that they were dead. To end up a mutilated corpse was a rough punishment for nothing more sinful than a little ignorance. Francis screwed up his vivid blue eyes. With good news to report, Fynn would have sent a man back to him at once.

Francis was ashamed to recall it now, but when he had first heard about the rebellion in Mashonaland, he had been overjoyed. His ivory hunting with Fynn had netted less money than he had hoped, and he had been on the point of arranging a transfer from the 9th Hussars to a cheaper, Indian regiment. Now, on active service, he would enjoy higher pay and better chances for promotion. He was lucky that the 9th had been the only regiment of imperial cavalry in Natal. His first action after receiving confirmation of the posting had been to telegraph Heywood Fynn, hoping to grab the American for the regiment. He had done even better, securing him as a scout for his own squadron.

On his return to the tented camp, Francis saw Fynn and his men trotting back through the people's maize gardens. There was no sign of Haslam and his wife. Instead a tall black man and a large woman were walking close to Fynn's horse—doubtless they would soon be giving him a revolting account of the couple's murder.

As they reached the picket line, Francis recognized the gangling fellow as the elderly preacher who had come to greet Clara Haslam those months ago. "Get on with it," he wanted to shout. The old man was limping along steadily as if he had all day, which he probably did.

"Where are the Haslams?" roared Francis as Fynn dismounted.

"The old guy speaks English."

"They are gone to Mungora," volunteered Philemon.

Francis eyed him closely. "Did they say when they'd be back here?"

"Maybe they will go south and not come here again."

Fynn sucked in his cheeks. "They sure won't like what they see in Belingwe."

Francis moved closer to Philemon. "If they do choose to return here, when will they be back?"

"Mungora is six days' journey. Already they are gone nine."

"So they could be here in three or four days?"

"It is possible."

Francis was relieved that they were apparently alive, but disappointed not to be able to take them with him. Now they would probably be tracked down and killed somewhere else.

"Three days, four days," grunted Fynn. "With niggers, that could mean any damn thing."

Francis slapped him on the back. "Come on, Fynn. How many kaffirs have you met like this one?" He indicated Philemon's patched frock coat and uneven chalk-striped trousers.

"If he looked like the goddamn Pope, Vaughan, we still couldn't wait."

"We can spare three days," snapped Francis, immediately irritated with himself for speaking of future plans in public. He glanced at the woman.

"Who is she?"

"Mponda's queen."

Francis frowned. "Is that a joke? I suppose she's told you where her husband is?"

"I haven't whipped her yet." Fynn grinned through his beard and raised a hand. "Now, that is a joke."

The old African's head bobbed up and down excitably. "She's a Christian woman, sir. She knows nothing."

Francis muttered to Fynn, "What do *you* think she knows?"

The American shrugged. "Maybe he's got a dozen wives. Some he talks to, some he don't. I'll talk some more to her."

"Well, do it now." Francis smiled at Philemon. "You can go home, old man."

As Fynn walked away with Chizuva, Francis wished he were less dependent on the American—and not just for his linguistic skills. Though Francis had engaged native "friendlies" as trackers, none had ever rivaled Fynn in drawing accurate deductions from different types of evidence. The American's present hunch was that Mponda had left here three weeks earlier and would soon join forces with Mucheri, chief of the land around Belingwe. Mucheri had burned Belingwe and killed all the prospectors, with some men vanishing as if they had never existed—tossed down mine shafts and blown to bits with dynamite. In the hotel room where Fynn and Francis first met Clara, they had found twenty charred bodies, male and female, roped together and burned alive.

Francis was returning from an inspection of the outposts when Fynn came up and told him he had let the queen go. "The old guy was right; she knows nothing." Fynn's gray eyes searched Francis's. "Reckon you'd want to stay on here to save an *ugly* woman?"

Francis felt his cheeks burn. "We're talking about her husband too," he insisted.

Fynn pulled a long face. "I just hope those savages don't reach Charter before we do."

Francis was not impressed by this elephantine hint that he would be endangering white lives if he stayed on here for a few more days. There would be delays later, regardless of how long they stayed here.

Francis said affably, "You know what's wrong with you, Fynn?"

"I don't always agree with you?"

"You let your prejudices warp your judgment."

"The hell I do."

"You hate missionaries."

"What of it?"

"It's stopped you using your brain. We can't afford not to wait for Haslam."

"He'll pray for us?"

"He'll know where the chief's gone."

"Chiefs don't trust missionaries," snorted Fynn, shaking his mane of grizzled hair.

"You're too cynical. The old chap said the queen's a Christian. Why shouldn't the chief be one too?"

Fynn blew strands of beard away from his mouth. "Yeah, but what does being a Christian mean to a chief?"

"You tell me."

"That Haslam gave him a shotgun and two hundred cartridges."

"Pure prejudice," said Francis coolly, starting to walk toward the mess tent. But Fynn's barbed remark about Clara had stuck in his flesh. If she really had been ugly, *would* he have found so many reasons for staying on? As a boy the chivalrous tales of Froissart and Malory had been his bedtime reading. Even now he was susceptible to damsels in distress, especially the haunting dark-haired kind favored by Dante Gabriel Rossetti.

Soon after his capture, Simon was blindfolded and forced to walk for a whole day with only a little water and some sorghum stems to chew. As he was dragged along by a leather halter, which chafed his neck, he stopped himself from crying by thinking of Christ's crown of thorns and the spear in his side. His feet were cut by sharp stones, but he was scarcely aware of it. He knew this plain well from his days as a herdboy, and once or twice he heard a flute and tried to pause; but always he was dragged onward. Although the sun's heat on his skin gave him an idea of the direction in which he was being taken, when the blindfold was finally removed he did not know where he was.

Fires had recently been lit. Crude, misshapen grass huts, like those built by Bushmen, were ranged around the opening of a cave at the base of a rocky hill. The men squatting by the fires were either Venda or their Makalaka servants. An ominous figure wearing a grass skirt and a leopardskin cap emerged from the cave. Fearing that his death was close, Simon closed his eyes and said the Lord's Prayer. When he opened them, he saw Nashu's face, framed by twists of greasy hair that fell like lizards' tails to his shoulders. The nganga folded his arms and gazed at Simon with unblinking eyes before indicating to the boy that he should squat. Expecting an ax-blow at the base of his skull, Simon prayed again.

"I want to talk with the leader of the white soldiers." The strange high-pitched voice continued: "You will help me, Ganda."

"Help you?" faltered Simon.

"You know his tongue. You must tell him I know where he can find Mponda."

"If you tell me, I can tell him." Though dazed with relief, Simon was shaking.

"Fool! How can I trust you?" He lashed Simon across the cheek with his giraffe-tail whisk. "Your master loves Mponda. I must tell the white man myself."

"Then why did your dog drag me here?"

"You must bring me something from the white man, something to show he will not harm me. A paper with his God's words on it. A ring of yellow metal or some other fetish. Deceive me, and I will kill your master."

"My master is here?" cried Simon thankfully. Again he felt the lash of the giraffe tail.

"Silence. Nobody questions Nashu."

At dawn, Simon, again blindfolded, was led away by the same Makalaka.

During the second day at Mponda's kraal, the camp was hit by an unusually heavy storm. The latrines flooded, and no amount of sand taken to the horse lines and spread there made them any less slippery. Francis was sitting under an umbrella in his sodden tent, writing up his staff diary, when his orderly, Corporal Winter, brought in a bedraggled boy and a large, very black native who had been spotted near the outposts. The boy was wearing a shirt and khaki trousers. Francis was about to shout for Musa, his translator, when the boy spoke to him in English. Francis was soon listening to Simon's account of his capture and release.

Nobody said a word until Corporal Winter blurted out, "Think it's some kind of trick, sir?"

Francis said sharply to Simon, "You say this man is an nganga. Then why does he want to betray his own chief's hiding place?"

"Nashu hates him. His daughter was one of the chief's rejected wives. She killed herself."

"The witch doctor wants revenge?"

"Yes, sah."

He frowned at Simon. "How can I be sure you're not in league with him and trying to lead me into a trap?"

"Nashu tried to kill me. Master will tell you."

"I look forward to it," remarked Francis dryly. As Simon started to cry, Francis noticed cuts on the boy's neck and cheeks. He said gently, "I've decided to trust you. You will be given a watch and the Queen's photograph for your nganga. You and your friend must have something to eat. Take them to the cookhouse, corporal."

Francis flicked at the air with his riding crop and laughed to himself. When would be the best time to tell Fynn? Perhaps when he next started to moan about being delayed here. "While you've been fooling about with your tracks and footprints, I've found out where the chief is hiding." Fynn's face would be a treat.

CHAPTER 17

As the light grew brighter, Clara saw Mponda's crag and could not help being moved by the familiar landmark. Since the rains, the hard and barren plain with its rash of anthills had vanished under a sea of green, gashed here and there by the dark earth of freshly dug gardens. The water in the dam shone like silver.

A trumpet sounded from beyond the maize gardens: a tripping flow of notes that sang in her ears. Could it really mean what she imagined? A great bubble of emotion swelled within her. As they came down from the ridge and saw the neat rows of tents, she wept. They were going to live. Surely they were going to live.

When they reached their house, Simon was nowhere to be seen. Robert ran to the mission and returned soon afterward with the news that the boy had been missing for three days. Philemon had last seen him on the morning when the soldiers had ridden in.

Though she, too, was worried about Simon, relief outweighed all Clara's other emotions. Now they would be able to leave with the soldiers and never have to endure long and terrifying weeks awaiting the arrival of their murderers. She went into the bedroom, meaning to put on some dry, clean clothes, but instead she lay down to savor her deliverance in peace and solitude. With no need to anticipate danger, her senses were blissfully at rest. As soon as Simon could be found, she would ask him to fetch water. She was imagining stepping into the hipbath, when she fell asleep.

Robert hurried through the village, which was strangely quiet and empty. By this hour in the morning, the boys would have gone to pasture with the cattle, but since no women were pounding maize and sifting meal, he feared that the soldiers had already misbehaved. The rapes and shootings in '93 had left him hating all troops, whether volunteers or regulars, and the possibility that Simon might have been hurt or detained by such men enraged him.

The soldiers had cut down every tree and shrub within three hundred yards of their camp—an act of vandalism that was presumably intended to deny cover to attackers—and a breach had been made in the southern side of the dam, to create a drinking stream for the cavalry horses. That the troopers were draining off precious water, which would otherwise have been available to the villagers during the dry season, shocked Robert, since they could easily have fetched water in buckets. When he stumbled upon two soldiers on lookout duty, his anger over Simon's disappearance made him tremble. On demanding to be taken to the men's commander, he was led to a tent guarded by a sentry. As he came closer, the flap was raised from within, and a young officer with fair, unruly hair came bounding out.

"Are you in command here?" asked the missionary doubtfully.

"Indeed I am," said Francis, smiling broadly as he retreated a few steps to lift the flap. "Do come in, Mr. Haslam. My name's Vaughan . . . Captain Vaughan." He indicated a case of claret for Robert to sit on, while he perched himself on an upended ammunition box.

Robert studied his handsome host suspiciously. "Did my houseboy come to your camp, Captain?"

"He did."

The young man's brisk tone grated on Robert. "Told you my name, did he? Where is he now?"

"Running an errand."

"I'll wait for him, then."

Vaughan pulled a face. "I'm afraid he won't be back till tomorrow."

"You've sent him into the bush?" Robert was dumbfounded.

"He'll tell you about it in the morning."

"I want to know now."

"It's better he should tell you himself," insisted Francis, ignoring his visitor's agitation. "You must come and dine with me tomorrow . . . you and Mrs. Haslam. Mr. Fynn and I brought your wife up here from Belingwe. Perhaps she mentioned it?"

"Yes, but the only name that stuck was that trader fellow's. He used to sell liquor here."

"Not anymore. He's in charge of my scouts now."

Robert frowned. "Why have you come to Mponda's kraal, Captain?"

"To take you and Mrs. Haslam to safety."

Robert was confused by the man's friendly manner. "I can't believe you only want to rescue whites. What are your orders, sir?"

"To end the rebellion and capture its leaders." Vaughan smiled self-deprecatingly. "Not on my own, you understand. General Carrington has three thousand men at his disposal."

"How can you tell who's a rebel and who isn't?"

"We keep our eyes open. Some rebels are good enough to introduce themselves ... by attacking us."

"With spears?" inquired Robert coldly. "I suppose you punish them with your Maxim guns?"

Vaughan's eyes were mildly reproachful. "Spears are no joke in woodland, Mr. Haslam. In fact, they have guns too. The native police went over to them with seven hundred rifles. We're often shot at."

"Don't tell me you're surprised."

"Of course I'm not." That easy smile again, as if, thought Robert, the man was amused by him. "They hate our guts." Vaughan rose and held out a formal hand. "Shall we say seven o'clock tomorrow evening? You and Mrs. Haslam?"

On reaching home, Robert was dismayed by Clara's eagerness to hear about the soldiers. Her cheeks were flushed and she was breathless as she ran up to him, for all the world like a young girl longing for the diversion of a military parade.

"So how many of them are there, Robert?"

"I didn't ask," he replied flatly.

"Did you talk to anyone in particular?"

He looked at her sadly. "Don't you want to know about Simon?"

"He's fine. You'd be mad with grief if he weren't." She clapped her hands like a child. "*Now,* who did you talk to?"

"Young chap called Vaughan. Says he brought you up here from Belingwe."

Her shriek of joy astounded Robert. He might have just told her that the rebellion was over and Mponda was coming home. She seemed to understand his confusion, for she took his hand and said gently, "It's just wonderful luck for us that it's him."

Robert shrugged. "He seemed a typical cavalry officer to me."

"Are most of them kind and considerate, Robert? Well, Captain Vaughan is. He may even ask your advice."

"I fear he has a less delightful associate. An American trader who sold brandy to the Venda."

"Heywood Fynn?"

"The very one."

Clara laughed cheerfully. "Poor old Fynn. He only *seems* rough and insensitive. Oh, Robert, he was awfully good to me."

Robert laid a hand on each of her shoulders. "Understand this, Clara: Vaughan has orders to put down the rebellion. That means he'll shoot people and burn villages."

"Of course he won't. He'll stop the murders."

"I'm telling you, Clara, Vaughan and his cronies will kill thousands. Revenge is ugly. I've seen it before."

"You're wrong about him," she insisted with finality.

He let his hands slip from her shoulders. "He's asked us to dine with him tomorrow."

"Splendid! You'll be able to judge how wrong you are."

Robert lowered his eyes. "My dear, I mean to send a note of refusal."

"But why?"

"Because," he replied gravely, "any man who joins the army knows he may be ordered to butcher patriots."

Clara felt dazed. Robert *couldn't* be turning his back on their only chance of survival. She said urgently, "We have to leave with Captain Vaughan. Surely we must, Robert."

"We don't at all."

"But if we stay, what happens to us?" She was too shocked to feel anger.

He said in his most reasonable voice, "These soldiers will attract enemies from miles around—thousands of warriors. They'll be wiped out."

"How many men would it take to kill the two of us here?" she cried.

He seemed astonished by the question. "We're Mponda's friends. Who would want to kill us?"

"Mponda's enemies, of course. One man with a spear—that's all it would take."

After a silence, he murmured, "All right. We'll dine with Vaughan and his officers. But don't think I'll leave here with them."

Looking at the confident scarecrow facing her, Clara felt pity as well as anger. Robert would probably talk down to Francis without any awareness of covert smiles and stifled laughter from the other officers. Clara's eagerness to meet them was replaced by an equally vehement disinclination.

When Simon came home early the following morning, wearing a hussar busby and a pair of overlarge riding boots, Robert embraced him tearfully. He looked no worse for his walk through the bush, except for some grazes around his neck. After Robert's initial relief was over, he scolded the boy fiercely, telling him he should never have gone anywhere near Captain Vaughan and his men. Surely he knew that soldiers killed people and led immoral lives. Simon then told him about his abduction and Nashu's determination to betray Mponda. Robert was disgusted by the nganga's treachery and scandalized to learn that Simon had arranged a meeting between Nashu and Vaughan.

He looked at the boy reproachfully. "How did Nashu persuade you?"

Simon became tearful. "He said he would kill you, master, if I didn't take his message to the soldiers."

Simon's unhappy face made Robert repeat to himself, "May he who is without guilt cast the first stone." He should have explained to the boy why Mponda had joined the rebels and why no black person ought ever to betray him. But in the past he had found it too painful to talk about the deceptions practiced by Cecil Rhodes on Lobenguela and other chiefs. And now that the murders had started, Robert felt he could not speak of earlier crimes by the whites without seeming to be excusing black atrocities. I should have spoken out strongly years ago. Instead I preached the vanity of earthly possessions to Africans witnessing the theft of their country.

"You must never wear a soldier's uniform," said Robert, lifting the busby from the boy's head.

"The soldiers are my friends, master."

Simon's innocence touched Robert. He said very gently, "They sent you through the bush. Would friends do that?"

"But, master, I have told you. Nashu said he would kill you if I did not go back to him. The soldiers didn't make me go. I wanted to."

"Has Nashu already told the soldiers' leader where Mponda is?"

"He will tell him soon."

Robert bowed his head. "We must pray for you, my poor misguided boy."

Obediently, Simon knelt beside his master. He tried to concentrate on praying, but he could not tear his eyes away from his beautiful soldier's hat. If only he could reach out and take it.

Two days after the missionary's return, Heywood Fynn was stunned to spot the nganga, leaving Francis Vaughan's tent soon after dawn. The sentry had been perfectly placed to see Nashu, and yet he did nothing, so Fynn knew that the visit had been sanctioned. Because, in the past, Francis had kept nothing from him, it was painful to realize that he was no longer confided in.

Since the American mistrusted Nashu, Francis's behavior alarmed him. A year earlier, Fynn had himself been a victim of the nganga's genius for extortion. Whenever Nashu had advised Mponda not to deal with a particular trader, the chief had invariably acted on his advice. Fynn had therefore paid Nashu with brandy and tobacco to guarantee his neutrality, but by doing so, he inadvertently led Haslam to think he was selling cheap liquor to the tribe. The missionary denounced him to Mponda, who promptly refused to trade with him. When Fynn asked Nashu to tell Mponda what had really happened, the nganga had denied all knowledge and had burned one of his wagons to punish him for speaking out of turn.

Later in the day, seeing Nashu and his henchmen drinking porter from several leather fire buckets, Fynn stalked away and on an angry impulse snatched some potassium from one of the squadron's veterinary chests. He unsheathed his knife and cut this lump into several pieces, before approaching Nashu and his cronies with an exaggerated show of deference.

"Greetings, Master of the Owls," he simpered, bowing low. "I owe you thanks. When you burned my wagon, you gave me the gift of fire."

There were mutterings of anger and incredulity.

"You have the gift of fire?" growled Nashu. "Why tell lies to grown men?"

"Lies?" Fynn tugged at his beard, as if greatly surprised. "The Lightning Bird sits in my hand when I set fire to water."

"The Lightning Bird cannot belong to living man," gasped the nganga, amazed at this blasphemy. "Not even Mwari makes water burn."

"You reckon I can't do it?"

Fynn waited for their jeers to subside, looking from man to man. Their disbelief lasted until the moment when he flung the potassium into the beer bucket closest to Nashu. A violet flash lit the whole circle of faces, and the surface of the beer hissed and seethed as if bewitched. Nashu recoiled in terror.

Fynn bowed respectfully to the witch doctor. "Thank you for the gift of fire, Great Lion." Francis would have a real job to patch things up with the little troublemaker now.

An hour before she and Robert were due to leave for the soldiers' camp, Clara was agitated by her memories of Francis Vaughan's kindness. While Fynn had made no secret of his dislike for missionaries and his doubts for her safety, Francis had simply tried to bolster her confidence. Most people, he had said, would act like her and start a new life if they only had the guts.

What should she wear for the evening? She could not put on faded cotton and act the devoted missionary wife, nodding agreement with Robert's every word. Despite the murders at Mungora, he was counting on her to stay behind with him when the soldiers left. But she needn't. She could go away with the hussars if she wanted, and he would be powerless to stop her.

Should she beautify herself for her meeting with these cavalrymen? She had a sudden vision of herself standing in the midst of rustling tissue paper and thrilling to the whisper of taffeta and tulle as she held up an evening gown from Ince's. The bodice would be cut low, her breasts supported enticingly. Just two years, and already her bosom had become smaller and her features more pronounced. Tears shone in her eyes, but she did not give way to them. Instead she chose a favorite wasp-waisted bodice, worn on the steamship passage. Why not wear the dress tonight, since it fitted to perfection? Yet she hesitated. They might think her a dissatisfied wife, eager to attract the first white men to cross her path in this godforsaken spot. She tossed the bodice aside and chose a nondescript dress in gray velvet.

The more Clara thought about meeting Francis again, the

more clearly she remembered their shared journey and her misgivings on approaching Mponda's kraal. It embarrassed her to imagine what Francis had thought then, and what he must think now, having met Robert.

They sat on camp stools and boxes on either side of a trestle table lit by two gasogene lamps: seven young men, none older than thirty, and most exuding a superiority that Clara disliked. There was no dazzling white tablecloth in the mess tent, only bare boards, and although Clara had expected scarlet mess jackets, everyone wore blue undress uniforms—everyone, that is, except Fynn, who sported his usual worn buckskins. Though the roast bustard was tough, they ate off china plates and drank claret in wineglasses. When big beetles began to clatter on the lamps' globes, troopers fixed up muslin nets across the tent's entrance.

Francis Vaughan presided benignly at the head of the table. Impregnable within his armor of patrician good manners, he chatted affably to his officers about nothing in particular. He had greeted Clara in the same easy style, like a casual acquaintance at home. She wondered what this African tragedy meant to him and guessed it signified very little. Yet there was something so disarming about his smiling lips under his straw-colored mustache that she could not think him cynical. He rarely looked at her, but when he did, his cornflower-blue eyes were kindly rather than prying.

Fynn's gaze was sharper. "Will you tell us this, Mrs. Haslam: Did you ever talk that chief into divorcin' his wives?" The American resumed stripping a bone with his teeth.

"Why not ask me, Mr. Fynn?" interrupted Robert.

The American chewed energetically, pleased to have the attention of everyone at the table. "It's like this, see: Mrs. Haslam and me, we had ourselves a disputation 'bout chiefs and their wives when we was travelin' up here."

"What did Mrs. Haslam say?" asked Robert, curiosity getting the better of irritation.

Fynn grinned at him. "She said chiefs had to quit assin' around and put their extra wives out to grass if they wanted to be Christian folk."

Robert looked pained, and Clara supposed it had upset him to be reminded that she had come to Africa parroting his views. The tension eased around the table when Francis gave Robert a friendly smile.

"Well, *did* you convert the chief, Mr. Haslam?"

"I did, sir."

"Then aren't you surprised he's joined the rebels?"

"Not in the least. He wants to free his country from foreign intruders."

Francis lowered his voice. "Did you warn him he would be defeated?"

Robert burst out, "He's prepared to die for his country."

"Is he also prepared to murder a few hundred women and children before he does?"

"He's a Christian, sir."

"Christians!" sneered Fynn. "Haven't they stained the earth red for centuries in the name of Jesus?"

Clara held her breath as Robert leaned across the table. "That's really quite something coming from you, Fynn. No more wars in America, so you come here to fight. No matter for whom. You'd work for the devil himself if he paid you."

Francis took an unhurried sip of wine. "Actually, Mr. Haslam, he's working for me at the moment."

There was an explosion of mirth from the officers. Robert went very red.

"No, sir, he's *not* working for you," contradicted Robert, raising his voice above the laughter. "Mr. Rhodes's company pays the War Office for your regiment to be here, and you pay Mr. Fynn from that money."

Francis put down his glass, and for the first time affability vanished. "You can't possibly speak from knowledge, Mr. Haslam."

"It's how things were done in '93," insisted Robert, turning on Fynn again. "Answer me this: Is Mr. Rhodes a swindler or is he not?"

Fynn's eyes narrowed. "You'd better believe he's not."

"Why had I better believe it?" mocked Robert. "I happen to know that Mr. Rhodes had Chief Lobenguela's permission to dig a few holes, *not* to occupy his whole country."

Without warning, Fynn crashed a fist down on the table, making every glass and plate jump. "Lobenguela signed an agreement," he thundered. "That ol' savage took guns and money from the chartered company in exchange for granting concessions."

"He didn't understand what he signed." Robert gazed straight at Fynn. "The man who says he did is a damned liar."

Clara's cheeks were burning. With his powerful build, Fynn could flatten Robert if he chose. But before the American could react, a red-haired officer, sitting to Francis's right, remarked sharply, "The niggers may love you, sir, but they don't love us. Visit our wounded sometime."

Clara sensed the emotional bond among the hussars and their common hatred of Robert's arguments. As if oblivious to the anger he had aroused, Robert remarked calmly, "Of course I'm sorry for your wounded, but they shouldn't have come here in the first place. None of you should."

"Soldiers don't choose their postings," said Francis mildly.

Robert looked at him with pity. "How can you bear to surrender your moral sovereignty to others?"

An officer with a badly sunburned face said, "We trust our leaders."

Robert shook his head sadly. "Christ is the only leader to trust."

As angry glances began to be aimed at Clara too, Francis smiled at her with such friendliness that she could have wept. He asked, "Do *you* think so badly of us, Mrs. Haslam?"

"I . . . I'm glad you're here," she croaked. "We found two settlers murdered at Mungora. We might have died on our way there."

"We're all very glad you didn't," soothed Francis. "You mustn't think us butchers, Mr. Haslam. We admire many of these people."

Robert nodded sagely. "Might one ask how this admiration expresses itself?"

Francis stared ahead of him. "I can't claim we've been handing out presents." There was a wistfulness about him, which Clara liked. "Just a little incident. Nothing remarkable, mind. I was spying out the land among some rocks near a stream, when there was a rattle of trinkets and the grass suddenly parted. A glistening Matabele warrior was standing with his back to me, only yards away. He had those cows'-tail plumes on his knees and carried a great oxhide shield. He was so still he might have been cast in bronze. I could hardly breathe. Took me an age to raise my revolver, but at last I had it pointed at his head. Pure luck I was downwind, or he'd have smelled me. Anyway, he dropped his weapons and knelt down to drink. As I touched the trigger, I saw it all in my mind: his body pitching forward, blood swirling in the water. I decided not to shoot him till he stopped drinking. God, how that man drank! Great sucking mouthfuls, as if he'd never stop.'' Francis looked around the table, reliving the moment. ''Do you know, I simply couldn't squeeze that trigger, so I let him go.''

Robert said dryly, ''Is it so noteworthy not to kill a helpless man in cold blood?''

''Helpless? These savages?'' stammered the red-haired officer. ''We saw things in Belingwe I can't even tell you. ... I'd have shot him in the guts and roasted him alive if I'd had the same chance.''

''Me too,'' echoed another officer.

''I wouldn't bet on it,'' said Francis. ''If he'd seen me, of course I'd have stopped him telling anyone else. But he saw nothing. He was a man on his own, doing something we all have to do.''

''What of it?'' muttered the sunburned officer.

''Is it really so hard to grasp?'' Clara blushed as Francis gazed straight at her. ''Do *you* think it's hard to understand, Mrs. Haslam?''

''Not at all,'' she stammered. ''A man drinking is just a man. But hiding in the grass, he's an enemy.''

Francis smiled at his brother officers. ''You see, gentlemen? Not so hard after all.'' His eyes sparkled with amusement. ''You know the way leopards move? All that pent-up power, coupled with incredible grace—that's what he made me think of.''

''Lucky for him he wasn't lame or fat,'' commented Robert.

Francis clapped appreciatively. ''You have a sense of humor, sir. I'm sure you'll need it.''

Later, the conversation ranged over such subjects as remedies for snakebite, linguistic misunderstandings, and the African idea of dressmaking. With clothes under discussion, an officer whose lips were disfigured by veld sores asked Clara if she often dressed as smartly as tonight. She could not help looking down her nose, duchess-like. ''My husband and I always dress for dinner.''

Most of the diners laughed, but Clara caught the red-haired lieutenant glancing surreptitiously from Robert to her and back again, as if bemused. And did she detect the same confusion in Francis Vaughan's eyes?

When she and Robert were leaving, Francis came with them

as far as the outposts. Men sprang to attention as he passed. The sky had cleared and the moon was bright. Distant trees and rocks stood out clearly. A trumpet startled Clara.

Robert said grimly to Francis Vaughan, "You're asking for an attack with your fires and trumpets."

"I have scouts out all around us, Mr. Haslam. Some are miles away in the bush."

"That won't stop you being surrounded. Your machine guns won't help you at night."

"They certainly won't." Francis laughed. "But we don't intend to sit around. In fact, we'll be gone within forty-eight hours."

The frogs around the dam lake were croaking in long pulses of merging sound. Robert faced Francis solemnly. "Don't expect us to leave with you, Captain."

Francis moved closer to Clara. His voice was warm and concerned. "Is that what you want, Mrs. Haslam?"

"I don't . . ."

Francis smiled encouragingly. "Your husband's wrong about my column's chances."

"Am I, Vaughan? You wouldn't be the first to be caught with exhausted horses and hunted down."

"Anything's possible," agreed Francis. "Perhaps I'll lure thousands onto my Maxims."

"Is that what you want?"

"Of course not. I want these chiefs to return home without bloodshed." He moved closer to Robert. "Come and help me."

"I can't desert my people."

"I'd hate to hear in a month or two that you're both dead."

Francis's concern struck Clara as so clearly genuine that she was mortified by Robert's refusal to acknowledge it. Away to their right, lanterns were moving among the dark shapes of the horses in the lines. When Robert finally spoke, it was dismissively, "Don't worry about us, young man. We are guided by Him who never fails."

The following morning, Francis was in an ugly mood, having just heard that Nashu had decamped after being humiliated by Fynn in a manner calculated to earn his lasting hatred. The American was cutting a skin into strips for new reins when Francis burst into his tent.

"Don't you realize Nashu could have led us to Mponda's lair?"

Fynn was incredulous. "You'd have followed that little bastard anyplace he led?" He put down his knife. "That's the last thing you should have done. Mponda's no more a Christian than my ass. He's a rebel, same as Nashu. They hatched this plot together. You're lucky as hell I got rid of him."

There had been a heavy shower earlier, and now the sun was beating down on the damp canvas, making it hot and sticky inside. "You should have talked to me before doing anything so bloody stupid," shouted Francis. "Nashu hates Mponda. He blames the chief for his daughter's death."

"What if he does? This is a war between black and white. Nashu's going to fight us first before settling old scores."

"Wrong again, Fynn. Nashu wants to oust Mponda in favor of Makufa. He wanted to use us against the chief. That was fine by me. But you've wrecked it all."

"Jesus Christ, Vaughan. Are you crazy? If you'd kept him with you, every goddamn rebel in Mashonaland would have known where we was headin'."

"We're his special weapon. Would he want us blunted?" Francis could feel sweat dripping down his back. Fynn's know-it-all manner was intolerable. But what could he do about it? Because the American was not in the army, the only disciplinary sanction against him was dismissal, and Francis could not afford to lose his best scout. Fynn sat chewing tobacco stolidly. Francis said, "Will you do something for me? Just make yourself agreeable to Haslam for the next twenty-four hours."

Fynn spat a stream of amber tobacco juice onto the ground. "That ol' mission maggot! He'll betray us too." He grinned at Francis, showing his teeth through his beard. "You want me to be nice to him so he'll bring along that sweet little wife o' his. Am I right?"

"No, you're not," snapped Francis. "Haslam can persuade Mponda not to fight us to the death."

"More likely he'll tell him all our plans. They're pals, Vaughan."

"Haslam's spent ten years of his life making Mponda a Christian. *Ten years.* He'll do anything to see he isn't killed."

The American shrugged. "Christians don't think rational about death."

"But you'll watch your tongue when he's around?"

Fynn laughed cheerlessly. "Don't you worry, Vaughan. I won't do nothin' to stop you feastin' your eyes on that little wife of his."

"To hell with that," muttered Francis, ducking down to leave. "Old man Haslam's the one I want to feast my eyes on."

Outside again in the open air, Francis hardly noticed the pleasantly cooling breeze. Yesterday he had promised Fynn that he would strike camp the following morning, and this left precious little time for working on the missionary. Francis had already decided to ask Clara to help him; if she could only be persuaded to tell Haslam that she wouldn't stay on here, then he would probably agree to leave with her. The thought of being alone with Clara disturbed Francis, especially when he recalled Fynn's knowing remarks. Perhaps he really had allowed his admiration for her to be obvious. But who wouldn't admire a woman who had endured what she had and still been able to joke about dressing for dinner?

Before Francis could set out to find the Haslams, an afternoon storm broke and within minutes the canvas sail erected over the sick-horse lines had collapsed under the weight of water it contained. In the ensuing stampede, several horses were seriously injured, and as Francis arrived on the scene, the veterinary officer was struggling to restrain one of them. Francis helped the vet to strap up the stallion's damaged leg with a stirrup leather, while the terrified creature thrashed and twisted, showing the whites of his eyes. Changing into dry clothes afterward, Francis tried not to feel bitter because he now had to humor a man who was ready to risk his wife's life for no good reason. But a cooperative Haslam could do more to safeguard the squadron than a hundred extra men.

Francis left the camp in watery sunlight and walked into a patchwork of native shambas, where the tassels of the growing maize hung down like pale-green horses' tails. Knowing the missionary would deplore his entering the village with an armed escort, Francis had strapped a Colt repeating carbine to his leg in case any heroic old warrior felt tempted.

Beyond the shambas, a few boys raced after a quail, which whirred up into the air and was struck down by one of their clubs, to the sound of loud applause from some women pounding grain.

A week after first entering the village, Francis still found the absence of all the young men strangely unnerving.

At the mission, Philemon explained that his master was seeing sick people. Across the room, a woman was cracking nuts and an old man was making a basket. Flies buzzed loudly. Francis pushed open a door and revealed a dozen people squatting on the floor. Malaria sufferers shook and shivered, and a young woman hid horribly inflamed eyes behind a filthy cloth. Francis moved closer to Haslam.

"I didn't know you were a doctor, Mr. Haslam."

"I'm not. Anyone can dispense simple remedies. An old coat can save a man with pneumonia."

Haslam laid a hand on Francis's arm and led him to a man who lay motionless on the ground. He pointed to an angry-looking raised weal on the man's thigh. "There's a harrabene worm in his leg. The thing started life as an egg under his toenail. It can't be extracted without surgery. He'll die unless your army surgeon will help him."

"I'll send some men with a stretcher."

"Unless he's cured, some poor innocent will be accused of witchcraft."

The smell was so vile that Francis was thankful to be led into the kitchen, where Simon was chopping vegetables.

"Where's the hat I gave you?" asked Francis.

"Simon's no soldier," said Robert, "but he knows plenty of ways to cook a goat and even makes flying ants taste wonderful."

Francis was expecting this recital of the boy's virtues to continue, when Haslam unexpectedly steered him out onto the veranda. "What can I do for you, Captain?"

"You can help me save Chief Mponda's life."

"Don't be absurd. You're the only man who can do that—by ordering your men home."

"I'd face a court-martial if I did."

"What can *I* possibly do?"

"Convince him that I'll spare him if his followers lay down their arms and return here."

"How can I be sure you won't use me to trick him?"

"You'll have to take my word for it." The missionary's face remained closed and hostile, so Francis appealed again, "If you won't help me, I'll have to storm his stronghold. I'll lose men, maybe a great many; but I'll end up killing him and most of his warriors.''

"Unless *he* kills you and all your soldiers.'' Haslam smiled bleakly. "It's happened before.''

"Believe me, Mr. Haslam, we'll be fine.''

"You think so?'' The older man moved closer, his stubbly chin jutting. "Tell me this, sir. What would be more welcome in the eyes of God? The death of a man defending his country, or the death of a stranger out to rob him?''

Francis studied his boots. "I imagine God would prefer it if neither of them died. If that's what *you* would like, come to my camp at dawn tomorrow.'' Receiving no answer, Francis walked away.

In the schoolroom, Clara was reading aloud. Shortly before Paul had been murdered, she had started *Gulliver's Travels* with the children, and so when several pupils sought her out and begged her to continue, she had agreed. At this uncertain time, she was glad to be occupied, and as always, she was delighted by their questions. Could he *really* have eaten so many cows and pigs and drunk so much milk, even allowing for his size? Would Chief Mponda employ a Gulliver against his enemies if he ever found one?

Being used to frequent whisperings while she read, Clara was surprised by a sudden silence. She looked up from the book and saw Francis Vaughan standing elegantly in the doorway.

He raised his hands in apology. "Please go on. I love to hear you speak the language.''

"You wouldn't if you knew how badly I do it.'' She was afflicted by a strange breathlessness.

The children remained deathly quiet. She noticed Francis's gun and said to them in their own tongue, "Don't be afraid.'' He looked strained, with his mouth bracketed by grim lines.

He asked, "Can I talk to you for a moment?''

"Of course.''

His insouciance of the evening before was gone, and he seemed ill at ease. "Am I right to think you may agree to come away with us?''

"Have you spoken to my husband?''

"He wasn't encouraging." Francis hung his head as if too dejected to continue. A moment later, he brightened. "He said soldiers are wrong to delegate moral responsibility. Surely that means he wants you to make your own decisions?"

"It means nothing of the sort." Clara's vehemence surprised her and left Francis speechless. His presence had robbed her of control and judgment. She wanted to behave normally but couldn't. She said harshly, "Stop being dishonest. You know I'll have a dreadful struggle to persuade him to come away from here."

He flicked a lock of hair from his forehead. "Mrs. Haslam, all I want is to get my men home with as little bloodshed as possible."

She stared at his polished boots and said quietly, "How do you end a rebellion without bloodshed?"

Francis came closer. "If your husband will help me, I'm sure we can save the chief and his men." He lowered his voice. "Anyone can see how much Mr. Haslam loves you. Please get him to come with me."

A wave of disappointment broke over her. So *that* was why he was strained and distraught: not in case *she* chose to stay behind but in case *Robert* did.

"Did he refuse you outright?" she asked.

"Very nearly."

She smiled wanly. "I'm not surprised. Robert sees you as Mr. Rhodes's stooge."

Francis drew back. "This country will be settled come what may. If the English lose heart, the Germans won't."

Noticing that the children seemed cowed by his presence, Francis sat down on one of the earth benches to seem less threatening. He turned humbly to Clara. "How can I win Mr. Haslam over?"

"Resign your commission." The words were out before she could stop them.

He got up as if she had slapped him. "Please understand this, Mrs. Haslam: My men are no more than boys . . . nineteen or twenty, most of them. I'm ready to eat a lot of humble pie to avoid writing letters of condolence to their parents."

Depression engulfed her. He thought her hard as nails, but she *couldn't* speak kindly to him while all he wanted was to secure Robert's cooperation. She said, "I can't influence him. He's decided to stay, and that's what he'll do."

He regarded her with unexpected sympathy. "You really mustn't underestimate his feelings for you. Tell him you're going to leave. Be firm. I know he'll think twice about staying."

"How do you know?"

He became deadly serious. "Because he'd be mad to risk losing you." The compliment was so unexpected that she felt a tearful tightness in her throat. "I'm afraid your husband was right about one thing: we really may be wiped out unless he's with us. I'd be very grateful if you could convince him that I've no intention of tricking the chief."

"I'll try," she whispered.

"Thank you." He brought his hands together as if in prayer. "We leave at dawn."

As Francis walked away, he passed through a shaft of sunlight, which made his hair shine like a golden helmet. For several seconds afterward, Clara's eyes remained fixed on the empty doorway.

The tents had all come down, though the sky was still crusted with stars. The men had breakfasted on biscuits and coffee, and the horses stood saddled in their lines. Francis watched the cloaked forms of the outlying pickets tramping in through the gloom. The wagons were ready, and the oxen stood in their places on either side of the poles. As the stars became paler, pink light glowed over the earth's eastern rim.

So where were the Haslams? Francis could hardly believe that Clara had failed with her husband. And where was she herself? Perhaps Haslam had been the persuasive one, causing a change of heart at the eleventh hour.

As Heywood Fynn rode up beside Francis, golden rays blazed on the horizon. The American reported that the advance screen of scouts was already moving forward. Francis knew he must now give the order to mount and form column. In the distance he could hear the shrill voices of herdboys driving their beasts to pasture. Dawn had broken. Francis turned to his trumpeter. Moments later, the notes of the order rang out across the veld.

Fynn shook his head as though bemused by Francis's obtuseness. "Still hoping, huh? I'm glad to be shut of 'em."

Francis mounted his stallion and kneed him around. "It's

grand news, is it? The chief fights to the last man, and Haslam's wife is raped and murdered! Hip, hip, hooray!''

''You've got it all twisted up. Haslam hates us.'' Around them, troop commanders were getting their men into column. ''Risks kill, Vaughan—like trustin' missionaries, and lettin' Nashu walk free.''

''He had my word of honor.''

''Honor can cost plenty,'' muttered Fynn as he turned his horse.

Francis felt chilled. From Fynn—more than from anyone— he wanted support, not carping. He was distraught that a brave and unhappy woman had chosen to face death with her husband rather than give herself a chance to live, and he bitterly reproached himself for failing to convince her. She had a strange talent for confusing him.

On every side, the bush stretched away, bereft of landmarks, indifferent to man. A thousand horsemen could lose themselves as completely here as fishes in an ocean. As the column snaked along, Francis glanced over his shoulder, and from time to time he would raise his field glasses. He did so again after a longer interval, fearing that it was already too late. But, to his astonishment, a small covered cart trembled in the twin circle of his lenses. He felt a surge of wild elation. Clara had chosen life. As the vehicle came closer, he saw that she was not alone, and raised his slouch hat in salute. She had persuaded her husband after all. She'd damn well done it.

CHAPTER 18

By the time she had spent three days with the column, Clara had accustomed herself to the frustratingly slow pace of the ox wagons, but she had not grown used to the condescension of the young officers. She had no idea whether their standoffishness was due to snobbery or to a continuing resentment against Robert for the views he had expressed before they left. Although none ignored her completely—perhaps because they had been told to be polite—their greetings seemed at best halfhearted. Out of all of them, only Francis Vaughan appeared genuinely eager to talk to her.

Whenever he did, Clara felt pleased but agitated in case Francis was talking to her only in order to gain Robert's goodwill. This possibility upset Clara more than she cared to admit to herself. There was no reason for Francis to treat her in any particular way, so why feel that he should? She certainly found him attractive—most honest women would admit the same. But since the morals of the cavalry officers she had met at home had been largely absent, she was glad she could not call her feelings love.

They were passing through dark woods, which made the young soldiers jittery and had kept the scouts busy for several hours before they permitted the column to proceed. Exotic lilies grew on the forest floor under the shadow of tall mahogany trees, and underfoot, the peaty ground sucked at the horses' hooves. Occasionally, the distant crashes caused by feeding elephants alarmed the troopers.

At last the column emerged into a terrain as brimful of light as a Dutch landscape. As they passed a village, with huts clustering in the midst of plantain groves, distant drums were thudding. The column halted, and a wagon became bogged down, obliging twenty men to push it out.

Francis Vaughan came striding toward the missionary's Cape cart. Clara was sitting beside Robert under the hood, and as usual in Captain Vaughan's presence, flickers of nervousness troubled her. Relations between the two men had been tense ever since Robert had refused to say where he thought Mponda might be hiding. All he had agreed to do was speak to Mponda if he could be found.

Francis lifted his slouch hat in greeting and waved to Simon, who was gathering mushrooms beside the track.

"I'd be glad if you could come and look at something, Mr. Haslam." Even when Francis was worried, his voice sounded calm and friendly.

Tramping along behind them both, Clara saw nothing unusual, until Francis pointed. At the head of the column, some objects were lying in the middle of the track. Above a heap of broken pot shards and ashes, an impaled cockerel's head had been mounted on a stick.

"What does it mean?" asked Francis.

Robert compressed his lips. "It's a witch doctor's pitiful attempt to stop disease visiting the village."

"Fynn doesn't think so," remarked Francis. Flies were buzzing around the severed head.

"What does he say?" asked Clara.

"That it's a warning to us."

"He's wrong," said Robert with finality.

Francis's puzzlement was plain to see. Clara guessed he had at least expected a discussion. Back in the Cape cart, she asked her husband, "Do you believe what you told Captain Vaughan?"

He gave her a martyred look. "I don't make a habit of lying."

"Lies aren't always bad," said Clara. "The soldiers might have attacked the village if you'd said those things were a threat." She glanced at him. "Is that why you lied?"

Robert picked up the reins and twisted them between his fingers. "Signs are always hard to interpret."

"Master is right," declared Simon loyally, from the raised seat behind them. "Different ngangas have different charms."

Clara was sure Robert had misled Francis, but perhaps no great harm would come of it. Francis would surely be as likely to believe Fynn's opinion.

That night, they camped on higher ground, three miles from the village. Clara and Robert were obliged to sleep on the floor of the cart after finding that their groundsheet had been gnawed by rats. The hours Clara had spent squashed up against her husband on their last journey had been hateful to her, and even now he thought it his right to pull up her skirt and force himself into her. While Clara felt violated, Robert resented her physical coolness and thought it no coincidence that she had become more distant after the arrival of the soldiers. Her attentiveness to Captain Vaughan confused him. If she was merely being polite, why was she always distracted after talking to the man?

During the night, Clara was woken by noises from the camp. Knowing she was frightened, Robert reassured her, saying that some horses had probably broken loose. She went back to sleep, but at dawn, Francis woke them both without apologizing. He was white-faced with anger. "Three of my men have been brutally murdered."

Clara was shaking as Robert began calmly buttoning his shirt. "I'm very sorry to hear that, Captain. Where were they?"

"On outpost duty. They were stripped naked and their stomachs slashed open."

"The Venda think it releases a man's ghost from his body."

"So it's a favor?" gasped Francis.

"Of course not. They don't want hostile spirits to haunt the place of burial."

"You lied about that stuff on the path."

"You needn't worry about pagan charms," said Robert, slipping his arms into his faded frock coat. "Your men terrify the natives—that's your real problem. Scared people are always dangerous."

With an immense effort, Francis folded his arms. "You expect me to believe that scared people creep out at night and murder armed men?"

"Desperation does strange things, Vaughan."

"Not *that* strange," snapped Francis, turning on his heel.

Less than an hour later, Robert saw flames rising from the distant huts. He caught his wife's arm. "Isn't that what I said he'd do? Burn whole villages. Your sweet-natured captain."

While the village burned, Robert prayed. Shortly before the column moved on again, he thrust his way into the little knot of officers that had gathered around Francis.

"Why the brutality, sir?" cried Robert. "Women and children didn't kill your men."

Clara feared that Francis might fail to rebut Robert's accusation. She had sworn to him that Francis was humane and honorable.

Having vented his anger, Francis eyed Robert with strained good humor. "Come come, Mr. Haslam, don't jump to conclusions. Nothing was done till the people had fled."

"Just nigger houses, were they?" growled Robert.

Francis met his gaze. "It's hardly like burning an English town. These places can be built up again in a week."

"What about their grain? Takes rather longer to replace."

"My men had orders not to burn it."

"But they killed people, I suppose?"

"I'm told one native was killed. He'd shot one of my people in the arm." A faint smile parted Francis's lips. "Will you report me to the Aborigine Protection Society?"

Robert said scornfully, "Wouldn't *you* fight foreign soldiers if they came to burn your home?"

Stung at last, Francis said, "The victims' water bottles were found in *that* village." He gazed for a moment at the rising smoke before mounting his horse.

Lieutenant Carew, one of Francis's subalterns, rode up beside him. "Don't know how you kept your temper, sir."

"He's right, in a way." Francis sighed.

"Really, sir?" Carew's face creased with puzzlement under his tropical helmet.

"You'd fight pretty hard, wouldn't you, Carew, if Chinamen invaded England?"

"*We're* not savages."

"We were when the Romans came. And we fought tooth and nail then."

"I bet we didn't slaughter their children after pretending to be friends."

"I wouldn't count on it."

Carew was twenty-four, only six years younger than his commander. Francis often felt twenty years older; and as for his men, they seemed like children: poorly educated, easily frightened, and held together only by their sergeants' example. Yet to winkle well-armed natives out of caves and drive them down from hilltops would require courage and outstanding marksmanship.

Carew took off his helmet and mopped his brow. His reddish-colored hair was dark with sweat. It upset Francis that the squadron had been issued hot and cumbersome pith helmets instead of light slouch hats. The chin strap had left a white line on Carew's brick-red skin.

"Who killed our men, sir?"

Francis stroked his mustache. "They weren't killed by members of a native army. So don't worry about that."

"How can you be sure, sir?"

"Fynn's been over the ground for miles." Francis flicked a mosquito from his horse's neck. "Our poor fellows were caught off guard by local natives. It's a popular uprising."

"They must have crept up so quietly . . . I don't like to think of it, sir."

"Then you mustn't," said Francis gently. He too lived in terror of waking up to the bowel-loosening realization that thousands of savages were closing in. In nightmares, he had watched the leaf-shaped blade of an assegai pressing slowly through the fibers of his coat. On this open plain they would be safe. But among rocks and scrub, they would be unable to deploy the quick-firing guns that alone could preserve them against overwhelming odds.

Five miles ahead of the column, Heywood Fynn was on his knees, examining the spoor of an army on the move and gleaning from the flattened grass and the scores of nutshells and chewed sorghum stems that several thousand men had recently passed by. One find that alarmed him more than the rest was a black ostrich feather such as Matabele warriors wore. If a Matabele impi had entered Mashonaland, a small column like Vaughan's would be annihilated by it.

Two days after the murders, Fynn was still enraged that the victims had each been stabbed thirty or forty times. The American consoled himself with the knowledge that he had disobeyed Vaughan's order not to destroy native grain. In order to avoid detection, he had poured water into the storage pits; and despite his fondness for native women, he had ignored another of Vaughan's prohibitions when he turned a blind eye to acts of copulation bordering on rape. He was still tormented by his memory of one white woman's corpse in Belingwe—a spear had been thrust up her vagina, and the point was sticking out through her neck.

Even before discovering that a native force was in the region, Fynn had decided to reconnoiter the supposed location of Mponda's headquarters with exceptional care. He had never shared Francis's belief in the reliability of Nashu's information and meant to spend at least ten days checking it. While this went on, to keep out of trouble, the main column would have to remain where it was—too far away to render him any assistance. But Fynn had a plan for giving his men additional protection. Because he believed that Nashu was in league with Mponda and intended to spring a trap, he thought it would be only prudent to take Haslam with him to plead for the lives of his scouts should they be captured. But with Francis expecting the missionary to persuade Mponda to lay down his arms, Fynn feared his commander would not agree to let Haslam out of his sight.

It was early evening when Fynn made his request. As he and Francis walked along the camp's thornbush perimeter, the American had no idea what the Englishman was thinking. Some guinea fowl dipped down to roost in trees away to their right. Francis let out a low breath. "All right, Fynn, I'll risk it. He can go with you."

Fynn seized Francis's hand. "You won't regret it, I promise."

"He may refuse to accompany you. I told you to be more respectful."

"Shall I go ask him now?"

Francis shook his head. "We'll do the asking tomorrow. I want time to think what to say."

The following morning dawned gray with rain hissing down steadily. The missionary was seated on a box, holding an umbrella over his head while his boy shaved him. His wife was reading a book under the canopy of their cart.

After greeting the Haslams, Francis launched into his theme. He stressed that Fynn would be taking less than twenty men and that such a small contingent could not possibly pose a threat to Mponda. "In fact," continued Francis eagerly, "this scouting expedition may provide the best opportunity we'll ever get for a meeting with the chief." He smiled encouragingly at Robert. "What do you think?"

Fynn and Francis stood, getting wet, while Robert pondered. At last the missionary announced, "I'll go, but it won't be for your sake, Vaughan. I'll do it because Mr. Fynn's men will commit fewer crimes if I'm with them."

Francis noticed that Clara was distressed and guessed she felt humiliated. He said quietly to Robert, "I expect you'll want to discuss things first with Mrs. Haslam?"

"She trusts my judgment, sir."

Francis was mortified; his effort to spare Clara's feelings had merely made things worse for her.

As the moment for the American's departure approached, the sky darkened to deep purple. The scouts were greasing their gun barrels and waxing their boots against the wet. Walking beside his friend, Francis weighed up the dangers of their situation, acknowledging that the presence of an unknown impi meant that in addition to Mponda's men, there were several thousand rebels in the area. He knew he ought to consider rejoining General Carrington's field force at once, but as always, the fact that he would be able to continue his career only if he could make a success of the campaign made him reluctant to order a pullback. Instead he would await the scouts' findings.

Francis gazed at Fynn's powerful neck and familiar grizzled hair. The man could be absurdly touchy, but Francis could not imagine being able to bear his responsibilities without Fynn's support. With his short legs and giant's torso, the American reminded him of a tough and confident boy who had plenty of growing still to do. Fynn grinned broadly.

"I'm mighty grateful, Vaughan."

Francis was touched. If anyone should be grateful, it was he.

CHAPTER 19

s Robert rode away with the scouts, Clara's heart told her it was admirable that her husband should be ready to risk his life as a mediator in the hope of saving Mponda; but her brain told her that it was futile to save a man whose survival would only lead to civil war.

Two days later, the vanguard of Francis's force—about thirty men—were riding through a tract of thick bush when, without warning, they blundered into a kraal. In the pandemonium of screaming children and bleating goats, a trooper panicked and fired a shot, which badly wounded a child. Spears were thrown at the soldiers, and more shots were fired in return; one of these killed an old man.

When the main column came on the scene, cooking pots were still bubbling and pigs had resumed their search for food. The entire population had fled, save for the white-haired man spread-eagled on the path and the injured girl, now bleeding to death in the arms of a trooper.

In the evening, soon after the girl's agony ended, the man who had shot her was tied to a wagon wheel and flogged, on Francis's orders. From fifty yards away, Clara heard the *whoosh* of the cane, followed by the first slashing blow. And every time thereafter, in the split second before the stroke, she felt as if she were falling through the air.

Soon after the trooper had been dragged sobbing to the M.O.'s tent, a hussar approached Clara with a note. Still shaken by the summary justice, she did her best to behave normally toward this young messenger, who was often to be seen waiting for orders outside Francis's tent. His sandy hair was closely cropped, and his face was pleasing in spite of crooked teeth. Clara read the message.

"Is there any answer, madam?"

"You can tell Captain Vaughan I'm happy to dine with

him.'' The hussar was leaving, when Clara surrendered to an impulse to question him. ''Does the captain always send *you* as his postman?'' She smiled apologetically. ''I'm afraid I don't know your name.''

''Corporal Winter. I'm the captain's orderly . . . a bit like being an errand boy.''

''It's that bad?''

''I shouldn't really say, madam.''

Clara lowered her voice conspiratorially. ''I won't give you away.''

''I stopped a bullet in Ashanti, so the captain's kept me in cotton wool ever since.''

''You like him, then?''

''He's a real good'un. But he still won't let me join the scouts. They're the cream: the column's ears and eyes.''

She nodded, then asked abruptly, ''Would *you* have flogged that man?''

Winter looked amazed. ''Would I, hell! Till the bastard begged. Men can't go blasting off their guns every time a nigger sneezes. There's got to be discipline.''

When Corporal Winter had gone, Clara splashed her face with rainwater from a bucket. Whatever anyone said, the trooper's punishment had been barbaric. What could be gained by lashing a man already tormented by guilt? And why burn a village when the perpetrators of an outrage were sure to be miles away? Yet Francis was no ogre. Whenever Clara spoke to him, his eyes conveyed kindness. But would he turn brutal, as Robert had predicted? She could not think so.

Clara's thick walking boots were hidden by her long skirt. She put on a white shirt that Simon had just ironed, and then she knotted a necktie. It made her look like a governess, but this austere garb suited her. At first she pinned up her hair, but then she let it hang freely to her shoulders, in striking contrast to her prim costume.

On entering the mess marquee, Clara was redirected to Captain Vaughan's tent. Corporal Winter ushered her in. Everything was more informal than when she and Robert had dined with all the officers. This evening, only three men welcomed her, and none were in uniform. Francis sported a dilapidated tweed coat and flannel trousers, and the other two were similarly dressed.

Francis rose at once, and in a friendly and cheerful way reintroduced her to his colleagues. Although Clara would have been very surprised to hear it, he had been dismayed by their last meeting. Now he noticed with misgiving that her lovely face expressed the same emotional fervor. Her clothes made him think of a village schoolmistress. But what a strange one! She was so vividly alive that her moods showed as clearly in her face as squalls on water. He found the slight hoarseness of her voice enchanting. She was made for pleasure, so by what streak of perversity had she chosen Haslam and his self-denying creed?

Francis listened with a glassy smile as his red-haired colleague, Carew, mumbled flatteringly about "the selfless devotion of missionaries" and how wonderful it was that "there are still men and women today, ready to face years of disappointment without expecting any reward."

Francis chose that precise moment to offer Clara a glass of wine. He caught her eye as she hesitated to reach out for it. "Will Mr. Carew be disillusioned if I accept?" Her stage whisper delighted Francis.

Carew blushed, fearing he had been gauche. "I'll turn a blind eye."

"Good lad!" Francis laughed, handing over the glass.

While they ate roast antelope with tinned peas, Francis's friend Matthew Arnot asked Clara about herself. Arnot had swarthy good looks and a sardonic manner that many people mistook for mockery. Clara refused to be nettled and answered his questions straightforwardly. Her father, she said, owned a pottery that produced crockery; nothing like Minton or Chelsea—cheap stuff but profitable enough for a provincial business. Francis enjoyed her ironic tone.

"By Jove! An heiress!" gasped Carew.

"Nothing to spend it on here." Arnot sighed.

"It's all bosh anyway." She laughed. "I might have a dozen brothers and sisters, for all you know."

"But do you?" demanded Arnot.

She put down her knife and fork and leaned across the folding table. "Do tell me about *your* expectations, Mr. Arnot."

"Matthew's going to be revoltingly rich," said Francis gloomily.

"But will it spoil his character?" asked Clara.

Arnot grinned at her. "You mean camels through needles' eyes and all that biblical stuff?"

Clara said with mocking severity, "Is that any way to talk to a missionary's wife?"

"I'd say it calls for a whipping," cried Carew.

Clara's mood changed in an instant. "How long will it take that poor man's back to heal?"

Francis felt his cheeks glowing. "A week or two," he replied, aware that it would take twice that time.

She was staring at him with a knowing wisdom he disliked. "It's not as if his suffering will bring that child to life again."

"No," agreed Francis, "but it should rule out similar accidents."

Clara regarded him sadly. "You can't be sure of that."

"Not unless we all leave the country, and I mean missionaries too."

"Missionaries don't go round killing people."

"They do worse," he said, at once regretting his words. "I shouldn't have said that. I'm sorry."

"Don't be," she said softly. "Just finish what you started to say."

Francis could not read her mind at all. Was she furiously angry and controlling it, or was she genuinely curious? He said, "I'm no expert on the natives, but their warriors seem totally bound up with their customs. Not just on Sundays but seven days a week . . . So to tell them they'll burn in hell if they don't wear trousers and come to chapel seems cruel. I was going to say it might be kinder to kill them, but it was more than I really meant."

"Well, thank you for telling me."

"You're not angry?"

She looked at him gravely, then smiled. "Do you really expect me to share all my husband's views?" She took a sip of wine and turned to the others. "Is that what you'll all expect from your good little wives?"

"Unless I marry a bluestocking," muttered Carew, winking at Arnot.

Clara noticed. "I bet you were all beastly children."

"That's a bit stiff," objected Arnot.

"Admit you bullied boys who funked their fences in the hunting field."

"Don't look at me." Francis laughed. "I was brought up in London and only rode at my uncle's place."

"And what about practical jokes?"

Francis could not help grinning. Arnot would certainly have made life a misery for sensitive boys at Eton. Clara announced that as a tradesman's daughter, she had been ostracized by the local landowners' children on the only occasion when she had followed the local hunt.

"Some of my best female friends are members of the lower orders," muttered Arnot.

"Let's draw a veil over that," said Francis.

Clara then told them about her mother's generosity to fallen women, gazing at Arnot while she did. Later, she made amends by laughing about the unsuitable presents her mother had sent out to Africa: winter gloves, silk dresses, and sporting blazers.

Francis clapped his hands. "Good for her! Africans look much better in stuff like that than in their dreary mission clobber."

"You're certainly right there." As Clara smiled at him, Francis felt caught up in a strange spell of intimacy.

When he escorted Clara back to her Cape cart through the moonlit lines, Francis sensed that she was tense and wondered whether she was worried about Haslam. He couldn't help hoping that she wasn't. Around them, frogs throbbed and croaked endlessly. "Penny for your thoughts," he asked.

"I don't know you well enough to say." Francis had posted a sentry near the cart, and tonight the man was on duty for the first time. As Clara caught sight of him, she asked, "Surely I'm perfectly safe? Your men see me as a sort of nun, don't they? The missionary's wife."

Francis studied the ground. "Let's just say that their eyesight's fine."

Clara blushed fiercely, and Francis could think of nothing to say. So at length he murmured a polite "Good night" and walked away toward his tent. Almost at once he wished he had stayed, but he had always found intimate silences—especially the unexpected ones—unendurable.

With a little coaching from Arthur Winter, Clara could soon recognize most of the soldiers' trumpet calls. After hearing "Horses In," she would go and watch the horses being driven in by the grazing guards. On one particular afternoon, she watched each man catch his own mount and tie him to the lines stretched between wagon wheels. Every trooper stood by his horse's head while the animal ate—touching proof, she imagined, of the bond between horse and man. But when she made this observation to Matthew Arnot, he laughed.

"If your life depended on the speed of your horse, Mrs. Haslam, wouldn't you make sure he got the whole of his corn ration?"

"So they don't care a jot for their horses?"

"That's not what I meant."

"Then why were you teasing me, Mr. Arnot?"

He made a show of being contrite. "You do tend to be rather serious about everything, ma'am."

"Is there much to laugh about just now?"

"Plenty." He raised a black eyebrow. "What about the gallant captain's drooling glances?"

Blood rushed to Clara's cheeks. "That's a lie."

He threw up his hands as if on the stage. "I beg you not to upset yourself. I thought you'd be flattered."

"I'm not."

Arnot snapped his fingers. "Goddammit! I keep forgetting who you're married to. So does my brave commander."

Clara began to walk away. Not long before, she would have thought Matthew Arnot witty, but now she found herself imagining him joking after he'd heard that Robert had been killed.

Early next morning, Francis told Clara that he and Mark Carew intended to take a picnic up onto the nearby hill, which shielded the camp's northern aspect. Would she care to come too? Apparently there were some rock paintings up there and an ancient ruin at the summit.

"Is Mr. Arnot coming?" she asked, blushing at the memory of what he had told her.

"No; I'm afraid he'll be on duty in the camp."

"What a shame."

For a moment Francis appeared to have taken her seriously, but then he smiled. "He's not *that* bad, is he?"

"Worse."

"Poor old Matt's not half as cynical as he pretends to be."

"That still makes him twice as cynical as anyone I know."

As Francis applauded her, Clara felt pleasantly elated. With Robert away, she was discovering that her old self still existed.

A good-natured mare was produced, and Clara and the two officers rode forth, with three troopers and two pack mules bringing up the rear. In single file, they picked their way through the granite boulders at the foot of the hill and then began to climb fairly steeply through long grass that brushed the flanks of their horses. Mixed in with the new growth were dried seed pods and prickly stalks, which, since Clara was riding sidesaddle, made her regret not choosing a thicker skirt. The hillside was uncannily silent, since no voices of herdboys or women floated up from the fields. All the local people had fled when the column first arrived.

The sun was hot enough to make Clara glad to reach the checkered shade of a few misasa trees. To her right were some soldiers' observation posts where the cliff plunged sharply, almost at the men's feet, affording an endless vista of tawny scrub. Somewhere out there in the haze, cattle and herdsmen would be moving away to avoid the white men. And beyond them, perhaps, a sight that every hussar dreaded: a well-armed impi, sweeping south.

As Francis came up beside her, Clara asked how many men he had on the hill.

"Not many. About forty in all; but they can see for miles, so they won't be surprised."

The party rode on at a leisurely pace, climbing gradually to a natural amphitheater walled in by rocky crags. From the plain, these tiered ledges had looked as if built with massive hewn stones. Now it was clear that the rocks had been carved by natural forces, and that the anticipated "ruin" was chimerical. Francis was admitting this to his companions, when screams rang out and heads appeared on the skyline. Carew and the troopers drew their carbines. Clara was too surprised to feel fear as she scrambled from her horse.

"Don't fire till they move," whispered Francis.

The heads moved in unison. Carbines were raised and then rapidly lowered. A troop of baboons came loping down the slope. A grizzled veteran led, while mothers with infants on their backs brought up the rear. Enraged to find trespassers in their stronghold, they shrieked and jabbered as they shambled away.

Laughing with relief, everyone helped to unload the pack mules. The troopers set up a small folding table and camp stools

under the purple shade of a fig tree. Wine bottles, glasses, a preserved ham, curried prawns, rice, and tinned fruit were all extracted
from the mules' panniers. After laying the table, the men re-
mounted and rode away. The other horses were left to graze on
the far side of the plateau. While Carew struggled to free a camera
from the straps around his neck, Francis joked about his habit of
festooning himself with water bottles, binoculars, compasses, and
map cases, regardless of the length of his journey.

As they were finishing their meal, some marauding bees attacked. Nobody was stung, but in batting them away with his hand,
Mark Carew knocked his glass from the table. He bent down and
retrieved it from the ground, then let out a cry. His first thought
was a snake, but he could see no fang marks.

"Was it a bee?" asked Francis.

"I can't see a sting."

Francis studied Carew's hand. "Probably a scorpion."

Thinking this likely, Carew decided to return to camp to see
the medical officer.

As soon as she was alone with Francis, Clara's recollection
of Arnot's remarks made her feel jittery. But Francis himself remained perfectly calm, finishing his plate of tinned fruit. Indeed,
his tone was almost offhand when, after wiping his fingers, he
asked, "Were you always religious, Mrs. Haslam?"

The question was disconcerting. She said briskly, "I lost my
faith after my mother's death."

"You aren't a believer?" He was dumbfounded.

"Later, my husband—of course, he wasn't that then—came
and preached in my town, and I found that . . . that I was after all."

"You'd mislaid your faith rather than lost it?"

"It seemed to have been there all the time."

"What a lucky thing." Francis spoke so solemnly that she
couldn't believe he was mocking her, as Arnot certainly would
have done in the same situation.

She murmured, "I'd rather talk about something else. Religious feelings are so personal . . . especially for someone like me."
She tried to lighten her tone. "You wouldn't like me to ask you
whether you're frightened when fighting . . . or whether you're as
brave as you used to be a year ago."

He folded his arms. "I wouldn't mind, actually."

"Then tell me," she challenged.

"I feel more frightened these days, but I hide it better." He smiled confidingly. "Don't tell the men. Could wreck their morale."

"That wouldn't do," she responded, wondering why his face gave her such pleasure. Was it the way his lips met so firmly under his fair mustache? Or simply how he looked at her? She could not believe that with such kindly eyes, he could be anything but honorable. And as she thought this, she felt ashamed for having been less than honest herself. Unaccountably, she felt tearful.

"Is anything wrong?"

"No, really, I'm fine. It's just that I should have trusted you. Things happened out here—horrible things—and God was no help to me. He still isn't." She felt delicious relief to have confessed.

His eyes were full of concern. "That's awful . . . I mean, for anyone in your position." He placed a hand on hers for several seconds. Even when he stood up and moved away, she felt the pressure of his palm. He clapped on his slouch hat and smiled. "Let's find those rock paintings, Mrs. Haslam."

She nodded, thinking how much nicer it would have been if he were in his tweed coat again and not in a khaki uniform and Sam Browne belt. He fed their horses some bread and took a rifle from a leather case attached to his saddle.

"Could be leopards up in the rocks. They're very partial to young baboons."

As they clambered over the rocks, heat radiated from them as if from a giant's oven. They paused to regain their breath on a narrow shelf-like terrace. Already their horses looked very small. The rocks became steeper and the handholds farther apart. Francis offered Clara his hand, and she was glad to take it. They reached a grassy ledge and froze. On the ground, just yards away, was an empty calabash and some spilled grain. Among the Venda, hills were often reputed to be holy places. Clara gazed at the grain. Was this a priest's offering? She was about to speak, when Francis pressed a hand to her mouth so rapidly that he hurt her lips.

The ledge they were on went back farther than the others, being more like a small plateau than a terrace. In the center, a large rock stood alone. Twenty yards behind it, the cliff surged upward to its topmost ridge. The rocks resembled a mighty drystone wall, the gaps between them opening out into caves and fissures. Clara's legs were trembling. Could men be hiding in those recesses?

Their progress from ledge to ledge could easily have been observed. Francis raised a finger to his mouth and, beckoning her closer to him, pointed to the central rock. She understood at once: they needed to take cover.

As they ran for the rock, a man in a skirt of leopard tails emerged from behind it. He froze before flinging himself out of sight again. Francis jerked back the bolt of his rifle, too late to fire.

The two of them crouched together behind the rock in the baking sunlight, with no idea how many men lay hidden only yards away. Francis took out his revolver, slipped off the safety catch, and handed the weapon to her. He indicated that she was to cover the right of the rock, while he would take the left. The blood was roaring in her ears. Her hat had fallen off in the dash to the rock, and the sun was burning her neck and cheek.

In time, the three troopers would return and, finding their horses still waiting, start to search. She clung to this thought as to a buoy in a storm. But again and again the corpses of the Frenchman and his wife filled her mind. As a child she had seen the young son of her father's coachman killed by a horse—the awful cracking noise of hoof against skull still haunted her. One moment laughing; the next, stone dead on the cobbles.

Her heart was beating so fast she feared it might burst. Above her on the rock she saw little orange lizards darting after flies. Sweat was trickling between her breasts and down her back. Dark patches had appeared at the armpits of Francis's uniform. The stippled wooden handle of the gun felt slippery in her hands.

Soon after thirst started to torment her, Francis took a canteen from his pocket and handed it to her. She drank gratefully and returned it. A little later, he offered her his hat to shade her burning face. Being darker-skinned, she gave it back again after a while. Occasionally, faint sounds came from behind the rock, but what they meant, Clara could not say.

The sun was inching closer to the upper crags when, far to their right, a man emerged from a slit in the rock-face. Clara cried out. Francis swung around and fired almost in the same movement. A huge man now sprang from behind their rock, wielding an ax. Clara screamed. Francis swung with his rifle butt and caught him in the ribs. The ax crashed wide and struck sparks from the rock. Francis swung again with his rifle but slipped. The ax flashed above him. Clara raised her revolver and fired. The man crumpled sideways. She fired again, hitting him in the neck. Francis was on his feet as another man peered around the side of the rock. Without time to aim, Francis fired from the hip and missed. The tribesman flinched and discharged his flintlock into the ground. Before Francis could fire again, his adversary dropped his gun and fled.

Francis grabbed Clara's hand. They half slid, half scrambled down the steepest rocks until reaching the next substantial ledge. An overhang gave them shelter from anything that could be hurled from above. Clara was trembling uncontrollably and would have fallen if Francis had not held her.

"You saved my life," he murmured.

"We saved each other's." A great sob broke in her throat.

His cheek was touching hers, but she did not turn away. Behind the rock, it had been as if everything that mattered to her had been about to be snatched away, his life more than hers. And now that he was suddenly restored to her, she felt his value more deeply. She remembered the ax poised above him and relived the split second before she fired—the barrel of her revolver shaking so much that she had shut her eyes as she squeezed the trigger. On opening them, she had expected to see Francis dead, his face upturned, hair wet with blood: the last sight she would ever see before she suffered the same fate.

She held Francis more tightly. Then, as if this were a dream, she drew back and looked at him, alive—dear God, alive—those cornflower eyes, that straight fair hair like a boy's. She touched his face, leaned forward, and kissed him on the lips, a soft, sweet kiss that left her weaker than before.

"Forgive me," she sighed as they drew apart.

For answer he kissed her again. "My darling," he whispered. "My darling."

As they held each other, she prayed: May I never turn my back on love because it is alive and hurts. He was looking at her with eyes that were helpless but repentant, as if he feared he had wronged her. She desperately wanted to tell him not to be sorry. Instead of speaking, she reached out and held his lapels. Then, drawing him closer, she tilted back her head. They kissed, then parted, breathing deeply like swimmers.

Far below, the troopers were dismounting after hearing the shots. Francis shouted to them to shoot anyone on the rocks above. Before leaving the ledge, he took Clara's hand and kissed it gently on the palm and on the fingers—a vow, she told herself, while fearing it might be a valediction.

CHAPTER 20

On Fynn's orders, Robert Haslam was wearing his jacket turned inside out, with the pale lining exposed, since the black cloth had been judged to be too eye-catching against gray rocks and sandy scrub. Fynn was squatting next to him in the shade of a stunted acacia, slicing thin strips from a lump of dried meat with his hunting knife. Four scouts were nearby, observing the hillside, shielding their field glasses to prevent their flashing in the sun. Today they were closer than usual to the people they were seeking.

Robert turned to Fynn. "If they spot us at this distance, won't they rush at us?"

"No, sir. They'll think we're tryin' to lure them into a bigger force. So they'll work around back of us."

Fynn had observed this particular hillside several times before, because he had noticed that the number of cooking fires had been steadily increasing. Robert could make out the glint of guns and assegais as men moved on the skyline. Fynn began to edge his way cautiously around the hill, making sketches of every cave opening he could spot. Past experience told Robert that the American would next try to capture a young woman from a neighboring village, to question her about the men. The first time this had happened, Robert had anticipated torture. But on that occasion and on all others, fear alone had elicited a flood of information.

Without the daily routines of life at the mission, Robert felt disoriented and lonely. He feared that the social chatter of the cavalry officers might make Clara nostalgic for the life she had abandoned. Their lascivious glances troubled him. May I never fall victim to mistrust and jealousy, he prayed. These young men were pitiable. Their carefree hedonism was no help against impending death. Robert pulled himself into a kneeling position. "O merciful God who knoweth that every unrepented sin is a fountain of fresh error, guide these poor sinners back, of their own volition, onto the one true path that leads to Thy salvation. Grant this, I pray, for the sake of Thy Son, Jesus Christ, Amen.''

That night, under the stars, men stirred in their sleep, while others kept watch. They had all been soaked to the skin in a late shower, but a fire was out of the question. An hour earlier, a man had lit a cheroot and Fynn had kicked him black and blue for betraying their position. Every night, the American went around rapping men's feet through their horse blankets. If they took off their boots at night, the patrol could not ride off at a moment's notice. Robert reflected sadly that most Christians could learn a lot about dedication from Mr. Heywood Fynn.

Not long after his lucky escape, Francis Vaughan sat in his tent, writing to Clara. On his table lay the torn scraps of earlier attempts. Easy to apologize for placing her in danger; simple to express anger with his incompetent scouts; a pleasure to praise her courage. The problem was how to refer to the kisses, the memory of which still delighted him, and at the same time tell her that they could never repeat such behavior. In a few days' time, her husband, at great risk to himself, might meet Chief Mponda and be instrumental in saving all their lives. To deceive him would be despicable.

Francis fiddled with his smoking lamp and then wrote: "Please be generous enough to forget an incident which I now greatly regret and cannot excuse." He sighed aloud and scored through the paper. The inescapable fact was that *she* had kissed him first and had done so deliberately. He remembered her pulling back to look at him before slowly leaning forward. So how could he apologize without insulting her? Was it even chivalrous to speak of regret? It certainly wasn't truthful. *And she had saved his life.*

No other woman of his acquaintance would have been brave enough to endure the ordeal they had shared without going to pieces. And Clara had moral courage too: the sort required for her to admit she had lost her faith. The sadness of her situation haunted him. Even on first meeting her in that crowded hotel supper room, he had hated to think what Africa might do to her.

In the end Francis abandoned his efforts to settle everything in a letter and instead wrote a simple note in which he asked her to meet him by the stream above the horses' drinking pool. He asked Corporal Winter to deliver the note, feeling relieved, although nothing had been decided. Only by talking to her in person would he be able to admit how he felt and yet insist upon honorable behavior.

"Take it to her," Francis repeated, puzzled by Winter's hesitation.

"She was asking things about you, sir."

"Like what, Corporal?"

"Whether I enjoyed being your orderly."

"I trust you said you loved it?"

"Of course I did." He coughed nervously. "Have you considered my request, sir?"

"Not that again."

"It's what I really want to do, sir."

Preoccupied with Clara, Francis suddenly lost the will to keep opposing his orderly's desire to be a scout. In truth, he felt he had no right to do so. Arthur Winter was a widow's only son and had been shot through both legs eighteen months earlier while rescuing a gravely wounded trooper, but could that justify shielding him from his own nature forever?

"Very well, Corporal. You can report to Mr. Fynn when he returns. But don't blame me if you come to a sticky end."

Before Arthur Winter could blurt out his thanks, Francis had ducked back into his tent.

Ever since Robert Haslam's departure, Simon had been despairing. He worried constantly about what might happen to him if his master was killed. Would Mrs. Robert take him to England with her, or would he be sent back to the kraal, as if he had never learned to live like a white man?

One day, he saw the soldiers playing a strange game in which they hit a ball and ran between some sticks stuck in the ground. A large man, whose beard resembled the straggling fibers on a maize cob, told him it was called cricket. Later, he explained the rules and let Simon try to hit the ball. Like all the white men, this soldier's face and neck were burned red brown. Simon knew his name was Sergeant, because that was what the men had called him. When he washed at the stream, his chest and back looked whiter than ivory.

It was strange how very naked white men looked without their clothes. A black skin was sufficient clothing in itself. But Simon enjoyed seeing the soldiers splashing each other in the water. They laughed and frolicked like boys and no longer frightened him, as they did on their horses.

This day, when most of the men had returned to their tents, Simon remained perched on the trunk of a fallen tree, watching Sergeant getting dressed. The boy asked, "Please, what are the bandages you tie around your legs?"

"We call them puttees."

Simon stared beyond the half-dressed soldier. A pale-blue shape was moving through the elephant grass. Simon had washed that very dress yesterday. Forgetting about Sergeant, Simon slipped down from his perch and set off in pursuit of his master's wife.

To prevent anyone's suspecting that he and Clara were heading for the same place, Francis Vaughan chose a circuitous route. On arrival, he looked around with satisfaction. It really was a splendidly secluded spot, shielded on one side by a tangle of papyrus reeds and on the other by a grove of palmyras.

During the night, Francis had slept badly and awakened drenched in sweat. In his dream, a dozen men had emerged from behind the well-remembered rock; and although he shot them, one by one, they kept on coming. As he turned to speak to Clara, a spear was thrust into her neck. On waking, Francis had felt steadier only after drinking some brandy.

Waiting for Clara, he felt shaky again. Don't be a fool, he told himself. Just be firm with her. Yet the moment he saw her wonderfully expressive face, framed by its twin curtains of black hair, his resolution melted away. Wanting to be cool and lucid, he could hardly think at all. He took in neither the blueness of her dress nor its delicate darker stripes. The long grass parted with a shushing sound as she approached. Just a dark-haired woman walking by a stream, he told himself, as the telltale signs grew worse: shakiness, confusion, and the treacherous conviction he sometimes had when listening to music: that something he had been born desiring but had never found might yet be within his grasp.

His feet moved; his lips smiled, and he heard himself say quite calmly, "But wasn't that a shocking day? I had nightmares. I doubt if I'll recover for months."

"Don't things like that happen to you all the time?" She looked at him so directly that he could feel himself blushing.

"God, no!" He laughed. "We soldiers are hardly ever in danger."

"Not even from married women?"

"Once in a blue moon."

She sounded put out that he had not answered honestly. "I'd heard that cavalry officers often console neglected wives."

He said, "I suppose that's better than compromising unmarried girls." She was smiling at him—ironically, he thought—and he found himself babbling defensively about the practice in many regiments of denying promotion to officers who married before reaching their mid-thirties. "So what's to be done in the meantime? Live like monks?"

"I understand the problem," she said, with a sympathy that surprised him. "Please don't see me as an innocent. I knew all sorts before I married." His longing for her was like a deep thirst. Her poor face and neck had been burned by the sun during their ordeal the day before. "Why did you ask me to come here?" she whispered.

He said wretchedly, "I owed it to you to say in person what I knew I had to. Your husband's ready to lay down his life for us. How can I stab him in the back?"

"He doesn't care a jot for you or your men. He's only interested in saving Mponda. That man always mattered more to him than anything. . . ." Her eyes were filling. "I may be dead in a month. We all may be."

Seeing her close to tears, he could not bear to remain aloof. His right hand hovered over her shoulder, and his left clasped her arm. They embraced, and he tipped her straw hat back to prevent the brim from hitting his face. Then he kissed her lightly on her cheeks and throat, and with a long sigh of relaxation she let her body mold itself to his.

When they had drawn apart, he could not remember what had seemed so important to him minutes earlier. He thought of what might lie ahead, the deaths and suffering, and couldn't understand why he had thought it more honorable to renounce Clara than to cherish her. Why *should* she be punished indefinitely for misplaced idealism and a foolish choice of husband? Francis's eye was caught by some black-and-orange spotted beetles moving purposefully in the grass. He smiled to himself. While he weighed scruples, a world at his feet was going its own way.

They walked toward the palmyras. Beyond them, Francis knew they must choose different paths or risk being seen together. He recalled a boyhood daydream in which he was Sir Lancelot trapped in Guinevere's chamber. Outside, armed knights were waiting to kill him when he emerged.

Ahead of them, a guinea fowl rose with a whir of wings. Suspecting someone must be hiding in the grass, Francis ran forward. A dark-skinned figure darted across the path toward a belt of scrub. Francis raised his revolver, but felt such a blow on his wrist that he almost dropped it.

"Don't!" gasped Clara, rubbing her hand where she had hit his arm. She was breathing hard from running after him. "It's only Simon. Robert's boy."

"You're sure?"

"Of course."

"Shouldn't I try to frighten him?"

"We don't know if he saw anything."

"I could threaten him anyway."

"It wouldn't work. He'd happily die for Robert."

Francis kissed her again. "He won't hurt you if he finds out?"

"I doubt it."

"Will he believe the boy?"

"Probably."

They walked in silence beside the stream as brown flycatchers swooped across the water. "Dear God," he said. "One day I nearly get you killed; the next, I get you into this."

"No, Francis. We got ourselves into it."

For all her courage, Francis sensed how shocked she was at being discovered. It was impossible to know how the missionary would react. He might rebuke Francis for immorality in front of his men. Or, out of pique, he might refuse to talk to Mponda. When Francis embraced Clara again, she clung to him. And as they kissed, tenderness and need awoke desire. He turned away from her for a moment, as if still able to choose another course. But he knew that the die was cast.

When Clara remembered the incredible coyness of much-chaperoned young ladies in Sarston, she could hardly credit her temerity. A murderer, in the eyes of the faithful, had been scarcely more iniquitous than the woman taken in adultery. Love affairs were "criminal liaisons"—at best "squalid." Even within marriage, passion was deplorable.

Yet it was after midnight, and here she was, waiting for Francis without any sense of guilt or shame. Quite the contrary: she was overwhelmed by a tormenting fear in case he failed to appear. On learning that she was sleeping in her husband's Cape cart, he had given orders for a tent to be put up for her. Gazing at the taut canvas above her, Clara willed time onward. The evening had passed so slowly that she wondered how her life would crawl on from one day to the next if he let her down.

That afternoon, he had taken her out shooting. For the last two nights, lions had been heard behind the hill: a threatening, primordial sound, the memory of which still had the power to frighten Clara in broad daylight. According to Francis, they dared approach humans only if they had first made a kill in the immediate vicinity, and the absence of vultures proved they had not.

Clara had never hunted and did not want to. But she was happy to crawl along a damp gully beside Francis in pursuit of a gazelle with pointed horns. Flies buzzed around their faces, and mosquitoes whined near their ears. Unaware of being watched, the little buck had urinated before trotting off. Unaccountably, they had lost him. But Francis persevered, staring hard at the ground, even crossing a broad shelf of rock where no hoofprints were visible. At last he had found the spoor again: just a few stalks of crushed grass and some spots of damp earth. Seeing Francis on his knees, concentrating so hard, Clara longed to go up to him and kiss his neck; instead she crawled along behind him. And then they had come upon the buck again: this time quietly nibbling the new grass between some thorn trees. Although Francis's excitement was infectious, she hesitated when offered his rifle. Yet how could she decline it? He was offering to her as a gift the outcome of his careful stalking.

He breathed close to her ear, "Perfect specimen. Aim low. Don't harm the head."

As she looked down the barrel, she whispered, "No, Francis. He's yours."

"Go on," he urged hoarsely.

She felt both scared and excited. Which would be worse, to miss or to kill? To end a graceful life she could never restore, or to disappoint Francis? A tickbird squawked loudly, and the startled gazelle took several bounding leaps, tottering on landing. Clara fired. Something shot upward where the buck had been standing— something like a divot of turf. After a stunned silence, Francis gasped, "Christ almighty! Didn't I say, 'Don't harm the head,' and you go and blast the damned thing right off!"

Still on her knees, she had started to cry, and suddenly he had knelt to embrace her. She wanted to swim into his body, and the pain of not being able to was intense. But he loved her. Surely he did?

Then he had picked up his rifle and asked, "Can I come to you tonight?"

His obvious fear of rejection had persuaded her. He felt as she did and therefore must not suffer. "Yes," she had whispered. "Yes, my love."

So Clara lay waiting in the darkness of her tent, listening to the dry scuffling of insects and the yelping of jackals. A thread of intimacy and danger seemed to vibrate in the air. Arnot resented his commander and would be able to wreck Francis's career if he found out about them. And there was danger from Simon too—if he had seen nothing by the stream, he might see them now. The risks Francis was taking on her account made Clara feel weak with tenderness.

He crept into the tent so quietly that she gasped with shock. As she rolled over toward him, his face came slowly down on hers. For a moment she held her lips closed against his. The sooner a thing started, the sooner it ended. Let it never be over but always in expectation—something mysterious and forbidden waiting to come about. And then she could no longer bear to wait but parted her lips and hung for a long time on his mouth. His hands were touching her hair and then her neck, slipping inside her nightdress and tracing the outline of her breasts. He paused to remove his shirt; his skin felt dry and hot, and his heart was thudding as if he had been running. As he loosened his trousers, she lifted her nightdress over her head. His hands came forward and took a bare breast in each. Then he caressed her body with an explorer's pleasure. Robert had never touched her like this. His lovemaking had always been self-absorbed—as if he would stifle his compulsion if he could—whereas Francis was reaching out to her with every nerve.

She could not see his body when he had finally wriggled out of his boots and trousers, but she could feel his penis brushing against her stomach as he moved.

"Darling," he was murmuring, "darling."

A hand was moving gently across her bottom, pressing one cheek and then the other. It slipped down between them, and a finger traced its way along the split. She opened her thighs and let him touch her properly, though she had never allowed Robert to do the same. She wanted Francis so badly that she moved onto her back, holding him tightly as he rolled on top of her, lacing her arms around his neck. He kissed her face and neck as she guided him into her. Already she was moving her head from side to side, ecstatic, overwhelmed.

It was two hours later, and still reassuringly dark. In less than an hour, light would begin to glow opaquely through the canvas, and he would have to leave. He had just rolled off her for the second time, and she could feel his warmth lingering on her breasts and stomach. She reached out for his hand and clasped it. Her body was still humming with pleasure, but already sadness was undermining contentment. Inevitable questions were crowding in on her. How had he learned to make love so beautifully? How many affairs had he had? Longing to know him better, she started with inquiries about his family. And the more he told her, the more she warmed to him. His father had died years ago; his mother was not well off; his sister was the paid companion of an old lady in a country town.

From time to time, a horse would whinny in the lines, reminding her of the male world that would soon reclaim him. He told her about the absurd snobberies that bedeviled the lives of poorer officers like himself. How there were certain makers of cheap saddles and tack who could be patronized only at grave social cost to the purchaser. An officer breaking this taboo generally resorted to the secret removal of all the telltale embossed rivet heads and then plundered a worn-out but expensive saddle in order to reuse its rivets.

"I can't see *you* doing that."

"I suppose you think me too noble to stoop to such ploys?"

She kissed him on the forehead. "Of course I do."

He tapped her lips gently with his index finger. "You're quite wrong. My family made sacrifices for me, so I must justify their faith by climbing the greasy pole. Poor men were often forced out of the regiment. I survived as a subaltern only because I was a natural polo player."

She tried to get him to tell her whether he had stayed on at Mponda's village solely to await her return.

"What would you think of me if I made my military plans fit in with personal wishes?"

"I'd love you even more."

"Liar. You'd want me to put my men first, like any decent commander."

Because she had always thought Francis above life's ordinary struggles, Clara was disturbed to learn that unless he received favorable mention in his general's dispatches, he would not gain the promotion that alone would enable him to meet his regimental bills.

Moving her fingers across her lover's stomach—marble smooth, apart from a sprinkling of hairs around his navel—she was struck that in a few hours, and in the dimmest of lights, she had mapped Francis's body more accurately by touch than she had ever done with Robert's in all their time together. She loved the way Francis repaid her attentions, stroking her hair and saying whatever bizarre endearment occurred to him. It might be to compliment her on, of all things, her elbows. She had grown so used to Robert's habit of never speaking unless having something of substance to say that Francis's chatter came as a delightful surprise.

Panic rocked her when she thought of Fynn and Robert returning in a few days. What would she and Francis do then? Even a furtive squeeze of the hand would be difficult. She forced herself to smile and said, "At Mponda's village, when people asked if anyone had heard any news, the usual reply was *masepa hela,* which means literally 'only dung,' the word they also use for gossip and lies."

He leaned on an elbow and sighed, "Let's hope that's what they'll say if news about us leaks out."

Clara blurted out unhappily, "I'd rather they thought it true." At once she sensed his dismay. "I'm sure they won't," she reassured him. But tears were spilling from her eyes. What hope could there be for them? Scandal would harm his career. Naturally he would wish to avoid it for the sake of his family. If Simon had seen them together and told Robert, Francis would probably expect her to patch things up with her husband. And why should she complain? Hadn't she made a point of telling him she knew how cavalry officers behaved with unhappy wives? And what could he have read into that, except that he could trust her to treat an affair lightheartedly?

And in the future, Robert would expect his marital rights as before. He would speak again about their souls being open to one another, and she would want to die when she remembered an experience that had *really* been like that.

CHAPTER 21

Five days after Clara Haslam had become his lover, Captain Vaughan was with the squadron's veterinary officer, discussing the recent increase in horse sickness. The vet had no idea what caused the illness, except that, being a disease of the rainy season, it was likely to have something to do with dampness and cooler temperatures. A threat to the horses was a worse danger to the squadron than malaria, but Francis could not stop thinking of Clara, even while inspecting the tongue of a dying mare and discussing the failure of quinine injections.

Francis had been with Clara the previous night and the night before that; and on both occasions he had sensed a new desperation in her lovemaking. Even when soaked in each other's sweat, they were left afterward nursing solitary fears, neither daring to test the other's ultimate intentions. With Robert's return drawing closer, the course of their love no longer resembled the clear and sparkling stream Francis had briefly imagined it to be. Darker now, it contained hidden depths and dangers.

For Clara's sake, Francis longed to make promises about the future, but he desisted for fear of alienating Haslam and thus throwing away his men's best chance of survival: a bloodless truce brokered by the missionary with Mponda.

That evening, loud cheers were heard coming from the camp's northern perimeter—sounds that could only mean that Fynn and Robert had returned. In future, Francis knew, he would be able to exchange only a few rushed words with Clara. Even now he shied away from calculating the consequences of their discovery. Haslam was as likely to forgive her as he was to set about destroying her seducer's career. Not even knowing whether Simon had seen him with Clara, Francis could only wait.

When he came upon Fynn in the horse lines, Francis was dismayed to learn that Haslam had already hurried away to find

252

his wife. The American clasped Francis's hand and pumped it up and down. "You ain't lookin' too good, Vaughan." He showed his strong yellow teeth. "You been busy nights?"

Francis gestured impatiently. "Out with it, man. What did you find? Do we live or die?"

"Strangest thing, Vaughan—not a sign of that goddamned impi."

"Isn't that good?"

"Yeah, but it's hard to explain." Fynn undid his horse's girth and lifted off the saddle.

"What about Nashu? Any sign?"

"If I ever see that little son of bitch, I'll kill him."

"So he didn't join forces with Mponda after all?"

"Ain't no evidence either way. He may have."

Francis shook his head. "I'm sure he still hates the chief."

When Fynn described the well-defended hill where Mponda had his stronghold, Francis was shaken. It had been impossible for Haslam to get near enough to make contact with the chief. For the first time in several days, Francis focused entirely upon the fighting ahead. According to Fynn, the chief's neighbor, Mucheri, had left a thousand warriors with Mponda before moving north, for the chief now appeared to have almost three thousand men with him. How they could be dislodged from their caves and crags, Francis could not imagine. More than ever, he needed Haslam to act as mediator. But supposing that the two men met: would Mponda agree to lay down his arms until he had first seen evidence that his enemies had enough men and guns to punish him? Francis did not think so and therefore decided that Haslam should not be asked to negotiate until after the chief had been given a serious jolt.

It was dark by the time Francis had finished discussing the situation with his officers. Unlike Carew and the others, Arnot had refused to accept Fynn's assurance that the impi had left the region. In his opinion, Mponda was being used by the Matabele as bait to lure the squadron into an ambush. Francis chose to believe Fynn.

His men were eating supper by their campfires before Francis persuaded himself that he could no longer decently postpone welcoming Robert Haslam. To delay now would be blatant discourtesy. Outside the missionary's tent, Francis took a long breath and then announced himself. On getting no reply, he glanced inside and saw Clara sitting by herself. Francis could hardly bear to look at her unhappy face.

"Has the boy told him?"

"I can't tell."

Francis moved closer to her. "If Haslam knew, he'd say something to you, surely."

"Maybe not at once. Robert thinks a lot. He'll need to know what God wants him to do."

"What might that be?"

She sighed heavily. "God knows." A pale smile parted her lips. "At the moment, Robert's obsessed with the state of my faith. My need to give myself entirely to Jesus. He's talked of little else since he returned. If the strain gets the better of me, I'll probably tell him about us myself." She gazed at Francis as if challenging him to deny her right to be truthful.

"Would that help you?"

"It might take my mind off you."

He said gently, "Neither of us willed or wanted this. But we're in its grip, and we have to be brave for a while."

She looked at him between dark lashes, her eyes bright with anger. "Till we get over it? Is that what you mean?"

"No," he cried. "Till it's clear what we should do." Determined not to speak of love, he found he could not help himself. "I have to be near you. You know that. But how can anything be decided at a time like this?"

She did not answer, but Francis recognized the truth of his situation. If Clara left her husband, there would be a scandal, and his career would be ended. His uncle would cut off his allowance, and without even his army pay, he would be penniless. Only a simpleton would expect Clara's pious father to bail them out. Francis wanted to comfort her, but he could not find the words. Instead he said, "I must talk to your husband about Mponda."

"Robert's out there somewhere . . . praying with your men."

The thought of the wronged husband on his knees, surrounded by docile troopers, was both sad and comical, yet Francis could find no humor in the image. Already Clara was paying heavily for their brief happiness—more heavily than he. Soon Haslam would be forcing himself on her.

Just as Clara had predicted, Francis found the missionary praying with a small group of soldiers. The sight jarred his conscience more than he had expected, although many officers of his acquaintance would think it a grand joke to roger a missionary's wife. As Haslam rose from his knees, his face, dusty and unshaven, looked drained, but if Simon had given him bad news, Francis could detect no sign of it. In fact, the missionary was entirely calm as Francis explained to him why he meant to give Mponda a bloody nose before trying to persuade him to lay down his arms.

Haslam asked mildly, "What if *he* teaches *you* a lesson?"

Francis could not help grinning. "I'd wish I'd asked you to talk to him first."

"That's just what you *should* do." The man's vehemence took Francis by surprise. He was holding a Bible, and its brass-bound corners caught the red glow of a nearby fire.

Francis tried to sound tolerantly amused. "You think he'll go trotting home just because you ask him nicely?"

"To ask in the name of Jesus is no ordinary request."

"He could still refuse you. And I'd have lost my only chance to surprise him. That's why I can't let you see him first."

"You'll never surprise him," predicted the missionary. "Mponda is always watching for enemies."

Haslam's conviction was very demoralizing and gave Francis his first inkling of how Mponda had been driven to put away his wives. He said more sharply than he intended, "He'll fight harder if I let him think my men are scared."

"They *are* scared, Mr. Vaughan."

"Fear is normal, sir," snapped Francis. "I'll thank you not to talk to my men about death."

"I spoke to them of faith."

"The only faith they need is faith in their officers."

The missionary's gaze was loftily compassionate. Francis told himself that all salvationists had to pretend to be morally superior in order to make their message convincing. But he still could not bear to think of the disdain Clara might soon be facing.

After parting with Haslam, Francis plunged into the mess tent and, pushing past Arnot and several other officers, demanded whiskey.

On the third day of their northward march, Francis gave orders for the column to continue by night. It pleased Heywood Fynn that this decision had been based on his estimate of the time it would take to reach Mponda's stronghold and on his recommendation of a dawn attack. Guiding the squadron by night held no fears for him, and he was never happier than when striding out in the darkness at the head of several hundred silent and trusting men. Beside him, for the first time, strode Arthur Winter, who was entranced to see his hero studying his compass inside an upturned hat by the hidden light of a match, and listened to Fynn as if to God when he gave hints for remembering the shapes of individual hills. Arthur was disappointed that the night was not quite dark enough for them to be obliged to kneel on the ground and feel for tracks with their hands.

Smoking and talking were forbidden in the column, and apart from the occasional cough of a man or snort of a horse, the only sounds to be heard were the creaking of saddles and the soft thud of hooves—until an NCO's half-tame dog began to yelp at the scent of a buck. Fynn had warned what would happen to noisy dogs, and he himself knifed it.

Open country caused Fynn few qualms, but whenever rocky ridges and gullies delayed him, he thought of the Matabele. Vaughan's four hundred men could be wiped out in an hour if an impi surprised them. In a rocky pass, four horses lost their footing and fell among the rocks. One had to be shot, and the other three were too lame to continue. It being after midnight, Francis decided to leave these animals behind, along with the ox wagons, which could be brought on at first light. The surefooted battery mules, carrying the barrels of the Maxims on their backs, would continue with the column.

Francis walked along the line of wagons toward the Haslams' Cape cart and was greeted brusquely by Robert. "Why must we travel by night, sir? No consideration for man or beast."

"I mean to reach the chief's stronghold by dawn."

"No point, Mr. Vaughan. He'll be ready for you night or day."

"Let's wait and see," replied Francis, sounding unruffled. "In any case, I want you to come with the column tonight; I may decide you should speak to the chief sooner rather than later."

"Mrs. Haslam must come too."

"I'll find horses for you both."

"What about my cart?"

"Your boy can bring it on with the wagons at first light." Francis was always pained to see Clara sitting beside her husband, but he could not resist glancing at her whenever he had the chance.

For miles the column struggled through thornbushes until, at last, they came to higher ground, where the scrub thinned. An hour before dawn, they were within sight of the hills where Mponda had gone to earth. Fynn had made many drawings of a rocky promontory, honeycombed with caves, and now this elevated headland rose before them, jutting into a green sea of vegetation. The American's drawings showed it as joined, on its northern side, to the adjacent hill by a gently sloping neck. Mponda would clearly expect the soldiers' main onslaught to be delivered here, and Francis decided to encourage this idea by sending a strong party to capture the neck, while he made his real push on the steeper southern slopes.

Fynn argued that Mponda would divide his force in two, with one group defending the hill and the other kept mobile to attack any besiegers from behind. With this in mind, Francis placed fifty men and a Maxim under the American's direction, with orders to defend the hussars' rear and to guard their horses while they attacked the hill on foot.

The hussars dismounted and off-saddled near a stream to fill their water bottles. Tension crackled in the air as the men waited to set off on this final leg of their march to the hill. Before they did, every man was given a piece of chocolate, a few biscuits, and some dried meat. Each troop commander was handed his orders and a map. While Francis was encouraging any men who looked scared, he was alarmed to see the missionary addressing a knot of troopers.

"My friends, listen to a Shona parable."

Francis touched him on the shoulder. "Quieter, Mr. Haslam, or not at all."

"Brethren," continued Robert Haslam, in a loud whisper. "God sent a chameleon with this message for mankind: 'Though you must die, you will live again.' The chameleon was overtaken by a serpent, which reached mankind first and said, 'If anyone comes and says that you live after dying, it's all lies. You perish as an ox, and that's an end of it.' When the chameleon arrived, people laughed at him. 'Oh, it's you at last. Don't bother with your message; we know it's nonsense.' " Haslam raised his arms as if to quell amusement. "My friends, don't listen to cynics; trust the chameleon. God offers eternal life to all his children, wherever they may be."

Seeing no harm in this parable, Francis went in search of Fynn, whom he found unloading muzzles, barrels, wheels, and ammunition belts from the backs of the mules.

"I want you to look after the Haslams for me."

Fynn stroked his beard. "You reckon God'll look after *me* if I do?" He chuckled quietly. "My idea o' salvation is two hundred rounds a minute from outa these little fellers." He slapped the side of a machine gun barrel.

Before moving off with his men, Francis checked his Lee-Metford carbine and the single-action Colt that Clara had used so tellingly. He released the catch and flicked the empty cylinder, watching it spin noiselessly. He wanted Clara to have it again today, not only because he was afraid for her but as a token of everything they had shared. But she was near her husband, and he found no opportunity to give it to her. Fynn's protection would have to be enough.

The sky was already brightening as Francis led his men toward the hill. Here and there in the half-light, the monotonous browns and greens of the scrub were flecked with mauve and white convolvulus and more startlingly with what looked like a splattering of blood on plant and tree. Suddenly the spots moved. Francis hoped that the restless dartings of these scarlet weaverbirds would not betray his position to enemy eyes.

By nine o'clock, the sun was hot enough to make men crawl under thornbushes. The troopers nearest to Francis had been held back as a reserve. Through his Zeiss binoculars, Francis watched three hundred of his men advancing in straggling lines up the southern face of Mponda's hill. A deep central gully, choked with rocks and scrub, obliged the hussars to clamber up on either side of it along two parallel ridges that resembled bony fingers. These rose to a knobbly line of crags, which looked like knuckles.

As Francis moved his glasses, he saw dark heads and shoulders bobbing about among the rocks, apparently reinforcing the tribesmen already there. A runner informed him that the hussars had taken possession of the neck with scarcely a shot being fired. This could only mean that Mponda's main force was not on the northern side of the hill at all but right here, on the southern slopes, behind these knuckle-like crags. As if to confirm this, a ragged volley rang out and several men fell. The hussars on the slope now dropped behind rocks or flattened themselves under overhanging ledges.

Francis scribbled an order for the runner to take back to Lieutenant Carew on the neck. If Carew's detachment could get around the hill without descending at all, they should be able to take Mponda's main body in the rear within an hour or so. In the meantime, the soldiers faced a new danger. Warriors were working their way down into the gully between the ridges and, from there, were able to subject the hussars on the ridges to a vicious cross fire. Nor could these natives in the gully be easily expelled, since they had crawled so close to his own men that Francis could not risk ordering his seven-pounder field gun into action. The only way to flush them out would be to drag a Maxim right up the gully— a task made extremely hazardous by the rugged terrain.

So what should he do? Francis was still pondering when the *rat-tat-tat* of Fynn's Maxim stammered out sharply in the bush about a mile from where they had left him. Francis's head swam. If Fynn and his men were annihilated, the hussars on the slopes would be caught between two native forces. For a moment Francis considered ordering his trumpeter to sound the recall. The men on the ridges would then be able to fall back and go to the aid of Fynn and the Haslams. But to leave the hill while Mark Carew was up there somewhere, preparing to attack Mponda's rear, would be to murder him and his men. Francis told himself that so long as Fynn's Maxim kept firing, he needn't worry. Someone coughed quietly. Francis turned and saw Sergeant Barnes's large red face. Sweat was dripping freely from under his melon-shaped pith helmet. A drop dangled on the end of his nose.

"What is it, Sergeant?"

"Sorry for mentioning it, sir, but those niggers—the ones coming down like that—" He pointed to the gully, then lowered his voice so that the trumpeter, waiting for Francis's orders, should not hear him. "I don't like the look of them, sir."

"Quite so, Sergeant," snapped Francis, enraged that the man should think it necessary to proffer advice. "I intend to take a Maxim up there to give 'em snuff."

At that moment, Fynn's Maxim stopped firing. Francis felt as if someone had punched him in the stomach. For several seconds he could only think of Clara lying dead; then other thoughts raced. Either the gun had jammed or the gunner had been hit. No; either the danger was over or the whole party had been overwhelmed. Barnes was trying to speak, so Francis shouted at him to be quiet. Even if the Maxim was done for, there still ought to be rifle fire going on. Not everyone could have died in an instant. Relief swept through him. The silence *must* mean that the danger was over.

He spun around. "Well, Sergeant? Where's my gun crew? I want six first-class marksmen, four pioneers, and four mules."

Sergeant Barnes fiddled with his sword hilt. "Who will be leading them, sir?" Francis recognized the fear in Barnes's voice. A year from retirement, he was desperate to avoid a hero's death.

"I will, Sergeant," replied Francis.

"Is that wise, sir?"

Francis did not know whether to be touched by the man's concern for him or irritated by his doubts about the outcome. He said quietly, "If I'm killed, Mr. Arnot will take command."

As the sergeant cast his eyes up to the crags, frantic efforts were being made to bring down a wounded man. One of the rescuers twisted and fell. Francis showed no emotion. It had been an article of faith at the Staff College that loss of composure in front of his men cost an officer their respect.

Twenty minutes later, Francis himself was crouching behind a rock halfway up the gully. He was bruised, breathless, and soaked with sweat; but at least he was no longer thinking about Clara. His immediate opponent was an old native who knew how to use a Martini-Henry rifle and was an expert at concealment. A few paces behind Francis was his trumpeter, and six paces from him was a dead mule. The other three animals had been sent down after efforts to drag the Maxim over jagged rocks had been abandoned. The gun being little use at the bottom of the gully, Francis and his marksmen had clawed their way higher without it, hoping to achieve with their rifles what the Maxim might have done. Slowly but surely, Francis and his little band were driving out the native snipers.

With the air cracking and whining as bullets ricocheted off rocks at crazy angles, Francis fought his fear by compiling a visual inventory of all the odd spots from which his adversary's grizzled head had bobbed up when he fired. He even managed to enjoy his men's repertoire of tricks: tossing a coat to tempt a snapshot; throwing an arm out and screaming as if hit, then shooting the triumphant native if he tried to look. One of these men had served in Afghanistan, another in Zululand, and thanks to their daring, Francis was able to press onward.

He dropped down into a new cleft between two rocks and almost fell over a body—the old warrior's. The man's thigh had been smashed by a ricochet, but this had not caused his death. In his agony, with all his ammunition gone, the veteran had wedged his assegai in a crevice and flung himself forward so that the blade severed his windpipe. Flies were buzzing inside his gaping mouth. As Francis moved again, he felt his hat struck from his head as if by a stick. He picked it up and saw a neat hole in the crown. Francis was still shocked and breathless when a roll of musketry echoed from behind the ridges. A distant cheer went up. Carew was attacking.

"Trumpeter!" gasped Francis. "Sound the charge!"

As the notes rang out, the men on the ridges scrambled forward again, magically restored to life. Francis was laughing. How many cavalrymen in history had charged like this, on their hands and knees?

When it dawned upon the hussars that they were no longer being fired upon from above, their pace quickened. Francis joined them as they swarmed over the granite ledges that had thwarted them when defended. Clutching at the roots of rockfigs and trusting to precarious tufts of grass as handholds, the troopers helped each other up, scenting victory.

Francis dropped down onto the litter of loose rocks and stones behind the crags and found Mponda's men in full retreat. From the continuous firing, he had expected to see hundreds dead, but there were no more than forty bodies, and not one dressed like a chief or headman. Up here, the hillside was seamed with cracks and wider openings. Francis watched hussars scrabbling at these cave entrances, tearing down barricades of rocks and branches. Again and again puffs of smoke and flashes spurted from concealed loopholes.

When the obstacles had been cleared from the mouth of one of the caves, three troopers entered with their bayonets held before them, as if they were about to prize some dangerous crustacean from its shell. But shots from within sent them reeling back. Seconds later, one was dragged out from the cave by his comrades, stone dead. After six other men had been shot in identical circumstances, Francis told his trumpeter to sound "cease firing." The odds had swung against the attackers. In these low-roofed caves, they had no means of knowing what lay just yards away in the darkness.

Soon after Francis had ordered a general recall, he learned from Sergeant Barnes that Matthew Arnot had been killed on the ridges. Carew was still slapping his men on their backs and shouting for three cheers. Francis's elation vanished. Arnot, with his dark good looks and suave self-confidence, had seemed far above an ordinary soldier's casual death.

While making arrangements for the removal of the men who had been killed, Francis acknowledged that his small success had been bought too dearly. Only the lucky timing of Carew's arrival behind the hilltop crags had denied Mponda the honors of the day. Would the hussars fare so well in a second encounter? Francis doubted it. The moment had arrived to see what Robert Haslam could do.

By the time mauve evening light was falling upon bush and hill, a laager had been made, its sides formed from the squadron's wagons and from felled trees and thornbushes. Pickets had been sent out and Maxims strategically placed. The dead had been buried close to Mponda's hill, and now the living, including eighteen wounded, were preparing to spend the night in a shallow valley flanked by a mopane wood.

The sun was sinking below the hills when Francis was buttonholed by Heywood Fynn and asked to walk out with him beyond the picket lines. Assuming that the American had found evidence of an impending attack, Francis followed with a heavy heart. After a few yards, he was unlucky enough to touch a buffalo bean plant with his hand. The discomfort never lasted more than an hour or two, but the burning sensation at the outset was severe enough to stop him from worrying about whatever Fynn might be on the point of revealing. Francis's shock was therefore all the greater when they came upon two young Matabele warriors trussed up like wild animals and guarded by three scouts. One of these guards was Francis's former orderly, Arthur Winter.

The captives were wearing traditional oxtail anklets, which would have fluttered if the men were running but hung down now, bloodstained and bedraggled. The warriors were young and had been beaten so badly that they could hardly open their eyes. Both were vainly trying to hide their fear.

"Who the hell did this to them?" shouted Francis.

"I did," growled Fynn. "We gotta know who these guys are."

"They may be spies from that impi, sir," stammered Arthur Winter.

"They may be spying for Mponda," pointed out Francis. "We know he has some Matabele in his force."

Fynn cleared his throat and spat. "We're kiddin' ourselves if we don't figure a link with that big impi."

Francis nodded toward the captives. "Where did they come from?"

"Over there," said Fynn, indicating the opposite direction from Mponda's stronghold.

"They could still have come from Mponda's hill." Francis knew he sounded too eager to believe this.

Fynn was exasperated. "If they crawled up the bed of the stream and doubled back, sure they could have come from the hill." The American thrust his face closer. "But maybe they came from just where their tracks tell us they did."

Francis said quietly, "All right, I take your point. But *don't* torture them."

"Are you nuts, Vaughan?" Fynn was beside himself. "They'd skin us alive without thinkin' twice. There may be three thousand savages on our trail."

Fear moved in Francis like a living thing. "No torture," he insisted.

"Then how do we make 'em talk?" grated Fynn. "I'm not gonna die for your principles."

Something had to be suggested quickly. Francis said, "We'll stage a mock execution tonight. Hoist them off their feet for a few seconds. They'll talk."

Fynn shook his head. "We hang 'em proper or not at all. If folk get the idea they was hanged and came alive, they're gonna reckon we couldn't kill them."

Francis cried, "You think Haslam will help us if we murder our prisoners?"

"Who says we tell him? Send me six men who can button their mouths."

Francis let out a long breath. "All right, Fynn. You speak

their language. Tell them they'll be hanged unless they talk, but remember, *I* decide the outcome.''

In camp again, Francis told Sergeant Barnes what he wanted and asked that the quartermaster and all others involved keep whatever happened to themselves. Then he visited the wounded. One hussar had been shot in the genitals; five had lost limbs, and four of these would probably be dead in a week. The exception was a young trooper whose passion had been football and who had lost his right leg. While talking to him, Francis was absurdly conscious of his smarting hand.

Francis had given orders for an encircling ring of fires to be built so that his Maxim gunners could see to shoot down attackers in the darkness before they could reach the tents and horses. As night fell, the firelit trunks of the closest mopane trees were etched brightly against the black wood behind.

In the same glowing light, Francis saw Robert Haslam hurrying toward him. His gray hair was disordered, and his eyes were bright and staring.

''Why have you been avoiding me, Mr. Vaughan?''

''I've had much on my hands.''

''Blood, sir. You have *that* on your hands.''

''Blood?'' faltered Francis, fearing that Clara had been hurt.

''Don't play the fool with me,'' rasped the missionary. ''I speak of the blood of the innocent men you shot and killed today.''

''I regret all deaths, natives and settlers,'' murmured Francis, relieved but still wary. ''I hope today's events will make Mponda keener to oblige us.''

Haslam said scornfully, ''Some men aren't cowed by force.''

''But they respond to appeals.'' Francis smiled encouragingly. ''Mponda will agree to go home if you tell him there'll be no reprisals. He'll believe what you say.'' Francis paused. ''Can he read?'' Haslam nodded. ''Then write to him tonight, and I'll find a way to get your letter to him in the morning.''

''Understand this, Vaughan. I'll refuse to meet him if you send soldiers to escort me. I won't be used by you to trick him.''

''There'll be no double-crossing.''

''You're quite right, Captain. But do you know why there'll be no double-crossing?'' Robert seemed amused by Francis's silence. ''It's because I'll be taking my wife with me and no one else.''

''That's mad!'' gasped Francis, dismayed to find his knees shaking. ''Africans aren't disciplined like white troops.''

The missionary smiled blandly. "Mrs. Haslam has asked to come. She says if she's with me, Mponda's men will know you can't intend treachery." Haslam eyed Francis sadly. "I'm not a fool, Vaughan. I know you mean to follow my tracks when I go to meet him—you and your assassins. If Mponda dies, his men surrender: you think that's your best chance, don't you? So what would it matter if you hit me too?"

Francis stared at him, appalled. "That's a lie. Mrs. Haslam can't think that I'd murder you unless she goes too. I don't believe it."

The missionary's face had become deathly pale. "How do you presume to know my wife's thoughts?"

"Because ... because I know she thinks ..."

"Thinks you honorable?" Haslam's smile became a sneer.

Francis said, "Did Simon tell you?"

"Tell me what?" Again that cold mockery.

"That I love your wife," declared Francis.

"No, sir, he didn't. *She* told me, this morning."

Francis's mouth hung open. "Is *that* why you think I might kill you? So I could have her afterward?"

"Yes," he hissed.

Francis looked at Haslam's suffering face and shuddered. Could the man have any idea of the guilt Clara must be feeling in order to have made her offer? For no other reason would she be prepared to risk her life.

As Robert Haslam walked away, Francis watched him helplessly. Was there any way he could stop Clara? Everything he knew about her character made him fear there was not.

Francis arrived, to see the ropes already in place on the branch of a spreading kachere tree. Although the sky was inky black, the distant fires threw a ghostly light on the proceedings. Joined wrist to wrist, the two Matabele sidled along like crabs so that both could keep to the twisting game path and avoid prickly grasses on either side.

As they gazed incuriously at the pair of ropes and nooses, Francis caught his breath. A sight he had relied upon to breed immediate terror meant nothing to them. Not a thing. But why should it? Clearly they had never seen a hanging. Francis had said "no torture" to Fynn because he had thought that if threatened with hanging, the prisoners would reach the breaking point long before their feet left the ground. Now they would have to be half throttled before they knew the meaning of those innocuous-looking ropes.

While the men were untied from each other and had their hands and ankles pinioned, Fynn talked to them in their own language. They remained unconcerned and listless, retreating further into a world of their own. Francis's old regimental M.O. in India had often regaled the mess with tales of botched hangings. When the drop had been too long, heads had come off; when too short, death had been by strangulation. In such cases, he claimed to have heard heartbeats twenty minutes after men had been suspended. Francis found he had forgotten the only really important fact. How long could people live if hanged without a drop?

"Let's get 'em up now, Sergeant," he rasped.

Barnes adjusted the nooses. Almost at once, the branch began to creak as troopers heaved on the twin pulleys. Francis heard someone say, "Like a bleedin' Christmas tree." The prisoners were writhing as they rotated slowly. Their bodies, which had looked so lithe and light a few moments before, now seemed incalculably heavy. One hunched his chin deep into his shoulders; the other's neck had somehow been bent right back. Francis was aghast as the tribesman's whole body jerked convulsively like a hooked fish.

"Get ahold of him," yelled Fynn. But before anyone moved, there was a muffled crack. The man became limp. When lifted down, though still alive, he could not move a finger.

"Broke his own goddamn neck," muttered Fynn in stunned admiration.

An awful choking noise was coming from the throat of the other man. Francis wanted to block his ears but forced clenched fists deeper into his pockets. And I was the one who hated the idea of torture. He bore the noise for almost a minute longer, before yelling, "Take him down, Sergeant."

The man was still gasping and retching, as Fynn peppered him with question after question. Again and again he waited for an answer. In vain.

"Pull him up," groaned Francis.

The process was repeated twice more before Francis could bear it no longer and declared the experiment at an end. The survi-

vor's loincloth had slipped, and his penis dragged in the grit as he
sank to the earth on naked buttocks.

"They beat us real good, huh?" grunted Fynn. He pointed
to the other Matabele, motionless but still breathing. "Can't just
leave 'im, Vaughan." He touched his holster meaningfully.

"I agree," blurted out Francis. "The second one stays our
prisoner. That means alive."

As he was passing through the picket lines, Francis heard a
shot and, after several seconds, another. On the point of running
back, he paused. The deed was done and could not be changed.
He tried to believe that Fynn had used two bullets on the same
man, but his doubts remained. Shame bore down on him. "A gentleman," his mother had often said, "is a man who would never
knowingly inflict pain upon another human being."

An orange moon faded to dull silver as it drifted above
Mponda's hill. Gazing at it, Clara felt calmer than she had for
days. Now that she was going with her husband on his mission,
she no longer reproached herself. Their account was in balance
again. He would always blame her, of course, but there were things
she would never forgive *him*—among them, letting Mponda trust
him, almost as if he himself were Christ.

In the small hours she lay sleepless, while Robert wrote by
candlelight. Even at this eleventh hour, she could not bring herself
to ask him whether he expected to live or die. The missionary who
died was no longer needed by God. As Robert's pen scratched
across the paper, she wondered what pleasure he had ever got out
of his life and whether he felt regrets. She doubted it. To give and
not to count the cost had been his golden rule. Did he think of
Philemon now, or Hannah and Mabo, and did he miss them? It
shocked her not to know.

After she had confessed her affair to Robert, he had been
dumbfounded, having imagined that her pious upbringing would
have made such a betrayal impossible. Never sensual himself, he
had detected no sensuality in her. Grief and bitterness had
washed through him slowly, as if numbed nerves were recovering one by one.

He had told her that a picture in an anti-slavery pamphlet,
which he had seen in boyhood, had never left him: a howling

Negro in the Deep South running from a white man with a gun. Now, once again, white men with guns were breaking his heart. How could she love any man prepared to exact vengeance on simple tribesmen for defending their homes? Clara had not argued, but in her mind she had defended her lover. Francis had not come to Africa by choice and had never condoned the settlers' brutality. Instead he had forbidden the burning of grain and had begged Robert to help him save lives.

When Clara fell asleep, she dreamed that she had been hit by a bullet and that Francis was holding her. She awakened before dawn, longing to tell him that her feelings were unchanged but guessing there would be no chance before she left. Watch fires still glowed on Mponda's hill, and a cool night breeze made Clara shiver. She knew the danger she faced but, despite her fear, could not risk living the rest of her life believing, if Robert died, that her presence could have saved him.

Chapter 22

Fynn's scouts had been out at dawn, quartering the whole valley in their search for fresh tracks, and had summoned Francis to consider various "discoveries." Barely four hundred yards from the camp, an ox had been driven along a game path by a barefooted man. Moist dung and pristine tracks established that the journey had been made during the night. Fynn deduced more: the driver was lame in his left foot and used a stick. Such a man would not have gone on a nocturnal excursion, reasoned the American, unless he had been taking supplies to the rebels.

Even in the present situation, Francis took pleasure in the progress made by Fynn's two newest scouts. Both were town boys. Arthur Winter, Francis's erstwhile orderly, had been an assistant in a department store and had never even seen the countryside before joining the army. Fynn indicated to Francis that he should follow Arthur, who was soon pointing to a particular spot in the grass beside the path. Though Francis himself would have walked straight by, he now saw the clear impression made by the ball of a foot.

Arthur coughed diffidently. "You can see the toes too, sir, splayed out like before jumping."

Francis knelt down and could indeed see the toe marks. And there on the opposite side of the path was another indentation, this time made by a heel—exactly the kind of imprint that would be left by a man landing after a leap. Someone had jumped across the path in order not to leave his footprints on the trodden earth.

"Follow me, please, sir," asked Winter, delighted to have his commanding officer's undivided attention.

Just yards away, similar prints showed that this person had not been alone in crossing the path. Arthur Winter's excitement was mixed with alarm as he pointed to more and more footprints. Francis merely smiled and remarked, "Well done, Corporal. I see you're learning fast."

Fynn snarled, "You gotta believe this, Vaughan: there's a second force out there, and they're spoilin' for somethin'."

Francis said sharply, "Were *none* of these tracks made by Mponda's men?"

Arthur ran an anxious hand through his cropped hair. "We looked all over, sir, but we couldn't find no tracks comin' from there." He jerked his head toward the chief's hill.

What Francis had most dreaded was coming true: there really was another force close by. "Are they made by Matabele?" he asked, nodding toward the tracks, praying the answer would be no.

"Some may be," replied Fynn. He produced a few harmless-looking fronds from his pocket. "The Matabele use this plant's leaves to stopper their beer pots. It's not a common plant around here."

"Take a sniff, sir," suggested Arthur, holding out a leaf to Francis.

The smell of beer was faint but undeniable. Francis said to Fynn, "You want to leave now and so do I, but we must wait till Haslam's had his chat with Mponda."

"You'll let Haslam risk his neck while these guys are prowlin' all over and there's an impi out there?" Fynn was shocked.

"Your scouts can follow him closely."

"For Christ's sake, Vaughan, they'll jus' get a great view when the Holy Joe gets his head blown off."

"Nonsense," cried Francis. "Mponda dotes on Haslam. He's going to lay out the red carpet."

"How come he's expecting him?"

Francis smiled serenely, "I've been lucky. The pickets captured an old man at first light. He's on his way to Mponda with a letter from Haslam."

"The chief can read?"

"His own language, yes."

"Why won't your old nigger toss the letter away?"

Francis grinned. "We've held on to something he's fond of."

"His loincloth?" scoffed the American.

"His son. And some goats."

Arthur and the other young scout laughed, while Fynn remained grim-faced. "Did the pickets blindfold the son of a bitch before letting him in?"

"Of course. I promise you that Mponda won't learn a thing

about the camp from him.'' Francis guessed that Fynn was uneasy because he thought the column's only African interpreter spoke English too badly to translate accurately. ''The old man understood us, and we understood him,'' soothed Francis. ''He said Mponda can't be killed by bullets because he's drunk the white man's holy medicine. And this is the bad bit: he thinks everyone who follows Mponda will be bulletproof too.''

''Thanks a lot, Jesus,'' sighed Fynn.

Later that morning, Francis went outside the perimeter to make a drawing of the graves of Matthew Arnot and the others. As a child, Francis had often drawn and painted for pleasure. Nowadays he rarely drew anything except for money. His sketches of military subjects had often been bought for a few guineas by magazines like *The Illustrated London News* and *Black & White*. He meant to send today's drawings as gifts to the dead men's next of kin.

On returning to camp, Francis spotted Clara watching a party of hussars building a barricade out of earth-filled sacks. Since, by some miracle, Haslam was not with her, Francis hurried over to her with a pounding heart.

''Please don't go with him,'' he implored.

''I must.'' Her voice was small and tight.

''You could die in front of me. I couldn't bear it.'' His throat ached with the effort of not shouting.

''Not here, Francis,'' she whispered. ''If Robert dies, people will say you sent him to his death.''

''You mean you're risking your life to stop tittle-tattle?''

''Try to understand,'' she moaned. ''White men hate endangering their women. Every native knows that. So if I'm seen at Robert's side, they'll know he can't be trying any tricks. No one will fire at us.''

''Clara, Clara,'' he groaned. ''Will you never stop trying to do the right thing?''

''It's hard to explain it to you, Francis, but I know if I don't do this, you and I will never be happy again.''

Francis pointed to a man near the Maxim pit on the other side of the camp. ''Suppose you were standing where that man is. Would I know your sex? Not a chance—unless you happened to be balancing a pot on your head.'' He kicked at the grass. ''If I had any sense, I'd stop this whole wretched business.''

''And condemn hundreds to death?''

Her faith in Haslam mortified Francis. He said gently, "Your husband may fail. Mponda may tell him to go to hell. I can't bear to be responsible for harming you."

"It's my decision ... nothing to do with you."

"Is it really?" he said dryly. "Guilt for what we've done doesn't come into it, I suppose."

"No," she said, stretching out a hand.

He held it for a moment, certain that she was lying to make things easier for him. His brave, generous, obstinate Clara. "I love you."

"I love you too." She squeezed his fingers. "Francis, will you do something for me?" He nodded. "Promise not to follow us."

"If you really want that." But he knew, even as he spoke, that he would not be able to stay away while she was shot at. Somehow she had to be saved from herself. If only Haslam had insisted on going alone, how simple everything would have been.

At midday, Fynn came up to Francis while he was supervising the laying of mines filled with rock-blasting explosive. Elsewhere, Francis had ordered the scattering of broken bottles to slow down barefooted attackers, but Fynn was unimpressed by all his arrangements. He said brusquely, "Ever ask yourself why these spies keep comin' so close and stayin'?"

Francis frowned. Wasn't the answer obvious? "To study our defenses."

"But why send so many scouts? A few could have told 'em about trenches and pits. We found spoor for risin' eighty men."

"Perhaps they feel safer coming in strength." Francis was alarmed by the American's persistence.

"A lot of these fellers stay out there in the mopane woods all day long, just watchin' us." Fynn raised a warning finger. "So don' let Haslam go anyplace till I find out more."

"Of course not. I don't want him harmed either." Since Francis liked and trusted Fynn, he had been thankful to learn that the second of the two Matabele prisoners had not been shot and was recovering under guard. It hurt Francis that Fynn appeared to think him ready to risk Haslam's life unnecessarily, maybe for personal reasons. There was a moral core to the American's nature, which, though well hidden, made Francis miserable to be misunderstood by him. Wanting to please Fynn before he set out, Francis promised to strike camp the moment Haslam had met Mponda. But Fynn was not pleased. With his grizzled hair and white-flecked beard, he reminded Francis of a truculent and brave old badger.

"You should do it soon as I'm back, if I say so."

A few hours later, Fynn rode into the bush with his gun across his knees, vowing to identify the spies in the mopane woods. If they were having dealings with Mponda, or if they were part of a Matabele impi, he would shortly find out.

Watching him leave with Arthur Winter and another of his young scouts, Francis experienced a sudden chill—less physical fear than superstitious dread. Was it possible, wondered Francis, that Nashu had sent him here not to destroy Mponda, as he had imagined, but to be destroyed by him?

Beyond the mopane woods, the ground sloped uphill steeply. Fynn and his two companions came to a belt of dark-foliaged trees, which were in turn replaced by thick bamboos. The ground was sodden and the air hot and steamy. Their horses' ears were laid back as they slipped and slithered. Bamboos whipped across their forelegs, and the smell of elephant droppings made them snort with fear.

At last the bamboos ended, and a moorland slope began. Tussocks of coarse grass made the going so rough that they dismounted to save their horses. Before them lay a deep valley, and beyond it blue hills. Until now, it had been easy to follow the tracks of the men who had spied on their camp. But here their footprints were lost in the boggy spaces between the tussocks. Hoping to find the spoor again on the far side of the valley, they hurried on, concealing themselves by descending in a shallow ravine, alongside a fast-flowing stream. Fynn took a metal cup from his saddle and, to amuse his companions, scooped a little gravel from the stream's bed. Having picked out the loose stones and earth, he washed the rest, leaving a fine residue of iron ore at the bottom of the cup. After repeating this process several times, he swirled the tail of fine grit to one side. To the stupefaction of the young scouts, a few specks of gold appeared.

"Just a 'color.' " Fynn laughed. "Plenty o' streams have colors and nothin' else."

While scrutinizing the opposite hilltop through his binoculars, Fynn related how he had once spent time prospecting in the Mogollon Mountains in Arizona and had lost everything he owned on the venture. When the scouts splashed their faces in the stream, he warned them that too much washing encouraged bush sores. Was there nothing this man hadn't seen or done? They knew there were other American scouts in Mashonaland, but for Arthur Winter and his friend Wilfred Birch, Heywood Fynn was unique.

On setting out, he had told them a story about Mr. Haslam. The missionary, he said, had first won the respect of Chief Mponda because of a bizarre event. In 1886, Haslam had shot an ox in celebration of his first wife's birthday. The bullet had passed through the animal, ricocheted off a tree behind it, and landed inches from the missionary's feet. A woman passerby who had witnessed this freak shot saw him calmly pick up the spent bullet and put it in his pocket, just as the ox sank to its knees. Mponda heard the news within the hour and decided that Haslam must be a great nganga. Who else could call back bullets at will?

The scouts found the tracks again exactly where Fynn had anticipated. The young men were at once affected by their mentor's gravity. As always, Fynn questioned them about their observations. How could they be sure of the age of these tracks? They whispered their answers: no rain had fallen on the footprints; few seeds had blown across them; the edges of some of the imprints were still damp; grasses that had been bent or broken by the natives' feet had not yet dried or withered. Arthur knew that their enemies must be very close. The utmost caution was essential.

At the brow of the next hill, they left their horses under some trees. Before reaching the top, Fynn ordered Arthur to go on alone. He liked his young apprentices to show what they could do. Arthur chose to crawl and did not breach the skyline until finding a tree stump to peer around. These two young townies almost made Fynn wish that he had had a son.

Arthur moved his head gingerly to the side of the stump, and feared he would faint. Too scared to make a sound or raise his head, he slewed around on his stomach and scrambled back toward Fynn and Wilfred on all fours.

"Niggers," he gasped. "Hundreds of them." Many had been

hiding in the long grass, but he had seen enough headdresses and spears to fancy there must be a small army out there.

"How far?" cried Fynn, already running back toward their horses.

"Hundred yards. Could be less."

As his two companions swung up into their saddles, Fynn studied the terrain in the direction from which they had just come. Warriors were crawling out of the elephant grass in the valley bottom. His mind was working fast. The men Arthur had just seen over the brow of the hill had shown themselves deliberately, so Fynn guessed they wanted him to turn back and retrace his steps toward the men coming up from the valley bottom. He and his young scouts could probably ride through these warriors in the elephant grass, but once they were past them, the boggy ground would slow down their horses to a trot, giving the running spearmen a fine chance to overtake and kill them.

At any second, warriors would appear on the skyline, intent on forcing them back toward the men in the valley bottom.

"We've gotta ride straight at 'em," announced Fynn. The two young men looked back nervously, as if wishing to retrace their steps. "Hell no!" cried Fynn, pointing to the brow of the hill as he mounted. They loaded their rifles, and Fynn kneed his horse around. "Stay close," he urged. Then, with a whoop and a yell, he thumped in his heels as if heading for a jump.

They flew over the brow of the hill knee-to-knee. A gently dropping slope stretched ahead, spotted with bushes and stunted thorn trees. Not a soul was to be seen. Fynn signed to them to trot. These tribesmen were cleverer than he had expected. Were they luring him and his friends forward into a ring that would close behind them? He turned sharply and saw men racing from bush to bush far to his left. The trap was already being sprung. With no time to guess where the circle would be weakest, he acted on instinct and rode hard to the left.

"If I fall, leave me," he shouted. "Get through and warn Vaughan."

The three of them were already galloping as they came up to their enemies. Fynn's wrists were strong enough for him to hold a rifle in one hand, and he fired now from the saddle, hoping to unsettle the natives' aim. His bullets kicked up dust around the bushes ahead. Arthur drew his sword and Wilfred his revolver.

Fynn saw heads and shoulders weaving among the bushes. The tribesmen's rifles began to crackle. Bullets whipped past with weird little *phit, phit* noises or a shrill *wh-e-e-e-w* as they flicked off the ground. Arthur was ahead, just to the right. Wilfred was level, to Fynn's left. The thunder of hooves and his own thumping heartbeats filled Fynn's ears. The sun flashed on Arthur's sword as he slashed and cut, carrying the weight of his horse into the blows. Men spun backward, shields and spears lifting in the air.

Fifty yards away, a tribesman with a Martini-Henry dropped on one knee and drew a steady bead on Arthur. Fynn fired the last two bullets in his magazine but missed with both. The native squeezed the trigger. Arthur's horse fell heavily in a tangle of legs and saddlery. Fynn was past in a flash but not too fast to see Arthur rolled onto the ground by a man with a short assegai. Fynn tried to turn his horse, but the animal refused, desperate to leave the fray. Crashing a boot along his horse's jaw, he swung him around by main force. As Wilfred galloped by, Fynn roared at him to keep riding, then he broke the cardinal rule of a scout's duty to his column and rode back to help his fallen comrade.

Arthur was kneeling behind his horse's body. Bright blood was oozing from his thigh. A knot of spearmen faced him at a distance, intimidated by his carbine. Closing from behind, Fynn shouted and discharged his rifle. He hit one man with a lucky shot, and as he charged, the others turned and fled. Dismounting, he hoisted Arthur up onto his own stallion, before running back to the young corporal's horse and cutting the ammunition pockets from the saddle.

Fynn mounted in front of Arthur, and they rode on. The tribesmen's deadly tactic soon became clear. They would creep into bushes, wait till he had passed, and then jump out and fire at his back. Arthur, clinging on behind, was terrified.

"Wilfred's broken through," Fynn reassured him.

Ahead, more warriors were blocking their escape. These men wore Matabele headrings, unlike the more numerous Venda, with their ostrich feathers. Fynn fired and missed. Seeing antiquated wide-bore guns leveled at him, he lowered his head to protect his eyes. A volley of birdshot peppered his scalp and his horse's shoulders. The maddened animal burst forward as if in the final furlong of a race.

Fynn and Arthur were level with their enemies now. Wielding his rifle like a club, Fynn sent two men spinning away.

Blood from his head was blinding him. Warriors were closing in, their skin kilts swinging as they ran. One seized Fynn's foot but lost his grip. To Fynn's amazement, the way ahead seemed clear. Yet something had happened. Something was horribly wrong. Why was his horse not moving faster? The animal was rising and falling on the spot, up and down like a hobbyhorse. A hundred yards away, natives were pointing and starting in pursuit.

Fynn dismounted. A spear was sticking in his horse's belly, just beside the girth. The poor creature was finished. So it was the end for him and Arthur too. As the dying animal's forelegs splayed out, Arthur slipped to the ground, his face gray with pain and terror. The muscles at the back of his thigh had been torn apart by a spearpoint, and he was bleeding profusely. Fynn carried him ten yards to a tall anthill, then ran back to his horse. Many a time the dilation of his stallion's nostrils or the pointing of his ears had warned Fynn of danger. Today the horse had done his best to save him. Fynn held his revolver out of sight and nuzzled against the animal's neck. The stallion whinnied for the last time, as if being brought his corn. Then Fynn sent a bullet through his brain.

Bowed down by his saddle and everything attached to it, the American staggered back to the anthill. With two rifles and plentiful ammunition, he and Arthur might last fifteen minutes. More if they were very unlucky.

Fynn loaded their four guns. He then bandaged Arthur's leg and gave him water and brandy. He knew the Africans would not move in for the kill until they had completely surrounded the anthill. When the attack came, it would be from all sides and would culminate with a dash. Seeing tears welling from Arthur's eyes, Fynn squeezed his hand.

"You won't let them . . . ?"

"I won't," Fynn promised, mentally kissing the bullets in his revolver.

"Why don't they come, Mr. Fynn?"

"They won't be long."

Arthur whispered, "Why can't we end it now? Why should we wait?"

"Say we kill maybe ten or twenty . . . That's a handy few who ain't gonna be botherin' Captain Vaughan."

"I can't even stand."

Fynn moved the saddle, scraped out a shallow depression behind it with his knife, and scooped away the loose soil with his hands. "Lie here and shoot around the cantle." He helped the wounded man position himself. Arthur's breeches were stained with blood and excrement.

Fynn listened hard but could hear no rattle of trinkets or spears against shields. The Africans were still far enough away for him to risk clambering onto the anthill. From the top he could see natives converging from every side, a couple of hundred at least. They were approaching gingerly, using the bushes and thorn trees for cover. He raised his rifle and shot three of them. In retaliation, bullets sang past so close that Fynn half slid, half fell down the anthill to the ground.

He swiped at the inferno of flies buzzing around Arthur's legs. The boy was weeping openly, and with each sob his heels gave a little jerk. High above, vultures circled in the pale-blue sky. Fynn tried not to imagine the images that had caused the boy's terror—and yet his own bowels were loosening. The nearest bushes were less than a dozen yards away. They would come running and leaping across that flat ground in seconds: firing, screaming, flinging spears. Would that leave him time to use his revolver?

Fynn had been almost as close to death before. When he was three, his mother had hidden him from the Sioux in a stack of newly shocked corn. He had lived because it had been too green to burn. Since then he might have died at the hands of a score of enemies: the Apache, cattle rustlers, outlaws, Mexicans, the Zulus in Natal, and in '93 the Matabele. And now, three years later, his sands of time had finally run out.

The torment of waiting made him long to fling himself into the open, away from the sheltering pile of clay. Or he could reach down and lift death to his temple. Instead he knelt beside Arthur.

"Not long now." He eased the neck of his brandy flask between Arthur's teeth. "These men are warriors. . . . Remember the guys we strung up? We can do well too."

For a time Fynn could not hear the approaching men above the sound of his own breathing, but soon the swish of grass was unmistakable. They were close enough to stand in the open and pour in a single lethal volley. But that was not their way. Already individuals were cutting loose with wild and uncoordinated shots.

"Don't waste your bullets, Arthur. Pick your man."

And then Fynn saw the blur of war paint on rich brown skin, and he was firing. Flame spurted from muzzle loaders, an oxhide shield loomed close enough to touch. A wind seemed to whip

across Arthur's shirt, scorching his back with a raw red furrow.
He leapt up with a scream and fell against the anthill. Released
from fear by rage and pain, he swiveled with incredible speed.
His rifle came up to his shoulder, and he shot three men with
six bullets.

Fynn was picking up his second rifle when a shot sent him
spinning around. Blood welled from his shoulder. Yet his arm still
functioned. The bullet had clipped his collarbone, missing both
nerve and artery. Arthur's gun was silent, its magazine empty.
Fynn tossed him his revolver.

Around the anthill lay dead and wounded men. Only moans
and cries broke the stillness. The first onslaught was over. Fynn
knew it was no more than a lull: an interlude before the final act.
His heart was hammering. A strange, high-pitched voice cut
through the silence, the speaker's words distorted by some kind
of horn.

"Won't the Lightning Bird help you?" sneered the voice. At
once, Fynn knew that Nashu was speaking. The American remembered making the nganga's beer catch fire and claiming to have
tamed the Lightning Bird.

"What does he say?" gasped Arthur. Fynn motioned to him
to be quiet.

"Only the eagle can safely offend," rasped the screeching
voice.

Fynn knew this Venda proverb well. The eagle could afford
to offend because he could fly away. Fynn yelled back, "The lion
that roars has not yet caught his prey."

"The Lightning Bird will kill you and the Umfundisi too."

Silence again. So *that* was why so many men had been creeping close to the camp. Nashu was desperate to kill the missionary
before he could persuade Mponda to make peace. One day Nashu
would surely kill Mponda too and replace him with Makufa. But
that would be after Mponda had been weakened by the hussars.
What a fool Vaughan had been to think he could use a man like
Nashu without being used by him. In the end the nganga would
probably betray the English to the Matabele.

Fynn was binding up his shoulder when he smelled fire. This
puzzled him, since the grass on the hilltop was scarcely dry enough
to burn. Only when he saw Nashu's men dragging up smoking
branches of mimosa and thorn did he understand the Lightning
Bird's revenge.

Arthur was slumped against the saddle, fighting the pain of stiffening wounds. His head was thrown back, and his eyes were tightly closed. At any moment he might smell his fate. The revolver lay in the dust, inches from the young man's hand. Fynn reached for it. Haslam would say a man should prepare for his death. Prepare to be burned alive? Fynn lifted the gun to Arthur's head and squeezed the trigger. No second shot was needed. The smoke was thicker now. Fynn spun the cylinder. Three bullets left. He pressed the barrel to his temple, then let it drop.

Why sneak away when he could meet it squarely? He flung down the gun and, like a sprinter, burst from the shelter of the anthill. He leapt a burning barrier and ran on, blinded by smoke. Already he could hear their pounding feet. The fleetest were soon at his shoulder. He heard the rattle of their ornaments, smelled their grease. Others pressed in from every side. An assegai pierced his side; another entered behind his knee, bringing him crashing down. Fynn made no effort to roll aside as the fatal spear was driven between his ribs.

CHAPTER 23

Ordinary men could be killed, but not *him*, not Heywood Fynn. Wilfred's cracked and dust-caked lips were trembling as he related the manner of Fynn's suicidal turning back. When Francis had heard as much as the trooper could tell him, he was shaken and grief-stricken but not really surprised. He and Fynn had often enacted half-mocking images of each other: Francis the quixotic gentleman, part English hypocrite, part chivalrous fool; Fynn the brutal pioneer, hard-bitten, cynical, realistic. Fynn a realist? He was a man who had done everything for adventure, nothing for luxury or gain, never settling, never prospering, drawn only by the raw life of the frontier.

Wilfred was looking at him with deepening anxiety. Francis realized that he was scowling. Why couldn't poor Arthur have been the one to escape? Why should it have been this nondescript Trooper Birch—this boy who couldn't say whether two hundred or two thousand men were about to attack? Arthur would surely have done better than that. And Fynn, miraculous Fynn—he would have told him not only their numbers but their intentions.

In the early afternoon a messenger arrived at the camp and said that he had orders from Chief Mponda to lead the Umfundisi to a secret meeting place. But if anyone attempted to follow, the messenger explained, he had instructions to turn back.

What was to be done? wondered Francis. Fynn's killers could be an advance guard of the impi, part of Mponda's force, or even a different group entirely. So should Haslam be allowed to leave the camp when native regiments were threatening on every side? The answer ought to be no; but this was the direst of emergencies. Only the missionary's personal pleas could now dissuade Mponda from launching a mass onslaught on the column. The problem would be how to stop Clara from going too.

The sun was blazing down and the midday silence still hung

over the camp as Captain Vaughan laid his plans. He and half a dozen men would tail Robert Haslam (or both Haslams), along with the chief's messenger, as closely as they could without betraying themselves. A long way behind, a cavalry troop would follow, leading their horses. Francis's trumpeter would be at his side to summon these men should the need arise. Meanwhile the camp, with Carew in charge, would remain in readiness.

As Francis strode toward the Haslams' tent, he was terrified for Clara. Because his duty to his column meant that he had to encourage Haslam's mission, the best he could hope for would be to shame her husband into leaving her behind.

Outside the missionary's tent, Simon was grinding coffee beans with a stone. On catching sight of Francis, the boy darted inside with the speed of a gecko. So now I'm the devil incarnate, thought Francis, saddened to recall the boy's former friendliness. Francis had decided to break the news of Fynn's death, before telling them that the chief's messenger had arrived. That way, he hoped to make Haslam nervous about taking Clara with him.

In fact, the missionary received the news of Fynn's death calmly. Not so Clara, whose hands shot up to her mouth. "How did it happen?"

"A trap. He might have escaped if he hadn't tried to save his companion."

Tears brimmed in her eyes. "Who was with him?"

"Corporal Winter."

"How horrible!"

Robert Haslam sighed. "Sadly, Clara, those who live by the sword really *do* die by it."

Francis said sharply, "They're not the only ones, sir. When a chief loses faith in his mentor, he murders him."

"What point are you making, Captain?"

The missionary's bland manner struck Francis as contemptuous. "Mponda may blame you for failing to stop my attack on his stronghold."

Haslam shrugged. "I've no means of knowing until I speak to him."

"Then how can it be safe for your wife to go with you? This isn't speculation anymore. The chief has agreed to meet you."

The missionary raised bushy eyebrows. "Do soldiers expect to be safe when *they* do their duty?"

"Of course not," snapped Francis.

"Then why should Christ's soldiers expect anything different?"

"Soldiers don't take their wives to the front line," cried Francis.

"Africa is our front line, sir—the whole country. I can't tell Mrs. Haslam where her duty lies. She is the best judge of that."

Clara said quietly, "Mr. Fynn's death makes it even more important for Robert to meet Mponda. I know I can give him a better chance."

"I'm afraid I forbid you to go," said Francis.

"Then *I* won't go, sir," announced the missionary.

Francis's cheeks were burning. "What compels you to endanger your wife's life?"

"You misunderstand, Captain. Mrs. Haslam is a free woman entitled to do what she thinks is right. How can I deny her that?"

Francis moved closer. "Don't fool yourself, Haslam. She's only going with you out of guilt."

The missionary clapped his hands, almost with glee. "Christians are supposed to feel guilt, sir. They seek redemption for it by prayer and good deeds."

Francis turned to Clara. "You're forcing me to call it off."

"Francis," she whispered, "you can't place more value on my life than on the lives of all your soldiers."

Francis met her gaze for several seconds, but she did not waver. He knew her too well to suppose that there was a chance of changing her mind.

With nothing more to be said, he remarked that he would return in an hour to wish them farewell.

The bush was thick and tangled; and as Francis and the members of his small patrol crawled forward, thorns pierced their breeches and tore their hands. Working around termite mounds and across streambeds, they struggled to keep in sight the three tiny figures almost half a mile ahead of them. Francis dropped his field glasses with a cry as a puff adder slithered past, inches from his face.

At last the Haslams and their guide reached a belt of trees and disappeared from view, allowing their pursuers to get up and run. Francis used a helio mirror to signal to his troops a thousand yards away, permitting them to come forward. Entering the wood, he gestured to his men to move cautiously. If the messenger saw any bolting antelope, he might decide to guide the Haslams no further.

Beyond the mopane trees, low hills rose on either side of a valley that narrowed to a gorge, blocked at its far end by limestone cliffs. Shadows in the cliffs could indicate caves, and already Francis saw how easy it would be for the chief to cut off anyone entering the valley. Fearfully he scanned the hills in case men were moving among the stunted trees that pimpled the slopes. In the baking valley bottom, acacias trembled in mirages, and the three human figures blurred and dissolved in the haze. Francis hated losing sight of the Haslams for a moment, but he was relieved to know that when the chief's guide looked back, he too would see everything undulating as if under water.

Finding the absence of game curious, Francis kept glancing at the hills, wanting to summon more men but telling himself it would be criminal to panic and give orders that might stop the vital meeting between Haslam and the chief from taking place.

As the valley became narrower, instinct told Francis that he must move forward to be within sprinting distance of the Haslams by the time they entered the limestone cul-de-sac. Hemmed in by rocks and thorn trees, he kept looking from side to side. Suddenly his heart rose up to choke him. Dark shapes were moving parallel on the slopes to his left. Unable to see anybody straight ahead, he waved his men on, dashing forward with Sergeant Barnes and his trumpeter beside him.

When Francis sighted the Haslams again, they were much closer than he had expected, perhaps two hundred paces away. He signaled to his men to get down and raised his field glasses. A tall and stately African was walking toward Robert and Clara, the heat haze making him appear to float in the air. Mponda must have stepped from a cave in the limestone. Francis scanned the rock face in case other men were creeping out, but the chief was alone. He had kept his word.

Francis lowered his glasses and felt horribly ashamed. The situation was pitiful. Because he had not trusted the chief and had followed the Haslams, warriors had been sent to protect Mponda. Francis could see it all very clearly now. Quite soon the warriors would attack him and his hussars, and if by then Robert was talking to Mponda, the meeting would be broken off in anger, and Robert and Clara would be blamed for leading the chief's enemies into the valley. They might even be killed for it.

Unable to think or even look about him for several seconds, Francis suddenly came to a decision and indicated that he wanted his men to move closer to the missionary.

Standing magisterially in the shadow of the limestone cliff, Mponda was as much at home among these rocks as in his own kraal. Clara could not take her eyes off him. His sudden appearance had been magical—not that there was anything insubstantial about him. He stood as solidly as a statue in his lionskin cloak. Beneath a headband of white and black beads, his face was careworn, and yet he was plainly relieved to see Robert. After Herida's death, Clara had blotted out her memories of Mponda's affection for her husband; but when the two men clasped each other, she could not help being moved.

Mponda stepped back and said in Venda to Robert, "Long ago you told me that soldiers are evil. Why do you live with them now, Umfundisi?"

"To make peace between you all."

"What do you wish me to do?"

"Go home to your kraal."

Mponda sighed. "Will the soldiers go home, Umfundisi?"

"No, my friend, they will not. But if you kill them, more will surely come. One day you will have to learn to live in peace with them."

Mponda said gravely, "Some things are worse than death. To throw one's people's pride to the hyenas is worse."

"Ask yourself this, Mponda. Do dead men have pride? Do fatherless children have it?"

Clara had been concentrating so hard on understanding what was being said that she was unaware of anything amiss until Mponda pointed in fury. A band of warriors had broken from cover, and its leaders were already springing toward them. A spear landed with a metallic clatter. Some of the attackers had guns and were firing as they ran.

"Hide, Clara," roared Robert.

Mponda reeled sideways, clutching his shoulder, as Clara began to run. She turned for a moment, looking for Robert, but he was not following. She reached a fallen tree, vaulted it, and crouched down, forcing her body in under the curve of the trunk. She refused to imagine what fate awaited her.

As Nashu ran, his body felt weightless as the wind. I am the hunting dog that never stops until he kills; I am the leopard that leaps on his prey from a tree. His heart was throbbing wildly, like a drum beating out the madjukwa roll: the call to the spirits. Revenge is the sweetest of all pleasures when the gods delight in it. Nashu raised his spear and shook it. Mponda and the white umfundisi had wronged him and killed his daughter. They had also betrayed the ancestors. Now they would die.

The nganga and his most devoted followers had been tracking the soldiers since they had left Mponda's kraal. Nashu had known in his bones that the white leader would try to use the umfundisi as bait to catch Mponda. Otherwise why bring the troublemaker along with him? A secret meeting would surely take place between the chief and his teacher. Fearing he might never get a better chance to kill them both, Nashu had thrown a ring of spies around the camp, watching it constantly, day and night. At last he had been rewarded.

On this long-awaited day, it had come as no surprise to Nashu that some of the soldiers had followed a long way behind the teacher and his wife. Of course white men would have to be on hand when Mponda met his umfundisi. How else could they hope to capture the chief? But the soldiers would not dare follow too close. If the chief's men spotted them, Mponda would not come to the meeting place. It delighted Nashu that the white men would have to keep their distance. This would give his own men enough time to race ahead and strike first. No white man without his horse could outpace a Venda warrior in the bush. Nashu knew that if his men failed to arrive before the soldiers, the missionary would be saved and Mponda would be taken alive. Because the chief shared the white men's religion, he might one day be allowed to return to his people, to reimpose foreign beliefs. The umfundisi would be there to help him renew his heresy. Nashu swore that this would never happen.

Just where the valley narrowed, the leading group of soldiers had started to move, so much faster than before that the nganga had briefly lost sight of them. So he had been obliged to order his men to break cover and run. He himself had scrambled up a termite mound to look ahead and with his own eyes had seen Mponda and the umfundisi talking together. In that instant his men had bounded toward them like lions. A flash of color had caught the nganga's eye. The teacher's wife was fleeing; but the black-coated umfundisi did not flee.

That evil man traced a magic sign in the air—like two sticks across one another—but his spell did not stop the men who soon tumbled him to the ground and stabbed him. Nashu leapt for joy. They were washing their spears in the blood of his daughter's enemy. The chief was wounded too, and as another bullet rocked Mponda, Nashu expected him to run. Instead he knelt beside the umfundisi's corpse. Only as a warrior ran at him with a spear did he rise and start to stumble away. The soldiers' ugly metal horn rang out. "Kill him," roared Nashu. "Be quick!"

Though losing blood, Mponda ran with loping strides. Guns crackled. Could no one lay him low? The soldiers were shooting too, and at last another bullet hit the chief. He staggered and ran on, carrying the bullet with him like a wounded elephant. Another shot made him falter, but still he did not fall. And then Nashu knew that Mponda was safe. The nganga's men were turning back. "Imbagha, ingulube!" Nashu screamed. Dogs, cowardly swine. The fools believed the nonsense about the white man's medicine making a man live forever. They thought their bullets were being turned to water and were terrified.

Nashu walked back along the valley, glaring at the ground. Although he had failed to kill the chief, the white men might still choke Mponda with a rope if they blamed him for the teacher's death. The nganga had already summoned the Matabele to deal with the soldiers. Some white horsemen galloped past him. "Women!" he screamed, not deigning to hide. *Men* fought on their feet, not on an animal's back. The hussars saw and heard him—a wiry little man, decked out with claws and feathers and jabbering to himself. Lieutenant Carew dismissed him from his mind. All he cared about was reaching his commander's side. He certainly did not intend to delay his arrival by taking potshots at simpletons on the way.

The shouting had ceased, and the noise of firing was becoming faint. Even after Clara had heard a trumpet call, she remained behind her fallen tree. When she crept out, the warriors had gone.

She looked around and saw a cloud of flies. Seconds later, she was screaming. Across Robert's whole torso, blood flowed as if he had been flayed alive. Glazed eyes stared heavenward. Petals of ripped flesh revealed white ribs. "Don't faint . . . don't faint." She reached down and held his dead hand. "O Lord . . . O Lord, forgive us all."

There were shouts again, this time in English. In the distance Mponda was running. Hussars raced past Clara. She heard roars of "Halt!" Then a stutter of firing. "No!" she screamed. "No!" She tried to run between Mponda and his pursuers, but already the soldiers were past her. She saw Mponda stagger as he ran. The soldiers were gaining on him—among them was Francis. She called his name, knowing, even as she did, that it was useless. Mponda ran on. At the base of the cliff, he turned for a moment. Then he was gone.

She felt a hand on her arm. "Don't worry, ma'am, they'll get him."

Clara gazed in astonishment at a kindly sweating face—the sergeant she had often seen in camp.

"You don't understand," she gasped.

Behind her, horsemen were fanning out across the valley in a protective crescent. Orders were shouted, and men were dismounting. Sergeant Barnes remained by Clara's side as she walked on toward the cliff. Ahead was the entrance to a cave with several dozen men gathered outside it.

A red-haired officer approached her. Lieutenant Carew cleared his throat. "The captain and two volunteers went in after him, ma'am. The chief left a spoor of blood spots. One of our chaps hit him."

"How long has the captain been gone?"

The officer glanced at his wristwatch. "Three minutes."

"Will anyone else go in . . . to help?"

"He left orders forbidding it."

"How long will you wait here?"

"Captain Vaughan said fifteen minutes."

So that was it. If Francis was not out in a dozen minutes, he would be presumed dead. Somehow Clara's legs continued to support her. If he killed Mponda, it would be unjust, terrible; but if Francis himself was dragged out dead, how would she survive it? As if by magnetism, her eyes were drawn repeatedly to the dark opening. Blackness must have wrapped around him like a blind-fold. Images of her lover's bleeding limbs flashed into her mind.

A muffled shot was heard and, seconds later, another. Such flat, matter-of-fact bangs, but every man at the cliff's base stood frozen.

And then they were there, blinking in the sunlight. Mponda was supported between two troopers, his right leg dragging, blood dripping from an arm. Francis followed them, cradling an injured hand. Released from her prison, Clara could breathe again.

Robert Haslam's body was lifted up and roped to a horse's back. As Clara rode behind, she wept not just for his death but for his confidence in God's protection. His hands were hanging down below the horse's belly. With them, he had built their house and the village dam. If there is no eternal life, she found herself asking, what then for Robert? What had his life meant?

CHAPTER 24

The drumming began while Robert Haslam's funeral was in progress. A sequence of slow, ominous thumps would be followed by silence, and then by a pattern of faster, more urgent beats. Dark bloodstains spotted the canvas sack into which the missionary's body had been sewn, reminding all those present of the violent end that many of them might soon be sharing. As Francis read the words of the burial service in the fading light, his wounded hand and arm throbbed sharply, exacerbated by the tightness of his sling. Head down in his prayer book, he managed to stop himself from glancing at Clara when the first scattering of earth pattered down on the corpse and Simon's high-pitched sobbing rose to a crescendo. Francis was never going to forget that his decision to disregard Fynn's final advice had cost the missionary his life.

Clara looked so frail and unhappy that Francis longed to go and comfort her, and he would have done so if fear of being disrespectful to the dead man's memory had not prevented him. Clara, he guessed, would behave befittingly, for though she had stopped loving the man, she would still grieve for him. To avoid seeming to be eager to resume their liaison without interruption, Francis merely murmured some words of sympathy at the end of the service and walked away.

"Francis," she gasped, snatching at his unhurt arm. "You must never risk your life again like that. Never!" He felt as bewildered as if she had hit him on the head. Her husband's corpse was scarcely covered, and yet she was speaking like this. There was something in her eyes that had nothing to do with love. She was angry.

He said pleadingly, "Tell me what I can do."

Her long silence dismayed him. At last she gave a painful sigh that came from the depths of her lungs. "If you love me, Francis, please be truthful." She moved closer. "Did you send Robert to meet Mponda simply so you could capture him?"

"It never entered my mind." He placed a hand on his heart. "I swear to you."

"But you followed us."

"Yes," he shouted back. "To protect you, of course. What else?"

"Then why did you risk your life hunting down Mponda?"

"For God's sake, Clara! He'd just ordered your husband's execution."

Her eyes were bright with indignation. "He tried to stop those men. He was furious."

"But those men—" said Francis, "they *must* have been Mponda's people, acting on his orders. Who else could have known about the meeting?"

She said sharply, "Give me one reason why he wanted to kill Robert."

"Mponda blamed him for bringing my men here in the first place."

"Nonsense!" she cried. "Mponda was delighted to see Robert. He couldn't have been acting. I was there, Francis."

"He had to put you at your ease until his thugs arrived."

"They weren't his men." She cradled her face in her hands. "Why won't you believe me?"

"I could ask you the same," he sighed. "Fynn reckoned that Nashu directed me to this place on Mponda's orders. He was right, Clara. Nashu only pretended to betray the chief. Nashu *and* Mponda sucked us into the trap we're in." Francis tried to smile. "So please don't tell me *I* set out to trick *him*."

"Do you deny that you broke your promise not to follow us?"

"I couldn't bear to let anyone harm you."

Tears formed in her eyes, and Francis himself was too upset to speak. It was intolerable that she still believed he had behaved dishonorably. If he really had used Haslam as bait to lure the chief, what sort of man would it make him? The drums were becoming louder, and although Francis longed to make his peace with Clara, he had too many duties to attend to before darkness came.

Outside the perimeter of the camp, horses were dragging logs across long grass to flatten it. Francis had given orders for every bush to be hacked down as far as the mopane trees, and this had not been done. Nor were the watch fires large enough to give his gunners the light they would need to repel a night attack.

After dealing with these matters, Francis hurried to the medical officer's wagon, where he expected to find that his native interpreter had found out by now what Mponda would offer in exchange for his freedom. It was a critical moment. If the chief was ready to cooperate, an all-out attack could still be avoided. Stay calm, Francis told himself, knowing that annihilation was the probable alternative. Stepping up onto the wagon's tailboard, he looked inside.

Mponda was lying on one of the truckle beds in the center of the vehicle. As he twisted from side to side, his torso shone with sweat. One of his eyes was opened unnaturally wide; the other, half closed, gave the bizarre impression of winking. The M.O., Dr. Lane, tugged anxiously at his muttonchop whiskers.

"Tore off his bandages. Won't accept chloroform."

Francis frowned. "Does he think we're trying to bewitch him?"

Dr. Lane shook his bald head. "Won't take help from his enemies—that's what your translator chap says. Damn shame. There's a bullet in his knee that'll cripple him if we don't get it out."

"What about his arm and shoulder?"

"Ought to come off, the arm. Gangrene already." The M.O. coughed to disguise his emotion. "He's a brave old rascal and no mistake." He shook his head. "How's your wound, Captain?"

Francis touched his sling. "Throbs a bit."

Tiptoeing ahead of his two troopers in the cave, Francis had seen a glint of blue and had flung himself forward fast enough to grab the point of Mponda's spear. The wounded chief had been too weak to thrust again. Francis still shuddered at the narrowness of his escape. A gashed palm was a small price to have paid. He turned to his interpreter, who was squatting beside the chief's bed. Nervous by nature, Seda looked even less at ease than usual.

Francis said gently, "Has the chief explained why he ordered Haslam's murder?"

Seda hung his head. "The chief will answer nothing to me, sah." The interpreter's face conveyed anguished apology. "All he says to me is fetch Mrs. Robert. I only speak with her, he says."

On his way to Clara's tent, Francis thought the drums sounded softer now, as if the noise was coming from farther away. Of course, it only meant that new native regiments were answering the call. A movement in the upper branches of the mopane trees made Francis look up: a flock of hooded vultures was silhouetted against the sky. If he'd been a more diligent boy at Harrow, he supposed, he would now be consoling himself with elegant classical allusions to Hades and its guardians.

Clara appeared to be asleep when he entered the tent, but she turned at once as he entered, her cool scrutiny telling him she had been awake.

"I had to come. Mponda won't speak to my interpreter. He says the chief will talk to you."

She swung her legs down from the camp bed. "You can't expect him to help unless you free him."

"It's not as easy as that. He's too badly hurt to walk. We might be able to strap him to a horse." He moved closer. "Might he agree to write a letter to his headmen?"

"None of them can read."

"Can I send Simon to talk to them?"

"You'd risk his life after what happened to Robert?" Her voice had risen to a screech of protest.

He raised placating hands. "We'll solve that later. All I need to know from Mponda now is the price he'll pay for his freedom."

"What do you want him to tell his people?"

"To surrender their guns and go home."

Clara's dismay was obvious. "Would *you* do that in his position?"

"I don't know. But if I can't get his guns, he'll use them to murder settlers."

"Not if he promises to go home peacefully."

Her naïveté dazed him. "Why would he keep his word?"

"Wouldn't you keep yours if you'd promised?"

"I'm bound by a code."

"He's a Christian, Francis."

He wanted to scream that the chief's treatment of his teacher had not been Christian, but he knew she would simply repeat that Mponda was guiltless of Robert's murder. Before he could think how to answer her, she hurried from the tent. He scrambled after her.

In the evening air, she said, "I must be on my own with him."

"Can't my interpreter stay?"

"Don't you trust me to tell you what is said?" Clara flicked some hair away from her face. "If I need help, I'll ask for it."

While Clara was closeted with Mponda, Francis inspected

the horse lines and tried not to think of the animals' terror in an attack. He slapped at mosquitoes and wished he could silence the frogs and cicadas even for a few minutes. Africa's fecundity revolted him. By now, scores of eggs would have been laid in Haslam's body.

As Francis waited for Clara to emerge from the hospital wagon, he chatted to his Maxim gunners, who were gazing across the firelit grass toward the woods. When his runners reported for duty, all of them were scared. Wilfred Birch could hardly speak. Francis was not surprised; Birch was the only one with any idea what to expect.

To make absolutely sure that she understood what Mponda was telling her, Clara summoned Simon. Again and again the chief denied bringing warriors to the meeting place. He had come alone to meet his friend because his headmen would have brought guns to the meeting. Many still hated Christians.

"Could any headmen have followed you at a distance, without you knowing?"

"No, Mrs. Robert. They could not."

"Then who killed the Umfundisi?"

"I do not know, Mrs. Robert." In spite of his pain and grief, the dying man radiated dignity. "Umfundisi said to me that to gain his life a man must lose it. I will soon find out." Clara did not trust herself to speak. "I *do* believe him." She nodded dumbly, moved in spite of herself by Mponda's faith in Robert—although, in the end, what sense did any of it make? A missionary labors for ten years to win an African ruler's trust, and then a young army officer turns up from nowhere and gives the chief a mortal wound.

A new thought rocked her. Suppose Robert had truly been what Mponda thought him: a holy man; a saint, even. What would that say about her? That she had betrayed a saint for a soldier who would stoop to any deceitfulness, provided it harmed his enemy? Francis had sworn that no soldiers would follow her and Robert, and he had broken his word.

Clara dipped a cloth in water and wiped the sweat from Mponda's brow. He knew that he was dying but showed no signs of fear. She leaned closer to one of his surprisingly small ears and said, "The chief soldier will allow you to join your own people if you swear to tell them to go home and give up their guns."

Raising his head with an immense effort, he gasped, "Jesus did not say to people, 'You cannot fight to keep your land.' I will not tell them to go."

Clara said, "If the soldiers free you, and then they try to get away, will your warriors stop them?"

Mponda let his head sink back again. "Who is it who eats last?" Not understanding, Clara looked to Simon, but he too was puzzled. Mponda smiled. "I will tell you who eats last. When hunger comes, the chief feeds his people first. Then he can eat. He shares his power like his food. He must ask his people's opinion."

"But if you are freed, will you advise your people to let the white men leave?"

"I will, Mrs. Robert."

"Will they listen?"

"When the old bull speaks, the bleating goats are silent." He chuckled and began to choke. He was so wet with sweat that his shoulders shone like molten bronze. Clara tried to get him to drink, but he was too weak to lift his head. At last Mponda said, "It is because Umfundisi wished it. . . . That is why I will spare the white men."

As Francis was talking to the crew of one of his field guns, Clara rushed up to relay Mponda's intentions and his account of Robert's death. "So you see the chief had nothing to do with it." She then explained that Mponda would let the hussars leave unharmed if he himself was freed. As she spoke, she felt again all the relief and pleasure she had experienced while talking to the chief.

When she stopped speaking, Francis simply tugged at the corner of his sling and said flatly, "So I free one of the most wanted rebels in Mashonaland, and what do I get in exchange?" He raised incredulous eyes. "Not a gun, not a bullet. Nothing."

"You'll stay alive . . . We all will."

"Save our skins, will we? What about the women who'll be killed with those guns I failed to capture? What about the settlers' children? I've no choice, Clara. If Mponda won't give up his guns, I must stay and try to kill as many as possible."

Clara said bitterly, "What else can they do except attack you, while you hold him prisoner?"

"They'll attack us whatever we do."

"If it makes no difference, you should free him anyway. He said he'd order his men home. I beg you to give him the chance."

"No," he cried angrily. "They'll see it as weakness. 'The white men are too scared to keep our chief a prisoner.' They'll sing that old song about him living forever. The white men couldn't kill him, so they had to let him go." He touched her arm and added in the gentler tones of the old Francis, "Destroy respect for white arms, and a whole brigade could be brushed aside like a fly."

"I can't agree with you"—she sighed—"but I do understand." Gratitude lit his exhausted face, and for a moment she felt close to him again. He believed what he said and was determined to save his men if he could. What did he think would happen? Was it just a matter of appearances now? Dying like men? She had to know what he thought. "Are we going to die, Francis?"

He gazed out across the flattened grass, toward the distant trees. "There's enough of them out there to eat us up several times over." He pulled a face. "Let's hope we stick in their throats."

He had spoken in his most matter-of-fact voice, but she saw vulnerability in the line of his jaw and in the dark shadows under his eyes. She thought of Shakespeare's lines: "Golden lads and girls all must,/As chimney-sweepers, come to dust." He must have known dozens who had died in India and West Africa: inexperienced boys straight from public school. The tightness at the corners of his mouth spoke of his effort to inspire confidence. Poor Francis. She recalled how much he had leaned on Fynn, and without thinking, she stepped forward and kissed him on the lips.

Before he could react, she was walking toward the doctor's wagon. She paused on the steps, and the stillness of the camp sent shivers down the backs of her legs. Around her, men were staring fearfully into the gloom beyond the line of fires. High above them all, the Southern Cross gleamed as if studded with bright nails.

Francis had ordered tents to be struck so that the enemy would have fewer targets for burning arrows. With fire in mind, he had sent relays of men down to the stream to fill buckets and barrels, and these had been stood near the wagons and in places where thornbush barriers could easily be ignited. The wagons had been brought to the heart of the camp to form a central laager, in which a last stand would be made if the outer defenses fell. Both the column's seven-pounders were loaded with case shot, and the gunners had orders to wait until the natives were within fifty paces. Francis had warned the Maxim crews to expect heavy sniping and always to have a man ready to leap into place the moment an operator was hit; there could be no excuse for belts jamming or anything else causing interruptions in fire.

While a quarter of the garrison kept watch, the rest slept. Some lay on their sides, others with arms outspread or knees drawn up, looking eerily like corpses. Above their blanketed forms, a crescent moon sailed serenely in the sky.

Moths, fluttering around the lamplit wagon in which Mponda lay, attracted night birds. Francis lifted the canvas flap and had the illusion of entering a shrine—not of Jesus, but of an ancient idol carved in ebony—until the all too mortal smell of gangrene filled his nostrils.

Francis murmured to Clara as she sat beside the chief, "Does he know he'll die without help?"

"Yes, but he still refuses it."

"I'm sorry."

"Are you, Francis?"

"You can't expect me to feel the same for him as your husband would have done."

Francis felt bitter to be placed in the wrong by her. Couldn't she see that Haslam had brought nothing but misery to his chosen tribe? So why must he be their martyred savior now? Francis's distaste for missionaries ran deep. What impudence to tell Africans that spiritual things were worth more than physical ones, when white prospectors were killing for gold.

He wanted to confide fully in Clara about their situation, but caution held him back. Perhaps he had already been too honest. If Clara let slip to Mponda that he was pessimistic, Francis feared it would destroy any chance he might otherwise have to bargain for his men's lives.

When Francis held out his revolver for her to take, Clara frowned as she weighed it in her hand.

"Shouldn't you keep it?"

"I couldn't hit a wounded elephant with my left hand."

"Better than nothing at close range, surely?"

"Things won't get *that* bad." He forced a smile. "A few natives may creep in undetected. That's the only reason to let you have it." After a silence, he said, "Will you ask the chief if there's anything he wants to say to me?"

Francis waited patiently while they spoke together in Venda. At last Clara announced, "He said, 'The black ants can swallow a herd of buffalo.' "

"So can the white ones. Anything else?"

Clara said thickly, "He hopes God will forgive you your sins."

"I return the compliment."

"He really meant it."

"I'm sorry. Please thank him."

As Francis stepped down from the wagon, he wondered if he would ever see Clara alive again.

The only tent that Francis had allowed to be left standing was Dr. Lane's hospital. Inside, the doctor and his assistants were laying out their instruments. A lookout post had been built at the center of the camp, but because of his wounded hand, Francis could not climb the ladder. So he sat on a chair placed within earshot of the men on the platform. His runners were close by, as was Seda, his interpreter. Mark Carew clattered down the ladder, his eyes red-rimmed with sleeplessness. James Gradwell, the youngest sub-altern in the column, followed him.

"What are the natives up to, sir? No signs of life at all." Carew sounded tense and querulous.

Francis shrugged. "Eating their breakfast, I daresay."

"At four in the morning?" faltered Gradwell.

"I was trying to be humorous," muttered Francis. "If I were in their shoes, I'd attack with the rising sun behind me."

"Christ almighty!" exclaimed Carew. "We won't see a bloody thing."

Young Gradwell looked so forlorn that Francis relented. "Don't worry; they'll be so close together, a blind man won't be able to miss."

"Do you really think so, sir?" Gradwell gulped. "Not another joke, I mean?"

Francis managed a fairly convincing laugh. "Of course it isn't."

As Carew and Gradwell clambered back onto the platform, Francis wished that occasionally people would try to make *him* feel better. He thought of the natives creeping down from the hills and through the bush, and the horror of it choked him—the feeling that something wild and implacable was closing in and could not be stopped. With their muscular, greased bodies and their kilts of catskin and monkey tail, these men were astonishingly vivid to him and yet utterly mysterious. They hid their penises within strange little reed cases, they sacrificed to ancestral spirits and believed that European inventiveness arose solely from taking medicine. White skin reminded them of ghosts and unbleached calico. They thought that men in shoes had no toes. And these were the people who meant to kill him and all his soldiers. It was so astonishing that for a moment, quite literally, it took his breath away.

Shortly before dawn, Francis fell asleep and did not wake even when Trooper Birch covered him with a blanket. Half an hour later, the notes of reveille had him scrambling to his feet, heart pounding. The sky was brightening fast. For the first time, he heard the sound of tramping feet and, suddenly, shouts and snatches of song. At first he thought his enemies were approaching on two sides. A rapid circuit of the camp told him that he was wrong; the sounds were coming from every direction.

Francis steadied his field glasses on top of the outer barricade. Warriors were assembling under their captains in the half-light. The Matabele were less numerous than the other natives and, unlike them, almost naked. They stood back and leaned on their spears, watching the proceedings superciliously. For what could these Venda herdsmen teach the martial Matabele about war? Their leaders wore lionskins, but would they stand firm in the place of killing when the fighting was hard? Francis sent a runner to the platform to make sure that these tall warriors were closely watched.

The shouting was becoming clearer. Francis asked Seda what it meant.

"It is their way, sah. They say the spears of the young men are thirsty. 'We will grind our spears on your bones. Like winnowed chaff you will be driven before our—' "

Seeing the woebegone faces of his runners, Francis laughed. "They're in for a surprise, eh?"

Although his enemies were too far away to be harmed, Francis gave the order to explode some mines. It might discourage them from digging sniping pits close to the barricades. Great fountains of earth leapt up into the air, showering the closest tribesmen with clods and stones; but very few of them retreated. Their shouting dwindled briefly to a murmur but soon rose again. Francis walked along the barricades, giving last-minute advice.

"Defend your front. Don't worry about anything else. . . . Remember, dead men don't sweat. A sweating corpse is faking, so finish him off."

Francis had split the camp into sectors and given orders for so many men from each of them to hold themselves in readiness to move to any sector that might be under pressure. If only he could foresee where the natives would drive home their main attack, what a blessing that would be! But at least they did not make use of the dazzling first light. It was much later when a tall warrior ran forward, brandishing an assegai with a long shaft. He threw off his leopardskin kaross and stood naked save for his loincloth. His spear was raised, his muscles were flexed, and as he flung his weapon, he shouted in a ringing voice, "Buya quasi!" The warriors behind him roared, "Bulala, bulala!," stamping their feet. Francis did not ask Seda to translate.

They attacked in long lines, slowly at first, but as Francis's sharpshooters started to pick them off at several hundred yards, they began to advance with stuttering rushes, flinging themselves down for a few seconds before worming their way forward on their stomachs, and then resuming their brief dashes. Francis wondered why none of these men were armed with rifles. If a few were to lie down and shoot at the hussars' firing line, they would greatly improve the chances for the rest to reach the outer perimeter. Then he realized that they were deliberately tempting his gunners, in a self-sacrificing effort to unmask the strength and number of his guns. Francis at once sent runners to the crews of each Maxim. No one was to fire unless the warriors came within twenty-five paces. Even when these attackers came close enough to hurl their spears, Francis did not countermand his order.

Only when a new and larger assault was launched did he signal to his gun crews, and as the first wave surged forward, the Maxims scythed them down. Within minutes, the attack was broken and many lay dead. Others dragged themselves away. After the guns ceased chattering, the cries of the wounded sounded very loud. Francis yelled up to his men on the lookout.

"Have the Matabele moved yet?"

James Gradwell looked down. "Not yet, sir."

Through his glasses, Francis saw that men were still emerging from the woods. Some were pulling thornbushes and logs. Would these be brought close to the camp's defenses to provide cover for snipers?

Trooper Birch stepped forward from the other runners. He looked pale and scared. "They'll light them, sir. Like when Mr. Fynn was killed."

Francis was not convinced. "They'll use branches to fire the grass?"

"I swear they will, sir."

"But it's too damp to burn properly."

Francis understood only when he noticed that they were carrying green boughs as well as dry kindling. A gentle breeze was blowing across the camp. Smoke, he thought. When their main thrust was launched, it would be through clouds of smoke. He raced over to the nearest seven-pounder and ordered the crew to elevate for eight hundred yards and open up. The more natives they could kill before the fires were burning, the better their chances of survival would be. Along the firing line, his men's bayonets caught the morning sunlight like pale flames.

As his field guns began lobbing case shot into the ranks of the waiting warriors, Francis struggled with his water flask. Damn his wounded hand. Because everyone knew that fear dried out the mouth, he disliked having to ask his runners to pour drinks for him. The exception was Wilfred Birch, whose terror made Francis pity him.

At first the natives lit their fires too far away, and the smoke failed to reach the camp. Regardless of shells and rifle fire, they came on steadily. At a heavy cost in lives, they built up a long line of smoldering heaps topped off with armfuls of damp grass. The billowing smoke made the hussars cough and rub their eyes, as moment by moment they waited for dark shapes to burst from the murk. From time to time, Francis ordered his Maxim gunners to fire into the smoke, in the hope that screams would betray his enemies' approach.

Suddenly the bellowing of oxen and the thunder of hooves

was heard. "From the north," yelled Carew from the lookout. Men raced toward the threatened quarter. Maxims were slewed around on their mountings. As the charging beasts loomed through the smoke, no one spotted the oxhide shields in among them, so perfectly did they blend. The points of spears could have been tips of horns, and windswept armlets nothing but flowing tails. Running with the oxen were scores of warriors, jabbing at the maddened creatures with their assegais, driving their great weight toward the earth-filled sacks that barred their way.

"Fire!" Francis roared, running along the barricade behind the riflemen, his scabbard thumping uselessly against his leg. The stammering rattle of the Maxims steadied him; the hussars were firing frantically, their fingers flying to triggers and bolts, plucking cartridges from bandoliers. The reek of cordite merged with the universal bonfire smoke.

"Your revolver!" shouted Francis to the bemused Birch. He had no time to explain that he had lent his own Colt to the missionary's widow and could not use his carbine with a damaged hand. Clara had known best. Even in his left hand the revolver felt useful. A spear fell at his feet and he scarcely noticed. Sergeant Barnes ran up.

"They're attacking from three sides, sir." Barnes swung his index finger around like a weather vane. His tone was accusing, as if it were somehow Francis's fault that after twenty-five years in the regiment he might never wear his long-service medal. The barricade behind the sergeant erupted. Oxen crashed through the wall of earth-filled sacks, pitching a hussar into the air. Another man fell under their hooves. Warriors were pouring through the breach. Hand-to-hand fights swayed back and forth: bayonet against assegai, rifle butt against club. There was no time to reload and no breath to spare, and many grim struggles took place in silence.

While battle raged about him, Francis sent his runners to make sure the Maxims continued firing into the smoke. If the numbers entering could be kept low, the camp might still survive. The inner laager had not yet been breached. From behind the wagons came the whinnying of frightened horses. Hussars were lying on their stomachs, firing between the spokes of the wagon wheels. Troopers were hit by their comrades' bullets. Africans killed each other by firing as they ran.

At last the Matabele entered the attack. With less smoke to

shield them, many fell early to the gusts of bullets that whipped the grass. But the numbers reaching the barricades did not seem small to the defenders. Like a black wave crested with white plumes, they swept down on the camp. Some were shot in the act of mounting the parapet, others while flinging aside the heaped up thornbushes at the base of the barricades.

Francis had begun to detach men from the outer defenses to fight the intruders inside the perimeter. He ordered his new groups to cover the backs of the riflemen at the barricades and to engage and kill all natives breaking through. Men on both sides fought like gladiators, for it was a case of kill or be killed. A man fought till he received his death blow or dropped from exhaustion. There was nowhere to run.

Francis saw many bullet holes in the canopy of the hospital wagon. Fearing for Clara's life, he ran toward it. A man with red-circled eyes and a chest dotted with white war paint crossed his path. Francis fired and missed. The warrior drew back his spear, poised to strike. As Francis flung up an impotent arm, the man cringed as if punched from behind. A red hole had appeared in the middle of his chest. Sergeant Barnes lowered his carbine.

"Bad business," he gasped, running up.

Francis could not smile. His lips were too dry, and his tongue felt like leather. "Thank you, Sergeant," he mumbled.

He looked around in puzzlement. The shooting had all but stopped. A ragged cheer went up along the defenses. Francis ran to see for himself. In several places, Africans lay in mounds across the face of the barricades. Dead cattle were scattered everywhere. Already vultures were landing. The cries of the wounded rose plaintively on every side. Francis hurried to the lookout.

"What do you think?" he shouted.

Carew came down the ladder, followed by an ecstatic James Gradwell. "We really showed 'em. Didn't we, sir?"

Carew said quietly, "There's as many as ever near the trees."

Francis nodded grimly and headed for the hospital tent. Dr. Lane's shirt was like a butcher's apron. The wounded lay waiting in rows. Raising his voice above the cries for water, Francis told Lane that he meant to carry Mponda outside so he could see how many of his people had died.

"Won't do any good, Captain."

"I'll be the judge of that, Doctor." But even as Francis replied, he knew that Lane was right.

Francis was leaving the tent, when Sergeant Barnes was brought in by three men. His lips foamed with blood, and his eyes were starting from his head. His hands were tugging at a spear buried deep in his abdomen. A trooper piped up, "One of their wounded did it, sir."

Francis's head was swimming. A minute earlier, Barnes had saved his life; now he was as good as dead. When he could trust himself to speak, Francis sent Birch racing away with orders for Carew. The officer was to disarm all wounded natives and, with Seda's help, to question them about their leaders' intentions. Only then did Francis turn toward the hospital wagon.

Clara had stayed with Mponda during the fighting. As soon as the firing stopped, she stepped down from the tailboard and peered out from the inner laager into the camp beyond. She swayed on her feet. Longing to turn back, she found herself rooted. Nothing had prepared her for the horror. Piles of bodies, black and white, lay under the pitiless sun, the wounded tangled up with the dead. Worse than the sights were the sounds: sobs, curses, pleas— a constant babble of noise, cut through by screams. And all the time the drone of thousands of flies.

"Water! Water!" She heard the word endlessly repeated. Shaking with shock, she looked about as if, miraculously, jugs of water might appear. Dr. Lane's scarlet face loomed before her.

"You must help me, Mrs. Haslam." He caught her roughly by the arm.

"Me?" Her heart was bumping, and she thought she might vomit. These men were so badly hurt she hardly dared look at, let alone touch, them.

"You can hold a cup of water, can't you?" His scorn reached her. "Get that boy of yours to help. Bandages must be tight enough to stop the blood. Come with me."

She hardly recognized the kindly man who had tended Mponda. He spoke harshly, and his face was contorted by rage and pity. The hairs on his arms were matted with blood. His shirt was torn and stained. Clara followed him humbly.

Ten minutes later, armed with scissors, bandages, a bucket, and a metal cup, she and Simon were working alongside Dr. Lane and his assistants. The stench of blood and excrement almost choked her, but the men's desperation overcame her fear. To hear grown men sob like children was terrible, and when she had to lift the wounded, or roll them over to bandage a limb, their groans were pitiable. Most were too badly hurt to be saved even by hands more skillful than hers. Their gratitude just to see her made Clara ashamed of her earlier dread. Many clutched at her dress to detain her, obliging her to tuck the hem into her waistband. Sweat trickled down her back, and her bodice stuck to her as if glued. Even the shock of kneeling down to help a man she then discovered was dead grew less as time passed. She found she could close a corpse's eyes without revulsion.

The most miserable sufferers were the wounded Africans. They gave no quarter in battle themselves, and therefore expected none now that they were prisoners. A man with a shattered thigh dashed away her cup when she offered it—though he was dying of thirst. She guessed he thought her a witch with a poisoned vessel. The Africans' eyes followed her every movement, as if a hidden knife might suddenly flash in her hand. Their terror sent an answering fear through her veins. Would she too be dying by evening, her body pierced and mutilated?

When Clara spotted Francis supervising repair work on the shattered barricades, she ran across to him, her hands red with the blood of men she had been tending. For everyone's sake she had to get through to him. She came up very close, so the men in the working party would not be able to hear her.

"It's not too late to save ourselves."

"By freeing him?"

His resentful tone dismayed her, but she said firmly, "I'm sure he'll persuade his headmen to let us go."

"How are you sure? He couldn't control the men who killed your husband. Why should these others listen to him? Least of all when he's sick."

"He's their chief."

"There are other tribes involved."

"How could they possibly attack us more fiercely if you free him?" Her voice was trembling. "Must I go down on my knees? I've never asked anything else from you."

He said sharply, "Africans respect strength, not whining."

"All right," she shouted, "fight to the death. It won't save any settlers or their families. But if Mponda sends his men home, think of the lives you'll have saved." With all her strength, Clara willed him to agree with her. "If you love me"—she whispered now—"free him." He looked so dazed and lost that she could not believe he would resist.

After a long pause, he said quietly, "I'll make no promises until my interpreter has finished with the prisoners."

Francis closed his eyes as Clara walked away. It had taken all his resolution not to give in to her. Moments before her arrival, he had learned that the Maxims' ammunition was running low and that the rest of his men had only enough cartridges to last two days at the present rate of firing. If the enemy abandoned caution and threw everything at the camp, the end would come swiftly. Francis's deepest instincts told him that on no account should he do anything indicating weakness.

The cries of the dying became more harrowing as the day went on. While Carew and Seda interrogated prisoners, Francis gave orders for canvas screens to be put up to shield wounded tribesmen from the full heat of the sun. Then he sat down under the shade of the lookout platform and wrote a pencil note to his mother on the pad he used when writing messages for his runners. It was not a long letter, and his writing was very clumsy, since he had to use his left hand.

Ibanula Camp, 13th July 1896

My dearest mother,

I am writing to you during a lull in the fighting. We are surrounded in country that does not favor a breakout, being hilly and heavily wooded. So we will have to stay on here and fight to a finish. Of course I blame myself, but we had a good chance to end the rebellion at a stroke, and with just a little luck might have pulled it off. I would do it all again, I know. We will do our best to fight on till the end. Please don't think I feel too badly. Of course I would rather live to be eighty. But when there's no help for something, it's much easier to face. My greatest regret is the pain my death will cause you, my dearest mother. Thanks to you I had a very happy boyhood. My period in the cavalry has also been a wonderful time for me. So please don't think I should be pitied. I would hate that.

Your loving son,
Francis

He thrust the letter into his shirt pocket, thinking that this garment would be less likely to be stripped from his body than his jacket. He wondered if Clara had written anything for her father and told himself that she would have died much sooner if he had left her behind at Mponda's kraal. Marrying Haslam had been the mistake that killed her. Yet nothing could make Francis feel less responsible. He wished he could have done as she had asked and freed the chief, but the Matabele would have thought he was trying to placate them. And why would they have relaxed their grip after that?

Whenever Francis closed his eyes, she was there—and in all the places he had once longed to take her: the Royal Academy for the Summer Exhibition, Hurlingham for the polo, Gunter's to eat ices, the garden of his childhood home to meet his mother. And now he knew that all his hopes had been delusions.

Mark Carew was striding across the trampled grass, looking haggard, with Seda following like a ghost in his pale blanket. Francis beckoned them away from the lookout so their words would not be overheard. Carew tossed his helmet to the ground. "If this goes on, they'll wipe us out. Every damn nigger says the same."

Francis found himself staring at a trail of blood spots on a patch of bare earth. He said calmly, "How long do they expect it to take?"

"A day or two. Some say less."

Francis thought of his dwindling ammunition. "Time doesn't worry them?"

"Nothing does," snorted Carew.

"What about their chief? Aren't they worried about him?"

"Why should they be? He can't be hurt by our bullets. They all think that. The white nganga made him drink the blood of Lord Jizzus, and now he'll live forever. We should show the stupid bastards." Carew's face was fiercely animated. "Their leaders told them they'd be safe because he'd turn our bullets into water. Most of them wouldn't have made it to the picket lines if they'd known the truth."

"Perhaps we *should* send him back," murmured Francis, as if thinking aloud. "They'd see his bullet wounds then."

Carew waved his hands dismissively. "What good would that do? They'd simply say we tried to kill him and failed. We must kill him, sir. It's our only chance."

"You mean I should ask the M.O. to overdo the morphia? No, no. Lane won't play that game."

"Who's talking of a game?" Carew's pale eyes were furiously reproachful. "Unless we've shot him by nightfall, we might as well shoot ourselves."

Francis knew he should respond with fury, but he could not. Instead he said quietly, "And afterward we send his body through the lines on a mule?"

"Exactly!" Carew grabbed Francis's arm above his sling, making him wince. "It'd be a terrible blow to their morale. Imagine it, sir. He's a god to them."

And Francis *did* imagine it—vividly. But he snapped back, "We can't shoot prisoners of war without a trial."

"Then try him, for God's sake. He's a rebel captured while offering armed resistance. Others have been tried for that."

"Only by civil courts. It's a rebellion, not a war, Lieutenant."

"How the hell do we get him to a civil court? The nearest is hundreds of miles away."

Francis smiled stiffly. "We can't shoot him unless he's violated the customs of war."

"He murdered the missionary," cried Carew triumphantly.

"Mrs. Haslam says the chief tried to save her husband."

Like a swordsman fighting for his life, Carew thrust again. "The rebels aim to kill all the whites, so Mponda must have sanctioned murder, sir. He's an important chief. How can he not be to blame?"

Trooper Birch ran up, shouting that the natives were relighting their fires. Already men were dashing to the barricades.

"Do we shoot him, or don't we?" screamed Carew, as his commander started toward the nearest Maxim.

"Save your ammunition till they're close," Francis roared.

While the rattle of shooting continued unabated, Clara remained with Mponda in the wagon. His eyes were dimmer, and his leg was shockingly bloated. When Mponda whispered her name, Clara did not dare ask him what she knew she must. If Francis would not save himself, she would beg Mponda to order his men to let the soldiers go.

For a long time the chief was absorbed in the business of breathing, his rib cage rising and falling as if an immense weight were resting on it. As soon as the pressure eases, I will ask him, Clara told herself. But before she could, he wheezed, "Until the white men came, my heart was happy eating honey and just living. I was like an ox. I did not know I could choose how to live."

"Umfundisi loved you very much."

"He saved me, Mrs. Robert."

Clara thought of the families in Mponda's village sitting outside their huts in the evening, eating together, then talking for hours around their fires or dancing late into the night; and Mponda's words haunted her: "My heart was happy . . . just living." Had Robert ever been happy just living? Perhaps in very early childhood. And she herself? Maybe before her mother had taught her about sin and salvation. And what of Mponda? Had he known one moment of peace after his conversion?

Clara braced herself to ask her question, but as she opened her mouth, Mponda gasped, "Are sinners punished here on earth, Mrs. Robert, as well as after death?"

"Why do you ask, my chief?"

"I did great wrong to Herida. Is that why I suffer?"

Clara's eyes filled with tears. "I'm sure God has forgiven you." She leaned closer to him, her heart thumping. How would he answer her? "My chief," she began, "if the white leader lets you return to your people, will you order your warriors to let the soldiers go?" She watched his face in anguish, for it conveyed no hint of emotion. His eyes were closed in their sunken sockets. At last his lips moved.

"The white leader insults me."

"He does not mean to."

"In his country," gasped the chief, "I would not ask him for favors if I had come across the sea with guns to fight."

"You wish your men to kill all the white soldiers?"

"No, I do not wish that. God has punished them already. For your sake, Mrs. Robert, I will ask my warriors to let them go. You may tell the white leader."

Clara felt faint with relief. Francis would surely grasp this heaven-sent chance. She squeezed Mponda's hand in gratitude and the next moment was flinging herself to the floor as a bullet tore through the canvas. Afterward, as her agitation subsided, she sat listening to Mponda's breathing, trying to concentrate on the dying man, whatever might be happening in the battle outside. How strange it was, after living through so much danger, still to feel afraid. She wanted with a great longing to know what was going on outside, and yet she could not bring herself to leave the wagon. The moment the attack was over, she would tell Francis what Mponda had said.

On the ledge beside the chief's bed she saw a giant grasshopper, four or five inches long. And although his wings were a beautiful shade of green, his expression was remarkably sinister. In front of him a tiny golden beetle was resting. From Clara's eyeline, the grasshopper looked as monstrous as she imagined he must from the little insect's viewpoint. She reached out and placed the beetle on her palm. He clicked open his golden armor and spread his wings. One flash in the lamplight, and he was gone.

CHAPTER 25

When the attackers finally fell back, it was midafternoon. Clara found soldiers crawling on their hands and knees, begging for help. Others sat on the ground, weeping with shock. In a line of dead bodies outside the hospital tent was Francis's runner, Wilfred Birch, intestines spilling from his stomach. She did not have to count corpses to know that the next attack would be the last.

As Clara approached the tent, Dr. Lane emerged, wild-eyed with anger.

"That bloody young fool is going to shoot him."

Stunned by the suffering around her, Clara could scarcely take in what he was telling her. "Shoot who?"

"The chief, of course," thundered Lane. "Vaughan's decided to try him by court-martial. His staff are doing the paperwork." Lane pointed to some men sitting at a table at the center of the laager. "They're sticking to the book in case there's trouble later."

Clara hurried across to see what documents they were copying. Over one man's shoulder, she read:

Order for the assembly of a Field General Court-Martial at Ibanula in Mashonaland this thirteenth day of July 1896.

Whereas complaint has been made to me, the undersigned Officer in command of the Gwelo Column, that the person named in the annexed Schedule has committed the offenses in the said Schedule, being offenses against the person of residents in the above named country, and I am of the opinion that it is not practicable that those offenses should be tried by an ordinary General Court-Martial—I therefore order the officers listed below to assemble at Ibanula Camp at 4:00 P.M. for the purpose of trying the said person by Field General Court-Martial.

At the foot of the page a space had been left for a signature, and beneath that had been written:

> *F. M. Vaughan, Capt. 9th Hussars*
> *President of the Court*
> *Commanding Gwelo Column*

On the table, Clara saw several copies of another document.

Charge Sheet

Mponda, Chief Induna of the Venda at Ibanula, is charged with:

1st Charge   Being a rebel in armed resistance to constituted authority: in that on 11 July 1896 at Ibanula he was captured in arms.

2nd Charge   Instigating murder: in that about 1st July he sent his men to attack and kill white miners near the Isanga River.

> *By Order*

> *M. de H. Carew, Lieut.*
> *Staff Officer*
> *Gwelo Column*

Clara ran back to Lane's wagon as the doctor was mounting the steps. "Can they try a dying man?"

"Vaughan can do anything he damn well likes if his men obey him."

"What if you refuse to let the chief leave the wagon?"

"He can try him in absentia."

"Will he really shoot him?"

"Undoubtedly."

Francis's eyes were bloodshot and his face unshaven. The ceaseless drums seemed to pulse in time with the throbbing of his hand. His sling was caked with dirt and dried blood. Clara approached him, looking so angry that all he wanted was to escape from her. He supposed the chief mattered to her so much because her husband had loved him and because she still felt guilty.

"How can you be so callous?" she cried.

"Callous?" he gasped, reacting in spite of himself, galled by the unfairness of it. "How can it be callous to want to save lives—my men's and countless natives'?"

"You can't have any idea how they'll react if you shoot him."

Francis said firmly, "If he dies, their morale will collapse."

She twisted a strand of black hair between her fingers. "Isn't it just as likely that they'll thirst for your blood?"

A faint smile moved his lips. "Can they get any thirstier?" He rose from his chair. "Please, Clara, try to be reasonable. He's dying anyway."

She stepped away from him. "He says he'll let your men go if you free him."

"Why should I believe him?"

"He's a Christian, a better one than I ever was."

Wanting to rage at her, Francis controlled himself and pointed to some wounded Africans. "Is he a Christian? Or him? Or the one with the scars? Use your head, Clara. Mponda split his tribe, and now he's dying. If I let him go, I throw away our only hope of survival."

She faced him pityingly. "It'll be murder if you shoot him. I can't believe it of you."

He said sharply, "Some of our prisoners say Mponda ordered the killing of miners on the Isanga River."

"Scared men will say anything to save their skins. The man's dying, Francis. He's helpless."

"We'll be helpless too before we're hacked to bits. And spare a thought for his people. What'll the British Army do to them if we're massacred?"

Clara gazed at him with blazing rectitude. "Some things must never be done, whatever the circumstances."

Not knowing how to answer her, he walked toward the laager where the court-martial would take place.

Ten minutes before four o'clock, Francis arrived with six troopers at the medical wagon. Dr. Lane stepped down, bristling with anger. "Dear God, Captain, the man will be dead within days. It's unheard of to try a man in his condition."

"It's unusual, I agree."

Francis told himself that somehow he must endure all the reproofs that came his way. But when Clara came out from the wagon, he did not know how he would survive the loathing in her eyes.

In lifting the stretcher down from the wagon, the soldiers jolted the dying man so severely that he cried out.

"Imagine he's Field Marshal Wolseley," roared Dr. Lane.

Clara caught Francis's arm. "He risked his life to meet Robert. Is this your reward?"

Francis did not reply but gently prized her fingers from his arm. Since Lane was a commissioned officer with the rank of captain, Francis had been unable to turn down the doctor's request to defend Mponda. He now feared that Lane would do the job well enough to arouse Clara's hopes of an acquittal.

When the stretcher was placed in front of the table, Francis gave orders for it to be tilted so that the chief could see his judges. Since Mponda had no feeling in his legs, he had to be strapped to the stretcher, or he would have slipped to the ground. The straps cut into his flesh, and his great head lolled sideways; but he made no sound.

At a quarter past four, the order convening the court was read aloud and signed by Francis. The charge sheet was also laid before the court. It too was read out and then signed by Carew in his capacity as prosecutor. Francis, as president, sat between the court's two other members: Lieutenant Gradwell and another subaltern, Richard Haydon. Both had been briefed by Carew and believed that their lives would be at stake if the prisoner was found not guilty.

While Seda was being sworn in as court interpreter, Mponda, whose eyes had been closed until then, interrupted. Long before

Seda had finished translating the chief's angry words, Francis guessed that Mponda wanted Clara to interpret for him. Since she was not appearing as a witness, he could see no good reason to deny the chief his wish. Clara was handed a Bible and asked to swear to interpret accurately at all times and to offer no opinions of her own. Then Francis swore in Seda as interpreter for the African prosecution witnesses. In a private aside, Francis asked Seda to raise his hand if he disagreed with Clara's translation on any point.

Francis had thought that Mponda might refuse to recognize the court; but through Clara he pleaded not guilty to both charges. The sight of her standing attentively beside the dying man, sometimes giving him water and at all times listening for the slightest sound he might make, was very painful to Francis. While it was noble to protect the sick, to do as he was doing was contrary to every canon of decent behavior. Yet whenever he heard a wounded man cry out, or caught the distant thump of drums, Francis's resolution was strengthened. The next attack would sweep them all away.

Carew rose to put the case for the prosecution. He began by calling as witnesses the two troopers who had accompanied Francis into the cave. Their evidence was supposed to prove the first charge: that Mponda was a rebel, captured in armed resistance to constituted authority. Both soldiers swore that when they called on Mponda to give himself up, he had first fired at them and then, when his gun had jammed, tried to stab Captain Vaughan with his assegai. Carew declared that this proved that the chief had been captured while offering armed resistance to authority after refusing to surrender.

Dr. Lane rose to cross-examine the troopers in turn.

"Trooper Morris," he asked in a gruff and kindly voice, "what would you do if you were chased into a cave by three armed men?"

"I don't know, sir."

"My dear chap, you must have some idea. Would you, for instance, call out, 'Here I am, come and get me, I've thrown down my weapons'?"

The trooper blushed with embarrassment as he said, "I think I'd say something like that, yes, sir."

"How very surprising. You wouldn't be terrified out of your wits and try to stop the three men getting near you?"

"We called out to the prisoner, quite friendly. 'Stop,' we told 'im. 'Lay down yer arms.' "

Lane nodded solemnly. "Might I ask what language you used, Trooper Morris?"

"There was no swearin' and cussin', sir. We used good language."

"The prisoner wouldn't have known that, would he? He doesn't speak English. For all he knew, you might have been threatening to shoot him."

"I suppose so, sir."

Only when the second charge, instigating murder, was dealt with did the prosecution fare better. They produced three prisoners who swore that the leaders of the raiding party that went to the Isanga River had made no secret of their intent to kill the white men there. Chief Mponda must have overheard them. No questions put by Dr. Lane, with Seda's help, could sway the witnesses.

Looking at these inscrutable tribesmen, Clara could not believe that they understood the significance of their testimony. Very often, at the mission, she had encountered natives who, out of simple politeness, said what they supposed their white listener wished to hear rather than what they knew to be true. Aware of the terrible danger that Mponda was in, Clara jumped up and asked the eldest of the three Africans in his own language if he was lying to please the soldiers.

Seda jumped up excitedly. "Captain, sir, she is asking questions."

Francis leaned across the table and said sharply, "No more of this, Mrs. Haslam. Only Dr. Lane and Lieutenant Carew may ask questions. The witnesses stated clearly that Chief Mponda sent men to the Isanga River knowing that they would kill the white miners there. The prosecution will now continue."

"Gentlemen, the point is this," said Carew, facing Francis and his brother officers behind the table. "The defendant, Chief Mponda, led armed men away from his kraal on an illegal expedition aimed at murdering the white residents of this country. Nobody had threatened his kraal or his people. Nobody had occupied his land. But he joined the rebellion as a leader, knowing that this would mean death for white settlers, including women and children."

Later, Dr. Lane refuted this by arguing that there was no evidence that whites had been killed while Mponda was actually commanding his force and that he could not reasonably be blamed for murders that took place while he was somewhere else. But since the African witnesses had plainly stated that the chief had known that murder was to be done, Clara sensed in her bones that Mponda was doomed. Her husband's beloved chief, his only convert and most brilliant pupil, was to be executed like a common criminal.

Dr. Lane wanted to ask Mponda whether he had ordered the deaths, and Clara put the question in Venda. The chief denied it so vehemently that she was utterly convinced. She turned to Francis and said in a voice cracking with emotion, "Chief Mponda swears those men are lying. He wanted his impi to drive the miners away from the area, but he did not want them killed."

Carew threw up his hands as if in amazement. "Then ask him this, Mrs. Haslam: How did he expect his men to behave if fired on by the miners?"

Clara exchanged words with Mponda and turned back to Carew. "He expected his men to defend themselves but not to surround the white men."

"In that case," persisted Carew, "ask him how all the miners came to be killed."

Ten minutes later, Dr. Lane was completing his final remarks for the defense. Mponda, he said, was a patriotic chief who had tried to defend his country and countrymen against people whom he thought of as invaders. He had lost control over his followers, but that did not make him guilty of instigating murder. He appealed to Francis and the two subalterns to respond in the spirit of British fair play and not to be a party to injustice.

When it was Mponda's turn to speak, he simply repeated that he had murdered no one. A brief recess followed, during which Francis and his two subalterns went through the formality of considering their verdict. On returning, Francis could not bring himself to look at Clara as she stood facing him across the table.

He said in a firm, clear voice, "This court finds the defendant, Chief Mponda, guilty on both charges and sentences him to suffer death by shooting. The sentence will be carried out at once."

As Clara translated his words for Mponda, the chief lifted his massive head from his chest and faced his judges with an expression of immense sorrow—whether for himself or for his accusers, Francis could not tell. Mponda's emaciated features expressed neither fear nor anger. His lids blinked upon eyes that looked straight through Francis to a world beyond him. The chief turned to Clara and said something in his own language. She answered and clasped his hand.

While the firing party assembled, Mponda was carried to the barricade on the eastern side of the camp. There, still tied to his stretcher, he was raised into a vertical position and propped against the palisade. As the firing squad shuffled into line, Clara stepped forward and placed something in his hand. Simon also came up and knelt beside him, while Clara said a prayer in Venda. When they withdrew, Carew brought the firing squad to attention. For what seemed an age, he fumbled to get his sword out of its scabbard. At last he raised it.

"Fire!" he shouted, as his sword flashed down.

Prrr-ah! The volley rang out. A light-brown wisp of smoke drifted toward the watchers. Something fell from Mponda's hand as his body sagged against his bonds. Walking forward to give the coup de grâce and feeling uneasy about firing with the revolver in his left hand, Francis paused. A pocket-sized Bible lay in the grass. Blood was flowing from Mponda's head and chest and splashing onto the earth. No tremor of life was visible. Francis replaced the revolver in its holster and picked up the book. Toward evening, he opened it and read the inscription. "To my dearest son, Robert, from his loving mother on the occasion of his christening, the second day of February 1857."

It was after dark when Francis finally handed Haslam's Bible to his widow. Clara took it without a word and turned her back.

Soon afterward, a procession set out from the camp. It was led by the young Matabele whom Francis had threatened to hang and was followed by Mponda's naked body, bent across a mule's back. Behind their dead chief hobbled strange courtiers, the African walking wounded, and then, on stretchers, were the more serious cases, carried by hussars. These sick and dying men were left on the grass a few hundred yards from the camp, while the soldiers scurried back to safety.

The moon was high and the black trees were etched sharply against the paler blue sky. The cortege paused at the margin of the trees, and Francis half expected to see a reverent throng come out to meet the chief. No one appeared, and after a few minutes the dark figures entered the wood.

Francis had decided that whatever the consequences, the column should march at dawn. He had lost one third of his men and could no longer defend the camp. If the enemy attacked his column on the march, the Maxims and field guns would be unlimbered, and they would fight to the death where they stood. That night, fifty of his men were buried—a demoralizing business for the burial parties. Then, for the first time in over a week, Francis slept several hours without waking. The whole column might be lost, but at last he knew he had done everything he could.

In the morning, in spite of Clara's bitterness and the stench of the corpses outside the camp, Francis felt as if hidden chains had fallen from him. Horses were being saddled, oxen brought to the pole and yoke, and everywhere there was quiet but purposeful bustle. Even many of the wounded, who had much to fear from a long march, were plainly relieved when lifted into the wagons. Only when the column had formed and was ready to move off did Francis feel fear again. Within an hour they would be either dead or free.

From a distance the mopane wood had looked dense and mysterious, but entering it, Francis saw that the trees were not close together at all. The pole-like trunks ranged from a few inches to a foot in diameter, and though growing to fifty feet or so, they put out few branches lower down. Since fallen timber was swiftly eaten by white ants, open vistas stretched in every direction between the trees, affording no cover at all.

Francis had sent forward two scouts with a trumpeter. When warning notes rang out, he did not call a halt and ignored the frightened glances being aimed at him. Lieutenant Gradwell rode over to remonstrate, only to be waved back to his place. A few minutes later, campfires were seen away to the right, with warriors standing around them. The trumpet's notes had not induced the natives to move from their position. Morning mist lay in streamers across the forest floor. Riding slightly ahead of the column, Francis heard the click of the hammers as the warriors brought their old-fashioned guns to full cock. Yet still they remained motionless, like figures on a frieze. Francis gave no new order, and the column proceeded at a stately trot. While his sling still prevented him from holding a sword or carbine, every mounted man behind him was ready to fire.

More regiments loomed ahead. Moment by moment, Francis expected shots. How easily these waiting spearmen could overwhelm his little column. But as before, the warriors guarded themselves against attack and stood their ground. Francis rode back behind his rear guard, afraid that the Africans would already be cutting off his line of retreat. He could hear nothing except the sounds of his own wagons and horsemen.

Mist had given the scene a dream-like quality in the first light. As the sun rose, the gray scarves burned away and the rebels could be seen with shocking clarity. A babel of shouts arose from their camps. Warriors were swarming among the trees. And still the column moved forward at the same pace. The natives were forming long lines in front of their night fires. They were carrying shields and guns. The column was well within their range.

Seeing Clara under the hood of her Cape cart, staring fixedly ahead, with Simon by her side, Francis could find nothing to say. She knew their situation as well as he did. Either Mponda's death had saved them, and the tribesmen were going to let them pass; or else these warriors were simply funneling them into the jaws of their strongest regiments. To see so many silent men, watching and waiting, was both terrifying and unearthly. It made Francis think of crowds lining a funeral route—as if they were already a column of the dead.

The hussars rode on for almost a mile between the trees, until there were no more camps. They rode in silence even after leaving the wood and crossing a broad clearing. Five hundred yards away, across the blowing grass, a herd of zebra was grazing calmly. From the direction of the wind, Francis knew there could be no men beyond them. He and his men had passed through the heart of a vast impi and emerged unscathed. Carew began to weep, and Francis himself could not utter a word. From somewhere behind him, he heard a man let out a cheer. A ripple of sound passed from one end of the column to the other. There was pandemonium: helmets were flung in the air, and cheers and laughter broke out all along the line.

The sun was setting, and deep shadows crept along the valley. The sight of maize gardens and village huts reminded Francis of everything he had found most idyllic about Africa. Children had been posted on anthills among the maize to keep the baboons away, and he could hear their piping voices wafted on the evening air. A boy and a girl scampered out of the tall yellow stalks and raced each other down the path to the riverbank. The peacefulness of the scene touched and pained him, since he knew he would never again see and hear such things without undercurrents of sadness.

While fearing that Clara would never forgive him, Francis yearned to hear her admit that the chief's death had saved the column. That morning, as if beauty were a sin, she had cropped her hair clumsily, as a naughty child might have done. Recalling how she had teased him about the peccadilloes of cavalry officers, he could hardly believe her the same person.

When, finally, he plucked up the courage to approach Clara, she was sitting beside Simon, who was blowing their evening fire into life. She had been washing clothes in a basin, and her sleeves were rolled up. Only weeks ago, Francis had kissed the hollows of those arms. Having dreaded a rebuff, he took heart a little from her decision to send Simon on an errand to the commissariat wagon.

She said in a lifeless voice, "What's it like to have played God and got away with it?"

"Don't ask that," he murmured. "I hated having to do it."

"How long will it be before you want something else as badly? Once you start breaking life's most sacred rules, you don't stop." She gave him a glance of cold appraisal. "Rules are for other people, aren't they, Francis? *You* can shoot an innocent chief. *You* can betray a man while he's risking his life for you. And that's fine, so long as ordinary people don't join in."

He raised a hand in appeal—his other hand, in the sling, throbbed constantly. "Only a few years ago," he said, "Mponda had his enemies clubbed to death. Why be sentimental about him?"

"Because he became a different person."

"If we'd broken out, I couldn't have dragged him along rough tracks in an unsprung wagon. Think of the pain."

"You could have left him behind. The prisoners would have cared for him."

"How long would he have lived?"

Her eyes were angry. "Even if he'd had no more than an hour to live, you still would not have had the right to shoot him."

As a young cornet, Francis had been sent to Kandahar. It had been just after the last Afghan war, when hundreds of men had been hanged by Lord Roberts in retribution for a massacre of British troops. Half of those executed could have played no part in what had happened. And how does my crime rate? he asked himself. Is it anything by comparison? The thought pleased him briefly, until the pain in his hand obliged him to reach for his flask.

"Want some?" he asked.

She shook her head, and he swallowed deeply, remembering how amused he had been the first time he had seen her drink. He understood her feeling of guilt for what he and she had done together, and he hated it. Haslam had been too old for her, had deceived her about the life she would lead in Africa, and might easily have caused her death. But because she had been unfaithful, she blamed herself for everything.

He said emotionally, "Things will seem different when you're in England."

She held herself very straight. "I mean to go back to Mponda's kraal. Philemon and the others must settle in a safer place. Simon can stay on and help them."

"Will you stay on too?"

"I don't know what I'll do. At some stage I'll spend a few months in England with my father. Then, who knows?"

He said in an even-tempered voice, "When you stop wanting to punish us both, a letter to my regiment will find me. I've never loved anyone as much." With his eyes filling, he walked away toward the big fire within the circle of wagons. The pain in his hand was almost a comfort, since it prevented his thinking of anything else. Later that evening, it ached so deeply and fiercely that a dozen times he was on the point of visiting Dr. Lane. But on each occasion, he recalled the kindly doctor's disgusted face after the trial and decided to dress the wound himself.

During the next few days, Francis thought often of his last conversation with Clara and what he might have said. Perhaps his fear of seeming pitiful had destroyed his chances. If he had begged on his knees, would he have been forgiven? Deep down, he doubted it.

Only once before had Francis known the bitterness of rejection; on that occasion he had been cast aside for being insufficiently well connected—a less hurtful situation than being found wanting in character. Francis's mother had taught him never to think himself so admirable as to deserve special exemption from trouble. He hoped the same mixture of pride and realism would sustain him now, with his professional future looking equally bleak. He would not be forgiven for losing so many men against "untrained natives," and Dr. Lane would probably make an official complaint against him for shooting Mponda. Yet if Haslam could have survived long enough to negotiate with Mponda, four thousand tribesmen might have returned to their villages without a shot being fired. Great careers had been founded on smaller successes.

Soon after the column had clattered into the tin-hut town of Charter, Clara announced that she intended to sell her Cape cart and to head south as soon as the next mail coach was allowed to run. Francis felt as if she had ripped out his heart and flung it away.

The following day, he had to acknowledge something he had been trying to ignore; his hand was not healing properly. The wound smelled peculiar, and black streaks had appeared in the ragged flesh that lay across the center of his palm. His arm was badly swollen below the elbow, and he was feverish. A visit to Dr. Lane could no longer be deferred.

CHAPTER 26

Clara's journey back to Mponda's kraal had taken two months of traveling, at first by mail coach and then in a trader's wagon. When she arrived, the women were returning from the fields and gardens, carrying great loads of firewood on their heads. As the cows were brought home, Clara held Simon's hand. He might so easily have been one of the herdboys riding, laughing, on a broad back or running alongside the herd, driving it onward. Instead he was condemned to look on, an outsider.

Familiar sights were all around: the dam, which Robert had built so laboriously; the khotla, where Mponda had humiliated Nashu. On their way to the mission, Clara and Simon were pointedly ignored by several children both remembered from the school. Not a soul came out to greet them.

The reason was soon apparent. Although her own house was still standing, the mission and the chapel had been burned to the ground. It came to her, with a twist of fear, that Makufa had already returned to claim his inheritance. Or if not Makufa, Nashu. Because Simon was too scared to climb the crag in search of his mother, Clara went up alone, thinking of the first time she had scrambled up this dusty, twisting path, following in Robert's footsteps.

Of all the chief's relations, only Chizuva would talk to her. Some few dozen warriors had returned from the north, and Nashu had ordered them to destroy the mission. The queen already knew that her husband was dead, so there had been no need to break the news. Chizuva told Clara that Simon's mother, along with Philemon, Mabo, Matiyo, and others, had left the village in the mission's ox wagon a month earlier, hoping to settle in Tuli or Mafeking. If no missionary could be found to welcome them, they planned to seek work in traders' stores or as watchmen or maids. Clara imagined them scrubbing floors and doing other menial jobs: they who had called themselves ''children of God.''

She stared at the ground for a long time before inquiring, "And you, Chizuva, what will you do?" The queen's skin had lost the well-oiled glossiness that Clara remembered from her days of grandeur.

"I will stay here. Makufa will not kill me when he comes. My ancestors will protect me."

Clara nodded sympathetically. She understood her return to her former faith. Poor woman; Christ had not brought her the blessings she had expected.

When Clara found Simon again, he seemed neither surprised nor even particularly upset by his mother's departure. He had always meant to remain with Robert. From the beginning, when Simon had annoyed her by saying only what would please Robert, Clara had guessed that he would choose not to sacrifice everything for his faith, preferring the path that offered a better way of life. Paul would not have done that; nor Philemon. Perhaps, thought Clara, if Philemon had stayed, she might have tried to start another school, but that was impossible now.

At times on her long and lonely journey here, Clara had believed she might possess the courage and inspiration to remain in Africa. But standing among the beehive huts and granaries, she realized that, like Robert, she had not been thinking of the everyday world. His vision had always been directed toward another place—another dimension, almost—somewhere beyond the daily pleasures and temptations of this earth. Life was proceeding most satisfactorily here. Young girls were singing as they helped their mothers prepare their evening meals; soon the menfolk would be home. Clara closed her eyes and imagined Herida's lovely smile. If Robert had never come here, she would still be alive, and so would Mponda.

She walked along the dam with Simon, recalling Robert's thankfulness that the drought had lasted long enough to cause suffering. Without misfortune, why would anyone think of Jesus? Why crave salvation, unless fearing hell? How she had hated such reasoning. Gazing across the placid lake, she thought that salvation was a tragic word. Life was not a preparation for anything except itself. Recently, Francis's actions had started to appear to her in a less negative light. If Robert could act morally for years and cause universal grief, should she be so sure that an immoral act, even the killing of a dying man, should be unreservedly condemned if many of its results were good? Memories came back to haunt her:

Francis rallying his men and handing her his revolver; Francis looking down on her in the darkness. Yet because he had chosen what he thought the least of the various evils facing him, she had left him without one kind word.

The old men sitting outside the cattle kraal were singing when Clara and Simon left Mponda's village next day. She had heard their song before. Death has no home, they sang. If we knew the place where death could be found, we would hurry there at once with our spears and clubs to fight him. But since nobody knows, what is there left for us to do but drink and sing and make love? Francis, who had never been crudely cynical, would nevertheless have enjoyed this song. As she thought this, she burst into tears.

In Cape Town, the busy streets with their fashionable shops disturbed Clara, reminding her of a time when such places had been her favorite haunts. New electric trams ran from central Adderley Street as far out as Claremont, and people all knew where they were going, and why. Most white women were smartly dressed as well as purposeful, making Clara feel like a shabby vagrant who had drifted in from the bush. On the journey from Mashonaland she had often felt sick, blaming the queasy motion of the mail coach or the heat in the train, but the persistence of the sensation after her arrival at the Cape suggested "nerves" as the likeliest explanation. She had read about people collapsing through nervous exhaustion at the end of a long ordeal, and perhaps this was to be her experience.

Lack of money was her most immediate worry, and she was obliged to borrow from the missionary society—only, she assured the secretary, until her father could send a telegram to the Standard Bank. She received tea and sympathy from the missionaries, who offered to find Simon suitable employment at the Cape and promised Clara a bed in a "respectable" lodging house. That same evening, they took her there.

Now she could have a bath and read by gaslight in the evening rather than by the pale glow of a stinking oil lamp. For the first time in months, she was able look at herself in a cheval glass. A strange young woman stared back at her, with heavy-lidded eyes, untidily cropped hair, and skin as brown as polished wood. Her image began to waver as a familiar bout of sickness turned to whirling dizziness. "I won't faint," she told herself, and fainted. As she came to, nausea overwhelmed her, and she vomited on the threadbare rug. She crawled on her hands and knees to the window, where the fresh air revived her. She must have cried out when she fell, because the owner of the boardinghouse came panting up the stairs to find out what was wrong.

A little later, this elderly widow returned, accompanied by a doctor. Clara lay on the bed, and he took in at once how thin and weather-beaten she was.

"Have you been eating properly?" he inquired gently. She explained that she had been traveling for several months. He took her pulse and asked her to open her mouth. He was a young man, recently qualified, she guessed. She would have to make sure the missionaries paid him. After examining her tongue, he asked, "Do you have any other symptoms?"

"Only nausea," she whispered.

"Are you married or single?"

"My husband is dead."

"I'm very sorry to hear that." He lowered his voice. "I must ask you a personal question, madam. Have your menses always been regular?"

"Not since I came to Africa."

"Are you late at present?"

"Yes, but it's nothing new."

"With respect, I think it is. To be frank, madam, I'm all but certain you will have a child." A tremendous silence followed his words. Clara felt that she must argue—as if by accepting his diagnosis passively she would somehow make it true. Yet she could not articulate a single word. He said, "You must get plenty of rest and make sure you eat more than you've been accustomed to." He left her with a bottle of iron tonic, a bill for his professional fee, and a feeling that an earthquake had just engulfed her future.

How could she lead a life of her own now? How become a teacher, or even a governess? And if earning her living was to be impossible, wouldn't she always have to depend on her father's money? In time, a second marriage might have brought her happiness. She was still young, and time was said to heal all wounds. But who would ever want to marry the mother of a dead man's child? Robert's chances of being the father seemed so much greater than Francis's that she hardly considered the possibility that the child might be his. She was a pregnant widow, destined to look after an aging father and bring up her child in his house.

The following day, feeling stronger, she walked along pleasant streets of gabled colonial houses. The mission secretary had said he would purchase a steamer ticket for her, and without arrangements to make herself, she was free to spend her time as she wished. Clara liked the old Dutch town best, with its pavements shaded by ancient oaks. The houses were mainly stuccoed and whitewashed, and a few were built from a peculiar type of blue stone. She had heard somewhere that it had been hewn by prisoners from the quarries on Robben Island.

She bought a newspaper near Government House and walked on, observing the passersby. The uniforms of the African servants and messengers were strikingly smart and clean. The grease-covered men and women of Mponda's kraal receded further into memory. She turned a corner and entered a coffee house. After choosing an inconspicuous corner table, she began to glance through her paper.

The stories were mostly about local politics or social events such as a meet of the Cape foxhounds or a reception given by the governor. She turned another page and read: CAVALRY OFFICER FACES BOARD OF INQUIRY. And there in front of her was a picture of Francis, with a sleeve of his full-dress coat pinned up to his chest. "Captain Vaughan, 9th Hussars, began his second day of evidence yesterday, before the military tribunal that is investigating the charge that he hazarded the lives of his men in Mashonaland in a negligent manner." Her eye raced down columns of print. Some words jumped out at her. "Captain Vaughan suffered the amputation of his right hand as a result of a wound inflicted during the campaign." She remembered the grimy sling he had been wearing when she had last spoken to him. With countless details to attend to, he had ignored the one matter most crucial to himself. She knew how much he had hoped that the campaign would win him promotion. Without an increased salary, he had expected his debts to force him out of the regiment. Even if he cleared his name, his career would be over. Such beautiful, gentle hands, she thought, and began to cry.

Clara crossed the large rectangular parade ground opposite the Castle and approached the sentries outside. Since the proceedings were closed to the public, she waited on a bench under a tall plane tree. She did not know whether she would try to talk to

Francis when he came out. But if she did, what could she say? I'm going to have a baby, but I think it's Robert's? The fact that she had made love to her husband more often than with him in the last month of Robert's life could easily devalue Francis's memory of the few nights they had managed to spend together.

She still thought him wrong to have shot Mponda, but it appalled her to think of men sitting in judgment on him for that or any other alleged professional failing. Unless they had lived through the same terror, what could they know? She wanted Francis to be aware that she sympathized. That was all. Suddenly she was bewildered. Suppose he comes out and, seeing me, thinks I've come to enjoy his troubles. But a strange perversity made her stay where she was. She had to *see* him—not to talk to but simply to look at. Would he be very much aged by what had happened? Would his confidence have gone, along with his graceful way of moving?

Half an hour later, when Captain Vaughan came out, accompanied by Mark Carew and several other officers and well-wishers, Clara was still sitting under her tree. She shrank behind her paper as he passed only yards away. His face was pale and his mouth bracketed with deep lines. She had never seen him in full-dress uniform and for a moment thought she was looking at a stranger. His sleeve was pinned up, as in the newspaper picture. When she heard his voice, it was exactly as she remembered it—warm, light-hearted, and with just a twist of irony. Her heart was beating at an impossible rate. She wanted to run after Francis; but his friends closed in and bore him away from her, their spurs ringing ever more faintly on the cobbles.

PART FOUR

CHAPTER 27

When Francis Vaughan returned to England after being acquitted by the disciplinary tribunal, he went to stay with his mother in Kent. She had moved from London to the country five years earlier to live more cheaply, so that additional funds would be available for her son and her daughter. In spite of such economies, she knew she could not hope to keep Francis in his regiment when it returned to the home country from Africa. His expenses would then exceed his salary by at least £400 per annum. At present, she rented a small house, little bigger than a cottage, in a sprawling village near Canterbury.

Ever since his return, Francis had affected an optimism about his future that his mother found heartbreaking. His handicap ruled out further active service and would therefore deny him promotion to field rank. He spoke of continuing his career by becoming a general's aide-de-camp or a home-based staff officer and increasing his income in this way. But he seemed blind to the competition he faced from ambitious able-bodied men.

"Don't you worry, Ma," Francis told her. "I'll have no problem riding at inspections and ceremonial occasions."

His mother smiled reassuringly and said she was sure he would not, although that was hardly the point, she felt. Even if he had not lost his right hand, the tribunal had damaged his reputation—acquittal or no acquittal. When she saw him practicing for hours with his left hand to improve his handwriting, it was all she could do not to cry. He, who had drawn and painted so beautifully as a boy, would never open a sketchbook again. She admired Francis's courage but feared it was an act put on to spare her feelings. In truth, she would have preferred him to admit the extent of the disaster. Then they could have wept together before sitting down to plan a different way of life. Snobbery against trade and commerce was diminishing all the time, and there was no doubt that the family needed money.

When he ought to have been considering other options, Francis was pinning all his hopes on his former colonel, who was widely tipped as the new inspector general of cavalry. Although his mother begged her son to keep an open mind, Francis behaved as if Major General Hewart's appointment was a foregone conclusion. His only worry was that the new inspector general might not recommend him to the War Office as one of his ADCs.

Each morning, Francis walked out into the village street, eager to meet the postman early on his rounds. His mother was sure that her son ought to leave the army, but whenever she caught sight of him striding past the lych-gate, she would pray that if his long-awaited letter did arrive, it would contain the news he longed to read.

One sunny autumn morning, he went out in his usual leisurely fashion but returned in breathless haste. Normally, when opening letters, Francis would sit at a table and press down with the weight of his injured arm on the envelope while slicing through the flap with a paper knife. In the street, he would have had to resort to the undignified stratagem of tearing it open with his teeth. From her bedroom, his mother heard his rapid footsteps in the hall and the sound of the dining room door being slammed. She imagined him getting a knife and sitting down to open his precious letter with a trembling hand. Then she heard his cry of dismay.

Major General Hewart had been passed over for the post of inspector general and had instead been offered the job of general officer commanding the North-West District of England. Francis's dream of a billet in Whitehall, only doors away from the adjutant general's and the commander in chief's offices, had become just that—a dream. He had told his mother, with a grin that had not concealed his seriousness, that when he was working only yards away from the Horse Guards, he would be in the perfect position to impress the most senior officers in the army. "My disability won't be a bar to promotion then. You'll see." Such thoughts could no longer be entertained. Hewart would end his career as a provincial GOC in the backwater of Chester, and his ADCs stood to gain little or nothing by their association with him.

Later that morning, a telegraph boy leaned his bicycle against the garden gate and sauntered up the path between the overblown roses. Francis took the proffered flimsy pink paper.

General Hewart wanted him to be his ADC in Chester. The

boy tugged at the strap of his pillbox hat. "Is there any answer for the sender, sir?"

Since no alternative occurred to him, Francis knew what had to be said. " 'I accept. Vaughan.' That's the answer."

When Francis went in and told his mother, she managed to hide her disappointment. It consoled her to think that this two-year appointment would bore Francis almost to death and persuade him that his future lay outside the army. To put pressure on him now would be unkind and pointless.

With the exception of "Caesar's Tower" and its adjacent buildings, Chester Castle had been largely demolished at the end of the eighteenth century, to be replaced by a barracks, the county hall, and the assize courts. In early October 1896, Francis took up residence in the old buildings by the round tower, where the GOC also had his office. General Hewart was a florid-faced man with a peppery manner but a sociable disposition. Because he was a life-long bachelor and his habits were of great importance to him, Francis tried to interfere with them as little as possible. The general had always valued social occasions and particularly enjoyed meeting the grander landowners of the county and entertaining them in return.

On the last Saturday in the month, General Hewart and his ADC set out from the castle in the official landau, bound for a weekend house party. As they clattered past the famous Chester Rows, with their black-and-white half-timbered shops and houses, Francis wondered whether their host and hostess would be as paralyzingly dull as Lord and Lady Farquhar had been ten days earlier. Their present destination was Holcroft Park, a large country house twenty-five miles to the southeast, owned by a Mr. Charles Vyner.

"Don't be fooled because he's only a commoner." The general chuckled. "His mother was Lord Sulgrave's only child. The title's gone, but the money certainly hasn't. Young Vyner's as rich as Croesus." Hewart moved confidingly closer on the landau's opulently padded leather seat. "That's not all, Vaughan. His wife's an heiress too. Lord Desmond's only girl."

Francis found it irksome to be expected to applaud the Vyners' good fortune. "Does Mr. Vyner find time to interest himself in the public good?" he asked innocently.

"I'm told his passion is his art collection."

"How lucky he has the means to indulge it," replied Francis, looking out at the warmly glowing fruits of the rowan and the hips of wild roses in the hedgerows.

Francis had studied the map before leaving. What struck him as more noteworthy than anything else encountered on their journey was the dark pall in the late-afternoon sky, just to the south, as they approached Holcroft Park. For under that smoke must lie the town of Sarston, where Clara Haslam had grown up. Whether she had returned there or had remained in Africa, he had no idea. And it was certainly most unlikely that these young aristocrats would know anything about a manufacturer's daughter. Until coming so close, Francis had told himself in vague terms that one day he would visit Sarston. His sudden agitation left him in no doubt that his return would now be sooner rather than later.

Mr. Vyner was a handsome young man, Francis decided, but in a refined and rather bloodless way. He presided at the head of his dining table with a look of scarcely concealed disdain when the less intellectual guests, such as the general, were speaking. An art critic, a picture dealer, and an archaeologist and his wife made up for the less cultivated country gentlemen and their ladies. Behind Mr. Vyner, on the dining room wall, was an immense Rubens depicting Salome with John the Baptist's head on a golden salver. Having seen so many dead men, and not long ago, Francis found the Baptist's glazed eyes disconcerting.

Earlier in the week, unknown to Francis, the general had written to their hostess, explaining that his ADC had lost a hand in the Mashonaland rebellion and requesting that any meat served to him should be cut up in advance. In fact, Lady Alice gave instructions that the job be done by a footman at the table. While this was happening, Vyner smiled at Francis. "No offense, you understand, but I'm morbidly intrigued to learn what happened to your hand afterward."

"I was in no state to ask."

Vyner turned to the general. "Didn't Lord Raglan give his arm a Christian burial?"

"That was Lord Uxbridge," replied General Hewart, pleased to be deferred to. "And it was his leg."

During this exchange, Francis had been aware of Lady Alice

Vyner's eyes upon him. She was restless and discontented. Soon after his arrival at the house, Francis had caught sight of her in the spotless austerity of a fashionable gray riding habit, lecturing her husband. In the candlelight, she was all smiles and gleaming jewels.

"Please forgive my husband's peculiar sense of humor," she begged Francis, and turned to her other guests. "We're lucky to have Captain Vaughan with us. A real live hero, I assure you. He captured a rebel chief single-handed in a cave. That's how he came to be stabbed with a poisoned spear. I read all about it in the *Morning Post*."

"I had two troopers with me, Lady Alice," murmured Francis, surprised by the expression of intense interest with which Charles Vyner suddenly regarded him.

For the rest of dinner, the archaeologist's young wife, who was sitting to Francis's right, plied him with flattering questions. What was the meaning of the miniature decorations on his mess jacket? Did he make a habit of being heroic? And so on.

Soon after the ladies had left the gentlemen, Mr. Vyner came and sat next to Francis. He puffed on his cigar and said nothing for a while.

Ever since Lady Alice had mentioned the *Morning Post*'s account of the incident that had cost the gallant captain so dear, Charles Vyner had been on edge. The same newspaper story had started with a description of the murder of Mr. Robert Haslam. Vyner vividly remembered his shock and confusion on first learning that Clara's husband was dead. Could it mean that she would be coming home to Sarston? Indeed, it had turned out to mean precisely that. And now Vyner found himself presented with an unexpected opportunity to gain information about Clara's life in Africa.

Many times since his own wedding, Charles had wondered whether he might have been happier with Clara. Would Alice ever have punished him as sublimely as Clara had that day in the art gallery? In no way. But with her realist's nature, nor would Alice ever have been guilty of the high-minded idiocy that had led Clara to marry a missionary. Yet what scathing contempt for wealth Clara had shown with that act, what scorn for personal safety. She had appeared to marry goodness incarnate while actually embracing a life of recklessness and danger.

Charles had held out for only three days, after learning that she had returned, before succumbing to his desire to call on her. She might reject him to start with, he thought, but what a mistress she would make in the end! All the amusing things she had said came back to him as he walked up the path to the door of her father's house. She had greeted him politely, but the moment he had given her a hint that his ultimate purposes might be amorous, she had become imperious.

"How dare you come here with your grubby proposition?" Her slanting, angrily averted eyes delighted him.

"That's not what I'd call it."

"What *would* you call it? I give you the whole dictionary." Mockery twisted the corners of her delicate mouth.

"An opportunity for mutual enjoyment," he murmured, daring everything on outrageous honesty.

"When I'm carrying my husband's child?" she cried.

"I'm very sorry. . . . I didn't know."

His tone had been wonderfully contrite, though really he had not been sorry at all. Lovely Clara would not easily find a second husband with the missionary's brat in her stomach. If he kept pressing her over a number of months, she would fall into his lap in the end. She had once been infatuated with him, and early passions invariably left the deepest marks. A sneaking smile flickered on his lips. The next moment, something whistled past his head and crashed to the ground near the gate.

"Laugh at me, would you?" she gasped, her hand still raised after hurling a ceramic pot. For years this ugly vessel had stood on her father's hall table. Now it lay in pieces across the path, along with the fern and the earth it had contained. "Go away— you arrogant, ridiculous man," she whispered with a throbbing tearfulness that overjoyed him. Recalling the way her lips had once opened in softly yielding response to his, he advanced a step. But only one. At that instant, she plucked a stick from her father's cast-iron umbrella stand and, with a deft flick, caught Charles on the shin. The door slammed in his face, and he had been left hopping on one leg in the middle of the path.

Vyner gave Francis a man-to-man smile. "So you knew Robert Haslam?"

"Not well," replied Francis, surprised that his host should even be aware of the dead missionary's name.

"Wasn't he killed on the day you were wounded?"

"That's right. A very brave man."

"I used to know his wife. She came from round here, you know." Vyner passed Francis the port. "Was she happy with Haslam?"

"Nobody's happy in a rebellion."

Vyner grinned at Francis. "You don't want to tell me, do you?"

"I don't, really."

"Aha. So you knew Clara well."

Francis shrugged. "She and her husband were with my column at a dangerous time."

"Meaning what?" Charles shook some ash off his cigar and waited. When it was clear Francis did not intend to answer, Vyner said quietly, "She came home pregnant, you know." Charles was amazed to see the color drain from the soldier's cheeks. "She didn't tell you?"

"I haven't seen her since I left Africa."

Vyner clapped him on the back. "Bad luck, old man!"

"I don't really want to talk about her, Mr. Vyner."

"Don't be so prim, man."

Francis managed to smile. "I'd call it propriety rather than primness. But perhaps you're right. I'll be frank with you, Vyner—I'd like to see her while I'm staying here."

"Perfectly understandable," murmured Vyner, with his characteristically ambiguous grin. "My coachman will take you over tomorrow."

The phaeton rattled into a small gaslit square, where the shops were down-at-heel and dowdy. There was a draper called J. & H. Ince, with rolls of material in the window and one or two dusty made-up dresses on dummies. It moved him to think that Clara might once have patronized such a place. Next door was a building society, where aspiring clerks would pay in their weekly shillings to finance a move from back-to-back terrace to bay-windowed semidetached. Through drawing room windows, Francis glimpsed orange-colored gas globes; every third or fourth house boasted terra-cotta embellishments. Clara's presence behind the walls of one of these modest houses made the whole town touching to him. His heart was beating faster as the carriage slowed down where granite sets gave way to cobbles. She was pregnant, perhaps with his child, but had made no attempt to contact him through his regiment. Must this mean that she had not forgiven him for Mponda's death? If it did, she might refuse to see him.

They bowled along past the sooty lodge gates of a municipal park and swept on toward the neo-Gothic Free Trade Hall. At last they turned a corner and entered the small enclave of Georgian streets that was all that was left of the old town. As the carriage came to a halt at the end of a Regency terrace, Francis tried to fortify himself with anger but failed. That she had chosen not to tell him that she might be carrying his child was something to weep over, not rant about.

The coachman pointed past a monkey puzzle tree to a dark-green door. "That's the one, sir."

"Did Mr. Vyner sometimes come here?"

"He did, sir. A few years back."

A maid came to the door, then Francis heard Clara's voice from the stairs. "Who is it, Helen?"

"A gentleman."

She came down to the landing and froze as she saw him framed in the doorway. "Show him into the dining room," she said softly to the girl. Francis assumed that someone else was in the house and that she did not want this person to see him. But he went into the dreary room like an obedient boy and waited. Two blue Bristol vases with cut-glass pendants cast reflections on the surface of the mahogany table. At the far end of the room hung a devotional painting by a follower of Holman Hunt, called *Christ Walking on the Water.* He wished that he could pray for a miracle, but he thought of Robert Haslam, and his prayer died unuttered. It came to Francis that this might be the last time he would ever be alone with Clara. He remembered Belingwe Camp and their first meeting. What advice would Heywood Fynn give him now?

The moment she entered the room, Francis took a long breath to steady himself. Outside, a street hawker was crying his wares. Clara closed the door and gestured to Francis to be seated. As she sat down opposite, he remembered her facing him accusingly across another table, while drums were beating and dying men cried out. He smiled, although his mouth felt as stiff as leather.

"It's so strange to see you here," he murmured.

"Did you come specially from London?" She sounded alarmed by the possibility.

He explained about his job in Chester and the coincidence

of his staying at Holcroft Park, then ended lamely: "I would have come anyway, in the end." She was wearing a tie and a wide white collar on a darker shirt, as if she were a schoolteacher. Her hair had grown, but she still wore it pinned up. He wondered if he had ever known her at all. Perhaps their affair had been an aberration, while her marriage to Haslam had been wholly in character. The sideboard was thickly strewn with fragments of colored earthenware—presumably samples brought home by her father for scrutiny.

She rested her elbows on the table and looked straight at him. "How do you like staying at Holcroft Park?"

"Not a lot. My host keeps asking me questions about your marriage."

"He once wanted to marry me himself. Lucky I was jilted. Lady Alice never looks happy."

An overwhelming attraction drew his gaze to her face. How charming she looked in her simple clothes. How young too. She had been through two years that would have destroyed many people, and the only evidence of it was a slightly more watchful expression about the eyes. He could not fathom her. "Are you still angry with me, Clara?"

She shook her head. "Nobody ought to be faced with the choices you had to make."

"Why didn't you write to me?" He tried not to sound querulous but feared he did.

"I was pregnant."

"What difference did that make?"

"You might have felt obliged to me. I think it's Robert's child."

"You still should have told me," he said unhappily, wondering how her pride would ever allow her to admit she needed him. "I don't care who the father is," he insisted. A long silence stretched his nerves to breaking. "You can't really doubt why I'm here. It's nothing to do with staying at Holcroft Park—that just made it sooner." He could feel himself blushing. Why had he rushed on like this before getting any sense of how she felt?

She stretched out her hands on the table. "When you killed that poor man . . . I can't describe what I felt, except that I was a vile, abominable woman to have loved you." She withdrew her hands, leaving a slight smudge on the polished mahogany. The silvery morning light shone on her black hair. He wanted to lean forward and touch her. She said quietly, "I went back to Mponda's kraal, you know. Makufa hadn't come home yet. I realized that there wouldn't be a civil war when he did." She looked past Francis at the heavy muslin curtains, as if reluctant to catch his eye. "It was a wonderful relief. I've had time to go over it all, Francis. Whatever the rights and wrongs of everything, you did what you thought you had to. I know I owe my life to you."

He tried to speak and failed at first. Finally he blurted out, "It means everything to hear you say that."

"It shouldn't," she said, almost sternly. Her eyes were sad and repentant. "I wept when I heard about your hand."

He managed to smile, though his throat felt tight. "I wasn't pleased about it myself. I'm afraid it spells finis for my career. I thought I might become a desk wallah, but it won't do. Not in the long run."

"At least you won't be killed charging at elephants." Her lips started to tremble. "I'm sorry, Francis. That came out wrong." She stared at the table. "I saw you in Cape Town, but I couldn't say anything. I was outside the Castle. I went there specially to see you."

"You did?" His joy was quite open.

"Of course." She raised her hands to her face for a moment. "I was ashamed of how I'd treated you."

"Oh, darling," he said. "You needn't have been."

"I can't believe it," she cried. "Can't believe I'm looking at you. I really loved you, Francis."

"But now?" he faltered, feeling as if he were tottering on the brink of great misery or great happiness.

"Of course I love you."

Although she smiled, he sensed a reflective sadness. Was she remembering how guilt had made her walk down that valley of death with her husband? And did she still need to think herself good? He feared he had made his love too obvious to her and had invited her pity by parading his lost career. He recalled a childhood prayer: "Whatsoever things are good, whatsoever things are pure, whatsoever things are lovely, think on these things." It would not be good or lovely to shatter a wounded man's dreams.

"Promise me . . ." he whispered, "promise not to lie to me."

She said gently, "Why should I need to lie? In a few months I shall give birth, and in the meantime you can be with me as much as you like. Isn't that enough for now? Remember when we couldn't even see a day ahead?''

He found himself looking at Christ walking on the water. The savior's clean white feet under his striped robe hovered several inches above evenly spaced green wavelets. A sigh escaped Francis's lips. Miracles could not reasonably be expected. He and Clara had loved each other in exquisitely perilous circumstances, as unlike the safe and sober present as it would be possible to imagine. But without fear of death to spice each moment, quieter pleasures could surely be enjoyed.

He asked pleasantly, ''What can one do for amusement in Sarston?''

She cast her eyes upward, as if assessing an infinity of choices. Then she said briskly, ''Get drunk, or go shopping for a hat.''

A grandfather clock boomed in the hall. Francis imagined Clara in front of a mirror, twisting her beautiful neck to look at a feathered hat from every angle. They would discuss other styles, and he would have the perfect excuse for gazing at her as much as he wanted for an hour. ''The hat,'' he declared, having no difficulty in sounding enthusiastic. ''Shall we choose it now?''